Am I dreaming?

There was no sign of Berrynose, but three other cats were sitting beside the nursery wall. Horror stiffened every hair on Jayfeather's pelt when he saw the muscular tabby shapes of Tigerstar and Hawkfrost, one with gleaming amber eyes, the other with ice blue. The third cat was a big brown tom with a crooked tail. Jayfeather had never seen him before. There was hunger in the eyes of the three spirit cats as they stared at the newborn kits.

"It's coming," Jayfeather whispered. "A battle between StarClan and the Dark Forest, and every warrior will be called upon to fight."

WARRIORS

THE NEW PROPHECY

POWER OF THREE

OMEN OF THE STARS

EXPLORE THE
WARRIORS
WORLD

Warriors Super Edition: Firestar's Quest
Warriors Super Edition: Bluestar's Prophecy
Warriors Super Edition: SkyClan's Destiny
Warriors Field Guide: Secrets of the Clans
Warriors: Cats of the Clans
Warriors: Code of the Clans
Warriors: Battles of the Clans

MANGA
The Lost Warrior
Warrior's Refuge
Warrior's Return
The Rise of Scourge
Tigerstar and Sasha #1: Into the Woods
Tigerstar and Sasha #2: Escape from the Forest
Tigerstar and Sasha #3: Return to the Clans
Ravenpaw's Path #1: Shattered Peace
Ravenpaw's Path #2: A Clan in Need
Ravenpaw's Path #3: The Heart of a Warrior

OMEN OF THE STARS

WARRIORS

THE FOURTH APPRENTICE

ERIN
HUNTER

HARPER

An Imprint of HarperCollinsPublishers

The Fourth Apprentice
Copyright © 2009 by Working Partners Limited
Warriors Adventure Game © 2009 by Working Partners Limited
Series created by Working Partners Limited

Library of Congress Cataloging-in-Publication Data
Hunter, Erin.
The fourth apprentice / Erin Hunter.—1st ed.
    p.   cm. (Warriors, omen of the stars ; [bk. 1])
ISBN 978-0-06-155511-4
[Fic]—dc22   2009014268
                                                   CIP
                                                    AC

Typography by Hilary Zarycky
11   12   13   14   15   LP/BR   10   9   8   7   6
❖
First paperback edition, 2011

Special thanks to Cherith Baldry

ALLEGIANCES

THUNDERCLAN

LEADER   FIRESTAR—ginger tom with a flame-colored pelt

DEPUTY   BRAMBLECLAW—dark brown tabby tom with amber eyes

MEDICINE CAT   JAYFEATHER—gray tabby tom

WARRIORS   (toms and she-cats without kits)

GRAYSTRIPE—long-haired gray tom

DUSTPELT—dark brown tabby tom

SANDSTORM—pale ginger she-cat with green eyes

BRACKENFUR—golden brown tabby tom

SORRELTAIL—tortoiseshell-and-white she-cat with amber eyes

CLOUDTAIL—long-haired white tom with blue eyes

BRIGHTHEART—white she-cat with ginger patches

THORNCLAW—golden brown tabby tom
APPRENTICE, BRIARPAW

SQUIRRELFLIGHT—dark ginger she-cat with green eyes

LEAFPOOL—light brown tabby she-cat with amber eyes, former medicine cat

SPIDERLEG—long-limbed black tom with brown underbelly and amber eyes

BIRCHFALL—light brown tabby tom

BERRYNOSE—cream-colored tom

HAZELTAIL—small gray-and-white she-cat
APPRENTICE, BLOSSOMPAW

MOUSEWHISKER—gray-and-white tom
APPRENTICE, BUMBLEPAW

CINDERHEART—gray tabby she-cat

LIONBLAZE—golden tabby tom

FOXLEAP—reddish tabby tom

ICECLOUD—white she-cat

TOADSTEP—black-and-white tom

ROSEPETAL—dark cream she-cat

MILLIE—striped gray tabby she-cat

APPRENTICES (more than six moons old, in training to become warriors)

BRIARPAW—dark brown she-cat

BLOSSOMPAW—tortoiseshell-and-white she-cat

BUMBLEPAW—very pale gray tom with black stripes

QUEENS (she-cats expecting or nursing kits)

FERNCLOUD—pale gray (with darker flecks) she-cat with green eyes

DAISY—cream long-furred cat from the horseplace

WHITEWING—white she-cat with green eyes, mother of Birchfall's kits: Dovekit (gray she-cat) and Ivykit (white tabby she-cat)

POPPYFROST—tortoiseshell she-cat, expecting Berrynose's kits

SHADOWCLAN

SHREWFOOT—gray she-cat with black feet

SCORCHFUR—dark gray tom

REDWILLOW—mottled brown-and-ginger tom

TIGERHEART—dark brown tabby tom

DAWNPELT—cream-furred she-cat

QUEENS **KINKFUR**—tabby she-cat with long fur that sticks out at all angles

IVYTAIL—black, white, and tortoiseshell she-cat

ELDERS **CEDARHEART**—dark gray tom

TALLPOPPY—long-legged light brown tabby she-cat

SNAKETAIL—dark brown tom with tabby-striped tail

WHITEWATER—white she-cat with long fur, blind in one eye

WINDCLAN

LEADER **ONESTAR**—brown tabby tom

DEPUTY **ASHFOOT**—gray she-cat

MEDICINE CAT **KESTRELFLIGHT**—mottled gray tom

WARRIORS **CROWFEATHER**—dark gray tom

OWLWHISKER—light brown tabby tom
APPRENTICE, WHISKERPAW (light brown tom)

WHITETAIL—small white she-cat

NIGHTCLOUD—black she-cat

GORSETAIL—very pale gray-and-white she-cat with blue eyes

WEASELFUR—ginger tom with white paws

HARESPRING—brown-and-white tom

LEAFTAIL—dark tabby tom with amber eyes

ANTPELT—brown tom with one black ear

EMBERFOOT—gray tom with two dark paws

HEATHERTAIL—light brown tabby she-cat with blue eyes
APPRENTICE, FURZEPAW (gray-and-white she-cat)

BREEZEPELT—black tom with amber eyes
APPRENTICE, BOULDERPAW (large pale gray tom)

SEDGEWHISKER—light brown tabby she-cat

SWALLOWTAIL—dark gray she-cat

SUNSTRIKE—tortoiseshell she-cat with large white mark on her forehead

ELDERS	**WEBFOOT**—dark gray tabby tom
	TORNEAR—tabby tom

RIVERCLAN

LEADER	**LEOPARDSTAR**—unusually spotted golden tabby she-cat
DEPUTY	**MISTYFOOT**—gray she-cat with blue eyes
MEDICINE CAT	**MOTHWING**—dappled golden she-cat
	APPRENTICE, WILLOWSHINE (gray tabby she-cat)
WARRIORS	**REEDWHISKER**—black tom
	APPRENTICE, HOLLOWPAW (dark brown tabby tom)
	RIPPLETAIL—dark gray tabby tom
	GRAYMIST—pale gray tabby she-cat
	APPRENTICE, TROUTPAW (pale gray tabby she-cat)
	MINTFUR—light gray tabby tom

ICEWING—white she-cat with blue eyes

MINNOWTAIL—dark gray she-cat
APPRENTICE, MOSSYPAW (brown-and-white she-cat)

PEBBLEFOOT—mottled gray tom
APPRENTICE, RUSHPAW (light brown tabby tom)

MALLOWNOSE—light brown tabby tom

ROBINWING—tortoiseshell-and-white tom

BEETLEWHISKER—brown-and-white tabby tom

PETALFUR—gray-and-white she-cat

GRASSPELT—light brown tom

QUEENS

DUSKFUR—brown tabby she-cat

MOSSPELT—tortoiseshell she-cat with blue eyes

ELDERS

BLACKCLAW—smoky black tom

VOLETOOTH—small brown tabby tom

DAWNFLOWER—pale gray she-cat

DAPPLENOSE—mottled gray she-cat

POUNCETAIL—ginger-and-white tom

CATS OUTSIDE CLANS

SMOKY—muscular gray-and-white tom who lives in a barn at the horseplace

FLOSS—small gray-and-white she-cat who lives at the horseplace

OTHER ANIMALS

MIDNIGHT—a star-gazing badger who lives by the sea

Hareview Campsite

Sanctuary
Cottage

Sadler Woods

Littlepine Road

Littlepine
Sailing
Center

Littlepine
Island

River Alba

Whitchurch Road

PROLOGUE

❧

Water poured over the lip of the rock in a smooth curve and roared down into a chasm. Far below, it tumbled and foamed into a pool. The rays of the setting sun set a myriad of trapped rainbows dancing in the spray.

Three cats sat on the edge of the river just upstream of the waterfall. They watched as a fourth cat approached, stalking delicately across the shaggy moss that covered the riverbank. Starlight sparkled at her paws and misted on her gray-blue fur.

The newcomer halted and raked the waiting cats with an icy blue stare. "In the name of all Clans, why did you choose to meet here?" she demanded, irritably shaking one forepaw. "It's far too wet, and I can't hear myself think."

Another she-cat, with ragged gray fur, rose to face her. "Stop complaining, Bluestar. I chose this place *because* it's damp and noisy. I have things to say that I don't want any other cat to overhear."

A golden tabby tom beckoned with his tail. "Come and sit by me. There's a dry spot just here."

Bluestar padded across to him and sat down with a

contemptuous sniff. "If this is dry, Lionheart, then I'm a mouse." Turning to the gray she-cat, she added, "Well, Yellowfang? What is it?"

"The prophecy has not been fulfilled," Yellowfang meowed. "The Three have come together at last, but two of the cats might not recognize the third."

"Are you sure we've got the right Three this time?" Bluestar asked sharply.

"You know we have." The speaker, a beautiful tortoiseshell-and-white she-cat, dipped her head gently toward the cat who had been her Clan leader. "Didn't we all have the same dream on the night the One was born?"

Bluestar flicked the tip of her tail. "You could be right, Spottedleaf. But so much has gone wrong that it's hard to trust anything now."

"Of course she's right." Yellowfang twitched her ears. "But if Jayfeather and Lionblaze don't recognize the One, there could be more trouble. I want to send them a sign."

"What?" Bluestar rose to her paws again, waving her tail commandingly as if she still held authority over the old medicine cat. "Yellowfang, have you forgotten that this prophecy isn't even ours? It could be dangerous to interfere with it. I think we should leave it alone."

Spottedleaf blinked, puzzled. "Dangerous?"

"Do you think it's a good idea to have cats in the Clans who are more powerful than the stars?" Bluestar challenged, facing each cat in turn. "More powerful than us, their warrior ancestors?" She swept her tail in a gesture to include her unseen

Clanmates, who were elsewhere in the beautiful, prey-filled forest. "What will become of ThunderClan if—"

"Have faith, Bluestar," Lionheart interrupted gently. "These are good and loyal cats."

"We thought that about Hollyleaf!" Bluestar retorted.

"We won't be wrong again," Yellowfang mewed. "Wherever the prophecy came from, we have to trust it. And we have to trust our Clanmates beside the lake."

Spottedleaf opened her jaws to speak, only to turn sharply at the sound of another cat brushing through the undergrowth a few fox-lengths farther upstream. A silver-furred she-cat burst out into the open and raced toward them, starlight swirling around her.

"Feathertail!" Bluestar exclaimed. "What are you doing here? Are you spying on us?"

"We're all Clanmates now," the former RiverClan warrior reminded her. "I guessed why you were meeting, and—"

"This is ThunderClan business, Feathertail," Yellowfang pointed out, with just a hint of her sharp yellow teeth.

"No, it's not!" Feathertail flashed back at her. "Jayfeather and Lionblaze are half WindClan—Crowfeather's sons." Her blue eyes filled with distress. "I care about what happens to them. I *have* to watch over them. And I grieve for Hollyleaf just as much as you do."

Spottedleaf stretched out her tail to touch the silver she-cat on the shoulder. "She's right. Let her stay."

Yellowfang shrugged. "They aren't your sons, Feathertail," she cautioned with unexpected gentleness. "We can warn them and guide them, but in the end they will go their own way."

"All sons and daughters do that, Yellowfang," Bluestar commented.

For a few heartbeats Yellowfang's expression darkened, and her amber gaze was fixed on the distance, as if she saw a lifetime of painful memories sketched in the sky. The sun was slipping down below the horizon, the red-streaked clouds fading to indigo. In the pool below the waterfall, the whirling foam shone pale in the shadows.

"So what do we do now?" Lionheart prompted. "Yellowfang, you mentioned sending a sign."

"I still think we shouldn't get involved," Bluestar insisted before Yellowfang could reply. "The third cat is already strong and clever, even if we don't know what her special power will be. If she's the right one, won't she figure everything out by herself?"

"We can't sit by and do nothing!" Feathertail protested, sinking her claws into the damp ground. "These young cats need our help."

"I think so, too," Lionheart agreed with a nod toward the silver she-cat. "If we had meddled more"—he glanced at Bluestar—"Hollyleaf might not have been lost."

Bluestar's neck fur bristled. "Hollyleaf made her own choices. These cats have to live their own lives. No cat can do it for them."

"No, but we can guide them," Spottedleaf meowed. "I agree with Yellowfang. I think we should send a sign."

"I can see you've all made up your minds." Bluestar sighed,

letting her neck fur lie flat again. "Very well, do what you wish."

"I will send an Omen." Yellowfang bowed her head; briefly the other cats saw beyond her matted fur and brusque manner to the deep wisdom of the medicine cat she had once been. "An Omen of the Stars."

"Which cat will you send it to?" Bluestar asked. "Lionblaze or Jayfeather?"

Yellowfang's amber gaze glowed in the last of the light as she turned toward her former Clan leader. "Neither," she meowed. "I will send it to the third cat."

CHAPTER 1

A full moon floated in a cloudless sky, casting thick black shadows across the island. The leaves of the Great Oak rustled in a hot breeze. Crouched between Sorreltail and Graystripe, Lionblaze felt as though he couldn't get enough air.

"You'd think it would be cooler at night," he grumbled.

"I know," Graystripe sighed, shifting uncomfortably on the dry, powdery soil. "This season just gets hotter and hotter. I can't even remember when it last rained."

Lionblaze stretched up to peer over the heads of the other cats at his brother, Jayfeather, who was sitting with the medicine cats. Onestar had just reported the death of Barkface, and Kestrelflight, the remaining WindClan medicine cat, looked rather nervous to be representing his Clan alone for the first time.

"Jayfeather says StarClan hasn't told him anything about the drought," Lionblaze mewed to Graystripe. "I wonder if any of the other medicine cats—"

He broke off as Firestar, the leader of ThunderClan, rose to his paws on the branch where he had been sitting while he waited for his turn to speak. RiverClan's leader, Leopardstar, glanced up from the branch just below, where she was crouching. Onestar, the leader of WindClan, was perched in the fork of a bough a few tail-lengths higher, while ShadowClan's leader, Blackstar, was visible just as a gleam of eyes among the clustering leaves above Onestar's branch.

"Like every other Clan, ThunderClan is troubled by the heat," Firestar began. "But we are coping well. Two of our apprentices have been made into warriors and received their warrior names: Toadstep and Rosepetal."

Lionblaze sprang to his paws. "Toadstep! Rosepetal!" he yowled. The rest of ThunderClan joined in, along with several cats from WindClan and ShadowClan, though Lionblaze noticed that the RiverClan warriors were silent, looking on with hostility in their eyes.

Who ruffled their fur? he wondered. It was mean-spirited for a whole Clan to refuse to greet a new warrior at a Gathering. He twitched his ears. He wouldn't forget this the next time Leopardstar announced a new RiverClan appointment.

The two new ThunderClan warriors ducked their heads in embarrassment, though their eyes shone as they were welcomed by the Clans. Cloudtail, Toadstep's former mentor, was puffed up with pride, while Squirrelflight, who had mentored Rosepetal, watched the young warriors with gleaming eyes.

"I'm still surprised Firestar picked Squirrelflight to be a mentor," Lionblaze muttered to himself. "After she told all those lies about us being her kits."

"Firestar knows what he's doing," Graystripe responded; Lionblaze winced as he realized the gray warrior had overheard every word of his criticism. "He trusts Squirrelflight, and he wants to show every cat that she's a good warrior and a valued member of ThunderClan."

"I suppose you're right." Lionblaze blinked miserably. He had loved and respected Squirrelflight so much when he thought she was his mother, but now he felt cold and empty when he looked at her. She had betrayed him, and his littermates, too deeply for forgiveness. Hadn't she?

"If you've quite finished . . ." Leopardstar spoke over the last of the yowls of welcome and rose to her paws, fixing Firestar with a glare. "RiverClan still has a report to make."

Firestar dipped his head courteously to the RiverClan leader and took a pace back, sitting down again with his tail wrapped around his paws. "Go ahead, Leopardstar."

The RiverClan leader was the last to speak at the Gathering; Lionblaze had seen her tail twitching impatiently while the other leaders made their reports. Now her piercing gaze traveled across the cats crowded together in the clearing, while her neck fur bristled in fury.

"Prey-stealers!" she hissed.

"What?" Lionblaze sprang to his paws; his startled yowl was lost in the clamor as more cats from ThunderClan, Wind-Clan, and ShadowClan leaped up to protest.

Leopardstar stared down at them, teeth bared, making no attempt to quell the tumult. Instinctively Lionblaze glanced upward, but there were no clouds to cover the moon; StarClan wasn't showing any anger at the outrageous accusation. *As if any of the other Clans would want to steal slimy, stinky fish!*

He noticed for the first time how thin the RiverClan leader looked, her bones sharp as flint beneath her dappled fur. The other RiverClan warriors were the same, Lionblaze realized, glancing around; even thinner than his own Clanmates and the ShadowClan warriors—and even thinner than the Wind-Clan cats, who looked skinny when they were full-fed.

"They're starving . . ." he murmured.

"We're all starving," Graystripe retorted.

Lionblaze let out a sigh. What the gray warrior said was true. In ThunderClan they had been forced to hunt and train at dawn and dusk in order to avoid the scorching heat of the day. In the hours surrounding sunhigh, the cats spent their time curled up sleeping in the precious shade at the foot of the walls of the stone hollow. For once the Clans were at peace, though Lionblaze suspected it was only because they were all too weak to fight, and no Clan had any prey worth fighting for.

Firestar rose to his paws again and raised his tail for silence. The caterwauling gradually died away and the cats sat down again, directing angry glares at the RiverClan leader.

"I'm sure you have good reason for accusing us all like that," Firestar meowed when he could make himself heard. "Would you like to explain?"

Leopardstar lashed her tail. "You have all been taking fish from the lake," she snarled. "And those fish belong to River-Clan."

"No, they don't," Blackstar objected, poking his head out from the foliage. "The lake borders all our territories. We're just as entitled to the fish as you are."

"Especially now," Onestar added. "We're all suffering from the drought. Prey is scarce in all our territories. If we can't eat fish, we'll starve."

Lionblaze stared at the two leaders in astonishment. Were ShadowClan and WindClan really so hungry that they'd been adding fish to their fresh-kill pile? Things must be *really* bad.

"But it's worse for us," Leopardstar insisted. "RiverClan doesn't eat any other kind of prey, so all the fish should belong to us."

"That's mouse-brained!" Squirrelflight sprang to her paws, her bushy tail lashing. "Are you saying that RiverClan can't eat any other prey? Are you admitting that your warriors are so incompetent they can't even catch a mouse?"

"Squirrelflight." Brambleclaw, the ThunderClan deputy, spoke commandingly as he rose from the oak root where he had been sitting with the other Clan deputies. His voice was coldly polite as he continued. "It's not your place to speak here. However," he added, looking up at Leopardstar, "she does have a point."

Lionblaze winced at Brambleclaw's tone, and he couldn't repress a twinge of sympathy for Squirrelflight as she sat down again, her head bent like an apprentice scolded in public by her mentor. Even after six moons, two whole seasons, Brambleclaw had not forgiven his former mate for claiming her sister Leafpool's kits as her own—and therefore his as well. Lionblaze still felt dazed whenever he reminded himself that Brambleclaw and Squirrelflight were not his real mother and father. He and his brother, Jayfeather, were the kits of the former ThunderClan medicine cat, Leafpool, and Crowfeather, a WindClan warrior. Since the truth came out, Brambleclaw and Squirrelflight had barely spoken to each other, and although Brambleclaw never punished Squirrelflight by giving her the hardest tasks or the most dangerous patrols, he made sure that their paths never crossed as they carried out their duties.

Squirrelflight's lie had been bad enough, but everything went wrong when she admitted what she had done. She had told the truth in a desperate attempt to save her kits from Ashfur's murderous fury at being passed over in favor of Brambleclaw, moons before Lionblaze and his littermates were born. Lionblaze's and Jayfeather's sister, Hollyleaf, had killed Ashfur to prevent him from revealing the secret at a Gathering. Then Hollyleaf vanished behind a fall of earth when she tried to escape through the tunnels to start a new life. Now the brothers had to accept that they were half-Clan, and that their father, Crowfeather, wanted nothing to do with them. And, on top of that, there were still suspicious looks from some of their own Clanmates, which made Lionblaze's pelt turn hot with rage.

As if we're suddenly going to turn disloyal because we've found out our father is a WindClan warrior! Who'd want to join those scrawny rabbit-munchers?

Lionblaze watched Jayfeather, wondering if he was thinking the same thing. His brother's sightless blue eyes were turned toward Brambleclaw, and his ears were alert, but it was hard to tell what was going through his mind. To Lionblaze's relief, the rest of the cats seemed too intent on what Leopardstar was saying to pay any attention to the rift between Brambleclaw and Squirrelflight.

"The fish in the lake belong to RiverClan," Leopardstar went on, her voice thin and high-pitched like wind through the reeds. "Any cat who tries to take them will feel our claws. From now on, I will instruct our border patrols to include the area around the water on every side."

"You can't do that!" Blackstar shouldered his way out of the leaves and leaped down to a lower branch, from where he could glare threateningly at Leopardstar. "Territories have never been extended into the lake."

Lionblaze pictured the lake as it had been, its waves lapping gently against grassy banks with only narrow strips of sand and pebbles here and there on the shore. Now the water had shrunk away into the middle, leaving wide stretches of mud that dried and cracked in the merciless greenleaf sun. Surely Leopardstar didn't want to claim those barren spaces as RiverClan territory?

"If any RiverClan patrols set paw on *our* territory," Onestar growled, baring his teeth, "they'll wish they hadn't."

"Leopardstar, listen." Lionblaze could tell that Firestar was trying hard to stay calm, even though the fur on his neck and shoulders was beginning to fluff up. "If you carry on like this, you're going to cause a war between the Clans. Cats will be injured. Haven't we got troubles enough without going to look for more?"

"Firestar's right," Sorreltail murmured into Lionblaze's ear.

"We should be trying to help one another, not fluffing up our fur ready for a fight."

Leopardstar crouched down as if she wanted to leap at the other leaders, letting out a wordless snarl and sliding out her claws.

This is a time of truce! Lionblaze thought, his eyes stretching wide in dismay. *A Clan leader attacking another cat at a Gathering? It can't happen!*

Firestar had tensed, bracing himself in case Leopardstar hurled herself at him. Instead she jumped down to the ground with a furious hiss, waving her tail for her warriors to gather around her.

"Stay away from our fish!" she spat as she led the way through the bushes that surrounded the clearing, toward the tree-bridge that led off the island. Her Clanmates followed her, shooting hostile looks at the other three Clans as they passed them. Murmurs of speculation and comment broke out as they left, but then Firestar's voice rang with authority above the noise.

"The Gathering is at an end! We must return to our territories until the next full moon. May StarClan light our paths!"

Lionblaze padded just behind his leader as the Thunder-Clan cats trekked around the edge of the lake toward their own territory. The water was barely visible, just a silver glimmer in the distance; pale moonlight reflected from the surface of the drying mud. Lionblaze wrinkled his nose at the smell of rotting fish.

If their prey stinks like that, RiverClan can have it!

Ahead of him, Brambleclaw trudged along next to Firestar, with Dustpelt and Ferncloud on the Clan leader's other side.

"What are we going to do?" the deputy asked. "Leopardstar *will* send out her patrols. What happens when we find them on our territory?"

Firestar twitched his ears. "We need to deal with this carefully," he meowed. "*Is* the bottom of the lake our territory? We would never have thought of claiming it when it was covered with water."

Dustpelt snorted. "If the dry land borders our territory, it's ours now. RiverClan has no rights to hunt or patrol there."

"But they look so hungry," Ferncloud mewed gently. "And ThunderClan never took fish from the lake anyway. Can't we let them have it?"

Dustpelt touched his nose briefly to his mate's ear. "Prey is scarce for us, too," he reminded her.

"We will not attack RiverClan warriors," Firestar decided. "Not unless they set paw on the ThunderClan territory within our scent marks—three tail-lengths from the shore, as we agreed when we came here. Brambleclaw, make sure that the patrols understand that when you send them out tomorrow."

"Of course, Firestar," the deputy replied, with a wave of his tail.

Lionblaze's pelt prickled. Even though he respected Firestar's conclusion because he was the Clan leader, Lionblaze wasn't sure that he had made the right decision this time.

Won't RiverClan think we're weak if we let them come around our side of the lake?

He jumped at the flick of a tail on his haunches and glanced around to see that Jayfeather had caught up to him.

"Leopardstar's got bees in her brain," his brother announced. "She'll never get away with this. Sooner or later, cats will get clawed."

"I know." Curiously, Lionblaze added, "I heard some ShadowClan cats at the Gathering saying that Leopardstar lost two lives recently. Is it true?"

Jayfeather gave him a curt nod. "Yes."

"She never announced it," Lionblaze commented.

Jayfeather halted, giving his brother a look of such sharp intelligence that Lionblaze found it hard to believe that his brilliant blue eyes couldn't see anything. "Come on, Lionblaze. When does a Clan leader ever announce they've lost a life? It would make them sound weak. Cats don't necessarily know how many lives their *own* leader has left."

"I suppose so," Lionblaze admitted, padding on.

"Leopardstar lost a life from a thorn scratch that got infected," Jayfeather continued. "And then straight after that she caught some kind of illness that made her terribly thirsty and weak, too. She couldn't even walk as far as the stream to get a drink."

"Mothwing and Willowshine told you all that?" Lionblaze asked, aware that medicine cats would confide in one another without thinking of the Clan rivalries that made warriors wary of saying too much.

"It doesn't matter how I found out," Jayfeather retorted. "I know, that's all."

Lionblaze suppressed a shiver. Even though he knew that Jayfeather's powers came from the prophecy, it still bothered him that his brother padded down paths that no cat, not even another medicine cat, had ever trodden before. Jayfeather *knew* things without being told—not even by StarClan. He could walk in other cats' dreams and learn their deepest secrets.

"I guess that's why Leopardstar is making such a nuisance of herself about the fish," Lionblaze murmured, pushing his uneasiness away. "She wants to prove to her Clan that she's still strong."

"She's going about it the wrong way," Jayfeather stated flatly. "She should know that she can't make the other Clans follow her orders. RiverClan will be worse off in the end than if they'd just struggled through the drought on their own territory, like the rest of us."

They were approaching the stream that marked the border between WindClan and ThunderClan. The water that had spilled into the lake with a rush and a gurgle just last newleaf had dwindled to a narrow stream of green slime, easily leaped over. Lionblaze drew a breath of relief as he plunged into the undergrowth beyond, under the familiar trees of his own territory.

"Maybe it'll all blow over," he meowed hopefully. "Leopardstar might see sense when she thinks about what the other leaders told her at the Gathering."

Jayfeather let out a contemptuous snort. "Hedgehogs will

fly before Leopardstar backs down. No, Lionblaze, the only thing that will solve our problem is for the lake to fill up again."

Lionblaze was padding through long, lush grass, his paws sinking into water at every step. A cool breeze ruffled his fur. Any moment now, he could put down his head and drink as much as he wanted, relieving the thirst that burned inside him like a thorn. A vole popped out of the reed bed in front of him, but before Lionblaze could leap on it, something hard poked him in the side. He woke up to find himself in his nest in the warriors' den, with Cloudtail standing over him. His fur felt sticky, and the air smelled of dust.

"Wake up," the white warrior meowed, giving Lionblaze another prod. "What are you, a dormouse?"

"Did you have to do that?" Lionblaze complained. "I was having this really great dream. . . ."

"And now you can go on a really great water patrol." Cloudtail's tone was unsympathetic. Since the streams that fed the lake had dried up, the only source of water was the shallow, brackish pool in the middle of the lake bed. Patrols went down several times a day to collect water for the Clan, in addition to hunting and patrolling as usual. The greenleaf nights seemed shorter than ever when every cat was tired out from extra duties.

Lionblaze's jaws gaped in an enormous yawn. "Okay, I'm coming."

He followed Cloudtail out of the den, shaking scraps of

moss from his pelt. The sky was pale with the first light of dawn, and although the sun had not yet risen the air was hot and heavy. Lionblaze groaned inwardly at the thought of yet another dry, scorching day.

Hazeltail, her apprentice, Blossompaw, Berrynose, and Icecloud were sitting outside the den; they rose to their paws as Cloudtail appeared with Lionblaze. None of them had been to the Gathering the night before, but Lionblaze could tell from their tense expressions that they knew about Leopardstar's threats.

"Let's go." Cloudtail waved his tail toward the thorn tunnel.

As Lionblaze padded through the forest behind the white warrior, he overheard Berrynose boasting to Icecloud: "River-Clan had better not mess with us when we get to the lake. I'll teach any cat not to get in my fur."

Icecloud murmured something in reply that Lionblaze didn't catch. *Berrynose thinks he's so great,* he thought. *But it's mouse-brained to go looking for trouble when none of us is strong enough for a battle.*

To his relief, Cloudtail took his patrol to the foot of a huge oak tree and instructed them to collect bundles of moss to soak in the lake. Berrynose couldn't go on telling Icecloud what a fantastic warrior he was when his jaws were stuffed with fluffy green stalks.

When they reached the lake, Cloudtail paused briefly at the edge, gazing out across the lake bottom. It looked dry and powdery near the bank, with jagged cracks stretching across it; farther out it glistened in the pale light of dawn. As he tried to work out where the mud ended and the water began, Lionblaze spotted the tiny figures of four cats, far out across the mud. He set down his bundle of moss and tasted the air; the faint scent of RiverClan wafted toward him, mingled with the familiar stink of dead fish.

"Now listen," Cloudtail began, setting down his own bundle. "RiverClan can't object to us taking water, and Firestar has already said that he doesn't want any fighting. Have you got that, Berrynose?" He gave the younger warrior a hard stare.

Reluctantly Berrynose nodded. " 'Kay," he mumbled around his mouthful of moss.

"Make sure you don't forget." With a final glare Cloudtail led his patrol out across the mud toward the distant lake.

The surface of the mud was hard at first, but as the patrol drew closer to the water Lionblaze found his paws sinking in at every step. "This is disgusting," he muttered, his words muffled by the moss as he tried to shake off the sticky, pale brown blobs. "I'll never get clean again."

As they approached the water's edge, he saw that the River-Clan cats had clustered together and were waiting for them, blocking their way: Reedwhisker and Graymist, with Otterheart and her apprentice, Sneezepaw. They all looked thin and exhausted, but their eyes glittered with hostility and their fur was bristling as if they would leap into battle for a couple of mousetails.

Reedwhisker stepped forward. "Have you forgotten what

Leopardstar told you at the Gathering last night?" he challenged. "The fish in the lake belong to RiverClan."

"We're not here to fish," Cloudtail replied calmly, setting down his moss. "We only want water. You're not going to deny us that, are you?"

"Are there no streams in your territory?" Graymist demanded.

"The streams have dried up, as you know very well." Lionblaze saw the tip of Cloudtail's tail twitch irritably as he answered; the fiery white warrior was finding it hard to control his temper. "We need water from the lake."

"And we'll take it whether you like it or not," Berrynose added, dropping his moss and taking a threatening step forward.

Instantly the four RiverClan cats slid out their claws. "The lake belongs to us," Otterheart hissed.

Blossompaw's eyes stretched wide in dismay and Hazeltail stepped forward, thrusting her apprentice behind her. Lionblaze braced himself and unsheathed his claws, ready to spring.

Cloudtail whipped around to face his patrol. "Keep your jaws shut!" he ordered Berrynose.

"Are you going to let them talk to us like that?" Berrynose challenged. "I'm not scared of them, even if you are."

Cloudtail stepped forward until he was nose to nose with the younger warrior, his eyes like chips of ice. "One more word and you'll be searching the elders for ticks for the next moon. Understand?"

Lionblaze felt a tingle of shock run beneath his fur. Cloud-tail was brisk at the best of times, but he'd never seen him this angry at one of his own Clanmates. It was as if collecting water was the most important thing in the world to Cloud-tail—and maybe it was, with his Clan weakened by thirst and getting weaker. Lionblaze wondered what would happen if RiverClan succeeded in preventing the other Clans from get-ting near the water. Would three of the four Clans die out?

Not waiting for Berrynose's response, Cloudtail swung around and addressed the RiverClan cats again. "I apologize for my warrior," he meowed. His voice was tight; Lionblaze could tell what an effort he was making to stay polite. "I think he must have caught a touch of the sun. Now, I'd appreciate it if you'd let us take some water."

For a heartbeat Reedwhisker paused. Lionblaze felt his paws itch with the urge to spring into battle. Cloudtail had warned them that they were too weak to fight, but he didn't know that Lionblaze was one of the Three and had the power to fight the fiercest battles without getting a single scratch. *But I know we've got problems enough without fighting one another.*

Finally Reedwhisker stepped back, gesturing with his tail for the rest of his patrol to do the same. "Take water, but no fish," he growled.

We're not here for fish. How many more times will we have to tell you that? Lionblaze thought.

"Thank you." Cloudtail dipped his head and padded up to the water's edge. Lionblaze followed, aware of the hostile gaze of the RiverClan cats boring into his back, watching his every move. His fury welled up again. *This is just stupid! Do they think I can smuggle a fish out under my pelt?*

He could see that his Clanmates were angry, too; Cloudtail's tail-tip twitched and Berrynose's eyes were blazing, though he had the sense to keep quiet. The she-cats' fur was bristling, and they glared over their shoulders at the RiverClan cats as they padded past.

Lionblaze soaked his moss in the lake water and lapped up a few mouthfuls. It was warm and tasted of earth and weeds, hardly quenching his thirst. He forced himself to swallow, wincing as the gritty liquid slid down his throat. The sun had risen, its harsh rays slashing across the tops of the trees, and there was no sign of a cloud from one horizon to the other.

How much longer can we go on like this?

CHAPTER 2

Jayfeather picked through the herbs in the storage cave at the back of his den. The leaves and stems felt dry and crackly, and their scents were musty. *I should be stocking up for leaf-fall,* he thought. *But how can I when there's no fresh growth?*

The pressure of being ThunderClan's only medicine cat weighed like a stone in his belly. He remembered all the times he had grumbled about Leafpool telling him what to do. Now he wished that she had never resigned as a medicine cat and gone to live in the warriors' den. *What does it matter that she had kits? She still knows all about herbs, and what to do when a cat is injured.*

His pelt prickled with the bitter memory of a few days ago, when Briarpaw had pelted into the camp and skidded to a halt in front of his den.

"Jayfeather!" she panted. "Come quick! Firestar's hurt!"

"What? Where?"

"A fox got him!" The young apprentice's voice was shaking with fear. "On the ShadowClan border, near the dead tree."

"Okay, I'm coming." Inwardly Jayfeather felt just as scared, but he forced himself to sound confident. "Go find Leafpool and tell her."

Briarpaw let out a startled gasp, but Jayfeather didn't pause to ask why. Grabbing a few stems of horsetail, he raced out through the thorn tunnel and headed for the ShadowClan border. Only when he was already on his way did he remember that Leafpool wasn't a medicine cat any longer.

Before he reached the dead tree, the scent of blood led him to his leader. Firestar was lying on his side in a clump of ferns, his breath coming harsh and shallow. Sandstorm and Graystripe were crouched over him while Thornclaw kept watch from the top of a tree stump.

"Thank StarClan!" Sandstorm exclaimed as Jayfeather dashed up. "Firestar, Jayfeather's here. Just hold on."

"What happened?" Jayfeather asked, running his paws gently over Firestar's side. His belly lurched as he discovered a long gash with blood still pulsing out of it.

"We were patrolling, and a fox leaped out at us," Graystripe replied. "We chased it off, but . . ." His voice choked.

"Find some cobwebs," Jayfeather ordered. He began to chew up the horsetail to make a poultice. *Where's Leafpool?* he asked himself in agony. *I don't know if I'm doing the right thing.*

He patted the poultice onto the gash in his leader's side, binding it with the cobwebs that Graystripe thrust into his paws, but before he had finished he heard Firestar's breathing grow slower and slower, until at last it stopped.

"He's losing a life," Sandstorm whispered.

Jayfeather went on numbly fixing the poultice in place, so that when Firestar recovered he wouldn't lose any more blood. The time seemed to stretch out unnaturally, and Jayfeather's mind whirled as he tried to count up how many lives his leader had left.

That wasn't his last life, was it? It couldn't be!

He had almost given up hope, when Firestar gave a cough, his breathing started up again, and he raised his head. "Thanks, Jayfeather," he mewed weakly. "Don't look so worried. I'll be fine in a few heartbeats."

But as Firestar set off back to camp, leaning on Graystripe's shoulder, with Sandstorm padding along anxiously on his other side and Thornclaw bringing up the rear, Jayfeather hadn't been able to forgive himself. *I needed Leafpool, and she wasn't here.* His former mentor hadn't appeared until they were within sight of the stone hollow. She had been hunting on the WindClan border, and it had taken Briarpaw all that time to find her.

"You did your best," she reassured Jayfeather when he told her what had happened. "Sometimes that's all you can do."

But Jayfeather wasn't convinced; he knew that Leafpool would have saved Firestar if she had been there.

My Clan leader lost a life because of me, he told himself bitterly. *What sort of medicine cat does that make me?*

Now he finished sorting through the herbs, picked up a mouthful of ragwort, and set off for the elders' den. When he ducked under the outer boughs of the hazel bush, he found Mousefur curled up near the trunk, snoring gently, while Longtail and the old loner, Purdy, sat side by side in the shade of the rock wall.

"So this badger, see, was out lookin' for trouble, an' I

tracked it—" Purdy broke off as Jayfeather entered the den. "Hello, young 'un! What can we do for you?"

"Eat these herbs." Jayfeather dropped the stems and divided them carefully into three. "It's ragwort; it'll keep your strength up."

He heard Purdy's wheezing breath as the old loner padded up and prodded the herbs with one paw. "That stuff? Looks funny to me."

"Never mind what it looks like," Jayfeather hissed through gritted teeth. "Just eat it. You too, Longtail."

"Okay." The blind elder padded across and licked up the herbs. "Come on, Purdy," he mewed through the mouthful. "You know they'll do you good." His voice was hoarse, and his paw steps were unsteady. Every hair on Jayfeather's pelt prickled with anxiety. The whole Clan was hungry and thirsty, but Longtail seemed to be suffering particularly badly. Jayfeather suspected he was giving his share of water and food to Mousefur.

If I can get Purdy on his own, I'll ask him.

Purdy grunted disbelievingly, but Jayfeather heard him chewing up the ragwort. "Tastes foul," the old loner complained.

Jayfeather picked up the remaining herbs and padded across to Mousefur. The elder was already waking up, roused by the sound of voices. "What do you want?" she demanded. "Can't a cat get any sleep around here?"

She sounded as cranky as ever, which reassured Jayfeather that at least she was managing to cope with the heat. *When*

Mousefur sounds nice and sweet, I'll really start worrying!

"Ragwort," he meowed. "You need to eat it."

Mousefur let out a sigh. "I suppose you'll nag me until I do. Well, while I'm eating it, you can tell me what went on at the Gathering last night."

Jayfeather waited until he heard the old cat beginning to nibble on the herbs, then launched into an account of the previous night's Gathering.

"What?" Mousefur choked on a ragwort leaf when Jayfeather came to the point where Leopardstar had laid claim to the lake and all the fish. "She can't do that!"

Jayfeather shrugged. "She's done it. She said that River-Clan deserves to have all the fish because they can't eat any other sort of prey."

"And StarClan let her get away with it?" Mousefur hissed. "There were no clouds covering the moon?"

"If there had been, the Gathering would have broken up."

"What are our warrior ancestors thinking?" Mousefur snarled. "How could they stand by and let that mange-ridden she-cat decide that no other Clans can use the lake?"

Jayfeather couldn't answer her. He hadn't received any signs from StarClan recently, not since the beginning of the hot weather. *Leafpool would have heard from StarClan by now,* he thought. *They would have told her what to do to help the Clan.*

Leaving Mousefur muttering darkly over the last of the ragwort, Jayfeather pushed his way out of the elders' den and headed into the clearing. Passing the apprentices' den, he picked up a couple of unexpected scents. "Now what's going on?" he meowed irritably.

He padded across to the den and stuck his head through the bracken that covered the entrance. He could hear muffled whispering and rustling among the moss and bracken of the apprentices' nests.

"Dovekit! Ivykit!" he growled. "Come out of there. You're not apprentices yet."

The two kits scampered out of the den, stifling *mrrows* of laughter as they halted beside Jayfeather and shook scraps of moss from their fur.

"We were only looking!" Dovekit protested. "We'll be apprentices any day now, so we wanted to choose good places for our new nests."

"Side by side," Ivykit added. "We're going to do all our training together."

"That's right," Dovekit mewed. "And we're never going on patrol with any other cats."

Jayfeather let out a snort, not knowing whether he felt amused or frustrated. "In your dreams, kits. The other apprentices will tell you where you're going to sleep. And your mentors will tell you when to patrol, and who to go with."

The two kits were silent for a couple of heartbeats. Then Dovekit burst out, "We don't care! Come on, Ivykit, let's tell Whitewing that we looked in the den!"

Jayfeather stayed where he was for a moment as the two kits bundled off toward the nursery. There was an ache in his chest as he remembered when he had been a kit and believed he had a mother to boast to. Now he only had Leafpool.

As though the thought had called her up, his real mother's scent drifted toward him as she emerged from the thorn tunnel with the rest of a hunting patrol. Tasting the air, Jayfeather could tell that Dustpelt, Brackenfur, and even the apprentice Bumblepaw were carrying fresh-kill, but Leafpool had nothing.

Jayfeather's lip curled into a sneer. *All she's caught is fleas! She's a medicine cat, not a warrior. She should be helping me, not trying to pretend that her entire history vanished on the day the truth came out.*

He heard Leafpool's paw steps padding toward him, but he didn't want to talk to her. He turned his head away, and felt her sadness as she passed him. She didn't try to speak, but he could pick up her loneliness and sense of defeat as sharply as if they were his own. *It's as if she's given up every scrap of fight she ever had!*

Jayfeather could sense the awkwardness of the rest of the patrol, too, as if they didn't know how to treat Leafpool anymore. She had been their trusted medicine cat for so long that they didn't want to punish her for loving a WindClan cat once, but it seemed as if they no longer knew how to treat her as a much-loved and loyal Clanmate.

The hunting patrol started to put their prey on the fresh-kill pile. Brightheart followed them in through the thorn tunnel; Jayfeather caught the tang of the yarrow she was carrying.

"That's great, Brightheart," he called. "I wasn't sure you'd be able to find any, and we're totally out."

"There're a few plants near the old Twoleg nest,"

Brightheart mumbled around her mouthful of stems as she headed for the medicine cat's den.

Many seasons ago, a former medicine cat, Cinderpelt, had taught Brightheart the basic uses of herbs and how to treat minor wounds and illnesses. Ever since Jayfeather had become the only ThunderClan medicine cat, Brightheart had been helping him by gathering herbs and dealing with straightforward injuries. He knew she could never be his real apprentice—she was older than him, and committed to being a warrior—but he was grateful for her support.

Besides, I don't need to choose an apprentice yet. That was for older medicine cats; he felt countless moons stretching out ahead of him, thrumming beneath his paws like the ancient footprints he walked in by the Moonpool. And of course there was still the Prophecy to fulfill before it was his turn to join StarClan. *There will be three . . . who hold the power of the stars in their paws.*

The sun was well above the trees by now, beating down so that Jayfeather's fur felt as if it were on fire. *I can almost smell the smoke!*

Then his nose twitched. The acrid scent tickling his nostrils really was smoke. His pelt prickling with fear, he tasted the air for a couple of heartbeats, just to be certain, and located the smell at the edge of the hollow, close to the elders' den.

"Fire!" he yowled, launching himself toward the smell of burning.

Almost in the same heartbeat, he stumbled as Dovekit hurtled past him, her pelt brushing his as she raced out into the center of the clearing.

"Fire!" she screeched. "The Clan is on fire!"

Jayfeather was impressed that she had smelled the smoke so quickly. *I thought my nose was the best in the Clan!* But there was no time to think about that now. He had to find the fire and put it out before it spread to the rest of the camp.

More caterwauling broke out behind Jayfeather as he ran toward the hazel bush. He scented Brackenfur racing beside him and snapped, "Get the elders out of their den!"

The ginger warrior veered away to the entrance; Jayfeather raced on past the den, guided by the scent of smoke. As he drew closer to the rock wall he could hear the crackle of flames. A wave of heat rolled out to meet him and he halted. Frustration at his blindness swept over him, fierce as the fire. *I don't know where to attack it!*

Then another cat shouldered him out of the way; Jayfeather picked up Graystripe's scent, with Firestar and Squirrelflight just behind him.

"We need water," the Clan leader mewed crisply. "Jayfeather, find some cats to go down to the lake."

"That'll take too long," Graystripe yelped. "Kick dust on the fire, quick!"

Jayfeather heard the sound of vigorous scraping, but the smoke and flames didn't die down. He turned away, about to obey Firestar's order, when he heard the sound of several cats racing over toward the fire.

"Cloudtail! Lionblaze!" Firestar exclaimed. "Thank Star-Clan!"

Jayfeather picked up the scent of wet moss as his brother

and several other cats brushed past him. There was a loud hissing sound, and the acrid smell of smoke suddenly became much stronger. It caught in his throat and he retreated, coughing.

Moments later, Lionblaze joined him. "That was close!" he panted. "If we hadn't come just then, the whole camp could have caught fire."

"You're sure the fire's out?" Jayfeather asked, blinking eyes that stung from the smoke.

"Firestar is checking." Lionblaze let out a long sigh. "And now I suppose we'll have to go get more water. I just hope the RiverClan cats have gone."

"RiverClan?" Jayfeather felt his neck fur begin to bristle.

"There was a patrol out there when we arrived," Lionblaze explained. "We nearly had to fight for a few mouthfuls of water. If the RiverClan cats are still there, they certainly won't welcome us back." His voice grew heavy with anger. "They looked as if they were counting every drop!"

Jayfeather's tail drooped as he stood beside his brother among the sooty remnants of the fire. Around him, cats were beginning to carry the burnt debris out of the camp; the sharp scent made him cough again.

Will the end of the Clans be like this? he wondered. *Just like the lake is shrinking? So ordinary, and frustrating, and so bitterly, painfully slow?*

Lionblaze touched his nose to Jayfeather's shoulder in a gesture of comfort. "Remember, we will be Three again," he murmured. "Whitewing's kits are Firestar's kin, too."

Jayfeather shrugged. "How can we be sure? Why hasn't StarClan sent us a sign?"

"We don't know that the prophecy came from them in the first place," his brother pointed out.

"But they—"

A loud yowl from across the clearing interrupted what Jayfeather was about to say. "Hey, Jayfeather!"

Jayfeather's whiskers twitched as he recognized the voice of the most annoying cat in the Clan. "What is it now, Berrynose?" he asked with a sigh, heading in his direction.

Berrynose padded up to meet him; Jayfeather detected the scent of Poppyfrost just behind him.

"Poppyfrost is having kits," the young warrior announced importantly. "*My* kits."

"Congratulations," Jayfeather murmured.

"I want you to tell her she's got to rest and take care of herself," Berrynose went on. "Having kits can be dangerous, right?"

"Well . . . sometimes," Jayfeather admitted.

"Yeah, I heard that the kits can come too soon, or they can be weak, or—"

"Berrynose," Poppyfrost interrupted; Jayfeather could pick up her distress as clearly as if she had caterwauled it to the whole camp. "I'm sure I'll be okay."

"Or the kits take too long in coming," Berrynose finished, as if his mate hadn't spoken.

"There can be problems, but . . ." Jayfeather padded forward until he could give Poppyfrost a good sniff. "She's a healthy she-cat," he went on. "There's no reason she can't carry on with her normal duties for now."

"What?" Berrynose sounded outraged. "That's not good enough! Poppyfrost, you go into the nursery right now, and let Ferncloud and Daisy take care of you."

"Really, there's no need—" Poppyfrost began, but Berrynose was already nudging her across the clearing toward the entrance to the nursery.

Jayfeather stood still as the sound of their paw steps retreated. *Why consult a medicine cat if you're not going to listen, mousebrain?*

Defeat suddenly flooded over Jayfeather like a huge wave. What was the point of having the power of the stars in his paws if even his own Clanmates didn't listen to him? "I don't know if we can do this on our own," he murmured to himself. "Two or three of us . . ."

CHAPTER 3
❧

Dovekit wriggled with excitement as Whitewing's tongue rasped around her ears and down her neck.

"Keep still," her mother scolded. "You can't go to your apprentice ceremony looking as if you've been pulled through the thorn barrier backward!"

Ivykit glanced over her shoulder from where she was crouched at the entrance to the nursery. "The cats are gathering out there already," she reported, her voice quivering with anticipation. "I think the whole Clan will come to see us become apprentices!"

Dovekit twisted away from her mother's tongue and scampered over the mossy floor of the nursery to join her sister. "Let's go!" she urged.

"It's not time yet," her mother told her. "We have to wait until Firestar calls the Clan together."

"It won't be long." The gentle mew came from Daisy, the cat from the horseplace. Dovekit understood that Daisy would never be a warrior; she and Ferncloud both stayed in the nursery to help each new queen with her kits.

Now Daisy was curled up beside Poppyfrost, who had moved into the nursery two sunrises before, her belly gently rounded with Berrynose's kits. Berrynose was Daisy's son, so these kits would be Daisy's kin too.

"Are you coming to see us made apprentices?" she asked the she-cats.

"Of course." Poppyfrost heaved herself to her paws and gave herself a quick grooming to get rid of the scraps of moss that clung to her pelt. "We wouldn't miss it for anything."

Dovekit gave her shoulders another wriggle; she felt as if she couldn't keep her paws still for another heartbeat. She was so excited that she could almost forget how thirsty she was. "I wonder who our mentors will be," she meowed.

Before Ivykit could reply, Firestar's flame-colored figure appeared on the Highledge and his voice rang out across the camp. "Let all cats old enough to catch their own prey join here beneath the Highledge for a Clan meeting."

Dovekit sprang up, ready to bounce out into the clearing, but her mother's tail reached out to hold her back. "Not yet," Whitewing murmured. "And you will *walk* out there like a sensible apprentice, not a little kit who doesn't know how to behave."

"Okay, okay," Dovekit muttered, trying to force down her impatience.

Ivykit echoed her sister, then added, "I think I'm going to be sick."

"Oh, no!" Dovekit let out a wail. *What will the Clan think of us if Ivykit is sick at her apprentice ceremony?*

"No, you're not," Whitewing mewed calmly. "You'll both behave yourselves and make me proud of you. Look, your father's come to get you."

Birchfall had appeared at the entrance to the nursery, looking down at his daughters with glowing eyes. "Come along, the Clan is waiting for you," he told them.

Ivykit sprang to her paws, and Dovekit flexed her claws while Whitewing gave her own pelt a quick grooming and came to join them. By this time the whole of ThunderClan had gathered in the clearing, beneath the Highledge. Dovekit felt the gaze of many eyes on her as she padded out of the nursery beside Ivykit, their mother and father following behind. Daisy, Ferncloud, and Poppyfrost brought up the rear, and sat down just outside the entrance.

Dovekit's heart was thumping so hard that she thought it was going to burst out of her chest, but she kept her head and her tail held high.

"I just know I'll forget what to do," Ivykit muttered into her ear.

Dovekit brushed herself against her sister's pelt. "You'll be fine."

Whitewing guided them toward the circle of waiting cats, who parted to let them in. Dovekit found herself standing between her sister and Squirrelflight, who gave her an encouraging nod.

"I've called you together for one of the most important moments in the life of a Clan," Firestar began. "Dovekit and Ivykit have reached their sixth moon, and it's time for them to become apprentices." He beckoned with his tail. "Come forward."

Dovekit wanted to do a big jump right into the middle of the circle, but at the last moment she remembered what her mother had told her and made herself walk slowly forward beside her sister.

"Dovekit," Firestar meowed, "from this day until you receive your warrior name, you will be called Dovepaw."

"Dovepaw!" The voices of her Clanmates rang out around her, making her pelt tingle as she heard her new name for the first time. "Dovepaw!"

"StarClan, I ask you to guide this new apprentice," Firestar went on, gazing up at the hot blue sky above the hollow. "Set her paws on the path she must follow to become a warrior."

Dovepaw suppressed a shiver as she thought of all the starry cats, her warrior ancestors, looking down on her as Firestar spoke to them.

"Lionblaze." Firestar flicked his tail toward the golden tabby warrior who stood close to the tumbled rocks that led up to the Highledge. "You will be mentor to Dovepaw. You are a loyal warrior and your battle skills are outstanding. I know that you will pass these qualities on to Dovepaw."

Lionblaze! Dovepaw's heart lurched as she gazed across the clearing at the golden-furred tom. *He's a great cat—but what if he doesn't like me?*

She bounded over to him, anxiously looking up into his amber eyes. She was astonished and delighted to see how pleased he looked as he bent his head to touch noses with her.

"I'll work really hard," she promised him in a whisper.

"So will I," Lionblaze replied. "We'll make a great team."

Dovepaw stood proudly beside him and listened as Firestar repeated the ceremony for her sister. Ivykit looked lonely and nervous all by herself in the middle of the circle of cats, but she kept her head up bravely, her gaze fixed on Firestar.

"Ivykit," Firestar meowed, "from this day until you receive your warrior name, you will be called Ivypaw. May StarClan watch over you and guide you in your journey to become a warrior." He paused for a heartbeat for the rest of the Clan to call Ivypaw by her new name, then swept his tail toward Cinderheart. "Cinderheart, you have shown courage and endurance in your apprenticeship, and I trust now that you will teach Ivypaw to follow in your path."

A murmur of approval rose up from the surrounding cats as Ivypaw scampered across the clearing to touch noses with Cinderheart. The gray warrior's blue eyes shone with joy as she welcomed her new apprentice.

"Dovepaw! Ivypaw!" the Clan called out.

Dovepaw felt as if she were about to burst with pride and happiness as her Clanmates crowded around to congratulate them both.

"What do we do now?" she asked Lionblaze eagerly.

"Nothing exciting, I'm afraid," he replied with a twitch of his ears. "The Clan needs water. We have to collect some moss, and then go down to the lake to soak it."

Dovepaw gave a little skip of excitement. "That's great! I'll get to see more of the territory." Glancing around for her sister, she added, "Can Ivypaw and Cinderheart come with us?"

"Of course." It was Cinderheart who replied, padding

toward them with Ivypaw bouncing at her side. "But we have to watch out for RiverClan. They might try to cause trouble."

"I thought RiverClan was on the other side of the lake?" Ivypaw asked, tipping her head on one side.

"Not anymore," Lionblaze growled. "Let's get going, and I'll explain on the way."

He led them through the thorn tunnel and headed in the direction of the lake. Dovepaw had never been more than a few fox-lengths outside the camp, but her excitement at seeing somewhere new was mixed with indignation at what Lionblaze and Cinderheart were telling them.

"But RiverClan can't just take the lake like that!" she protested. "Can they?"

"Why doesn't Firestar fight them?" Ivypaw mewed.

"Firestar doesn't like to cause trouble," Cinderheart explained. "He always tries to look for a solution that doesn't involve fighting. That's part of what makes him such a great leader."

Dovepaw wasn't sure that she understood. Even though she was only a new apprentice, she knew that Clans didn't trespass on one another's territory. That was part of the warrior code!

"Stick close to me and Cinderheart," Lionblaze warned them. "And whatever happens, *don't* mess with RiverClan."

Just so long as they don't mess with me or Ivypaw, Dovepaw thought.

Their mentors took them to the foot of a huge oak tree, where they collected balls of moss from the roots, and then onward to the lake. As they emerged from the trees onto the bank, Dovepaw's mouth dropped open, letting her moss fall.

"I thought the lake was huge!" she gasped. "Not just that little bit of water right over there." She felt a stab of disappointment. Why did the warriors make such a fuss about something that was not much bigger than a puddle?

"It usually comes right up to where we are now," Lionblaze told her. He angled his ears forward to where a narrow strip of pebbles gave way to dried mud. "It's only because of the drought that it's shrunk so much."

"The drought also means there haven't been so many Twolegs around this greenleaf," Cinderheart meowed. "So it isn't all bad." It sounded as if she was trying to convince herself as much as the apprentices.

"What if the lake shrinks away altogether?" Ivypaw asked.

"It won't," Cinderheart stated, though the look she exchanged with Lionblaze told Dovepaw that she wasn't completely certain. "It's bound to rain soon."

"Now that we're here, you might as well learn something about the territories," Lionblaze meowed. "This is Thunder-Clan territory, of course, and over there"—he swept his tail around in an arc—"is WindClan."

Dovepaw's gaze followed his pointing tail to where smooth grassy moorland swelled up to meet the sky. "There aren't many trees for hunting in," she remarked.

"No, WindClan cats like open spaces, so their territory's perfect for them," Cinderheart told her. "ShadowClan cats like pine trees, so they chose the territory over on that side."

Dovepaw and Ivypaw both examined the dark line of trees that bordered the lake on the other side of ThunderClan. "I'm glad I'm not a ShadowClan cat," Ivypaw mewed.

Dovepaw concentrated for a moment, trying to memorize everything that the scene in front of her could tell her. She could see a group of cats on the ShadowClan side, trekking across the barren ground toward the distant lake, and she drew in a long breath to taste their scent. On the WindClan side, cats were returning to the shore, and Dovepaw breathed in their scent, too.

"Ivypaw," she whispered, flicking her sister over one ear with her tail, "you should be picking up the scents of those cats over there. It's all stuff we need to know."

"What?" Ivypaw gave her a puzzled look, but before Dovepaw could say any more, she was interrupted by a loud exclamation from Lionblaze.

"Now what's happening?"

Dovepaw looked across the brittle brown mud and spotted a patrol of ThunderClan cats close to the water's edge. They seemed to be struggling, their backs arched and tails thrashing in the air. A couple of heartbeats later one of the warriors began racing back to the shore; as he drew closer she recognized Thornclaw.

"Trouble?" Lionblaze called.

"Berrynose and Spiderleg are stuck in the mud," Thornclaw panted, pausing briefly. "I need a branch or something to get them out."

"We'll come and help," Cinderheart told him, with a whisk

of her tail to beckon the two apprentices. "Come on, you two. Bring your moss, and watch where you're putting your paws."

As she led them out onto the mud, Dovepaw glanced back to see Thornclaw pull a long stick out from under the roots of an elder bush at the edge of the bank. Before he could carry it off, Jayfeather erupted from the undergrowth, a bundle of herbs in his jaws.

"Hey, that's mine!" he protested, spitting leaves everywhere. "Put it back!"

"Are you mouse-brained?" Thornclaw mumbled around the stick. "I need it. It's only a stick."

"It's *my* stick." Dovepaw was startled to see how worked up Jayfeather was, his eyes blazing and his neck fur bristling as if he was facing an enemy. "If you don't bring it back in one piece, I'll . . . I'll . . ."

"Okay, I'll bring back your stupid stick," Thornclaw snarled. "Keep your fur on."

He raced back across the mud with the stick in his jaws. Dovepaw and Ivypaw followed more slowly behind their mentors. Dovepaw was trying to lift each paw almost as soon as it touched the scorching ground. Her pads would be shriveled by the time she reached the water.

"Do you think the heat is getting to Jayfeather?" Ivypaw whispered. "Thornclaw's right. It's only a stick."

Dovepaw shrugged. "Maybe it's medicine cat stuff."

"Yes, but what happens to us if our medicine cat gets bees in his brain?"

Dovepaw didn't reply. They were drawing closer to the

edge of the lake, and she could see the glistening bodies of dead fish lying here and there; she almost choked as the smell rolled out to meet her. Suddenly the hard ground vanished, replaced with glossy warm mud that sucked at her paws. Her feet sank deeper with every step, and the surface shivered, as if it were waiting hungrily for her next paw step.

"Stay there," Lionblaze warned over his shoulder. Brownish-gray sludge flecked his pelt and clotted his belly fur. Just beyond him, Berrynose and Spiderleg were up to their haunches in mud.

The two warriors were thrashing helplessly, their pelts plastered to their sides by the brown slime. They didn't seem to be sinking past their belly fur, but they couldn't get a paw hold to drag themselves out.

"I'm glad they won't be sharing our den," Dovepaw murmured to Ivypaw. "They'll stink of mud and dead fish for a moon!"

Ivypaw nodded. "I bet they won't be sharing any cat's den until they get that stench off!" She wandered off to examine a dead fish lying a couple of fox-lengths away. Dovepaw stayed to watch as Thornclaw cautiously approached the mud hole, holding the stick at one end and stretching the rest of it out so that his Clanmates could grab it. Berrynose sank his claws into it and scrambled along it until he reached more solid ground, where Lionblaze and Cinderheart helped him to his paws.

"Filthy stuff!" he exclaimed, spitting out mud and shaking his pelt so that sticky drops flew everywhere.

Dovepaw leaped back to avoid being spattered. Meanwhile

Spiderleg clambered along the stick and stood panting at the edge of the muddy hole.

"Thanks," he meowed to Thornclaw. "I'll be more careful where I put my paws next time."

Thornclaw nodded. "You're welcome. You'd better go back to camp and get yourselves cleaned up."

Spiderleg and Berrynose plodded off, their heads and tails drooping, shedding mud from their pelts at every paw step.

"And now I suppose I'd better give the stick back to Jay-feather," Thornclaw went on, "or he'll be madder than a fox in a fit."

He set off toward the shore, only to halt after a few paces as a furious caterwaul came from farther around the lake. Dove-paw looked up in alarm. A mottled blue-gray tom was racing toward them, his tail streaming out behind him. Twitching her whiskers, Dovepaw picked up another unfamiliar scent, similar to the fish lying on the mud.

That must be RiverClan.

Thornclaw dropped the stick again. "Hey, Rainstorm!" he called. "What do you want?"

The RiverClan warrior ignored him and the rest of the cats who were clustered together a few tail-lengths away from the mud hole. He was heading straight for Ivypaw, who was still sniffing curiously at the dead fish.

"Prey-stealer!" he yowled. "Leave that alone! The fish are ours!"

Ivypaw spun around, her fur fluffing up and her eyes wide with terror at the sight of a full-grown RiverClan warrior bearing down on her.

"Mouse dung!" Cinderheart spat, bounding off to intercept Rainstorm before he could attack her apprentice. Dovepaw and Lionblaze raced after her.

Suddenly Lionblaze let out a yowl. "Rainstorm, watch out!"

Dovepaw realized that the RiverClan cat was heading straight for the mud hole. Too intent on Ivypaw, he seemed not to hear Lionblaze's warning. His flying paws slid into the deeper mud; he gave a screech of mingled fear and surprise as he rapidly sank up to his belly fur.

"Help!" he wailed. "Get me out of here!"

"Serves you right," Cinderheart meowed indignantly, halting at the edge of the mud hole and looking down at the struggling warrior. "Can't you see she's only an apprentice? This is her first time out of camp."

"I'm sorry." Ivypaw trotted up, looking anxious. "I wasn't going to eat the fish, honestly."

"I don't think any cat would want to eat it," Dovepaw added, coming to stand beside her sister. "Yuck!"

Rainstorm didn't reply. He had sunk into a deeper part of the hole than the two ThunderClan cats who had been trapped earlier; the mud was oozing around his shoulders, and his frantic efforts to climb out only made him sink farther.

"Keep still," Lionblaze mewed. "We'll get you out."

Thornclaw trotted up with the stick and pushed it out across the mud until Rainstorm could sink his claws into it. But he couldn't get a firm-enough hold to drag himself out, as if his struggles had already worn him out. Dovepaw pressed close against Ivypaw as she watched, her belly fluttering with anxiety. Even though the RiverClan warrior had been about to attack her sister, she didn't want to see him drown.

"Help . . . me . . ." Rainstorm rasped, stretching his neck to keep his muzzle clear of the mud.

"Oh, for StarClan's sake . . ." Lionblaze muttered. He crept up to the very edge of the hole, testing every paw step before he put his weight down, and leaned over so that he could sink his teeth into Rainstorm's scruff. He gave an enormous heave, and with a loud sucking noise the RiverClan tom scrambled free of the clinging mud and collapsed on one side, his chest heaving as he gasped for air.

"Consider yourself lucky," Thornclaw meowed unsympathetically. "Now take off. You shouldn't have been on this side of the lake at all."

Rainstorm's paws scrabbled, but when he tried to stand up his legs gave way and he fell onto the mud again.

"Now what are we going to do with him?" Cinderheart meowed. "He's never going to make it back to RiverClan in that state."

Lionblaze sighed. "There's no need for any of this, if River-Clan would just be reasonable. Are any of his Clanmates around?"

"Over there." Thornclaw pointed with his tail and Dove-paw spotted a group of RiverClan cats in the distance, close to ShadowClan territory. They were confronting the Shadow-Clan patrol she had seen heading to the waterside earlier.

Her whiskers quivered and she sensed they were having an argument.

"I'm not getting involved in that debate," Thornclaw decided. "If we go over there, we'll find ourselves fighting with ShadowClan as well as RiverClan. Come on." He prodded Rainstorm with one paw. "You can come back to our camp until you're fit to travel. It's not nearly as far as your own territory."

"Thanks," Rainstorm panted. He staggered to his paws, managing to stay upright this time; Lionblaze padded alongside him and gave him his shoulder to lean on. "Cinderheart, will you keep an eye on the apprentices while they collect the water?" he called. "I'll help Thornclaw get Rainstorm back to camp."

"Sure," Cinderheart replied.

Dovepaw watched the two ThunderClan warriors set off across the mud, flanking Rainstorm, who was still unsteady on his paws. "Hey!" she called after them. "Don't forget the stick!"

Thornclaw bounded back, his tail flicking irritably. "I don't know what's got into Jayfeather," he growled, snatching up the stick and carrying it away with him.

"Are you okay, Ivypaw?" Cinderheart asked, looking down at her apprentice with concern in her blue eyes.

"Yes, I'm fine," Ivypaw replied. "I'm sorry I was stupid about the fish. If I hadn't gone near it, Rainstorm wouldn't have fallen into the mud."

"It wasn't your fault!" Indignation surged through

Dovepaw. "He was being horrible."

"Dovepaw's right," Cinderheart mewed. "He had no need to come dashing over here like that. Now, pick up your moss, and we'll go collect the water. I want to get back to the hollow and find out what Firestar does when he hears about this."

CHAPTER 4

Lionblaze halted in the center of the clearing and let Rainstorm sink to the ground, where he sprawled on his side with his legs folded untidily beneath him. The RiverClan warrior looked like a mess: With mud plastering his fur to his sides, it was obvious how scrawny he was, as if he hadn't had a good meal in a moon. Lionblaze couldn't help feeling sorry for him.

RiverClan must be in big trouble if they get that angry about a dead fish.

Thornclaw had bounded away up the tumbled rocks to find Firestar in his den. Lionblaze was left to wait with Rainstorm and Jayfeather, who had joined them when they reached the shore and accompanied them back to camp. Lionblaze's shoulders ached from supporting Rainstorm on the long trek from the lake, and his mouth was parched with thirst. It was nearly sunhigh, and the air in the hollow was quivering with heat. The mud on Rainstorm's pelt was already baked dry.

If we hadn't run into all this trouble, we'd have been back with the water long ago, Lionblaze thought. *We should be resting when it's this hot.*

More of the ThunderClan cats were appearing from their dens, gazing curiously at the RiverClan warrior.

"What's *he* doing here?" Blossompaw emerged from the elders' den with a huge ball of bedding, dropped it, and bounced across the clearing to get a closer look. "Is he a prisoner?"

"No, he had an accident," Lionblaze explained. "He'll go back to RiverClan once he's rested."

"I don't see why he has to rest here." Mousefur had followed the apprentice out, guiding Longtail with her tail on his shoulder, and Purdy just behind. She gave Rainstorm a suspicious sniff. "Ugh! He smells like a rotting fish!"

"And where's our water?" Purdy added.

"Is Rainstorm hurt?" Brightheart asked more sympathetically. "Jayfeather, do you need me to get some herbs?"

"No, he's just exhausted," Jayfeather replied.

Lionblaze began to explain what had happened beside the lake. He left out the fact that Rainstorm had charged at Ivypaw; he hoped that the RiverClan warrior wouldn't really have hurt such a young apprentice, and there was no point in arousing more hostility.

"Some cat will need to keep an eye on him," Brambleclaw meowed when Lionblaze had finished telling the story. "We can't have him wandering around the camp."

"He doesn't look as if he'll be wandering anywhere for a while," Sandstorm pointed out with a flick of her ears.

The comments died away as Firestar appeared with Thornclaw and shouldered his way through the gathering crowd of cats until he stood in front of the RiverClan warrior. Rainstorm struggled to sit up and face him, though Lionblaze could tell how much effort it took.

Firestar dipped his head to the RiverClan tom with cool politeness. "Greetings, Rainstorm," he meowed. "Thornclaw told me what happened."

"Yes, I . . ." Rainstorm hesitated as if the words were choking him, then added, "I'm grateful to your warriors for helping me."

"We would help any cat in trouble," Firestar replied. "You'd better stay here until sunset, and then go home when it's cooler. Lionblaze will show you a quiet spot where you can sleep."

"I'll keep guard over him," Brambleclaw added.

"Good idea," Firestar meowed, while several of the other ThunderClan cats murmured agreement.

"Can he have some fresh-kill?" Ferncloud asked, her gentle gaze fixed sympathetically on Rainstorm.

"We don't have enough for ourselves," Thornclaw snapped, without waiting for the Clan leader to respond. "Firestar, I had an idea while we were bringing him back here. We saved his miserable life; why shouldn't ThunderClan get something out of it?"

Firestar turned to look at him, a puzzled expression on his face. "What do you mean?"

"Well, we've got one of RiverClan's warriors here. Why not send a message to Leopardstar that she can only have him back if she lets us have some fish?"

"What?" Rainstorm protested. "You can't do that!"

"We can do what we like, mange-pelt," Thornclaw retorted, unsheathing his claws. "Don't you think we deserve a reward for helping you?"

"That's right!" some cat exclaimed from the back of the crowd.

"Are you mouse-brained?" Jayfeather growled, whipping his head around to face the speaker. "What do *we* want with RiverClan's fish? It smells disgusting."

Glancing around, Lionblaze could see that several of the cats looked as if they agreed with Thornclaw, in spite of what Jayfeather had said. *Why not?* he thought. *We're hungry enough.* But the thought of keeping a Clan warrior prisoner made his pelt prickle with uneasiness.

"What do you think, Firestar?" Sandstorm prompted quietly.

Firestar was silent for a moment, while Rainstorm's gaze flickered from one cat to the next as if he could read his fate in their eyes.

"I think Thornclaw's right." Spiderleg, dried mud still clinging to his pelt, pushed his way to the front of the crowd. "Maybe it would teach RiverClan to stay away from our side of the lake."

"And to stop telling other Clans what they can do," Cloudtail added. "Leopardstar's getting way too big for her fur."

"No, they're just desperate," Brackenfur argued. "This heat—"

"It's hot over here, too," Mousefur snapped.

"Firestar?" Brambleclaw raised his tail to silence the arguing cats. "What do you want us to do?"

Finally Firestar shook his head. "I'm sorry, Thornclaw. I know you want what's best for the Clan, and I admit that I don't like turning down the chance of some extra food. But there's nothing in the warrior code that allows us to use a cat from another Clan to bargain with."

"That's right," Squirrelflight added, padding up to her father's side. "We would just be making things worse."

Thornclaw opened his jaws as if he was going to argue, then closed them again, shrugging. "Whatever you say, Firestar," he muttered.

"Brambleclaw, show Rainstorm where he can rest," Firestar instructed. "Later, when it's cooler, you can lead a patrol to escort him back to RiverClan."

Lionblaze crept into the shadow of a rock and managed to snatch some sleep. His dreams were dark and confused, and when he woke he felt almost as tired as when he had first curled up.

Long shadows stretched across the clearing as he padded to the pitifully small fresh-kill pile, and the sky above the trees was streaked with scarlet. The scorching heat of sunhigh had faded, but the air was still heavy and stale.

Maybe I can get some cats together for a hunting patrol.

"Hey, Lionblaze!"

Lionblaze swung around at the sound of Brambleclaw's voice. The Clan deputy was bounding toward him; Rainstorm followed more slowly. The RiverClan warrior's paw steps were firmer now, though he still looked exhausted.

"I'm leading a patrol to take Rainstorm home," Brambleclaw explained as he came up to Lionblaze. "I'd like you to come."

"Sure. Can I bring Dovepaw? It would be good experience for her."

At Brambleclaw's nod, he looked around for his apprentice and spotted her outside her new den with Ivypaw and Cinderheart. When he waved his tail, all three cats came trotting over.

Meanwhile, Brambleclaw ducked into the warriors' den and emerged with Brackenfur and Sorreltail. Lionblaze noticed that he hadn't chosen any of the cats who had wanted to keep Rainstorm hostage until RiverClan gave them some fish.

"We're going over to RiverClan with Rainstorm," Lionblaze told Dovepaw as she approached.

"Great!" Dovepaw gave a little bounce of excitement. "I'll get to see some other territories."

"Can't we go too?" Ivypaw asked, looking up at Cinderheart with disappointment in her eyes.

"Sorry, no," Cinderheart replied. "You'll both have to get used to being separated for your duties," she added to her downcast apprentice. "We'll go to the training clearing instead, and I'll teach you your first fighting moves."

"Great!" Ivypaw cheered up at once, her eyes gleaming. "Dovepaw, I'll flatten you when you get back!"

Dovepaw flicked her sister's nose with the tip of her tail. "You can try."

Brambleclaw gathered his patrol together with a sweep of his tail and led the way out of the thorn tunnel. As soon as they set off into the forest, Lionblaze realized that they were heading for ShadowClan territory.

"Wouldn't it be safer to go the other way, past WindClan?" he suggested.

Brambleclaw gave him a brief glance from thoughtful amber eyes. "We've had just as much trouble with WindClan lately," he replied. "Besides, it's farther that way, and I'm not sure how long Rainstorm will be able to keep going. I think that if we cut straight across the mud, staying between what's left of the lake and ShadowClan's territory, we shouldn't have any problems."

"I hope you're right," Lionblaze muttered.

They emerged from the trees not far from the stream that marked the border with ShadowClan. Lionblaze shot a dismayed glance at the exposed mud at the bottom. "This stream used to be full to the brim," he told Dovepaw as she padded up to stand beside him and peered down curiously at the empty stream. "Water flowed constantly into the lake, but now most of it is gone."

"Is that why the lake has shrunk?" Dovepaw asked, tipping her head to one side.

"Partly," Lionblaze replied.

"So why did the stream go away?"

"No cat knows. I suppose it must be the heat."

Dovepaw stared upstream to where the channel curved away, hidden beneath wilting clumps of fern. Her whiskers were quivering and her claws flexed in and out.

"There's nothing we can do about it," Lionblaze told her. "Let's keep going."

Dovepaw jumped as if he had startled her, though he

couldn't see what had sent her into such deep concentration.

"What—" he began, but at that moment a yowl interrupted him. "Lionblaze! Are you with this patrol or not?"

Brambleclaw had led the rest of the cats out onto the dried-up lake and paused, glancing back over his shoulder as he called out to Lionblaze.

"Sorry!" Lionblaze called back. With Dovepaw scampering behind him, he raced onto the hard brown mud and fell in at the back of the patrol. "Stay beside me," he warned Dovepaw. "And if we see any ShadowClan warriors, let Brambleclaw handle it."

"What if they attack us?" Dovepaw mewed; she looked excited rather than afraid.

"I don't think they will. But if they do," Lionblaze warned her, "stay out of it if you possibly can. You're not trained; a ShadowClan warrior could turn you into crow-food with one paw."

"Couldn't," Dovepaw muttered under her breath, just loud enough for her mentor to hear.

Lionblaze didn't scold her. He remembered what it had felt like to be an apprentice, desperate to prove himself and learn all the skills of a warrior. He liked this little she-cat; she was brave and curious, and he guessed she would learn quickly.

Are you the One? he wondered as he watched her padding purposefully across the mud, her gaze flicking from side to side as if she was checking for the approach of ShadowClan cats. *Or is it your sister? I wish StarClan would send us a sign.*

To his relief, there was no trace of ShadowClan patrols

as the ThunderClan cats trekked across the mud. Lionblaze couldn't help feeling as if hostile eyes were gazing at him from the undergrowth on the bank, but no cats appeared.

The last of the sunlight was fading and the moon had risen above the trees by the time the patrol reached the edge of RiverClan territory.

"You go ahead now," Brambleclaw meowed to Rainstorm. "Lead us to your camp."

"There's no need for you to go anywhere near our camp," Rainstorm retorted, sounding a bit more belligerent now that he was back on his own territory. "I'll be fine on my own from now on."

"I want Leopardstar to hear *our* side of what happened," Brambleclaw replied; only a tiny flick of the tip of his tail told Lionblaze that he was irritated. "And if she offers us some fish in return for looking after you, we won't say no."

"We don't have any prey to share with other Clans," Rainstorm snapped as he turned and led the way up the bank and onto RiverClan territory.

The RiverClan cats had made their camp on a wedge of land between two streams. Usually the waters ran high, but now the land was completely dry. The lush growth of plants that normally edged the stream had wilted and shriveled, exposing soil baked hard by the sun. The smell of rotting weed and dead fish hung in the air like smoke.

Lionblaze's fur prickled. They were trespassing on another Clan's territory, and even though they had good reason, the RiverClan cats might not see it that way.

"Will they drive us off?" Dovepaw asked in a whisper.

Lionblaze jumped; he had done his best to hide his worries from his apprentice, and he hadn't expected her to be so perceptive. "It's possible," he whispered back. "If there's any trouble, stay close to me. And keep your eyes and ears open."

As Rainstorm led the ThunderClan patrol across the dried-up streambed and up the bank on the other side, a gray-furred she-cat emerged from the undergrowth. Some of Lionblaze's anxiety faded as he recognized Mistyfoot, the RiverClan deputy. Mistyfoot was a reasonable cat, and she had been friendly to ThunderClan in the past.

But there was nothing friendly in Mistyfoot's tone as her blue gaze swept over the patrol. "What are you doing here?" she demanded. "And what happened to Rainstorm?"

"These cats kept me in their camp—" Rainstorm began.

"We *allowed him to stay* in our camp," Brambleclaw interrupted. "Lionblaze and Thornclaw rescued him when he fell into a muddy hole at the edge of the lake. If it wasn't for them, he would be hunting with StarClan by now."

"Is that true?" Mistyfoot asked Rainstorm.

The RiverClan warrior ducked his head. "Yes. And I'm grateful to them. But then they said that they wouldn't let me come back home unless Leopardstar gave them some fish."

"Really?" Mistyfoot's ears twitched up and she turned an inquiring gaze on Brambleclaw.

"We discussed that," Brambleclaw admitted, sounding slightly awkward. "But Firestar said it would be breaking the warrior code. So we let Rainstorm rest through the worst of the heat, and now we've brought him back. May we speak to Leopardstar?" he added politely.

"Leopardstar is busy." Mistyfoot's tone was unusually curt, and Lionblaze wondered if she was hiding something. "I'm grateful for your help," she went on, "and if we had fish to spare I would give you some, but we don't."

The two deputies were still for a couple of heartbeats, their gazes locked together. Lionblaze guessed that Brambleclaw was wondering whether to insist on seeing Leopardstar. *Come on, Brambleclaw. You're not going to win an argument, or a fight, right here in RiverClan's camp!*

Beside him, Dovepaw stood with her ears alert and her whiskers twitching, while her brilliant golden gaze seemed to bore through the undergrowth right into the RiverClan camp.

I wish she really could see what's going on there, Lionblaze thought. *There's something that RiverClan isn't telling us.*

Eventually Brambleclaw dipped his head. "Then we'll say good-bye, Mistyfoot. Please give Firestar's respects to Leopardstar. And may StarClan light your path."

Mistyfoot looked relieved. "And yours, Brambleclaw," she replied. "Thank you for helping our warrior." Beckoning to Rainstorm with her tail, she turned and disappeared into the undergrowth, heading for the center of the camp. Rainstorm gave an awkward nod to the ThunderClan cats, muttered, "Thanks," and followed her.

"Well!" Sorreltail exclaimed. "He could have sounded a bit more grateful! Any cat would think we'd pulled his tail out."

Brambleclaw shrugged. "No cat likes to admit they needed help from another Clan. Come on." He bounded back across the dried-up stream, making rapidly for the edge of the territory. Brackenfur and Sorreltail kept pace with him, and Lionblaze and Dovepaw brought up the rear, glancing over their shoulders every now and then to make sure no River-Clan cats were following them.

"Lionblaze," Dovepaw panted as her shorter legs struggled to keep up, "was that blue-furred cat the RiverClan deputy?"

"That's right: Mistyfoot. She's a great cat."

"She's very worried, isn't she?"

Lionblaze was faintly surprised at his apprentice's comment. He'd guessed there were things Mistyfoot wasn't telling them, but he wouldn't have said she was worried. "Every cat is worried about the drought and the shortage of prey," he pointed out.

Dovepaw shook her head. "Oh, I think it's more than that, don't you? I think she must be worried about the sick cat."

Lionblaze halted at the edge of the muddy bottom of the lake and stared at her. "What sick cat?"

"There's a very sick cat in the RiverClan camp," Dovepaw meowed, her pale golden eyes wide with surprise. "Couldn't you tell?"

CHAPTER 5

A paw clipping against her ear woke Dovepaw; keeping her eyes closed, she batted irritably at it. "Get off, Ivypaw! I need to sleep." Nearly a moon had passed since the apprentice ceremony, and the day before, their mentors had given them their first assessment, on the far side of the territory. Dovepaw couldn't remember ever being so tired. She'd never realized how nerve-racking it was to have invisible eyes watching her every move!

The paw cuffed her again, lightly, but with a hint of claws.

Dovepaw's eyes flew open. "Ivypaw, if you don't stop, I'll—"

She broke off, staring. Standing over her was a cat she had never seen before: a she-cat with matted gray fur and amber eyes. Her jaws were parted in the beginnings of a snarl, revealing two rows of snaggly teeth.

Dovepaw sprang up into a crouch, ready to tackle this strange cat who had managed to sneak into ThunderClan's camp. "Who are you? What do you want?" she growled, forcing her voice to stay steady.

"You," the strange cat replied.

Struggling not to panic, Dovepaw gazed around the apprentices' den. Moonlight filtering through the ferns that covered the entrance showed her Ivypaw and the rest of her denmates curled up and sound asleep.

"Ivypaw!" Dovepaw gave her sister a hard shove. "Wake up! Help!"

Ivypaw didn't move. Dovepaw looked up at the intruder, fear giving way to anger. "What have you done to her?"

"Nothing," the she-cat replied, annoyance sparking in her amber eyes. "Now do as you're told and follow me."

Dovepaw wanted to ask why she should do anything the she-cat told her, but something compelled her to rise to her paws and scramble out of the apprentices' den. The clearing lay silent in a wash of moonlight, the shadows lying black against the silver walls. Toadstep, on guard at the entrance to the thorn tunnel, was as still as a cat made of stone, and didn't twitch a whisker as the mysterious she-cat led Dovepaw out into the forest.

This is weird, Dovepaw thought. *What's happening to me?* Even the forest didn't look familiar; the sparse, shriveled undergrowth was full and lush, and the grass underneath her paws felt cool and fresh.

"Where are we going?" she called, stumbling over a fallen branch that lay in the shadow of a bramble thicket. "I shouldn't be sneaking out at night like this. I'll get into trouble. . . ."

"Stop complaining," the gray she-cat snapped. "You'll find out soon enough."

She led Dovepaw through the trees; gradually the

undergrowth thinned out and more moonlight broke through. A fresh breeze began to blow, bringing with it the scent of water. Dovepaw paused for a heartbeat to let it ruffle her fur, rejoicing in its coolness after so many days of unrelenting heat.

"Come on." The she-cat had halted beneath a tree a few fox-lengths ahead. "Come and look at this."

Dovepaw bounded over to her side and stared in astonishment. The trees gave way to a strip of rough grass; beyond it water stretched out almost as far as she could see, its ridged surface silvered by the moonlight. Gentle lapping filled her ears, steady as a queen licking a kit in the nursery.

"This—this is the lake!" she stammered. "But it's full! I've never seen so much water. Am I dreaming?"

"At last!" the she-cat commented sarcastically. "Are they filling the apprentices' heads with thistledown these days? Of course you're dreaming."

For the first time Dovepaw noticed the faint shimmer of starlight around the she-cat's paws. "Are you from StarClan?" she whispered.

"I am," the she-cat replied. "And once I was your Clan-mate."

"Then can't you do something to help ThunderClan?" Dovepaw asked; fear and excitement made her voice quiver. "We're having such a hard time."

"Hard times come to every Clan in every season," the old gray cat replied. "The warrior code doesn't offer the promise of an easy life. There will be much debate and fighting—"

"Fighting?" Dovepaw interrupted, horrified, then slapped her tail across her mouth. "Sorry," she mumbled.

"Blood is spilled in every generation," the she-cat went on. Her amber gaze softened, and Dovepaw became aware of an intense kindliness behind the rough exterior. "Yet there is always hope, just as the sun always rises."

Her figure began to fade; Dovepaw could see the silver waters of the lake through her gray fur.

"Don't go!" she begged.

The gray she-cat faded even more, until she was barely a wisp of smoke, and then entirely gone. As the last traces of her faded, Dovepaw thought that she heard her voice again, whispering gently into her ear.

After the sharp-eyed jay and the roaring lion, peace will come on dove's gentle wing.

Dovepaw woke with a start, her heart pounding, and sprang to her paws in one swift movement. *I'm here in my den! So it was a dream. . . .* Dawn light was filtering through the ferns at the entrance, and she could hear cats calling to one another in the clearing as they prepared for the new day.

Beside her, Ivypaw twitched an ear and blinked open her eyes. "What's the matter?" she muttered, her voice blurred with sleep. "Why are you jumping around like that?"

Bumblepaw's meow came from just behind Dovepaw, edged with annoyance. "Do you realize you just kicked moss all over me?"

"Sorry!" Dovepaw gasped. She had been sleeping in the

apprentices' den for almost a moon, but she still wasn't used to how crowded it was in there.

Already the dream was breaking up into scraps, fluttering away like leaves in leaf-fall as she tried to recapture them. *There was an old gray cat . . . a StarClan warrior. And the lake was full of water again.* She realized that her legs were heavy with tiredness and her paws felt as sore as if she really had walked to the lake and back in the middle of the night. *That's mouse-brained! It was just a dream.*

But there had been something important about the dream. The StarClan warrior had given her a message. She dug her claws deep into her mossy bedding, trying to recall the words, but they were gone. She let out a faint snort, half-amused and half-irritated. *Who do you think you are? A medicine cat? Why would a StarClan warrior come to give a message to you?*

Stretching her jaws in a huge yawn, she pushed the dream from her mind and wriggled out through the ferns into the clearing. The sky was growing brighter as the sun rose; the early patrols had left, and for a few heartbeats Dovepaw tracked Brackenfur and Sorreltail, who were stalking prey near the stream that marked the border with ShadowClan. Pricking her ears, she heard Sorreltail leap on a squirrel as it tried to escape up a tree, and Brackenfur padding over to touch his nose to her ear. "Great catch," he murmured.

Better not listen anymore, Dovepaw thought, shutting out Sorreltail's loving purr and listening instead to a couple of starlings having a noisy quarrel in the branches of the dead tree. Letting her senses range farther over the territory, she picked up a yowl of pain from the dawn patrol on the WindClan border, and then Berrynose's voice: "I trod on a thistle!"

Dovepaw let out a little *mrrow* of amusement as she pictured the cream-colored warrior hopping indignantly on three paws while he tried to pull out the prickles with his teeth. If she knew Berrynose, he'd blame the thistle.

"Great StarClan!" Dustpelt sounded angry and frustrated. "Will you sit still and let some cat help you? Rosepetal, sort him out, please, or we'll be here all day."

"Just another day in ThunderClan," Dovepaw whispered to herself.

And what about your dream? A voice seemed to speak in her mind.

"What about it?" Dovepaw muttered, firmly pushing the memories away again.

Slipping back into the den, she gave Ivypaw a sharp prod in the side. "Wake up, lazybones! Let's find Cinderheart and Lionblaze and see if they'll take us hunting."

Pride tingled through Dovepaw from ears to tail-tip as she carried her prey—a mouse and a blackbird—over to the fresh-kill pile and dropped it in front of the warriors who were gathered close by.

"Well done," Graystripe meowed, glancing up from the vole he was sharing with his mate, Millie. "At that rate, you'll be one of the best hunters in the Clan."

"And she's been an apprentice for less than a moon," Lionblaze added, padding up to deposit his own prey on the pile.

"She seems to know what the prey is going to do even before the prey does."

Whitewing, who was sharing tongues with Birchfall nearby, let out a purr of approval. "Good. I'm glad to hear you're working hard."

Dovepaw started to feel embarrassed. "I'm not that good," she protested as she dropped her catch. She didn't like being praised too much in front of Ivypaw, who had managed to kill only a single shrew. "I've just got a great mentor."

Then she went hot all over in case any cat thought she was criticizing Cinderheart. The gray she-cat didn't seem to have noticed anything wrong as she and Ivypaw set their own prey down, though Ivypaw cast an envious glance at her sister.

"Don't be upset," Dovepaw whispered. "It was just bad luck that you missed that squirrel."

Ivypaw gave an angry shrug. "Bad luck doesn't fill bellies."

"You can each take a piece of prey," Cinderheart meowed to the two apprentices. "You've worked hard this morning."

"Thanks!" Dovepaw chose a vole from the pile, and after hesitating Ivypaw took her own shrew. Dovepaw could sense that however hungry she was, her sister didn't want to take more than she'd managed to contribute.

Dovepaw's belly was yowling too, but as she crouched down to eat she forced herself not to gulp the vole down in a couple of ravenous bites. The sun had risen over the tops of the trees, its rays beating down mercilessly, and there would be no more hunting until it set.

"I don't know how much longer this drought can go on,"

Millie sighed, finishing her share of the vole and swiping her tongue over her whiskers. "How many more days without rain?"

"Only StarClan knows," Graystripe responded, touching his tail to his mate's shoulder in a comforting gesture.

"Then StarClan should do something about it!" Spiderleg looked up from where he sat on the other side of the fresh-kill pile with Hazeltail and Mousewhisker. "Do they expect us to survive without water?"

"There's hardly any left in the lake," Hazeltail added sorrowfully. "And the stream has dried up completely between us and ShadowClan."

"So where has all the water gone?" Mousewhisker asked with an irritable flick of his ears.

Dovepaw paused, puzzled, before taking another bite of her vole. "Don't you know why the stream has dried up?" she asked. "Isn't it because of the brown animals who are blocking it?"

Spiderleg stared at her. "What brown animals?"

Dovepaw swallowed her mouthful. "The ones who are dragging tree trunks and branches into the stream."

Glancing around, she realized that every cat beside the fresh-kill pile was staring at her. The vole she had just eaten suddenly weighed heavily in her belly. *Why are they looking so confused?*

The silence seemed to stretch on for a season. Eventually Lionblaze spoke in a quiet voice. "Dovepaw, what exactly are you meowing about?"

"The—the big brown animals," she stammered. "They're making a barrier in the stream, like our thorn barrier across the camp entrance. It's stopping the water from flowing. There are Twolegs watching them."

"Twolegs!" Mousewhisker gave a snort of amusement. "Are they sprouting wings and flying as well?"

"Don't be silly!" Dovepaw snapped. "They're watching the animals and pointing . . . something, some Twoleg stuff at them. Maybe the animals are blocking the river because the Twolegs told them to."

"And maybe hedgehogs fly," Spiderleg mewed with a sigh. "Lionblaze, you really ought to tell your apprentice not to make this stuff up. It's not funny, not when we're all suffering."

"That's right," Whitewing added. The approval in her eyes had changed to annoyance and embarrassment. "Dovepaw, what's come over you? This is a nice game to play with your sister, but it's not the sort of thing you should talk about in front of all your Clanmates."

Dovepaw sprang to her paws, the remains of her vole forgotten in her surge of anger. "It's *not* a game! And I'm *not* making it up! You have to know I'm not."

"I don't know anything of the sort," Spiderleg retorted. "Twolegs and big brown animals? It sounds like a tale for kits."

"Can't you hear them?" Dovepaw asked. All the other cats were looking at her uneasily, and she found it hard to meet their gaze.

"Don't be too hard on her." Graystripe flicked his tail at Spiderleg. "We all played games when we were apprentices."

"Maybe she's confused," Millie added kindly. "It could be the heat. Did you have a dream?" she asked Dovepaw.

"I didn't dream it, and it's *not* a game!" Dovepaw's anger was giving way to distress, her forepaws working in the earth of the camp floor. *Why are they all pretending they don't know about the stream?*

"Come on." Hazeltail got up and stretched. "Let's find a shady place to sleep. Maybe we can all dream about big brown animals." She padded off toward the edge of the clearing, followed by Spiderleg and Mousewhisker. Birchfall skirted the fresh-kill pile and halted in front of Dovepaw. His eyes were serious.

"If you're making things up for fun, then stop it and say you're sorry," he meowed. "If you're feeling ill, then go ask Jay-feather for some herbs. But stop bothering warriors who have better things to do than listen to nursery tales."

"It's not a nursery tale!" Dovepaw wanted to wail like a lost kit. *Even my own father is joining in!*

Birchfall exchanged a glance with Lionblaze, then padded away with Whitewing. Graystripe and Millie headed for the warriors' den. Cinderheart rose to her paws. "Get some rest now, Ivypaw. When it's cooler, I'll take you for some battle training."

"Thanks," Ivypaw mewed, watching her mentor as she followed the other warriors. She gave Dovepaw a hard shove. "Stop showing off."

Dovepaw stared at her, incredulous. "But, Ivypaw, you—"

"You're only doing it to get attention," Ivypaw hissed. Before Dovepaw could respond, she bounded away and vanished into the apprentices' den.

Dovepaw stayed crouched beside the fresh-kill pile, her head down, feeling utterly crushed. Every cat in the Clan had treated her like a piece of dirt, just because she knew about the brown animals. *Why are they pretending they don't know?* At least Lionblaze must have heard them; he was beside her when she sensed them, far upstream on the border with Shadow-Clan. Maybe it was some big secret that apprentices weren't supposed to know about? *He shouldn't have taken me to that empty stream, then!*

After a few moments, she felt the light touch of a nose against her ear, and looked up to see her mentor gazing down at her. His amber eyes were unreadable.

"Follow me," he meowed.

CHAPTER 6
❧

Dovepaw followed Lionblaze through the thorn tunnel and into the clearing just outside the camp. *Is he angry with me as well?* she wondered.

Lionblaze halted in the shade of a hazel thicket at the edge of the clearing and turned to face his apprentice. "Tell me what you can hear," he mewed.

Dovepaw was startled. Was this her punishment? "Waves lapping at the edge of the lake," she replied. "And the dawn patrol is on its way back." Brightening up a little, she added, "Berrynose trod on a thistle earlier. He was trying to balance on three paws while he pulled the prickles out with his teeth."

"Was he now?" Lionblaze murmured. "And where did this happen?"

"On the WindClan border, near the stepping-stones across the stream."

As Dovepaw spoke, the bracken at the other side of the clearing parted, and Dustpelt led his patrol into the open. Rosepetal, Foxtail, and Berrynose followed him; the cream-colored warrior was limping.

"Hey, Berrynose!" Lionblaze called. "What happened to you?"

Berrynose didn't reply, except for heaving a long sigh.

"He stepped on a thistle," Dustpelt snapped. "You would think no cat ever had a thorn in his paw before."

Lionblaze was silent until the patrol had vanished into the tunnel. Then he turned back to Dovepaw. Her fur prickled under the intensity of his gaze.

"Wait here," he ordered.

Dovepaw crouched down as he padded across the clearing and followed the patrol into the tunnel. Her belly was churning uncomfortably. *I don't understand what all this is about!*

A few heartbeats later, Lionblaze returned; Dovepaw stiffened when she saw that Jayfeather was with him. *Does Lionblaze think that I'm sick, too? Does he think I need a medicine cat?*

"This had better be important," Jayfeather grumbled as he crossed the clearing beside Lionblaze. "I'm in the middle of making a yarrow poultice."

"It is important," Lionblaze assured him, halting in front of Dovepaw. "I think she's the one."

"One what?" Dovepaw's nervousness made her voice sharp. "Don't talk about me like I'm not here."

Lionblaze ignored her. "She hears things," he explained to Jayfeather. "Not from StarClan. I mean from really far away." Turning to Dovepaw, he added, "Tell Jayfeather about the brown animals blocking the stream."

Reluctantly Dovepaw repeated the story she had told to her Clanmates around the fresh-kill pile. When she had finished she waited for Jayfeather to make fun of her like the others. *Why is Lionblaze making me go through all this again?*

Jayfeather was silent for a moment; when he spoke it was to Lionblaze. "Do you think she's telling the truth?"

Dovepaw's frustration spilled over. Before Lionblaze could reply, she sprang to her paws and confronted Jayfeather. "I don't understand why every cat thinks I'm making this up! There are animals blocking the stream; are you telling me that you can't hear them?"

Jayfeather answered her with another question. "Do you *just* hear them?"

Dovepaw shook her head; then she remembered that Jayfeather couldn't see her. "No, I know what they look like, too." Confusion swept over her. "I mean, I can't really see them, not like they're in front of me. But—but I know what they look like. They're brown, with stiff fur and flat tails. Oh, and they have big front teeth, which they use to cut the trees and branches."

"She saw Berrynose treading on a thistle, too," Lionblaze added. "While his patrol was at the other end of the Wind-Clan border."

Jayfeather's whiskers twitched. "So, you saw him and heard him," he mused. "Anything else? Did you feel his pain?"

"No," Dovepaw replied. "But I saw him stumble, and I heard him complain about the thorns in his pad. And I knew he was trying to pull them out with his teeth."

"That doesn't sound like messages from StarClan," Jayfeather remarked, turning to his brother. "It's more as if she can see and hear things that other cats can't."

"We need to test her," Lionblaze meowed.

"Do you mean I'm different from other cats?" Dovepaw asked, her brain whirling. Couldn't all cats tell what was happening around the territory? How did they know when trouble was coming, then? She felt her fur beginning to fluff up in panic. "Is there something wrong with me?"

"No," Lionblaze assured her, giving her a calming touch on her shoulder with the tip of his tail. "It—it means you're special."

"Can Ivypaw sense the same things?" Jayfeather asked.

Dovepaw shrugged. "We've never spoken about it. But . . . maybe not." Now that she thought about it, she had always been the one who commented on things happening far away, not her sister. A worm of fear crept into her belly. *I thought every cat could see and hear the same way I can. I don't want to be the only one.*

"We need to test her out," Lionblaze repeated. "Is that okay?" he added quickly as Dovepaw began to bristle up again.

She met his amber gaze, aware that something had changed in the last few moments. Lionblaze was no longer just her mentor, teaching her things and telling her what to do. Instead, his eyes held respect, perhaps even awe.

Weird, she thought. "I'm fine with being tested," she meowed. *Let's just get it over with, and then maybe life can get back to normal.*

"I'm going to go off somewhere and do something," Lionblaze told her. "When I get back, I want you to tell me what I did."

Dovepaw shrugged again. "Okay."

Without another word, Lionblaze dashed off into the

trees, heading toward the WindClan border. Dovepaw felt a bit strange being left alone in the clearing with Jayfeather. She didn't know the medicine cat like she knew the warriors, though she was well aware of his sharp tongue. But he didn't seem inclined to talk; he just crouched down with his paws tucked under him, so Dovepaw let her attention wander out into the forest.

Gradually she made sense of the confusion of noise that poured from the trees. A ShadowClan patrol was investigating the scent of a fox near the border; RiverClan warriors were making a fuss about the sticky mud at the edge of the shrunken lake, where Mistyfoot was scolding an apprentice. And farther away, at the very edge of her senses, one of the big brown animals was adding another piece of wood to the blockage in the stream.

She jumped when Jayfeather spoke. "Can you tell what Lionblaze is doing yet?"

Dovepaw swiveled her ears in the direction Lionblaze had gone, toward the WindClan border. But there was no sign of her mentor there. *Where could he have gone?* She investigated the abandoned Twoleg nest and the training clearing, where she picked up the sounds of Cinderheart and Ivypaw practicing battle moves. Still no Lionblaze.

Dovepaw focused her senses on the edge of the lake. *Yes! There he is!* She could hear him and scent him, heading down the bank to the pebbly lakeshore. *Did he think he would be able to trick me if he doubled back?*

Lionblaze's paw steps thudded on the dried mud. Pausing,

he glanced around, then bounded over to a lump of battered wood and started dragging it onto the pebbles. Dovepaw could hear them rasping and rolling as Lionblaze tugged the wood higher. When he had pulled it all the way up to the grass, he pulled a tendril of bramble out of a nearby thicket and laid it over the wood.

"Lionblaze, what are you doing?" Dovepaw heard Sandstorm's voice and spotted the ginger she-cat appearing around the edge of the thicket, with Leafpool, Briarpaw, and Bumblepaw just behind her. All four cats were carrying bundles of moss.

"Oh, hi, Sandstorm." Lionblaze sounded startled. "I'm . . . uh . . . just trying an experiment."

"Well, don't let me interrupt you." Sandstorm seemed puzzled as she waved her tail and led the two apprentices out onto the mud, heading for the water in the distance.

When Sandstorm had gone, Lionblaze ran back through the trees and arrived, panting, a few moments later. "Well?" he gasped. "Where did I go and what did I do?"

"You tried to trick me, didn't you?" Dovepaw began; she felt so self-conscious that every hair on her pelt was prickling. "You set off toward WindClan, but then you went down to the lake. And you found a piece of wood. . . ."

As she went on, she saw Jayfeather listening with his head to one side, his ears pricked. He didn't speak until she had finished. "Was she right?"

"Yes, every detail," Lionblaze replied.

Suddenly the air around the three cats seemed to crackle

with things unsaid, as if a greenleaf storm was about to break. Dovepaw drew a shaky breath.

"It's no big deal," she protested. "I thought every cat could tell what was going on, even if it's not right in front of us. We all have good hearing and sensitive whiskers, right?"

"Not *that* sensitive," Lionblaze meowed.

"Listen." Jayfeather leaned forward with an intensity in his sightless blue eyes. "There is a prophecy, Dovepaw," he began. "*There will be three, kin of your kin, who will hold the power of the stars in their paws.* It was given to Firestar a long time ago by a cat from another Clan, and it refers to three cats who will be more powerful than any others in the Clans—more powerful even than StarClan. Lionblaze—"

"But what has that got to do with us?" Dovepaw interrupted; suddenly she felt as if she didn't want to know the answer.

"Lionblaze and I are two of those cats," Jayfeather mewed with a flick of his ears. "And we believe that you are the third."

"What?" Horror and disbelief surged over Dovepaw; her voice came out like the squeak of a startled kit. "Me?" Spinning around, she fixed her gaze on her mentor. "Lionblaze, this can't be right! Please tell me that it isn't true!"

CHAPTER 7

Jayfeather winced at Dovepaw's dismay as she learned that she was different from all the other cats in her Clan, with a destiny greater even than StarClan. *Not that we know what our destiny is . . .* He heard Lionblaze sigh as she begged him to tell her it wasn't real.

"I can't tell you that, Dovepaw," his brother meowed. "Because it is true. I often wish it wasn't, believe me."

"Lionblaze and I both have special powers," Jayfeather put in. "He can't be beaten in battle, and I . . . well, I have more skills than other medicine cats." *No way am I telling her what they are! Not yet, anyway.*

"And you have especially strong senses," Lionblaze told her. "You can tell what's going on very far away. I started to wonder that day we went to RiverClan, when you told me there was a very sick cat in the camp. I didn't sense anything like that. You're a better hunter than you should be, with less than a moon's training. And no other cat knows anything about these animals you say are blocking the river. The way you could tell exactly what I did just now makes me think you could be right about them."

Dovepaw was silent for a few heartbeats; Jayfeather could hear her claws tearing at the grass. "This is mouse-brained!" she burst out at last. "I don't believe you. I don't want to be different!"

"What you want isn't—" Jayfeather began, then broke off as he heard the swishing sound of cats pushing their way through bracken. Sandstorm was in the lead, with more cats behind her, their scents almost drowned in the dank smell of mud.

"I'm sick of this," Sandstorm complained, her voice muffled so that Jayfeather could picture the soaked moss she held in her jaws. "RiverClan is behaving as if we have to ask their permission every time we want to go near the water."

"And I'm *covered* in mud," Briarpaw protested.

"We're all covered." Leafpool's voice was tired. "Once we take the water to our Clanmates, we can have a rest and lick it off."

"Yuck!" Bumblepaw exclaimed.

The sounds of the patrol faded as they headed into the thorn tunnel.

"We can't talk here," Jayfeather meowed. "We might as well announce everything to the Clan and be done with it."

"Then let's go farther into the forest where no cat can overhear us," Lionblaze suggested.

Jayfeather led the way along the old Twoleg path as far as the abandoned nest. The scent of catmint greeted him, soothing his worries and filling him with a deep sense of satisfaction. *If ThunderClan ever suffers from greencough again, we'll be well prepared.*

"Your catmint is flourishing," Lionblaze remarked as the three cats padded into the overgrown Twoleg garden. "It's weird that it grows so well in a drought."

"If it did, that *would* be weird," Jayfeather agreed. "I've been fetching soaked moss to water the roots. We can't afford to let it die."

Distracted for the moment from the problem of Dovepaw, Jayfeather moved confidently from plant to plant, guided by the strong scent of catmint, and gave each root a careful sniff to make sure that the fragile shoots were thriving.

"You must understand how I can tell what's going on all over the forest." Dovepaw padded up behind him, a challenge in her voice. "You know where every one of those plants is, even though you can't see them."

Jayfeather flicked up his ears, startled, while Lionblaze began, "Dovepaw, that's different—"

"It's okay," Jayfeather interrupted. It was refreshing to meet a cat who didn't tie herself into knots trying not to mention his blindness to his face. "Dovepaw has a good point. I know other cats are surprised when I know where things are. I've developed very good senses of smell and hearing," he went on to Dovepaw. "I suppose that's to make up for not being able to see. But I can't tell what's going on at the other side of the forest." A flicker of resentment crossed his mind. "Your powers are much greater than my senses."

"But I don't understand!" Jayfeather could tell that Dovepaw was trying very hard to keep her voice steady. "*Why* do I have these powers? What does the prophecy *mean*?"

"We're not sure," Lionblaze replied. "We felt just like you, at first. And we've struggled hard to understand it, but—"

"What's the matter with you?" Jayfeather cut in. "How can you not want to be more powerful than your Clanmates? To have a greater destiny, a mystery to solve? How can you not want to be one of the Three?"

"But we're not three, we're four!" Dovepaw spun around to face him. "What about Ivypaw? What are her special powers? What does the prophecy say about her?"

"Nothing," Jayfeather told her. "At first we didn't know whether the prophecy meant you or your sister. But you've made it pretty clear that you're the One."

"You just told us Ivypaw can't sense things at a distance, the way you do," Lionblaze pointed out.

"Not yet. But how do we know she won't?" Jayfeather dug his claws into the ground at the apprentice's stubborn tone. "Besides, she's my sister. I'm not going to do anything without her."

"You don't have any choice," Jayfeather snapped.

"Do you think we asked for this?" Lionblaze heaved a deep sigh. "I wish every day that I could just be an ordinary warrior, doing my best to help my Clan."

"But we've had to accept it," Jayfeather mewed.

He heard a scuffling sound from Dovepaw, as if the apprentice was flexing her claws in and out of the soil. "*I* don't have to accept it," she muttered mutinously.

"You do. Because of what you did today," Lionblaze meowed. Jayfeather could tell that he felt a strong sympathy for his apprentice. "You couldn't have made it clearer if you'd gone and yowled it from the Highledge."

Now Dovepaw was silent, and Jayfeather could sense her anger fading, replaced by uncertainty and fear. He let out a sigh, knowing what he had to tell her, even though he had hoped there would be no need. "You must have heard that we once had a sister," he began. "Hollyleaf. We—we thought that she was part of the prophecy, one of the Three."

"But she wasn't." To Jayfeather's relief, Lionblaze took up the story. "She tried so hard to figure out her special power, and how she could use it to help her Clan."

"So what made you realize that she wasn't one of the Three?" Dovepaw asked.

Grief and shame swept over Jayfeather, as sharp as when he first discovered that he wasn't the son of Squirrelflight and Brambleclaw. He could sense that his brother felt the same. What could they possibly tell this apprentice without tearing open the wounds that had threatened to destroy their Clan?

"How much do you know about Hollyleaf?" he asked Dovepaw.

"Not much." The young cat's voice was curious now. "I know she was your sister and she died in an accident in the tunnels. Ivypaw and I used to hear cats talking about her sometimes, but when they saw us listening they always changed the subject."

I'm not surprised, Jayfeather thought.

"We just realized that the prophecy didn't include her," Lionblaze stated flatly, in a tone that warned Dovepaw not to ask any more questions.

"So you made a mistake!" Dovepaw retorted. "How do you know that you're not making the same mistake again? Firestar has loads of kin in ThunderClan, not just Cloudtail and Whitewing!"

"Because—" Jayfeather began.

"I don't want to listen!" Dovepaw's voice was angry, and Jayfeather could picture her glaring at him with her neck fur bristling. He sensed deep fear within her, which she was trying to bury under her anger. "I don't care about special powers, unless they can help me to be a loyal warrior to ThunderClan. I don't want any part of any prophecy, especially one that's so vague you can't even be sure which cat it refers to!"

"Listen, you stupid furball!" Jayfeather spat. "Do you think *we* wanted things to be like this?" All his anger and frustration came spilling out, like a storm breaking over the forest, and he didn't even try to stop it. "We didn't choose to be part of the prophecy! We lost our sister because of it!"

His paws were shaking so much that he had to sit down. *Who sent the prophecy?* he wondered, yet again. *And why should we listen to it, when it causes so much pain?*

"I—I'm sorry," Dovepaw stammered. "But if it's so hard, why don't you ask Firestar about it?"

"Firestar has never spoken to us about it," Lionblaze replied. "He doesn't even know that we know he received the prophecy in the first place."

"Then how . . . ?" Dovepaw's voice was bewildered.

"I walked in his dreams," Jayfeather explained reluctantly.

He could tell how his intensity was scaring the young she-cat, and how hard she would find it to accept the darkness within his powers. But something was urging him on, an inner voice that seemed to warn him there was no time to wait for her to understand. "We don't know what the prophecy requires us to do," he went on, trying to keep his voice calm, "but we need to be ready. And that means having the courage to face up to our powers, whatever they are."

Dovepaw hesitated; Jayfeather could feel uncertainty coming off her in waves. "Wouldn't StarClan want me to learn to be a warrior first?" she meowed at last.

"I don't know. I'm not even sure that the prophecy comes from StarClan." Jayfeather hated to admit that, but it was true; no StarClan warrior had ever confirmed the prophecy for him.

"But you're right, Dovepaw." Lionblaze's voice was warm with approval. "The best thing you can do is get on with your warrior training. Let's go and get some more hunting practice, before the other cats send out a search party for us."

"Yes!" Dovepaw immediately sounded more cheerful. Jayfeather knew she was trying to push the prophecy to the back of her mind.

"Carry on," he mewed. "I'll stay here and take care of my plants. There are a few dead leaves that could do with pulling off." He heard Lionblaze's paw steps retreating, with Dovepaw following him; at the edge of the garden she halted and turned back.

"Jayfeather," she began hesitantly, "I had a dream. This

StarClan cat took me down to the lake, and it was full of water again."

"What was the cat like?" Lionblaze asked.

"Scary! She had messy gray fur and yellow eyes. And her teeth were all snaggly."

"That was Yellowfang," Jayfeather told her. "She used to be ThunderClan's medicine cat when the Clan lived in the old forest."

"Firestar talks about her sometimes," Lionblaze reassured his apprentice. "He says she's not as scary as she looks."

"Did she say why she came to you?" Jayfeather prompted.

"No . . ." Dovepaw sounded uncertain again. "If she did, I can't remember."

"And is this the only dream you've had?"

"The only one from StarClan. Do you think it's important?" Dovepaw mewed.

"Yes, but I don't know why." Jayfeather scraped his paw over the damp scented soil. "Let me know if you have any more, okay? Oh, and welcome to the Three."

CHAPTER 8

❧

Lionblaze pushed his way through the thorn tunnel and padded across the clearing toward the warriors' den. As soon as the sun had set, Brambleclaw had called him to patrol along the Shadow-Clan border, to make the best use they could of the cooler evening. Now Lionblaze felt as if his paws were going to drop off. He was so tired he wasn't even sure if he could make it as far as his den.

Moonlight washed over the clearing; Lionblaze shivered when he looked up at the sky and saw the moon swelling to the full. *There'll be a Gathering tomorrow night,* he thought. *It's been a whole moon since Leopardstar laid claim to all the fish in the lake. And things are no better—they're worse.*

With a massive effort he pushed his weariness away and veered from the warriors' den to head for the tumbled rocks that led up to the Highledge. *I've got to talk to Firestar.*

On the Highledge he paused for a moment, making sure he knew what he wanted to say, then called out softly, in case his leader was asleep. "Firestar?"

"Come in."

Firestar's voice was weary, and when Lionblaze stepped

into the den, he was shocked to see how thin and troubled the Clan leader looked. He crouched among the moss and bracken of his nest, his green gaze fixed on his paws. He blinked slowly as he raised his head to face Lionblaze.

"I'm sorry, Firestar," Lionblaze stammered, beginning to back out again. "You look tired, so—"

"No, I'm fine," Firestar reassured him. "If you want to talk, this is a good time."

Slightly encouraged, Lionblaze padded into the den, dipped his head to his leader, and sat beside the nest with his tail wrapped around his paws.

"How is Dovepaw's training going?" Firestar asked.

"Er . . . fine." Lionblaze wondered if Firestar had made the connection between Dovepaw and the prophecy. He must have heard about the story she had told earlier, about the brown animals blocking the river. Would Firestar believe her? And if he did, would he take this as a sign of great power? "She works hard. I think she's going to be one of the best hunters in the Clan."

Firestar nodded. "She has a good mentor," he mewed.

Lionblaze squirmed. "I do my best."

The Clan leader turned his brilliant green gaze on Lionblaze, moonlight reflecting in his eyes. "Just as Brambleclaw did," he murmured, "when he raised you as his own son."

Catching his breath, Lionblaze felt a hot core of rage beginning to grow in his belly, as if he had swallowed a burning acorn. *Why is Firestar bringing that up again now? I don't want to talk about it!*

"I know you and Jayfeather are angry that you were lied to," Firestar went on quietly. "I can understand that. But you shouldn't forget that you couldn't have had a better mother and father than Squirrelflight and Brambleclaw. Things could have been very different."

"I'm not mad at Brambleclaw," Lionblaze retorted. "He's a noble cat. I was proud when I thought he was my father. And he suffered from the lies just like the rest of us."

"Leafpool and Squirrelflight did what they thought was best for you and your littermates," Firestar meowed. "Would the truth have been easier to live with?"

"We have to live with it now," Lionblaze pointed out, making an effort not to lash his tail.

"I know." Firestar sighed. "Secrets never stay hidden forever. It takes a good deal of courage to face the truth." He paused with a brooding look, as if he was remembering something long past. "You don't need to punish Leafpool any more than she has already been punished," he went on. "She has lost everything she ever loved. And Squirrelflight has lost her mate. Do you think that's easy for her?"

They both deserved it! It took all Lionblaze's self-control not to hiss the words aloud. His anger threatened to overwhelm him; he didn't want to think about what Leafpool might be feeling.

"I take it that's not what you came to talk about?" Firestar asked, tilting his head to one side.

Lionblaze seized on the change of subject, glad to speak to his leader as a warrior of ThunderClan, not Firestar's troubled kin. "Have you heard the story Dovepaw told, about the brown animals blocking the stream that marks the Shadow-Clan border?"

Firestar nodded.

"I think she might be right," Lionblaze continued.

The ThunderClan leader blinked in surprise, opened his jaws to speak, then seemed to consider the possibility more carefully. "If she is, I don't see how she knows," he replied. His eyes narrowed, and Lionblaze suppressed a shiver at his piercing green gaze. *How much does Firestar know about us?*

"StarClan might have sent her a dream, I suppose," Firestar mewed after a moment. "She didn't mention that to you, did she?"

Lionblaze wished he could have said yes. It would be such a convenient explanation. But lying to his Clan leader would create more problems than it would solve. "No, she didn't," he replied.

"Hmm . . ." Firestar's whiskers quivered; he was obviously thinking deeply. "What she says makes sense," he continued eventually. "I don't mean about the brown animals. But there could be something blocking the stream so that the water doesn't reach us anymore."

"That's what I thought." Lionblaze was relieved to have a good reason for believing Dovepaw that meant he didn't have to reveal the truth about her senses.

"There's nothing in our territory," Firestar went on in a murmur, half to himself. "And there can't be anything in ShadowClan's territory either, or they would have unblocked it."

"It must be much farther upstream," Lionblaze mewed.

"Let me take a patrol to investigate. There might be something we can do."

"No, it's too dangerous." Firestar shook his head. "We don't know what might have caused the blockage. Besides, we would need to travel through ShadowClan territory. Blackstar would claw our ears off, and I couldn't blame him."

"So every cat has to suffer without water?" Lionblaze challenged him. "Jayfeather is doing his best to keep the Clan going, Firestar, but there's a limit to what any medicine cat can do. Much more of this, and cats are going to die of thirst."

"I know." Firestar let out a long sigh that told Lionblaze of his despair more clearly than words. "But journeying upstream . . . it's too much to take on, when we don't know for sure that the stream has been blocked."

"Then what are we going to do? Sit around waiting for rain?" Lionblaze's anger was flaring up again, until he felt as if it would shrivel every hair on his pelt. "StarClan hasn't sent us any messages to tell us when the drought might end. It's time we took our destiny into our own paws!" Frustrated, he scraped his claws along the rock floor of the den. Words hovered, unspoken: *You know that I'm more powerful than StarClan! Why won't you believe me when I tell you we can fix this?* But Lionblaze managed not to say them out loud.

"Very well, then," Firestar responded wearily. "If you're convinced that Dovepaw is right, I'll let you look into it. There doesn't seem to be anything else we can do to help. But I still won't allow a patrol of ThunderClan cats to travel upstream alone. You would never reach the blockage, even if it exists."

"But—" Lionblaze began.

"I said *alone*," Firestar interrupted. "If ShadowClan would join us, the mission would be a lot less dangerous. In fact, it would be best if we could form an expedition from all the Clans. Four Clans working together would be much stronger than one patrol alone."

"Would they agree?" Lionblaze asked doubtfully.

"We're all suffering from the lack of water." Firestar sounded more energetic now, as if the plan was renewing his strength. "Why shouldn't we all do something about it?"

Lionblaze shrugged. He found it hard to imagine Blackstar, Leopardstar, and Onestar agreeing to send warriors off into the unknown when life was so tough around the lake. But maybe they were desperate enough to consider it. *And if it's the only way to ease the drought,* he decided, *I'm sure I won't be the only cat who's up for it.*

"I will propose it at tomorrow's Gathering," Firestar mewed decisively.

When Lionblaze climbed down the tumbled rocks into the clearing, he found Dovepaw and Jayfeather waiting anxiously for him.

"I heard you in there with Firestar!" Dovepaw whispered. "What did he say?"

"If you heard us, don't you know what he said?" Lionblaze asked, disconcerted to realize that his apprentice might have been listening to everything that he and Firestar had discussed.

"I don't eavesdrop!" Dovepaw twitched her whiskers

indignantly. "That would be wrong."

"So what did he say?" Jayfeather prompted.

"He wants to send a patrol from all four Clans upstream, to see if we can unblock the stream," Lionblaze replied. "He's going to mention it at the Gathering tomorrow night."

"*All* the Clans?" Dovepaw's eyes stretched wide with dismay. "But—but what if they don't believe me?"

"Don't worry." Lionblaze rested his tail on his apprentice's shoulder. "Firestar isn't going to say it was your idea."

"He'll probably tell the other Clans that we should explore the area upstream, to find out where the water has gone." To Lionblaze's surprise, Jayfeather's eyes were gleaming.

Lionblaze couldn't share his brother's enthusiasm. Forcing the Clans to cooperate with one another seemed likely to cause more trouble than he was prepared to deal with. "You sound very keen on this idea," he commented.

"Of course." Jayfeather waved his tail. "All the Clans are suffering. It makes sense that we should work together to solve the problem."

CHAPTER 9

❧

Lionblaze gazed up at the full moon hanging above the empty bowl of the lake. It outlined the WindClan cats in silver as they headed around the shore on their way to the Gathering. They looked thinner than ever, and they trudged along with their heads down and their tails drooping as if they were too tired to go on putting one paw in front of another.

Lionblaze looked around at his Clanmates and realized they were just as exhausted. Only Dovepaw seemed to have any energy. Her fur was fluffed up with excitement, and every so often she would run on a few paces, then wait for Cinderheart and Lionblaze to catch up. Her ears were pricked and her whiskers quivering. Lionblaze wondered what she could sense, whether she was already listening to murmurs from the island.

There was no need to use the fallen tree to cross the lake to the island. There was no water left in this narrow channel; the lake bottom was exposed to the stars, tumbled with pebbles and bits of wood. Firestar led the way down, jumping gracefully through the scattered debris, his paws silent on the stones.

"I don't know why we came all this way around," Foxleap muttered. "We could have just walked straight across the lake from our own territory.

"I suppose so," Cinderheart agreed. "But we've always done it this way. Somehow it doesn't seem respectful to change."

Foxleap shrugged with a tired sigh.

Moonlight showed the lake robbed of all its old magnificence, reduced to a bowl of dust and stones. It felt strange to Lionblaze to be padding over an arid waste of pebbles where deep water had once rippled. Above him, the fallen tree didn't seem so high, either, as when he had to balance carefully on it with the dark lake lapping hungrily below.

The undergrowth on the island was brown and brittle all the way down to the shore. ThunderClan and WindClan mingled together as they padded quietly through it toward the clearing. Lionblaze spotted the WindClan deputy, Ashfoot, pacing beside Crowfeather; the deputy was Crowfeather's mother, Lionblaze remembered, with a sudden shock at the realization that he had more kin in WindClan.

He dropped back, hoping that Ashfoot and Crowfeather hadn't noticed him, and found himself walking just behind Squirrelflight and Thornclaw. Cinderheart was beside him, with Birchfall on his other side and Ivypaw and Dovepaw following. Together they pushed through the bushes that surrounded the clearing and emerged in the cold starlight, circled by pine trees. ShadowClan had already arrived. They greeted ThunderClan and WindClan with subdued nods. The shadows that flitted over the ground were as light and frail as fallen leaves; was it Lionblaze's imagination, or were the cats really making less noise with their half-starved paws?

While Firestar and Onestar were climbing the tree to join Blackstar, Lionblaze spotted Jayfeather padding over to touch noses with Littlecloud, the ShadowClan medicine cat. Nearby, Littlecloud's apprentice, Flametail, was sitting with his littermates Tigerheart and Dawnpelt.

Tigerheart sprang to his paws as soon as he saw Lionblaze. "Hi!" he called. "How are you doing?"

"Fine, thanks," Lionblaze replied curtly. As he turned away, he tried to ignore the hurt in the younger cat's eyes.

Moons ago, when Tigerheart and his littermates were newly apprenticed, their mother, Tawnypelt, had brought them to ThunderClan because a loner named Sol had taken over ShadowClan. Tawnypelt had been born and raised in ThunderClan; she and her kits had been welcomed, though cautiously, but had gone back to ShadowClan as soon as Sol had been driven out.

I thought they were my kin then, Lionblaze reflected sadly. *Brambleclaw is Tawnypelt's brother. . . . I liked them, especially Tigerheart. But now . . .*

"I wish they would leave me alone," he muttered aloud to Cinderheart. "They know I'm not their kin."

Cinderheart's blue eyes softened. "You can be friends without being kin," she pointed out. "And isn't it a good thing to have friends in another Clan instead of enemies?"

How could Cinderheart understand? She hasn't been betrayed by her parents. Lionblaze's gaze rested on Tigerheart and Dawnpelt. *I wonder if Tigerstar has visited them in their dreams, like he used to visit me in mine?* Tigerstar was Brambleclaw and Tawnypelt's father. He had been a warrior and deputy of ThunderClan, but he had been banished by Bluestar for plotting her death and became leader of ShadowClan. He had dreamed of ruling over all four Clans when he was alive, and he nursed that dream still, even though he now walked in the Dark Forest, with other cats who were denied entry to StarClan. He had come to Lionblaze at night, preying on their shared blood, to train him in the art of merciless fighting and brutal ambition. Lionblaze had learned everything eagerly, but as soon as he found out that Tigerstar was not his kin, he realized that the dead warrior had been using him for his own dark purposes.

Lionblaze forced his paws to carry him toward the young ShadowClan warriors, knowing that he ought to try making up for his unfriendliness, but before he could take more than a couple of steps he heard Onestar calling from the Great Oak.

"Has any cat seen Leopardstar and her Clan?" When nothing but shrugs and shaking heads answered his question, he added, "Weaselfur, go take a look, will you?"

The WindClan warrior pushed his way back through the bushes and returned a moment later. "There's a patrol on its way," he reported to his leader. "They're coming straight across the lake."

All the cats settled down to wait, their talk dying into silence. Lionblaze sat beside Cinderheart, with a guilty glance across the clearing at the ShadowClan cats. *Maybe I'll talk to them before we leave.*

Not many heartbeats had passed before Lionblaze heard more rustling in the bushes and Leopardstar emerged at the head of the RiverClan patrol. He felt his pelt bristle with shock when he saw how frail the RiverClan leader was, every bone visible beneath her spotted pelt and her eyes as dull as the mud left in the lake.

As soon as Leopardstar appeared, Dovepaw sat straight up, her eyes stretched wide with astonishment. Wriggling around to face Lionblaze, she leaned across to him and whispered in his ear, "That's the sick cat from the RiverClan camp!"

"Are you sure?" Lionblaze was taken aback. *That means Leopardstar has been sick for nearly a moon!*

Dovepaw nodded, and Lionblaze didn't ask her any more questions. He didn't want any other cat to overhear their conversation.

Leopardstar held her head high as she padded across the clearing with Mistyfoot behind her. She paused at the foot of the tree, gazing upward but making no attempt to leap; Mistyfoot murmured something to her.

"I think Mistyfoot is offering to help her," Cinderheart whispered into Lionblaze's ear. "Leopardstar must be really ill if she can't even jump into the tree."

But as Cinderheart spoke Leopardstar gave her head a decisive shake, gathered her haunches under her, and sprang. Her forepaws just scraped the lowest branch; she dug her claws in and after an undignified scramble managed to pull herself up. She crouched on the branch and glared at the cats below with fierce yellow eyes, as if daring any of them to comment on her awkward jump.

Lionblaze exchanged a glance with Foxleap, who sat next

to him. *Leopardstar looks as if she'll fall off that branch at any moment!* Then his gaze flicked to his brother, who was sitting at the foot of the tree with the other medicine cats, and he wondered if Jayfeather knew how weak Leopardstar was.

Firestar rose to his paws and let out a yowl to indicate that the Gathering had begun. Even though he was much thinner than usual, he still looked a lot healthier than Leopardstar. "Cats of all Clans," he began. "We are all suffering from the heat and the lack of water."

"What else is new?" Crowfeather called from a group of WindClan warriors.

Firestar ignored him. "The problem is getting worse. The stream between our territory and ShadowClan's has dried up. We think there's a possibility that there's a blockage up the stream. Some of the cats from my Clan want to explore and see if that's true."

As he spoke, his green gaze rested on Lionblaze, as if to reassure him that he didn't intend to name Dovepaw, or reveal that the cat who had the idea was only an apprentice. *Let's hope the other cats who heard her by the fresh-kill pile have the sense to keep their mouths shut.*

Lionblaze responded to his leader with a tiny nod; glancing at Dovepaw, he was relieved to see that she was listening as attentively as any other cat, but she didn't look as if she knew more than Firestar was telling.

"Your patrol will be trespassing on ShadowClan territory if they travel upstream," Blackstar growled in reply to Firestar's suggestion. "I will not allow it."

"I think we should send a patrol made up of cats from all four Clans," Firestar explained. He raised his tail for silence as a ripple of surprise passed through the clearing. "Remember what happened when Twolegs destroyed our home in the old forest?" he went on. "A patrol of six cats, representing all the Clans, went on a quest to find new territories. That was how we survived then; this could be the way to survive now."

Lionblaze felt a thrill of excitement pass through the clearing. Cats were springing to their paws, their pelts fluffing up and their tails waving.

"I'll go!" Tigerheart called out.

"So will I!" added Dawnpelt, her eyes shining. "It'll be a real warriors' quest!"

"I wasn't born when the Clans made the Great Journey," Lionblaze heard Foxleap meowing to Rosepetal. "But I bet it was exciting."

"I wonder what we'll find." Rosepetal's whiskers were quivering. "I bet a moon of dawn patrols it's Twolegs again."

"Or badgers," replied Foxleap. "I wouldn't put anything past badgers."

"I want to go," Dovepaw whispered to Lionblaze. "Do you think Firestar will choose an apprentice?"

"Don't worry," Lionblaze murmured in reply. "You're the one cat in all the Clans who *has* to go."

"You really think we could bring the water back?" It was Onestar who spoke; his voice was cautious, but hope was waking in his eyes.

"I think it's worth a try," Firestar responded.

"And who would be in charge of this joint patrol?" Blackstar asked, still sounding belligerent. "You?"

Firestar shook his head. "I don't think any Clan leader should go," he meowed. "Our Clans need us here. Besides, when we made the Great Journey, no cat was in charge. We learned to cooperate then, and there's no reason why we can't do that again. What do you think?"

Blackstar kept silent, apart from the sound of his claws scraping the bark on his branch. Onestar exchanged a glance with his deputy, Ashfoot, who was sitting on a root below, then gave a decisive nod. "I agree. It makes sense to involve all the Clans. WindClan is with you, Firestar."

"And so is ShadowClan." Blackstar fixed Firestar with a hard stare. "You'll be trekking through our territory, and you're not doing that without ShadowClan cats to keep an eye on you."

"Thank you, both of you." Lionblaze thought Firestar was trying to hide his surprise that he had gained the two leaders' consent so easily. "Leopardstar, what do you think?"

The RiverClan leader was gazing across the clearing as if she hadn't heard any of the discussion above her.

After a few heartbeats of awkward silence, Littlecloud rose to his paws. "If I may speak," he began, with a courteous nod to the leaders, "the situation now isn't quite the same as it was last time. The cats who went on the first quest were summoned by a prophecy." His gaze swept across the Clans until he found Brambleclaw, Crowfeather, and Tawnypelt. All three cats nodded; Lionblaze thought he could see memories flickering in their eyes.

Squirrelflight glanced across at Brambleclaw, and there was deep regret in the look she gave him. Lionblaze knew she hadn't been chosen by StarClan, but she had insisted on going with the others; she must be longing for that time before the lies and betrayals had come between her and her mate.

"StarClan deliberately chose those cats, one from each Clan," Littlecloud went on. "Who will choose these cats?" He paused to glance around at the other medicine cats, then added, "Has StarClan given you any hints about who should go?"

The other medicine cats, even Jayfeather, shook their heads. Lionblaze felt his belly tighten. Dovepaw *knew* that the big brown animals had blocked the stream. StarClan hadn't told them anything. *We can't wait for our warrior ancestors to save us! They know less about this than we do!*

For a moment, Lionblaze was afraid that Firestar would agree to wait for signs. Then the ThunderClan leader dipped his head to Littlecloud. "That's an important point," he meowed. "But if StarClan were going to send us signs this time, I think they would have sent them already. Each Clan leader is capable of choosing which cats should go to represent their Clans. StarClan trusts the four of us to do our best for our cats; that's why we received nine lives."

Murmurs of agreement rose from the clearing; Lionblaze saw that Onestar and Blackstar were nodding, too.

"The cats who go on the journey must be brave and strong," Firestar continued. "They must be capable of seeking out something they know little about, and willing to set aside Clan rivalry for the sake of every cat. I trust that all the leaders will make the right choice."

Lionblaze heaved a sigh of relief. That had gone much more smoothly than he had expected. The stream wouldn't be blocked for much longer! Then Leopardstar raised her head.

"Just like you, Firestar," she rasped. "Always coming up with a plan. Do you think I don't know what you really have in mind?"

Firestar looked down at her with bewilderment in his green eyes. "I'm not hiding anything," he assured her.

"Fox dung!" Leopardstar spat. Her thin, patchy pelt bristled along her bony spine. "This is a trick! You're just trying to cheat RiverClan out of our fish. You want to get rid of some of our warriors so that we can't keep up the patrols anymore."

"That doesn't make sense." Firestar didn't sound angry, just sympathetic. "Leopardstar, I can see you're not well—"

"I'm not a fool, Firestar." Leopardstar rejected the Thunder-Clan leader's pity with a snarl. Struggling to her paws, she swayed on the branch as if she was about to lose her balance and fall off. "I know you'd let RiverClan starve to save your precious Clan!"

"No, he wants to help," Onestar protested. "We all do."

"You all want our fish," Leopardstar snarled. "But you won't get it. RiverClan will *not* join this patrol."

The other three leaders glanced at one another in dismay, but before any of them could speak, Mistyfoot leaped up to her leader's branch. She crouched next to Leopardstar and spoke quietly into her ear.

Lionblaze strained to hear what she was saying and managed to pick up a few phrases. "They'll weaken themselves if they send their strongest warriors away. . . . We benefit more than the others if the lake is refilled."

Tension rose in the clearing as the other cats waited; Lionblaze could feel his pelt prickling as if a storm was coming. Leopardstar snapped at her deputy once or twice, but Mistyfoot persisted, her tail-tip resting gently on her leader's shoulder.

At length Mistyfoot rose to her paws, still keeping her tail on Leopardstar. "RiverClan will send cats with this patrol," she announced.

A few yowls of protest rose from the RiverClan warriors. "That's for Leopardstar to say, not you!" the elder Blackclaw spat.

"She already made her decision," Mallownose added. "Now you've made her look weak!"

Birchfall, sitting a couple of tail-lengths away from Lionblaze, let out a disdainful sniff. "Leopardstar couldn't look much weaker if she was dead," he commented.

Mistyfoot didn't try to argue; she just waited for the noise to die down. Then she dipped her head to Leopardstar and the other leaders and leaped to the ground again.

"Thank you, Leopardstar," Firestar mewed, stepping forward once more. "I promise, you won't regret this decision." He paused to give his chest fur a couple of thoughtful licks, then went on, "Each Clan must send two cats to the mouth of the dried-up stream on the second sunrise from now. The Clan deputies can escort them." His green eyes glowed in the moonlight and his voice rang through the clearing. "We will find the water! The Clans must survive!"

CHAPTER 10

As soon as Jayfeather woke on the morning after the Gathering, he could feel excitement buzzing around the camp like bees disturbed from their nest. Yawning and trying to shake off the dark dreams that had troubled his sleep, he pulled himself to his paws and swiped at a frond of fern that was clinging to his nose.

Don't they realize that the cats who go on the journey might never come back?

He stumbled drowsily out into the clearing and scented Firestar emerging from his den onto the Highledge. The Clan was gathering around to listen even before their leader yowled the words that would call a meeting. Jayfeather felt Mouse-whisker brush against his pelt, and he heard the thump of paws as Blossompaw, Briarpaw, and Bumblepaw rushed past him. Padding forward, he found a place for himself close to Lionblaze and Dovepaw.

"Cats of ThunderClan," Firestar began when the excited murmuring had died into silence. "At the Gathering last night, all four Clans decided to send two cats to explore the stream and find out if it really is blocked. I've decided that Lionblaze and Dovepaw will go to represent ThunderClan."

Even before Firestar had finished speaking, yowls of indignation rose into the still morning air.

"She's an apprentice!" Thornclaw protested. "We should send a strong warrior who can cope with the danger."

"Yeah, what's so special about her?" Berrynose added.

But all the disapproving voices were drowned out by Ivypaw's distraught wail. "Why do you get to go when I can't? Why doesn't Firestar send another warrior?"

"It's not because Firestar likes me better, or anything," Dovepaw reassured her sister. Jayfeather heard her pad over to Ivypaw and try to give her ear a comforting lick, but Ivypaw jerked away from her. "It's just that I was the first cat to think about something blocking the stream."

Jayfeather felt guilt flowing over her as she remembered that she was keeping her special senses, and everything she knew about the prophecy, a secret from her sister. *She'll have to get used to it, that's all.*

"I know," Ivypaw mewed wretchedly. "But I thought we would always do everything together."

"I wish we could, but we can't," Dovepaw replied.

"That's enough!" Squirrelflight's voice rose above the clamor of the protesting cats. "Firestar has made his decision. It's not for us to question it."

"That's right," Graystripe agreed. "Do you trust your leader or not?"

Gradually the noise died down, and Firestar spoke again. "Lionblaze and Dovepaw will leave at the next sunrise. The meeting is over."

The crowd of cats broke up into groups, muttering together

among themselves. For a few heartbeats Jayfeather lost track of Dovepaw, then located her near the fresh-kill pile with Icecloud and Foxleap. Picking up a surge of anxiety from the apprentice, he padded over to join them.

"How come you get chosen to go?" Foxleap was asking as Jayfeather approached. "How did you know about the stream, anyway?"

"Did you have a dream from StarClan?" Icecloud added eagerly. "What did they say to you?"

Jayfeather could tell that Dovepaw was beginning to panic. "So what, if she did have a dream?" he snapped, flicking his tail in Icecloud's direction. "That's between her and Firestar. Now, if you've nothing better to do, you can go down to the lake and get some water for the elders."

He heard an annoyed hiss from Foxleap, but the two young warriors turned and padded off without arguing.

"He talks to us as if he was our mentor," Icecloud complained in a whisper as they headed for the thorn tunnel.

"Jayfeather, I don't know what to tell them!" Dovepaw meowed as soon as the warriors were out of earshot. "I didn't have a dream, you know I didn't! I can *hear* those brown animals, *sense* them, just like I knew what Lionblaze was doing by the lake."

Jayfeather twitched his whiskers. "I know," he replied. "But only Lionblaze and I will understand that. As far as the other cats are concerned, this was a dream. Understand?"

Dovepaw hesitated. "I don't like lying to them," she meowed.

Jayfeather could feel her bewilderment, and he understood that her supersharp senses were perfectly natural to her. But she was being way too stubborn and narrow-minded. Frustration stabbed at him, sharp as a thorn. "Don't you want to be special?" he demanded. "Don't you like being chosen for a destiny greater than your Clanmates?"

"No, I don't!" Dovepaw spat back at him, then seemed to remember who she was talking to. "Sorry," she mumbled. "I don't like keeping secrets from my Clanmates, that's all."

"Then don't talk about it," Jayfeather advised. He sensed that the apprentice was about to go on arguing, when he scented Brightheart approaching. Dovepaw took the chance to scamper away across the clearing to where her sister was sitting outside the apprentices' den.

"Hi, Jayfeather," the she-cat called. "Do you want me to go and collect some traveling herbs for the journey?"

"Thanks, Brightheart, that would be great," Jayfeather replied. His mind began to race. He knew Brightheart was waiting for him to tell her what herbs she needed to look for.

Mouse dung! I'm not sure I can remember.

This would be the first time he had prepared the traveling-herbs mixture on his own. He tried to think what Leafpool had done when Brambleclaw and the rest left to search for Sol, but he was distracted by another, deeper worry. *I wish Lionblaze and Dovepaw weren't both going on the quest. What if they don't come back? The prophecy will never be fulfilled if I'm the only one left!*

He scented Leafpool as she padded past on her way to the fresh-kill pile. His pelt burned to ask her about the traveling herbs, but he forced his mouth to stay shut. *She's not a medicine cat anymore! She turned her back on that when she let herself fall in love with Crowfeather.*

"Sorry," he mumbled to Brightheart. "Just give me a couple of moments."

He could always ask Cinderheart, to see if her half-buried Cinderpelt memories would be able to tell her the list of herbs. *But that might cause more problems than it solves. Cinderheart has no idea that she was once ThunderClan's medicine cat.*

"It's okay," Brightheart mewed cheerfully. "I think I can remember the mixture, from when I ate the traveling herbs before I went to the Moonstone, back in the old forest. Let me see . . . there's sorrel in it, isn't there, and daisy? I remember that because I hate the taste!"

"That's right." To Jayfeather's relief, his memory was coming back. "And chamomile's another . . ."

"And burnet!" Brightheart finished triumphantly. "That's all, isn't it? I'll get onto it right away."

"Thanks, Brightheart." Jayfeather dipped his head. "The best place for sorrel is beside the old Twoleg path. And you'll probably find chamomile in the garden behind the Twoleg nest."

"Great!" The she-cat whisked away. "Hazeltail! Blossompaw!" she called. "Do you want to come with me and look for herbs?"

When the three cats had vanished into the thorn tunnel, Jayfeather sensed Leafpool still crouched beside the fresh-kill pile. A surge of emotion jolted him, so powerful that it almost carried him off his paws. Before he could stop himself, he was flung into Leafpool's memories.

He was looking through her eyes as she hurried through long grass and undergrowth, her heart pounding. The pungent taste of traveling herbs was in her mouth. The scents around her were strange to Jayfeather, and he realized that this memory must belong to the old forest, before the Clans were driven out. Leafpool was struggling with an agony of fear; Jayfeather sensed that she was completely focused on her sister. There was something that she didn't want Squirrelflight to do. . . .

Then Leafpool pushed her way through the branches of a bush and confronted Brambleclaw and Squirrelflight. Jayfeather was surprised by how much smaller and younger the cats looked. *This was before the Great Journey. Leafpool and Squirrelflight must have still been apprentices.*

Leafpool padded forward and laid her mouthful of leaves down in front of her sister and Brambleclaw. "I brought you some traveling herbs," she murmured. "You're going to need them where you're going."

Brambleclaw's eyes widened with outrage, and he began to accuse Squirrelflight of giving away their secret to her sister. *What secret?* Jayfeather wondered.

"She didn't need to tell me anything," Leafpool promised. "I just knew, that's all."

Jayfeather flinched. Leafpool and Squirrelflight had a connection he had never appreciated before—and now Leafpool was terrified that her sister was going away, and that they might never see each other again. *This is the beginning of the quest!* Jayfeather realized. *When the six cats went to find Midnight and learn the message StarClan had given her.*

He listened through Leafpool's ears as Squirrelflight poured out the whole story of Brambleclaw's dreams, and of the meeting with cats of other Clans. He was aware of Leafpool's deepening dismay, a chaos of feeling he could not penetrate, as if even in her memories there was something she was hiding. Leafpool tried hard to persuade Squirrelflight not to go, but Jayfeather could tell that she knew she had no hope of changing her sister's mind. *Squirrelflight hasn't changed much, then!* At last, sadly, Leafpool had to accept that Squirrelflight was leaving.

"You won't tell any cat where we've gone?" Squirrelflight insisted.

"I don't know where you're going—and neither do you," Leafpool pointed out. "But no, I won't say anything."

She watched as Squirrelflight and Brambleclaw licked up the traveling herbs, then in a sudden rush of anxiety tried to teach her sister everything she had learned from Cinderpelt, so that they could find the right herbs to help them while they were on their journey.

"We *will* come back," Squirrelflight promised.

Then the memory dissolved, and Jayfeather was sightless again, back in the clearing. As the rush of Leafpool's emotion died away, he sensed her watching him from the fresh-kill pile. She had deliberately given him this memory.

I know how you feel. I felt like this, too.

No, you didn't! Jayfeather flashed back angrily. *You and Squirrel-flight weren't part of a prophecy. If she hadn't come back, perhaps it would have been better for every cat.*

She rose to her paws and padded away, toward the warriors' den. The air as she left was sharp with sadness. For a couple of heartbeats Jayfeather was almost betrayed into sympathy. The memory had been so clear, and Leafpool's emotions so raw. He shook his head, trying to toss the weakness away.

If you'd told the truth in the beginning, you could have helped us with the prophecy. Hollyleaf might still be here. But she's gone now, and we have to do it on our own.

The sun was well above the trees by now, its rays burning down into the hollow as if the air had turned to flame. Jayfeather's paws itched to be doing something, but with Brightheart out collecting herbs he couldn't justify leaving the hollow.

I'll check the edges of the hollow for snakes. With every cat so excited, they'll never remember to keep a lookout.

As he padded across the clearing, he remembered the dreadful day when Honeyfern had been bitten by a snake that slipped out of one of the holes at the bottom of the cliff. There was nothing he or Leafpool could do to save her from the poison. Later, as the young cat's kin grieved for her, he and Leafpool had stuffed a mouse with deathberries and pushed it into the hole in the hope that the snake would eat it and die. But the venomous creature hadn't taken their bait. Jayfeather suspected it was lurking around, waiting for another chance to strike.

As he worked his way along the rock wall, checking that all the holes were still securely blocked with stones, Jayfeather picked up Purdy's scent and realized that the old loner was stretched out on the flat-topped rock, near where the snake had appeared. He could hear the old cat's rhythmic snoring, which ended abruptly in a snort as if Jayfeather's paw steps had disturbed his nap.

"You want to be careful up there," Jayfeather meowed, halting beside the rock. "You know the snake—"

"I know all about the snake, young 'un," Purdy interrupted. "And there's no sign of slippery creatures around here. I've been watchin'."

"That's great, Purdy." Jayfeather bit back a comment about how clever Purdy was to keep watch for snakes in his sleep. "But I've still got to check."

"I'll help you." Purdy flopped down from the rock, staggered to find his balance, and padded to Jayfeather's side. "I reckon you youngsters need some cat wi' a bit o' experience to show you what's what."

Oh, sure, Jayfeather thought as he went on checking the snake holes, pulling out bits of stone to give each opening a good sniff before he pushed the stone back and checked that the blockage was secure.

Purdy padded alongside him, offering helpful comments like, "You missed a gap there," just as Jayfeather was feeling around for a stone that would fit the space, or, "Are you sure you gave that hole a proper sniff?"

Jayfeather gritted his teeth. "Quite sure, Purdy, thanks."

StarClan help me not to claw his ears off!

"You'll miss your brother, I'm guessin'," Purdy went on. "But he'll be back before you know it, mark my words. It was just the same, y'know, when Brambleclaw and Squirrelpaw went off to find Midnight."

"Squirrel*flight*," Jayfeather corrected the old loner. *Don't you start as well! I've just had enough of that from Leafpool!*

"I remember the first time I met them," Purdy rambled on. "They were so young and so brave! I reckoned they all had bees in their brain, travelin' so far. But see how wrong I was? They found this place to live, after the Upwalkers wrecked their old home."

Jayfeather, flat on his belly in front of a suspicious-smelling hole, just grunted in agreement.

"Not that I ever had no trouble wi' Upwalkers," Purdy continued. "My Upwalker was right friendly. I'd got him well trained, see. He was 'specially good when the weather turned cold and huntin' was difficult. Always somethin' tasty to eat, an' a fire to sit beside . . ."

Jayfeather let the old loner's voice fade into the background of creaking branches and buzzing insects. He wished that the older cats would stop going on about the quest to find Midnight. He wanted to yowl out the words of his own prophecy so that every cat could hear it.

This is more important than anything that happened in the past!

"Okay, Purdy," he mewed, interrupting a long and convoluted story about a fox. "We're done here. Thanks for your help."

"Any time, young 'un." Jayfeather heard Purdy clambering back onto the flat-topped rock and settling himself in the sun. "You don't get foxes now like the ones when I was young . . ." he murmured drowsily.

As Jayfeather padded back toward his den, he heard Lionblaze and Dovepaw practicing battle moves beside the thorn barrier. He stopped, listening to Dovepaw leaping at Lionblaze and slicing her claws through the air, barely a whisker from his fur. Suddenly the quest was real. Lionblaze and Dovepaw would be gone the next morning, and the thought terrified Jayfeather more than he would have thought possible.

Just find these animals, and come back, he begged. *Whatever we have to do for the prophecy to come true, I can't do it on my own.*

CHAPTER 11

❧

Dovepaw stood on the rocks at the mouth of the stream that marked the border with ShadowClan. Even though the sun had only just cleared the horizon, the stones were hot under her pads, and the island at the far side of the lake was veiled in a shimmering haze of heat. The journey was about to begin—the quest that she had set in motion when she heard the animals that were blocking the stream—but Dovepaw couldn't push down her misery at leaving her sister behind. Before dawn, when Lionblaze had come to rouse her in the apprentices' den, Ivypaw had curled up and pretended to be asleep so that she didn't have to say good-bye.

Beside Dovepaw, Brambleclaw and Lionblaze were mewing quietly together. Not wanting to listen in on their conversation, Dovepaw let her senses range farther. She spotted a patrol of RiverClan warriors circling the pool of brackish water in the middle of the lake; they looked hungry and scared. Listening briefly to their complaints about the heat, she pushed her awareness farther still, and focused on the cats in the RiverClan camp. Soon she managed to identify Mistyfoot, Reedwhisker, and the golden-furred medicine cat, Mothwing, whom she had seen at the Gathering.

"I've done everything I can for Leopardstar," Mothwing was meowing anxiously. "But she still hasn't recovered from losing her last life."

Mistyfoot shook her head. "She hasn't had the chance to get her strength back. But there must be some herbs you can use to help her, Mothwing?"

"The herbs are all dried up." The medicine cat's mew was quiet. "I'm afraid Leopardstar is going to lose this life as well."

There was a stunned silence. *How many lives does Leopardstar have left?* Dovepaw wondered. At last the quiet was broken by Reedwhisker. "Then we have to hope that Firestar's plan works, and the cats we send find out what has happened to the water."

The sound of paw steps on the other side of the stream jerked Dovepaw back to her surroundings. Three cats had emerged from the dried-up grass on the opposite side of the stream and were padding down the stretch of pebbles to join her and her Clanmates.

Brambleclaw stepped forward to meet them. "Greetings, Russetfur," he meowed.

The dark ginger she-cat just grunted in response.

"She's the ShadowClan deputy, isn't she?" Dovepaw whispered to Lionblaze. "She looks really old!"

"She was one of the cats who made the Great Journey," Lionblaze murmured in reply. "But she's still a formidable warrior. Don't let her hear you calling her old!"

"These are ShadowClan's chosen cats," Russetfur meowed, waving her tail toward the younger warriors who had followed her down to the stream.

The two cats stepped forward and nodded to the Thunder-Clan patrol. Dovepaw recognized the golden tabby pelt of Tigerheart, Tawnypelt's son, from the Gathering, but the other warrior, an older dark brown tom, was a stranger to her.

"Who's that?" she whispered to Lionblaze.

"Toadfoot," her mentor told her. "He made the Great Journey, too, but he was a kit then."

"Wow! Kits made the Great Journey?"

Lionblaze nodded, but he motioned with his tail for Dovepaw to be quiet as Russetfur spoke again.

"Don't forget you'll be traveling through *our* territory to begin with," she growled. "Don't even think about stealing prey, because my warriors will be watching you."

Lionblaze let his gaze sweep across the burnt grass on either side of the stream. "What prey would that be?" he asked pointedly.

Russetfur bared her teeth in the beginning of a snarl. "Don't get clever with me, Lionblaze. And just because this quest was Firestar's idea, don't start thinking that Thunder-Clan cats are in charge."

"No cat thinks that," Brambleclaw mewed soothingly. "That wasn't how it worked on the first journey. They'll figure things out for themselves on the way."

Russetfur let out a snort. "What was Firestar thinking,

choosing an apprentice?" she demanded, with a glare at Dove-paw. "What use will she be?"

Dovepaw bristled. *I'm the one who knows about the animals block-ing the stream!*

A moment later her eyes flew wide with shock as Lionblaze meowed defensively, "She has to come. She's the one who knows why the stream is blocked."

Brambleclaw took a step forward, his eyes narrowed as he gazed at Lionblaze. His jaws opened, but he didn't speak. Dovepaw guessed that he wanted to say, "Mouse-brain!" but couldn't in front of the other Clan cats.

"*She* knows?" Toadfoot looked disbelieving. "How does she know?"

Lionblaze gulped, seeming to realize his mistake. "Oh, she . . . uh . . . yeah, she had a dream from StarClan," he explained awkwardly. "They told her all about it."

"Yeah, and hedgehogs fly," Toadfoot muttered.

Dovepaw stood up straighter and tried to look strong and capable, only to cringe when her belly let out a huge rumble. *Oh, no!*

Russetfur rolled her eyes, and Toadfoot flicked his ears contemptuously, but Dovepaw picked up a sympathetic glance from Tigerheart, and she started to feel a little better. Maybe at least one of the ShadowClan cats was friendly.

Lionblaze touched her shoulder with his tail-tip and angled his ears across the lake to point out three more cats approach-ing from the direction of RiverClan. As they drew closer, Dovepaw recognized Mistyfoot, along with a young gray-and-white she-cat and a dark gray tabby tom.

"Petalfur and Rippletail," Lionblaze whispered in her ear.

Mistyfoot dipped her head toward the other deputies, but she didn't approach. The three RiverClan cats stopped a little way off, waiting with a wary, reserved look on their faces. Dovepaw guessed that even though Leopardstar had been persuaded to let her warriors join in the quest, none of the RiverClan cats were happy about it.

Toadfoot let out a disdainful sniff and leaned over to murmur something to Tigerheart. Dovepaw picked up his soft words. "What a scrawny lot! Leopardstar must be saving her strongest warriors to guard the lake."

Dovepaw wasn't sure he was right. True, Petalfur and Rippletail looked hollow and ungroomed, but that seemed to be true of every cat in RiverClan. She wished the ShadowClan cats weren't so unfriendly. *This journey won't be much fun if we can't even greet one another!*

Russetfur raked her claws through the dried mud of the riverbed. "Where is WindClan?" she meowed impatiently. "I've got better things to do than stand here all day."

Looking past the ShadowClan deputy, Dovepaw spotted three cats racing down the hillside in WindClan territory and heading out across the dried-up lake. Ashfoot, the WindClan deputy, was in the lead, with two she-cats behind her: a small white one and a younger light brown tabby.

"Who are they?" Dovepaw asked her mentor. "I saw them at the Gathering, but no cat told me their names."

"Whitetail and Sedgewhisker," Lionblaze replied, peering

across the empty lake. "Good choice—Whitetail especially. She's an experienced warrior."

Dovepaw was pleased to see that the WindClan cats looked a lot friendlier. They raced up to the waiting cats with excitement shining in their eyes.

"Greetings," Ashfoot mewed as they skidded to a stop at the edge of the stream. "It's good to see you."

"And you, Ashfoot," Brambleclaw responded, dipping his head.

Russetfur's only reply was a grunt, and Mistyfoot didn't say anything at all.

"You know what you have to do," Brambleclaw went on.

"Find what's blocking the stream, and get rid of it," Lionblaze replied promptly, his tail flicking as if he couldn't wait to be on his way.

"Really?" Rippletail cast an alarmed glance at Mistyfoot. "I thought we were just supposed to find out what the problem is, and then come back to report."

Before the RiverClan deputy could reply, Russetfur let out a growl. "What's the matter? Is RiverClan too scared to take on a challenge?"

"Of course not!" Mistyfoot snapped, her blue eyes flashing. "But the safety of our Clanmates matters to us, even if it's not important to you."

"It's for the sake of our Clanmates that these cats are going," Russetfur snarled, letting her neck fur bristle.

Dovepaw's heart started to race; for a moment it seemed as if the two she-cats would hurl themselves at each other in a screeching fight. But then Ashfoot stepped forward.

"That's enough," she meowed. "We're working together now. The patrol must do whatever they can without risking their lives."

Dovepaw picked up a sigh from Toadfoot and saw him roll his eyes. Brambleclaw's ears snapped up; he had spotted the younger warrior, too. "You made the Great Journey, Toadfoot," he meowed with an edge to his voice. "You should remember how the four Clans worked together to help one another. It doesn't mean you won't come back to your own separate territories."

Toadfoot scuffled his forepaws on the dusty ground. "I was only a kit then," he mumbled. "I don't remember much."

"Try," Brambleclaw advised him drily. When there was no response from Toadfoot, he let his gaze sweep around to take in all the other cats. "Keep to the stream so that you can find your way back easily," he instructed them. "Don't get distracted; don't let foxes or kittypets chase you off course—"

"As if!" Toadfoot interrupted.

That cat is a real pain in the tail, Dovepaw thought. *Brambleclaw has more traveling experience than any cat. Why can't Toadfoot listen?*

Brambleclaw fixed the ShadowClan warrior with a glare from his amber eyes. "Take time to rest and eat when you can," he went on. "If you find the blockage, you won't be able to do anything if you're exhausted when you get there."

Even though Dovepaw knew that Brambleclaw's advice was good, she was starting to get impatient. She could hear the brown animals far up ahead, feel their scratching through the stones beneath her paws, and sense the effort they were making to hold the water back.

"Have you got ants in your pelt?" Lionblaze whispered.

"Sorry!" Dovepaw murmured, trying to keep still.

Brambleclaw stepped back to join the other deputies. Dovepaw glanced around, realizing that the cats who were to go on the quest were standing together for the first time. *I hardly know their names!* she thought, fighting back panic. Their different Clan scents filled her nose and made her feel dizzy; she drew closer to Lionblaze, feeling encouraged by how calm and strong he seemed among these restless, unfamiliar cats.

"May StarClan light your path," Ashfoot meowed solemnly. "And bring you all home safe."

CHAPTER 12

With the gazes of all four deputies on them, the patrol turned to leave and started to pad up the dry streambed. It wasn't wide enough for them to all walk next to one another; before they had gone more than a few paw steps, Toadfoot pushed his way to the front.

"This is our territory, you know," he growled.

It's just as much our territory! Lionblaze thought indignantly. *This stream is the border, mouse-brain!* He was aware of Dovepaw beside him, bristling as if she expected him to protest, but he kept silent, giving her just a tiny shake of his head.

"Sorry." The embarrassed mew came from Dovepaw's other side as Tigerheart squeezed past her to join his Clanmate at the head of the patrol.

Lionblaze couldn't help feeling sorry for him. It wasn't Tigerheart's fault that his Clanmate was being such a pain.

Following the ShadowClan cats' lead, the other cats fell into Clan pairs too, with Dovepaw bringing up the rear beside Lionblaze. Her head and tail were dropping in disappointment, as if she hadn't thought the journey would be so tense; Lionblaze guessed she'd looked forward to making friends with the cats from the other Clans.

"Don't worry." He bent his head to murmur into her ear. "It won't always be like this. It'll take a while to get to know the other cats."

Dovepaw blinked at him. "We don't have time to argue," she whispered back. "Whatever is blocking the stream, the brown animals are adding to it, making it stronger. The water might be trapped forever!"

Lionblaze touched her flank with the tip of his tail. "Not if we can do anything about it," he promised.

The streambed gradually became deeper, sheltered by crumbling banks of sand. Flat stretches of grass opened up on either side, and Lionblaze heard the strange thumping sounds and weird yowls of Twolegs up ahead.

"We're getting to the Twoleg greenleafplace," he mewed to Dovepaw. "Remember you heard the same sounds when I took you on your first tour of the territory?"

Dovepaw nodded. Her whiskers quivering with curiosity, she scrambled up the side of the stream before Lionblaze could stop her and peered over the top of the bank. Lionblaze sprang up beside her, his claws extended to drag her down again.

"They're huge!" Dovepaw couldn't hide a squeak of astonishment as she stared at the tall pink creatures that had no fur except for a tiny scrap on top of their heads. Three or four Twoleg kits were leaping about the clearing, throwing something brightly colored at one another, while the fully grown Twolegs sat outside the pelt-dens. *They're like moving trees,*

Lionblaze thought, his own curiosity making him forget the danger for a couple of heartbeats.

"Get down!" Toadfoot hissed furiously from behind them.

But it was too late. One of the Twoleg kits had spotted Dovepaw; she froze in horror as it ran toward her with its pink paws outstretched. Yowls came from the other Twolegs. The fully grown ones sprang to their hind paws and pounded across the clearing, where their kits were already gathering around.

"This way!" Toadfoot snapped.

As Lionblaze shoved Dovepaw down the bank, the ShadowClan warrior turned to lead the way upstream, but a huge Twoleg leaped into the streambed, blocking their path. Big, meaty paws groped down from the sky, reaching for the cats.

"No!" Petalfur screeched.

In a panic, Sedgewhisker tried to climb the steepest part of the bank and fell back in a whirl of flailing legs and tail. Rippletail whipped around and fled back downstream, but Twolegs were blocking that way, too. Pushing Dovepaw behind him, Lionblaze advanced on the first Twoleg, his fur fluffed up and his claws out.

"Over here!" Toadfoot's yowl rose above the noise. "Follow me!"

He had scrambled up at a place where the bank had slipped down into the stream and it was easier to climb out. Clambering after him, Lionblaze launched himself into the open with the rest of the patrol close behind.

Toadfoot led them straight across the clearing toward the

scatter of flimsy green pelt-dens. "No! This way!" he yowled when Whitetail and Sedgewhisker veered off toward the lake. "Stay together!"

The WindClan cats swerved back and the whole patrol streamed across the scorched grass, pursued by yowling Twolegs. Lionblaze raced along, his feet thudding on the hard ground. Fear fluffed out every hair on his pelt, but at the same time his paws tingled with excitement. *You can't catch us, stupid Twolegs!*

Toadfoot looped around one den and started to lead the cats back toward the stream. Lionblaze caught a glimpse of Petalfur and Rippletail; the RiverClan cats were dropping back, and Petalfur was limping.

"Lionblaze, look!" Dovepaw gasped; she had seen them, too.

Before Lionblaze could make a move, a young male Twoleg, bigger than the other kits, swooped down and grabbed Petalfur. As the Twoleg swung her up into the air, the RiverClan cat let out a terrified squeal and struggled to get free.

"Help!" Rippletail yowled. "Don't leave her!"

At the head of the patrol, Toadfoot turned and raced back toward the young Twoleg. "Make a circle!" he snapped. "If we want him to drop Petalfur, we'll have to show him we're not afraid to fight."

Whitetail, Sedgewhisker, and Rippletail exchanged horrified glances, but they ran into place, trembling, until they surrounded the Twoleg. Lionblaze slipped in between Dovepaw and Tigerheart. Taking their lead from Toadfoot, the patrol began to close in on the young Twoleg, stalking through the grass and hissing.

"Let her go!" Lionblaze snarled.

From behind him, a full-grown Twoleg let out a bellow. The young Twoleg dropped Petalfur; the RiverClan cat plunged to the ground and stood shakily on her paws.

"Quick!" Toadfoot gathered the patrol with a whisk of his tail and led them at full pelt past the young Twoleg. Ripple-tail ran beside Petalfur, guiding her by pressing up against her shoulder. More Twolegs were pounding toward them; the patrol split into two at a nod from Toadfoot, and veered into a pair of pelt-dens.

Lionblaze hurtled into the weird blue-green light with Dovepaw and Tigerheart behind him. Glancing back, he saw Dovepaw crash into a pile of hard Twoleg stuff that clattered and rolled all around her, almost carrying her off her paws. Recovering, she raced across a soft pelt laid on the ground and ducked under another pelt that was hanging from the roof of the den; it fell with a soft flop, burying her under stifling folds.

Dovepaw let out a terrified screech, clawing wildly to free herself.

"Help her!" Lionblaze snapped at Tigerheart, while he scrabbled at the bottom of the outer pelt, trying to find a way out.

Tigerheart tugged at the pelt until Dovepaw managed to thrust her head out; she gulped in air and dragged herself the rest of the way, shaking the pelt off her hindquarters as she regained her paws.

Lionblaze found a loose fold in the outer pelt and held it up in his teeth to make a gap. It tasted foul, like licking the trail left by a monster on the Thunderpath. Tigerheart wriggled through and Dovepaw followed, popping out into the harsh sunlight of the clearing. As Lionblaze wriggled out behind them, something heavy whizzed past his head and landed with a thump in a bramble thicket that bordered the clearing.

Dovepaw jumped in alarm, then plunged off again when she spotted Toadfoot just ahead. Lionblaze followed, making sure Tigerheart was still with them. Toadfoot led the patrol past the outlying pelt-dens and into the bracken at the edge of the clearing. As he thrust his way through it, Lionblaze picked up the ThunderClan scent marks and realized that he had crossed into his own territory.

The rest of the patrol bundled into the ferns beside him, where they crouched, panting, while the Twolegs in the clearing went on baying. Toadfoot was the last to arrive; he stood glaring at the rest of the cats with his tail lashing furiously.

"This is hopeless!" he hissed. "We can't even get out of our own territory without running into trouble. Thanks to that apprentice!" he added, turning his glare on Dovepaw.

Lionblaze saw Dovepaw stiffen, the fur on her neck and shoulders beginning to rise. *Toadfoot, you mouse-brain, it was you who led us straight into the Twolegs!* he thought. He stretched out his tail to give Dovepaw a calming touch on her shoulder. "Young cats are curious," he replied, his voice level. "If the Twolegs weren't crazy, this would never have happened."

Toadfoot let out an angry snort. "This quest is over before

it's begun," he growled. "We don't even know what we're going to find at the end of the stream. What makes us think we can refill the lake when we panic over a few Twolegs?"

"I think you're wrong," Whitetail stated; she was still trembling, but she stood squarely in front of the young ShadowClan warrior. "Okay, we had a narrow escape, but that doesn't mean we have to give up. We're not helping our Clans by staying in our own territories and watching the lake shrink even further."

Rippletail, who was crouched beside the shivering Petalfur, trying to comfort her, looked up at that, his neck fur bristling. "Are you trying to blame RiverClan? None of you realizes how hard this is for us. We need the lake for *food*!"

"No, I'm not blaming you!" Whitetail replied indignantly. "What did I say that would make you think that?"

Lionblaze rose to his paws and stepped between Whitetail and the enraged RiverClan warrior. "We're wasting time," he meowed. "We need to keep going. Next time we'll avoid the Twolegs."

"If there is a next time, you—" Toadfoot began.

"Hey, we survived, didn't we?" Tigerheart interrupted his Clanmate. Of all the cats, Lionblaze thought Tigerheart was the least affected by their danger; his eyes were gleaming, as if he had enjoyed the excitement. "We showed those dumb Twolegs! They were terrified! Who cares if we meet them again?" Turning to Dovepaw, he added, "Don't worry, I'll protect you."

Lionblaze felt faintly amused as he saw Dovepaw's jaws drop open in outrage. "I can protect myself!"

"We can all look after ourselves." Sedgewhisker unexpectedly backed Dovepaw up. "After all, that's why we were chosen, right? Because our Clans thought we had the best chance of solving the problem with the stream?"

"That's true," Lionblaze meowed.

Petalfur raised her head; she was still shaking so much she could hardly speak, but she gazed bravely at the other cats. "I think we should go on," she mewed. "I've watched my Clanmates starving around me, and I can't do that anymore! Thinking of that gives me courage."

"Well said, Petalfur," Whitetail mewed quietly.

"Then we keep going." Lionblaze spoke before Toadfoot had a chance to argue. With a glance at the ShadowClan warrior, he added, "And since we're in ThunderClan territory now, *I'll* take the lead."

CHAPTER 13

Lionblaze cast sidelong glances at Dovepaw as she padded beside him along the narrow trails underneath the ferns. Her fur was still standing on end from the encounter with the Twolegs, and he could see a ring of white around her eyes.

Were we wrong to bring her? he wondered. *She's been apprenticed for only a moon.* He shook his head. *No, we need her,* he told himself. Lionblaze thought of the time he had journeyed into the mountains with his littermates, to the Tribe of Rushing Water. They had only been apprentices then, and they'd managed fine. *Dovepaw will be fine, too. She has to be.*

The sun was rising higher in the sky when the cats approached the point where the stream veered off into ShadowClan territory. Lionblaze halted and gazed across the dried-up streambed into the pine forests, where brown needles covered the ground and the undergrowth was patchy.

Toadfoot padded up. "I think we should rest here for a while and eat," he meowed. He nodded toward the two River-Clan cats. "They look ready to fall over."

Lionblaze didn't like his sneering tone, and he didn't want to side with Toadfoot against the other Clans, but he had to admit that the ShadowClan warrior was right. All the cats were tired from fleeing the Twolegs, and from the increasing heat, but Rippletail and Petalfur looked exhausted. Petalfur had already flopped down on her side among the ferns, breathing heavily.

I'm not surprised the RiverClan cats are finding it hard, Lionblaze thought. *They're better at swimming than walking.*

"Okay, we'll rest." Lionblaze raised his voice so all the cats could hear him. "ThunderClan and ShadowClan will hunt, each in our own territories."

"We can hunt for ourselves," Whitetail pointed out with a glance at Sedgewhisker.

"Sure," the tabby she-cat agreed.

"That would be prey-stealing!" Toadfoot snapped.

Whitetail sighed. "But it's not stealing if you catch it and give it to us? Can't you just give us permission and make it easier for every cat?"

Lionblaze guessed she wanted to add *mouse-brain*, but she restrained herself. *At least Toadfoot didn't insult them by saying they only know how to catch rabbits,* he thought.

"We'll do it Toadfoot's way," he mewed peaceably to Whitetail. "I'm sure you'll get a chance to hunt for us all later." Even though he could see the WindClan warrior's point, he didn't want to risk them running into a ThunderClan or ShadowClan patrol. They'd had enough delays already with the Twolegs.

The WindClan she-cat hesitated for a moment, then gave him a curt nod.

Lionblaze led Dovepaw deeper into ThunderClan territory, feeling safer and more relaxed to be on familiar ground. "You go that way," he suggested to his apprentice, angling his ears around the edge of a hazel thicket. "There might be some prey under the bushes. I'll go this way and meet you back at the border."

"Okay." Dovepaw stalked off, setting her paws down lightly, her ears pricked and her jaws parted to scent the air.

I hope she finds something really good, Lionblaze thought as he watched her out of sight. *That'll show Toadfoot!* He padded into the trees in the opposite direction and almost at once spotted a squirrel out in the open, scraping at something underneath the leaves on the forest floor.

Excellent!

Dropping into the hunter's crouch, Lionblaze crept silently up on his prey, his belly fur brushing the ground. There was no wind to carry his scent, and he was sure he hadn't made a sound, but before he had covered half the distance the squirrel started up in alarm and launched itself toward the nearest tree.

"Mouse dung!" Lionblaze spat.

He hurled himself after it, realizing with a surge of triumph that there was something wrong with the squirrel; it was limping, so that he soon overtook it and killed it with a blow to the spine before it reached the tree.

I hope it hasn't got some horrible disease, he thought as he looked down at the limp body. He gave it a cautious sniff. It smelled fine—mouthwateringly good, in fact. Picking up his fresh-kill, he headed back toward the border. Dovepaw caught up to him when he was almost there, with a tiny mouse dangling from her jaws.

"Sorry," she mumbled around it. "This was all I could find."

Lionblaze sighed. If Dovepaw couldn't find any prey, then there wasn't any prey to be found. "Don't worry," he mewed. "It's better than nothing."

When they returned to the spot where the other cats were waiting, he found Rippletail and Petalfur drowsing in the shade of the ferns. Whitetail and Sedgewhisker sat beside them alertly, as if they were on watch.

"That squirrel looks good," Whitetail congratulated him as he dropped the fresh-kill on the edge of the stream. "And so does the mouse," she added to Dovepaw.

"No, it doesn't." Dovepaw dropped her prey with an annoyed flick of her tail. "If it was any smaller it would be a beetle."

"It's fine." Whitetail reached out to touch Dovepaw on the shoulder with her tail-tip. "We need every scrap of prey we can get."

"Hey, Toadfoot and Tigerheart are coming back!" Sedgewhisker meowed.

Lionblaze turned to see Toadfoot padding confidently through the pine trees, carrying a blackbird in his jaws. Tigerheart was a little way behind him, dragging something along the ground.

"The squirrel's not bad," Toadfoot mewed as he leaped

over the stream and dropped his prey beside Lionblaze's. "Pity about the mouse."

Lionblaze ignored him, watching as Tigerheart lugged his prey up to the bank of the stream, dropped it down into the dried-up bottom, then leaped down after it and clambered up the other side with the prey gripped in his jaws. It was a huge pigeon; tiny gray feathers clung all over Tigerheart's dark brown tabby pelt.

"Great catch!" Sedgewhisker exclaimed.

"Yes, great," Lionblaze added, stifling feelings of envy. He'd wanted to show Toadfoot that ThunderClan warriors were better hunters than ShadowClan any day. But Tigerheart's catch was impressive, and he wouldn't spoil the younger warrior's pride in it.

Toadfoot was looking quietly triumphant, but at least he didn't boast about his Clanmate's catch.

Tigerheart seemed a bit flustered. "I nearly missed it," he meowed. "It flew off, and I had to leap really high to get it."

"That's great!" Lionblaze told him. He was pleased to see the glow in Tigerheart's eyes and hoped he had made up for being unfriendly to him at the Gathering. Cinderheart had been right: It was better to have friends than enemies in the other Clans. And the young warrior was a real asset to his Clan.

I wonder if Tigerstar realizes that yet? Lionblaze wondered, feeling a cold claw run down his spine in spite of the heat.

The cats divided the prey and crouched down to eat. For the first time, Lionblaze felt a sense of companionship with these cats who only the day before had been his rivals. *Perhaps we can work together after all.*

Roused from their sleep, Petalfur and Rippletail ate as if they hadn't seen prey for a moon. By silent agreement the other cats drew back and let them fill their bellies.

"It won't help any of us if they're too weak to carry on," Whitetail whispered to Lionblaze.

When they had finished eating, Toadfoot took the lead again as the stream left the border and wound its way among the pine trees of ShadowClan territory. Lionblaze felt uneasy at the open spaces and the sight of so much sky above them; the sun cast the shadows of the pines over brown needles on the ground until he felt as if he were trekking across an enormous tabby pelt. After a while they spotted a ShadowClan patrol in the distance, headed by Rowanclaw; Toadfoot called out a greeting, but the ShadowClan cats didn't approach.

The sun was sliding down the sky when the patrol reached the edge of ShadowClan territory. Lionblaze halted as he crossed the scent markers and peered into the forest ahead. The stream ran between gray boulders covered with moss. A few fox-lengths ahead the ground changed; it became more broken, strewn with tumbled stones, and the pines gave way to gnarled trees, smaller and older than the ones he was used to in his own territory. Their branches were woven together like the roof of a den, with moss and ivy clinging to their pale trunks. But there still wasn't much undergrowth.

Not many places to hide, Lionblaze thought uneasily.

Whitetail padded up beside him with her jaws parted

to taste the air. "I think we should take turns leading," she meowed. She spoke with conviction, her air of authority reminding Lionblaze that she was the most senior warrior, even though she was so small.

"Fine," he responded, taking a pace back and waving his tail to let her go ahead.

Toadfoot opened his jaws as if he was going to object, then closed them again. With Whitetail in the lead, the cats jumped down into the bed of the stream and headed into the unknown forest. The trees closed over their heads; they padded forward in the dim green light, turning their heads to check for danger on each side. Lionblaze realized that the WindClan warrior had chosen the best cover available by keeping them in the empty stream, where they could duck down to hide if necessary.

"There's mud here!" Dovepaw exclaimed, shaking one forepaw in disgust. "I walked right into it."

"That's good," Rippletail meowed. "Where there's mud there might be water. It looks as if the stream here doesn't get as much direct sunlight."

The RiverClan warrior was right. A few tail-lengths farther on, Whitetail spotted a small puddle of water underneath the overhanging bank, behind the roots of an oak tree. All the cats gathered around to drink. It was warm and tasted muddy, but Lionblaze didn't think he'd ever lapped up anything so delicious.

When the cats had drunk their fill, they trudged onward. Every so often, Whitetail told one of them to leap up onto the bank and take a look around. When it was Lionblaze's turn, he spotted a pair of deer bounding light-footed through the trees. *We don't see many of those in ThunderClan,* he mused, *but there are plenty around here.* He spotted their cloven hoofprints marking the bank of the stream, and the moss on the trees had been chewed off as high as a deer could reach.

"I saw deer up there," he reported to Whitetail, leaping down into the streambed again.

The WindClan she-cat nodded. "They shouldn't bother us."

Padding onward, Lionblaze realized that he was beginning to enjoy himself, and he guessed his companions felt the same. The air under the trees was cool and damp; their bellies were full and their thirst quenched. They walked peacefully in silence, broken only by the occasional rustle of leaves from the forest, or the splash of a paw hitting a patch of mud. It would be easy, Lionblaze thought, to forget how serious their mission was.

Suddenly Dovepaw stopped dead, her neck fur bristling up. Her eyes were wide and scared as she turned to Lionblaze. "Dogs!" she whispered. "Coming from over there." She flicked her tail at an angle to the stream.

Lionblaze took a quick mouthful of air, but he couldn't detect any dog scent. He couldn't hear anything, either. But that didn't mean Dovepaw was wrong. There was no point in trying to outrun dogs, especially in unfamiliar territory, and they couldn't risk losing sight of the stream. There was only one answer.

"Dogs!" Lionblaze yowled, turning to face the rest of the patrol. "Quick! Climb a tree!"

The cats started milling around in confusion, tripping over one another in the narrow stream.

"What? Where?"

"I don't smell any dogs."

"How do you know?" Rippletail asked, genuine curiosity in his voice.

"There isn't time for this." Lionblaze forced his voice to carry above the babble. "Just climb a tree, okay?"

To his relief, Toadfoot and Tigerheart spun around and scrambled up the far bank of the stream, shooting up a nearby tree and peering down from a high branch. *At least they're safe.*

But the WindClan and RiverClan cats hadn't moved; they just shuffled their paws and cast awkward glances at one another.

"We don't climb trees," Whitetail pointed out.

"Oh, for StarClan's sake!" Without waiting to argue, Lionblaze, with Dovepaw helping him, bundled the four cats out of the streambed and nudged them toward the nearest tree. "Now climb!"

Sedgewhisker veered away, heading for a low-growing tree with twisted branches that made it easier to climb. "I think I can get up here," she meowed.

"No—come back!" Lionblaze called to her. "The dogs would follow you up there in no time. Look, you just dig your claws in," he explained as the she-cat bounded back. "Then use your hind paws to push you up the trunk. It's easy."

The cats looked scared and baffled. "I'll never do it." Sedgewhisker was shaking. "You go. I'll take my chances down here."

"We're not leaving you!" Dovepaw meowed fiercely.

Lionblaze struggled with fear and exasperation. He could hear the dogs now, their barking still faint in the distance, but growing louder with every heartbeat.

"Try this." Dovepaw bounded over to the nearest tree and leaped up the trunk until she could balance on the lowest branch. Scrambling down again, she added, "Come on, you can do it."

To Lionblaze's relief, Toadfoot and Tigerheart reappeared at his side. "We'll take one each," Toadfoot meowed, heading for Petalfur.

"Great, thanks." Lionblaze beckoned Sedgewhisker with a flick of his tail. "Tigerheart, you take Rippletail; Dovepaw, go with Whitetail."

The older WindClan warrior would be more confident, he guessed, and easier for an apprentice to cope with; besides, he suspected that Whitetail might have climbed a tree or two in the wooded area near the border with ThunderClan. Free to concentrate on the terrified Sedgewhisker, he shoved her over to the nearest tree. "Put your front claws here," he instructed, "and use that knot-hole there to give one hind paw leverage. Now, up you go."

Sedgewhisker did as he said, then froze, splayed out against the tree trunk with all four sets of claws digging into the bark. "I can't move," she choked out.

"Yes, you can," Lionblaze encouraged her. "And if you fall, you'll fall on your paws. Now bring one hind paw up to that hollow there. . . ."

Gradually, paw step by paw step, the WindClan cat edged up the tree with Lionblaze beside her. The dogs had almost reached them, noisily barking and plunging about in the sparse undergrowth. Their scent drifted thickly on the air, and Lionblaze took quick, shallow breaths as he tried not to taste it.

The trees they had chosen were hard to climb, to make sure that the dogs couldn't follow them, but it was slow going for the inexperienced cats. Glancing around, Lionblaze could see that Dovepaw and Whitetail had reached the safety of a high branch, while Tigerheart was shoving Rippletail into the fork between two branches. Toadfoot was still coaxing Petalfur up the trunk of the tree next to Lionblaze's.

"You're doing fine," the ShadowClan warrior growled, "but for StarClan's sake, don't look down."

Just as Sedgewhisker managed to claw her way onto a branch, the dogs erupted into view. There were two of them, with smooth, shiny pelts, one yellow and one black. They gamboled about, leaping into the stream and out again, and sniffing around the roots of the trees.

"At least they're not hunting us," Lionblaze meowed, crouching on the branch beside Sedgewhisker. "Stupid creatures; they have no idea we're here."

Just then, one of the dogs scented him and Sedgewhisker. It burst into a flurry of excited barking as it bounded over to their tree and jumped, reaching up the trunk with its front paws. Its jaws gaped and its long pink tongue lolled out.

Sedgewhisker let out a terrified squeal and slipped off

the branch, her paws flailing uselessly as she fell. Lionblaze flung himself forward, digging his hind claws into the branch while he grabbed at Sedgewhisker with his front paws. But he was a heartbeat too slow to get a firm hold. He could feel Sedgewhisker slipping through his grip, while the dog below leaped and barked in a frenzy of excitement. Sedgewhisker's eyes were stretched wide with terror, and her jaws gaped in a soundless wail for help.

Just as Lionblaze thought she was bound to fall, he saw Toadfoot hurtle through the air from the neighboring tree, leaving a panic-stricken Petalfur with both front legs wrapped around a branch.

By now both dogs were jumping up at the tree, snapping wildly at Sedgewhisker's dangling tail. For a moment Lionblaze was convinced that Toadfoot had leaped short and would fall into their jaws. Then the branch lurched alarmingly as he landed beside Lionblaze and reached down, sinking his front claws into Sedgewhisker's scruff.

Slowly the two warriors dragged the WindClan cat upward until she could sink her claws into the branch again. "Thank you! Oh, thank you!" she gasped, shaking so hard that she almost fell off again.

Lionblaze steadied her with his tail. "Thanks," he mewed to Toadfoot.

The ShadowClan cat grunted, with a barely visible nod, as if he was embarrassed to be caught helping cats from rival Clans.

Lionblaze heard Twolegs yowling through the trees. The

two dogs turned and loped off in the direction of the voices, casting reluctant glances back at the cats. When their noise had died away and the forest was quiet once more, Lionblaze guided Sedgewhisker down to the ground, while Toadfoot went back to his original tree to help Petalfur. All the cats descended shakily and gathered together beside the stream, crouching among the brittle stems of sun-dried grass.

"I think I've wrenched my shoulder," Sedgewhisker mewed, flexing her foreleg with a grimace. "I'm so sorry, Lionblaze. I'm being such a nuisance."

"Nonsense, you're fine," Lionblaze reassured her. "We can't all be good at everything. If we had to run away from something, you and Whitetail would outpace every cat."

"Not when my shoulder's hurting," Sedgewhisker muttered miserably.

"Mothwing taught me a bit about herbs before we left," Rippletail put in, giving Sedgewhisker's shoulder a sniff. "She says a poultice of elder leaves is good for sprains. Should I go look for some?"

"Good idea," Lionblaze replied. "But don't go far."

"I won't." Rippletail darted off, looking glad to be doing something useful.

"What are we going to do, if some of us can't even climb trees?" Tigerheart asked when the RiverClan cat had gone. "How can we hope to do what we have to?"

The young warrior's anxiety struck Lionblaze like a claw, especially since he had been so optimistic earlier. The other cats were murmuring in agreement.

"We don't even know what we have to face," Sedgewhisker pointed out. "I mean, how do we know that the stream has been blocked at all? It might just have dried up in the heat. We could be walking *forever!*" she ended with a wail.

Glancing at his apprentice, Lionblaze noticed that she was looking worried. He edged over to her and bent his head to whisper into her ear. "You're not wrong. I trust you."

Dovepaw looked a little more relieved, though Lionblaze saw that her claws were still working in the earth in front of her.

By this time the sun had almost gone; the sky above the trees was stained red, and shadows were gathering around the trunks.

"I think we should stay here for the night," Whitetail meowed. "We all need to rest—Sedgewhisker especially."

"But is it safe?" Petalfur asked, her voice edged with fear. "What if the dogs come back? Maybe we should sleep in the trees."

"No, you would probably fall out when you fell asleep," Toadfoot told her brusquely.

Petalfur's eyes stretched wide with alarm. "Then what are we going to do?"

"It'll be okay," Lionblaze reassured her. "We'll take turns to keep watch." Before any other cat could argue, he sprang to his paws. "Let's collect some fern and moss for bedding."

Dovepaw and Petalfur jumped down into the stream to look for moss, while Lionblaze and the others started to tear up fronds of dried bracken.

"You stay here and rest your shoulder," Lionblaze told Sedgewhisker. "Rippletail should be back soon."

By the time the RiverClan warrior came back with a bundle of elder leaves in his jaws, the other cats had formed bracken fronds into rough den walls, while Petalfur and Dovepaw had patted moss into nests.

"Here we are," Rippletail mewed cheerfully, dropping the leaves beside Sedgewhisker. "We'll chew these up and put them on your shoulder, and by morning you shouldn't have any more trouble."

Sedgewhisker blinked at him. "Thank you."

As the patrol found places for themselves in the makeshift den, Lionblaze realized how awkward it felt to be settling down with cats from rival Clans; each cat was huddling together with their Clanmate, and Tigerheart practically jumped out of his pelt when Petalfur accidentally flicked him with her tail.

"Sorry," she whispered, looking embarrassed.

Lionblaze nearly put his paw down on Whitetail's ear, and he flew back, brushing Toadfoot's pelt as he did so.

"Watch it!" the ShadowClan warrior growled.

Lionblaze gave him a brief nod of apology and jumped over the bracken wall to stand on the edge of the stream. "I'll take the first watch," he announced.

He crouched on the bank with his paws tucked under him but soon realized he was tired enough to sleep unless he kept moving. Forcing himself to his paws again, he patrolled up and down the bank, always keeping the den in sight. His ears were pricked and he kept tasting the air for any signs of danger.

There was nothing: The scent of the dogs was growing stale by now, and once he thought he caught a distant whiff of badger, but it was too far away to be a threat.

When he returned to the den, the waning moon was reflected in a pair of eyes staring up at him.

"Dovepaw!" he murmured, not wanting to wake the other cats. "You don't have to stay awake, you know."

"Don't I?" Dovepaw's voice was low but challenging. "If the dogs come back, I'm the one who'll hear them first."

"You're not responsible for our safety on your own," Lionblaze told her with a stab of sympathy. "We can help. Now go to sleep."

For a heartbeat he thought that Dovepaw might argue and he would have to remind her that he was her mentor. Then she let out a faint sigh and curled up, closing her eyes and wrapping her tail over her nose. Within moments, her steady breathing told Lionblaze that she was asleep.

Lionblaze sat beside her, separated from her only by the thin wall of bracken, and watched her as well as his surroundings. *I know what it's like to have a power no other cat understands,* he thought. *It's the loneliest feeling in the world.*

CHAPTER 14

As soon as the thorn barrier stopped quivering after Brambleclaw, Lionblaze, and Dovepaw pushed their way out of the hollow, Jayfeather turned and headed back to his den. Every hair on his pelt was tingling with doubt. *Eight cats are setting out on a quest based on what Dovepaw thinks she can see, hear, sense, or whatever, up a dried-out stream. It's hardly a prophecy from StarClan.*

What really bothered Jayfeather was that their warrior ancestors had said nothing to him about the quest, or about the brown animals that were blocking the stream. At the last meeting at the Moonpool, none of the other medicine cats had mentioned it, either. *Is StarClan waiting to see if the prophecy of the Three will save us? It's greater than them, after all.* Halting, Jayfeather lifted his nose to the sky he couldn't see. *Are any of our warrior ancestors watching us now?* he wondered.

The scamper of paws sounded from behind him, startling him out of his thoughts.

"Don't look at me like that!" Ivypaw's voice was raised in protest.

What now? Jayfeather asked himself, sighing.

"Well, stop being so grumpy," Briarpaw retorted. "No cat put ants in your pelt."

"You'd be grumpy if your littermates went off to save the Clans," Ivypaw snarled, "and left you doing stupid dumb training!"

Jayfeather heard the sound of a pebble being kicked, followed by an indignant yowl from Mousefur. "Watch it! Can't a cat go to make dirt anymore without being pelted with rocks?"

"Sor-ree . . ." Ivypaw muttered.

Jayfeather heard the elder padding away, annoyance buzzing out of her like bees from a hollow tree. He couldn't help feeling some sympathy with Ivypaw. *I've been left behind, too.*

"Ivypaw, control that bad temper right now!" Cinderheart came bounding up. "You should show respect to our elders."

"Sorry," Ivypaw repeated, sounding more miserable than angry now.

"I should think so. Later on we'll find a really good piece of fresh-kill for Mousefur, and you can take it to her. But not yet," Cinderheart continued, "because all of you are going to do battle training this morning."

"Oh, big deal!" Ivypaw wasn't impressed.

"No, it's great." Briarpaw sounded excited. "I'll help you, Ivypaw. I'll be doing my final assessment soon."

"Hey, slow down." Thornclaw padded up behind his apprentice. "Your assessment isn't for a couple of moons yet. Ivypaw's mentor will do her training. *You* need to concentrate on that leap and twist I showed you last time. You haven't got it quite right yet."

"Okay." Briarpaw seemed untroubled by her mentor's rebuke.

Hazeltail and Mousewhisker came up to join Blossompaw and Bumblepaw, and the whole crowd of mentors and apprentices headed out of camp, with plenty of pushing and excited squealing from the young cats.

Jayfeather sighed. *Sometimes I feel as old as Rock.*

The hollow felt very empty once the cats had gone. Jayfeather stood still for a moment longer, listening to the faint creak of branches above his head, then gave his pelt a shake. Striding forward, he crossed the clearing and followed Mousefur into the elders' den. Longtail was curled up asleep, his breath whistling through his nose, while Mousefur was settling into her nest with a crackle of dried bracken.

Purdy sat beside her. "I was just rememberin' the time when a couple o' rats tried to move into my Upwalker's den," he began. "I reckon you'd like to hear about that, so—"

"Hang on a moment, Purdy," Jayfeather interrupted. "I need to have a word with Mousefur."

"What now?" the old she-cat demanded. She still sounded annoyed; either she hadn't got over being hit by the pebble, or maybe it was the thought of listening to one of Purdy's interminable stories.

"I just need to check where the stone hit you," Jayfeather explained.

Mousefur let out a sigh. "I'll be fine, Jayfeather. There's no need to fuss."

"I'm only doing my job, Mousefur."

Another long sigh. "All right." Jayfeather heard the rustle of bracken as Mousefur stretched out in her nest. "It was just there, at the top of my leg."

Jayfeather padded forward and sniffed carefully. To his relief, he couldn't find any trace of a wound; Mousefur's skin hadn't even been broken. "I think you're fine," he mewed.

"I told you that," Mousefur snapped. "Young cats, thinking they know everything."

"Even so, if you feel any pain or start limping, let me know right away. Okay?"

"I'll see she does," Purdy put in. "Don't you worry none."

"Thanks, Purdy." Jayfeather headed out of the den, but before he could leave, the old loner spoke again.

"Don't dash off like that, young 'un. You'll enjoy hearin' this story as well. There were these rats, see . . ."

Jayfeather stood fidgeting impatiently near the entrance to the den. As soon as he heard movement in the clearing, he broke into Purdy's rambling tale. "Sorry. Gotta go. Could be an emergency." Without waiting for an answer, he squeezed under the branches of the elder bush and padded into the hollow.

Brambleclaw had returned from seeing off the questing cats; as Jayfeather drew nearer, he heard Firestar leaping down the tumbled rocks to join his deputy in the center of the camp.

"Well?" the Clan leader asked eagerly. "How did it go?"

"Fine," Brambleclaw replied. "All four Clans sent their cats, and they all set off upstream."

"Which cats have been chosen?"

"Toadfoot and Tigerheart from ShadowClan," Brambleclaw

began. "Sedgewhisker and Whitetail from WindClan, and Rippletail and Petalfur from RiverClan."

Jayfeather's ears flicked up in surprise. *That doesn't sound as if Leopardstar sent her strongest warriors. Doesn't she realize what dangers they'll be facing?*

If Firestar thought the same, he gave no sign of it. "I hope they can all get on together," he commented.

"They will," Brambleclaw promised. "They'll learn to rely on one another, and they'll come back stronger cats for the experience."

"We can only pray to StarClan that they come back at all," Firestar meowed. "And that they find out what happened to the water." He sighed, then went on in a brisker tone, "Meanwhile, we'd better start with the patrols before the day gets too hot. I'll lead a hunting patrol; can you organize the rest?"

"Sure, Firestar."

Jayfeather heard both cats pad away and begin calling to others inside the warriors' den. He listened briefly as his Clanmates pushed their way out through the branches, yawning and stretching, and then he turned away toward his den. Before he reached it, Firestar led his hunting patrol past him. Dustpelt brought up the rear; as he brushed past, Jayfeather felt a stab of pain at the base of the tabby warrior's spine. Pricking his ears toward the patrol, he detected a slight unevenness in Dustpelt's paw steps.

"Hey, Dustpelt!" he called. "Hang on a moment!"

"What?" Dustpelt sounded even more crabby than usual as he retraced his steps. "I'm supposed to be hunting with

Firestar, so make it quick."

"Have you hurt your back?" Jayfeather asked.

The brown tabby tom hesitated. "What makes you think that?"

"I'm a medicine cat," Jayfeather retorted drily. "If you're hurt, I've got some herbs that will help you."

"I don't need herbs," Dustpelt retorted; Jayfeather pictured his neck fur bristling up. "Save them for cats who are really ill."

"I've got plenty of what you need," Jayfeather assured him. He wasn't going to let Dustpelt deprive himself of medicine out of misplaced selflessness. His back would only get worse, and then he wouldn't be able to hunt at all. "Come see me when you get back."

"Okay, I will." Jayfeather thought he could sense relief behind Dustpelt's brusque tone. Quietly he added, "Thanks, Jayfeather."

"Make sure you don't forget!" Jayfeather called as Dustpelt bounded away to catch up to Firestar and the rest of the patrol. He reminded himself to have a word with Ferncloud if her mate didn't turn up for the herbs. Heading for his den once again, Jayfeather became aware of a cat's warm gaze resting on him. *Leafpool!* He could sense his mother's pride in him, for the way he had detected Dustpelt's injury and avoided wounding the warrior's dignity or sense of duty when offering him the herbs.

I don't want your pride, Jayfeather thought.

Suddenly the hollow felt as if it were closing in on him.

He couldn't stay here a moment longer with the stone cliffs pressing around him, trapping him beneath watchful eyes. He spun around and raced across the clearing, pushing through the thorn tunnel in the wake of the patrols. Once in the forest, he headed for the lake, missing the scents of cool, damp air that always drifted to meet him when he took this path. Now the forest felt strange and restless, crackling in the hot, dry breeze.

When he emerged on the bank of the lake, a tail-length from where the water used to lap against the shore, an unfamiliar emptiness stretched in front of him. He was used to sensing the cold, wet weight of the lake on his fur when he took a breath, but now there was nothing except dust. Pausing at the edge of the trees, Jayfeather located patrols from ThunderClan and WindClan heading for the lake. *They must have come for the water.* Farther out, he could hear a ShadowClan patrol arguing with the RiverClan warriors who were guarding the shrinking lake.

"You don't own the water," Russetfur snapped. "Every cat has the right to drink."

"And we have the right to the fish," Graymist retorted. "Touch so much as a single scale, and I'll claw your ears off." In spite of her threats, the RiverClan she-cat's voice was dull and fretful, as if she had little strength left.

It can't be much fun, stuck out here with no shade or rest, Jayfeather thought. He padded out onto the dried-up bed of the lake, feeling the pebbles rolling underneath his paws. Somewhere nearby, he knew, must be the opening from the tunnels where the underground river had washed them into the lake. But no cat had mentioned finding a hole in the lakebed; perhaps it had been filled up by one of the many mudslides, like the one Rainstorm had fallen into.

Jayfeather shivered in spite of the heat, remembering the mudslide that had trapped his sister, Hollyleaf, when the roof of the tunnel had fallen in. For a heartbeat he was standing there again in the rain-battered forest, desperately calling out to her. Then he shook himself, pulling himself away from the terrible memory.

"Hey, Poppyfrost!" Icecloud's cheerful voice brought him back to the scorched lake. The ThunderClan water patrol had arrived, Berrynose and Brightheart padding along with her.

There were more paw steps behind him, and Jayfeather realized that Poppyfrost had ventured out onto the lake bottom as well; she trotted up to the patrol, her steps sounding slow and heavy with the weight of her kits.

"Hi," she panted. "Isn't it hot? The lake is—"

"Shouldn't you be in the nursery?" Berrynose interrupted before his mate had the chance to mew more than a few words.

Jayfeather sensed that Poppyfrost was taken aback. "I just wanted to stretch my legs," she explained, "and see if the lake has shrunk any more."

"You're supposed to be resting," Berrynose pointed out with an edge to his voice. "What about our kits?"

"But I want a drink," Poppyfrost protested.

"Icecloud will bring you some water," Berrynose meowed,

before padding on toward the distant lake.

Brightheart's and Icecloud's embarrassment was so strong that Jayfeather could almost taste it. "Sure, Poppyfrost," Icecloud mumbled. "I'll bring you some moss."

"Thanks, but I can get my own." Poppyfrost sounded tense and brittle. "I'll see you later."

She trudged away from the patrol, following Berrynose, but not trying to catch up to him. When she passed Jayfeather, she halted. "It's okay for me to leave the nursery, isn't it?"

"Of course," Jayfeather replied. "Your kits aren't due for another moon."

"I thought so," Poppyfrost mewed. "Daisy said I wouldn't do them any harm if I took a walk." She let out a weary sigh. "Berrynose seems to want me to stay in the nursery forever! He says there isn't enough room for me in the warriors' den now."

Jayfeather scuffed the hot ground with his paw. "I'm sure he just wants to take care of you."

Poppyfrost didn't reply; she just let out a disbelieving snort and headed for the water.

Putting the tension out of his mind, Jayfeather returned to the shore and located his stick, carefully wedged under some elder roots a tail-length or so from the bank. Settling down in the shade of the elder bush, he ran his paw along the scratch marks. Faint whispers wreathed around his ears, and he recognized some of the voices from the time he spent with the ancient clan. He strained to hear what they were saying, but they were too quiet. A pang of sadness pierced him, like a thorn, that he had left them behind. They had been his friends, once—and he had helped to send them away from the lake forever. The spirits of the ancient cats seemed to be all around him now, brushing their tails along his pelt, mingling their scents with that of the dry lake.

What do you want? Jayfeather asked, sensing their anxiety.

But there was no reply.

Yowls from the edge of the water distracted him. Shoving the stick back under the roots, he crawled out from under the elder bush and rose to his paws.

"This is WindClan's part of the lake!" Jayfeather stiffened as he recognized Breezepelt's voice. "Get back to your own side."

"That's ridiculous!" Icecloud protested. "Our territories end three tail-lengths from the shore."

"The shore is where the water starts," Breezepelt growled. "And that makes this part of the lake WindClan territory. So get your tails out of here!"

"Do you want to make us?" That was Berrynose's voice; Jayfeather could imagine the cream-colored warrior squaring up for a fight, his fur bristling and his teeth bared in a snarl.

A fight is the last thing we need! Jayfeather bounded forward, his belly fur brushing the dust and loose pebbles of the dry lakebed. "Stop!" he yowled, thrusting himself between the two warriors. "What value does the lakebed have to any Clan?"

He heard an enraged snarl and scented Breezepelt nose to nose with him. "You would say that, *half-Clan cat!*"

Jayfeather was jolted by the wave of hatred coming from

the WindClan warrior. He took a step back, his nostrils flaring. "What has that got to do with—" he began.

Breezepelt pushed his face even closer to Jayfeather's. "Your mother betrayed my father as well as her Clan," he hissed. "You have no right to be a medicine cat. No right even to live among the Clans. I'll never forgive you for what you've done! Never!"

Jayfeather was too stunned to reply. He was aware of Berrynose bristling next to him. "I'll claw him for you if you want, Jayfeather!" the young warrior growled.

Jayfeather shook his head. What would that change? He heard paw steps approaching and scented Ashfoot, the WindClan deputy.

"What's going on here?" she demanded.

"Nothing," Breezepelt replied. "Just a misunderstanding about getting to the water."

Ashfoot turned to Jayfeather. "You should advise your warriors to keep to your own side of the lake," she warned. "To avoid future *misunderstandings.*"

Jayfeather wasn't about to quarrel, not with Breezepelt breathing venom at him. "Very well," he mewed, dipping his head to the deputy. Anger rose inside him as he picked up the smug feelings of triumph radiating from Breezepelt. "Come on," he added to the ThunderClan patrol. "We're doing no good here."

He could feel the fury of the ThunderClan cats as they padded beside him toward their own territory.

"I can't believe that mangy WindClan cat!" Icecloud spat.

"How dare he tell us where we can and can't go?"

"You should have let me get him!" Berrynose snarled.

"There was no call for what he said to you." Brightheart's mew was quieter, but Jayfeather could sense her shock.

He shrugged, not wanting to discuss the accusations Breezepelt had hurled at him, and to his relief Brightheart said nothing more. Leaving the patrol to head for the distant water, Jayfeather turned toward the shore, the hot wind ruffling his pelt. In spite of the heat, cold struck through him, bone-deep, and he felt the ancient cats wreathing around him once more.

Beware, Jay's Wing, one of them whispered. *Stormclouds are gathering on a dark breeze.*

CHAPTER 15

A *dry, dusty breeze swept over* Dovepaw, rattling the branches above her head. She blinked awake and stretched her jaws in a huge yawn. For a couple of heartbeats she couldn't remember where she was. *This isn't the apprentices' den! Where's Ivypaw?*

She scrambled up, panic surging through her, only to recognize the den that she and the other cats had built the night before, and the clearing where they had fled from the dogs. The others were still asleep, except for Lionblaze, who was sitting a couple of tail-lengths away on the bank of the stream.

"Hi," he purred. "I was awake when Whitetail finished her watch, so I took your shift."

Every hair on Dovepaw's pelt prickled with annoyance. Springing over the low bracken wall of the den, she stalked over to her mentor. "I can do my own shift!" she growled. "You don't have to treat me like a kit."

"You've only just been made an apprentice," Lionblaze reminded her.

Dovepaw bit back a yowl of frustration. "The prophecy doesn't care about that, does it?" she pointed out. "I had my power before I left the nursery. It's not like StarClan waited for me to grow up first."

Lionblaze opened his jaws to reply, but before he could speak a rustling noise came from the den and Sedgewhisker sat up, stretching. Her eyes were filled with shock as she looked around; then she seemed to remember where she was and stood up, shaking scraps of moss from her pelt.

"Hi, Sedgewhisker," Dovepaw called. "How's your shoulder?"

The WindClan she-cat flexed her leg experimentally, then looked up, purring with relief. "It's much better, thanks. I can hardly feel anything."

As she spoke, the other cats began stirring, looking tense when they realized how close they were to cats of other Clans.

"We should get on with hunting," Toadfoot announced, jumping out of his nest. "Before it gets too hot and all the prey is hiding down holes."

"Don't go too far," Lionblaze warned the cats as they scattered. "Remember, those dogs might still be around."

Dovepaw cast out her senses, but she couldn't pick up a trace of the dogs. *The stupid creatures are probably still asleep in their Twoleg's den.* What she did pick up was a squirrel somewhere among the trees on the other side of the stream; she leaped onto the far bank and headed toward it. *I'll make up for that miserable little mouse I caught yesterday.*

Slipping between the trees, she spotted the squirrel nibbling a seed at the foot of a beech tree. Dovepaw pressed herself to the ground, checked that the wind was blowing her scent away from her prey, and dropped into the hunter's crouch. Step by silent step, she pulled herself closer. *That's right . . . look the other way. . . .*

One swift blow of her paw brought the squirrel down, and she trotted proudly back to the others, who were gathering again beside the den. Lionblaze had killed a vole, while Tigerheart had a couple of shrews and Toadfoot had a mouse. Whitetail and Sedgewhisker had caught a rabbit together.

"You should teach us that technique of hunting as a pair," Lionblaze was suggesting as Dovepaw padded up with her fresh-kill. "It could be useful."

Whitetail acknowledged his words with a flick of her ears; Dovepaw guessed she didn't feel comfortable teaching anything to cats from another Clan.

As the cats settled down to eat, Rippletail and Petalfur drew back. "We didn't catch anything, so we can't eat," Petalfur meowed, with a longing look at the fresh-kill.

"Nonsense," Whitetail replied briskly. "How are you going to travel if your bellies are empty?"

"That's right," Lionblaze added. "On this journey, we all share. Come on, there's plenty."

The two RiverClan cats crept back again and Dovepaw dropped her squirrel in front of them. "Thanks," Rippletail muttered.

Dovepaw sensed their guilt and embarrassment as they started to eat, and she felt sorry for any cats who were so dependent on one kind of prey. No wonder the RiverClan cats were starving now that they couldn't find fish.

When every cat had finished eating, they set out again, with Toadfoot in the lead. They padded silently along the bed of the stream, almost as uncomfortable with one another as they had been at the start of the journey; Dovepaw could feel the tension rising, as if each one had realized all over again that they didn't know where they were going, or how they were going to get there.

Panic bubbled up inside her. *They're only here because of me. What if I'm wrong?*

Pausing, she struggled to block out all the sounds of the forest around her, then closed her eyes and cast her senses ahead. At once, sounds began to travel down the streambed to the stones underneath her paws: scratching, gnawing, the slap of trapped water, and the paw steps of large brown animals slipping over a pile of tree trunks. She sensed their bulky bodies as they dragged more branches out into the stream.

"Dovepaw?" She jumped at the sound of Petalfur's voice. "Are you okay?"

Dovepaw's eyes blinked open to see the RiverClan cat at the rear of the group looking back over her shoulder.

"Uh . . . sure," Dovepaw mewed, running to catch up. "I'm fine."

Reassured that the brown animals really were up ahead, she fell in beside Petalfur as they padded on. The foliage overhead was growing thicker, blocking out the fierce rays of the sun, so that it felt as if the cats were traveling through a cool, dimly lit tunnel. Dovepaw even spotted a pool of water underneath the overhanging bank.

"Look at that!" she exclaimed, giving Petalfur a friendly flick on the shoulder with her tail. "Maybe there are some fish in there."

Dovepaw had meant her words as gentle teasing, but the RiverClan she-cat's ears pricked. "Maybe there are."

She padded up to the edge of the pool and peered down into the unmoving green water. Rippletail came up to join her. "Fish?" he asked, tasting the air.

"Yes!" Petalfur's tail went straight up in the air. "There *are* fish. They must have survived here when the rest of the stream dried up."

"Do you think you can catch some?" Tigerheart asked curiously.

"Of course she can." Rippletail's eyes shone with pride.

"The rest of you stay back," Petalfur instructed, waving them away with her tail. "If your shadows fall on the water, the fish will know they're being hunted."

"Just like staying downwind of prey," Dovepaw murmured to Lionblaze as they retreated.

Rippletail and Petalfur crouched down at the edge of the pool and waited with their gazes fixed on the water. The wait stretched out. Dovepaw shifted her paws impatiently, then made herself stand still, wondering if fish could sense vibrations in the ground. Still they waited. Her legs ached and her fur itched; she stifled a yawn. *Is this really how RiverClan cats catch their prey? That fish had better be worth it.*

Suddenly Rippletail flashed one paw into the water and scooped a small silver fish out of the water in an arc of drops.

It fell onto the dry streambed, where it flopped and wriggled until Petalfur killed it with a swipe.

"There," she meowed. "The other fish have probably fled into the darkest corners now, but at least we have one piece of fresh-kill."

"Come and share," Rippletail offered. "You haven't lived until you've tasted fish!"

The two RiverClan cats watched with glowing eyes as their companions approached cautiously. Whitetail was the first to give the fish an experimental nibble.

"Er . . . no, thanks," she meowed, passing her tongue over her jaws. "I think I'll stick to rabbit."

"So will I," Sedgewhisker agreed, after barely tasting it. "Sorry, but I don't think I could ever get used to that."

"I bet I could!" Tigerheart meowed, taking a huge mouthful. "It's great!" he mumbled around it.

Dovepaw waited for Toadfoot and Lionblaze to take a share, then crouched down in front of the fish and bit into it cautiously. The flavor was strong, and not unpleasant, though she much preferred mouse or squirrel.

"Thanks, it's really . . . different," she mewed as she stepped back to let the RiverClan cats finish up the fish.

As they moved on, she realized that she had fish all over her paws and whiskers. *Mouse dung! Now I can't smell anything else!*

A little farther on the stream wound in a tight curve. Toadfoot, who had drawn some way ahead, halted. "Get up onto the bank now!" he ordered, spinning to face them.

"Why? What's the matter?" Lionblaze called.

"Just do it!" Toadfoot hissed. His fur was fluffed up and his eyes were wide.

His urgency spread to the other cats like a gust of wind. Dovepaw scrambled up the steep bank with her companions on either side of her, and Toadfoot led them under the trees, lashing his tail to hurry them along.

Tigerheart, straying back toward the bank of the stream, glanced down and froze. "Oh . . ." he breathed.

Curious, Dovepaw padded over to join him, aware of Toadfoot's annoyed hiss behind her. Bile rose into her throat and she swallowed when she saw why Toadfoot had moved them on so quickly. A dead deer lay in the stream, its legs sticking out stiffly and blocking the way. Flies were buzzing around it, and a sweetish, rotting scent rose up to hang lazily in the air.

Dovepaw backed away quickly as the other cats came to see what she and Tigerheart were staring at.

"Don't say I didn't warn you," Toadfoot mewed, cutting across their expressions of disgust. "I scented it—only faintly, because the wind's behind us—and I wanted to stay well clear."

"Quite right, too," Whitetail responded. "It might have died because of some sickness."

"More likely it died of thirst," Rippletail added sadly.

The cats padded on, leaping down into the stream again once they had left the body of the deer far behind. A somber mood hung over them like a gray cloud; Dovepaw guessed that they were all thinking about how much their Clanmates needed water back at the lake.

"I don't understand," Dovepaw muttered to Lionblaze. "I should have scented the deer before Toadfoot, and I didn't."

Lionblaze shrugged. "Like he said, the wind was behind us. Besides . . . no offense, Dovepaw, but you smell like fish."

Dovepaw let out a sigh. "Maybe—but I should have been more alert." *What else have I missed?*

A few heartbeats later, Tigerheart dropped back to walk alongside her. "Are you okay?" he asked, his voice full of concern.

"It was just a dead deer." Dovepaw tried to sound as if the sight hadn't shaken her. She didn't want Tigerheart to start treating her like a helpless kit. "Look!" she meowed, angling her ears forward in the direction they were traveling. "The trees are thinning out!"

Successfully distracted, Tigerheart bounded ahead to take a better look. The rest of the patrol quickened their pace, too, and climbed out of the streambed to stand in a line on the edge of the trees. Dovepaw gazed out across a field where fluffy grayish-white animals were nibbling at the grass.

"What are they?" Petalfur exclaimed in surprise. "They look as if they're made of cobwebs!"

"Oh, they're just sheep," Whitetail replied. "We see them all the time in WindClan."

"Their pelts make good linings for nests," Sedgewhisker added.

Whitetail took the lead as the patrol crept out into the field, following the line of the stream. Dovepaw felt uncomfortably exposed with nothing between her and the open sky, and she was grateful for the experience of the WindClan cats. Then behind her she heard a loud yapping and the scent of dog flooded over her, swamping her senses. Whipping around, she saw a Twoleg walking along the edge of the wood with a small brown-and-white dog trotting at its heels.

As soon as the dog scented the cats, it began racing toward them, yapping even louder. Dovepaw looked wildly around, but there were no trees to climb, except for the forest they had left.

"Run!" Toadfoot yowled.

Their paws pounding on the short grass, the patrol hurtled toward the opposite side of the field. Dovepaw cast a swift glance over her shoulder. "The dog's gaining on us!" she gasped.

Whitetail glanced back too, then let out a loud caterwaul. "Head for the sheep!"

"What?" Tigerheart almost fell over his own paws as he whirled around. "Why the sheep?"

"Twolegs never let dogs near sheep," Whitetail panted. "Maybe sheep are dangerous to dogs. Anyway, if we can reach them, we should be safe."

As she raced toward the sheep, Dovepaw's heart lurched with fear. But there was no choice, unless she wanted to stay out in the open with the dog. Along with the rest of the patrol, she dived among the legs of the weird animals.

The sheep had bunched together, uttering high-pitched cries that seemed to show the sheep were scared of the dog. Dovepaw caught a glimpse of it among the bulky gray bodies, dancing around a few tail-lengths from the sheep and still yapping its head off. The sheep began to swirl across the field, moving in one giant group. The cats had no choice but to move with them, frantically dodging skinny legs and sharp hooves. Dovepaw was squashed among the warm, greasy cobweb pelts, and she lost sight of the others. *Help! Where have they all gone?*

Above the noise of the sheep, she heard the Twoleg's voice raised in a commanding yowl. The dog's yapping broke off. Dovepaw couldn't see it anymore, but she heard its paws falter on the grass and then retreat as it trotted reluctantly back to its Twoleg.

Gradually the sheep slowed down, then stopped close to the hedge on the far side of the field, still letting out their piercing bleats. Dovepaw wriggled to the edge of the flock and spotted Tigerheart and Lionblaze emerging together a few tail-lengths away. Toadfoot followed them into the open, with Petalfur and Rippletail behind him. A few heartbeats later Whitetail and Sedgewhisker appeared farther down.

"We need to get out of the field!" Whitetail called. "Go through the hedge!"

Dovepaw obeyed, dragging herself under thorny branches that raked across her back, keeping her belly pressed to the dried leaves and debris on the ground. On the other side was a strip of grass with a stretch of black stone beyond it, where the patrol gathered together again and stood panting.

Dovepaw's eyes widened as she gazed at her companions. Their pelts were matted in clumps with wisps of sticky sheep-cobweb clinging to them, and a sour smell billowed around them like a cloud of flies. *I'm just as bad,* she thought disgustedly, pawing at a gray strand that clung to her shoulder. *But at least none of us is hurt.*

She bent her head to lick her chest fur, wincing at the foul taste, only to look up, startled, a moment later as the sound of thunder rolled around her. The sky was clear blue, with only a few tiny wisps of cloud being tossed by the wind. But the thunderous noise was growing louder still, and a bitter, burning scent swept over her.

Dovepaw glanced from side to side, confused by the noise and the stench and the sense of something huge and shining, solid as stone. . . .

"Get back!" Lionblaze screeched.

He shoved Dovepaw and Petalfur into the prickly hedge. Dovepaw stumbled and half fell among the thorns as a gigantic silver creature roared past on round black paws.

"What . . . what was that?" she stammered, picking herself up.

"A monster," Lionblaze told her, his voice tense. "They run along these Thunderpaths." He waved his tail at the stretch of flat black stone. "We saw lots of them when we went to the Twolegplace to find Sol."

"We had to cross Thunderpaths on the Great Journey, too," Whitetail added, "and there was one that went past the old forest. They're dangerous; we all need to be very careful."

Dovepaw warily approached the edge of the Thunderpath and gave it an experimental sniff. Her nose wrinkled at the bitter scent. The rest of the patrol stood alongside her;

Tigerheart set a paw cautiously on the hard black surface, then drew it back.

"We'd better stop hanging around," Lionblaze meowed, "and get across while it's still quiet." Padding over to Dovepaw, he murmured, "Is it safe? Are there any more monsters coming?"

Dovepaw extended her senses, listening for another of the terrifying creatures, but there was nothing in either direction. "It's okay," she whispered.

"Right." Lionblaze raised his voice. "Follow me as quick as you can, and don't stop!"

He thrust off from the grass verge and bounded across the Thunderpath. Dovepaw followed, keeping her gaze fixed on him, but aware of the other cats running alongside. They reached the strip of grass on the far side only to be brought up short by a fence of shiny, crisscrossing silver stuff that stretched up far above Dovepaw's head.

"Now what do we do?" Rippletail wailed. "We can't go any farther this way."

"Over here!" Toadfoot called from a few tail-lengths along the fence. "There's a hole I think we can wriggle through."

He flattened himself to the ground and pulled himself forward through a narrow gap at the bottom of the fence, standing up a few heartbeats later on the grass on the other side. "Come on, it's easy," he urged his companions.

Whitetail followed him through and then Dovepaw did the same, shivering at the touch of the hard Twoleg stuff against her back as she squirmed through the gap. The rest of the cats followed, with Lionblaze keeping watch until they were safely on the other side. Finally he struggled through, grunting with the effort as he pushed himself along.

Dovepaw stood still, looking around. A smooth field stretched in front of her, the grass much greener than she had seen it anywhere else since the heat and the drought began. Beyond it were Twoleg nests built of some kind of red rock. Dovepaw had never imagined that there could be so many Twoleg nests all in one place. Noise poured out from them like clap after clap of thunder; she shook as the din swept around her, flooding her senses. Twolegs were screeching and chattering, banging and roaring, in an endless surge of sound.

Desperately Dovepaw tried to block it out, to focus on the cats around her, and on what she could see directly in front of her. Only then did she realize what she *couldn't* see.

"Where's the stream?" she gasped.

CHAPTER 16

Lionblaze heard panic in his apprentice's wail and saw the fear in her eyes. Quietly he padded over to her and rested his tail on her shoulders. "Calm down," he murmured. "It'll be okay."

Rippletail was looking around. "Water doesn't run uphill," the RiverClan cat meowed, "so the stream must be somewhere over there." He pointed with his tail to a line of long grass at the bottom of a green slope.

"Let's check it out," Toadfoot suggested.

He let Rippletail take the lead as the cats trotted in single file alongside the silver fence. Before they had covered many fox-lengths, Lionblaze heard loud Twoleg voices coming from the other side of the field. A group of Twoleg kits erupted into the open, shouting noisily and kicking what looked like a smooth, round boulder with their hind paws.

"Hurry!" he called to his companions as the young Twolegs ran across the grass toward them.

Every cat picked up the pace until they were racing with their tails streaming out. Lionblaze felt the ground shake under his paws as the young Twolegs came nearer, still yowling and kicking the boulder-thing back and forth between them. With a gasp of relief he plunged into the cover of the long grass at the bottom of the slope, but his gasp changed to a screech of alarm as the ground gave way under his paws. He rolled and bumped down a shallow cliff, paws and tail thrashing, and landed with a thump on hard, pebble-strewn earth.

"It's the stream!" Petalfur mewed.

Dazed, Lionblaze sat up and looked around. He was back in the dry streambed, with overhanging grasses almost meeting above his head. His companions were scattered beside him, picking themselves up and examining scraped pads and snagged fur.

"I've swallowed every piece of the grit in this stream!" Tigerheart complained, spitting.

"No, you haven't," Toadfoot growled, giving his pelt a shake. "It's all over my fur!"

Lionblaze spotted Dovepaw crouching beside a jutting rock, her eyes glazed with fear. "I should have heard the Twolegs coming!" she whispered. "I should have known what was going to happen and warned you."

Lionblaze glanced over his shoulder at the other cats, who were getting ready to move off again. "Dovepaw has some gravel in her pad," he called. "We need to lick it out; we'll be with you in a couple of heartbeats."

Then he leaned over Dovepaw so that no other cat could hear what he was saying. "You're not responsible for all of us. You're on this mission because you were the first to sense the brown animals blocking the stream, but that doesn't mean that the rest of us can't hear and see things and protect ourselves."

Dovepaw blinked up at him unhappily. "I hate it here, so close to the Twolegplace," she murmured. "It's too much—all the sounds and scents and images in my head. I can't cope with it! I can only concentrate on what is close by." Her eyes widened into huge pools of misery. "It's like being blind!"

Lionblaze bent his head and touched his nose to her ear in a gesture of comfort. At the same time he pushed away a stab of worry that Dovepaw had needed to block out so much to cope with the stress of being in a strange territory. He realized how much he had been depending on her to tell them what was up ahead.

We'll be fine without her powers, he reassured himself. *After all, other cats have made journeys with just their ordinary senses.*

"It'll be okay," he mewed. "At least we've found the stream again." He could still hear the noise of Twolegs beyond the tall grass, their loud voices interspersed with thumps of the smooth boulder-thing.

"That can't possibly be a rock," Sedgewhisker observed, her ears quivering. "They would break their paws if it was."

Just as she finished speaking, the boulder crashed into the long grass ahead of them and lodged at the very edge of the bank. Tigerheart and Sedgewhisker darted forward to take a look at it.

"Be careful!" Whitetail and Toadfoot called out in the same heartbeat, then gave each other an embarrassed glance.

The two younger warriors didn't take any notice. Tigerheart

scrambled up the side of the streambed and gave the boulder a nudge with his nose.

"It's not a rock!" he meowed in surprise. "Look!" He gave the boulder another nudge and it bounced away from him, lighter than a twig.

"Mouse-brain!" Lionblaze hissed. He ran forward and gave the boulder a harder shove, sending it farther off. "Keep away," he warned Tigerheart and Sedgewhisker. "It's a Twoleg thing!"

Before the three cats could hide in the streambed again, one of the young Twolegs came blundering through the long grass, yowling to his companions. Lionblaze guessed that he was looking for the round thing.

"Hide!" he hissed. "Keep down!"

He crouched down beside Tigerheart and Sedgewhisker, feeling very exposed with only the grass stems to hide him. Tigerheart was tense with alarm, but Sedgewhisker seemed perfectly comfortable, keeping still and silent, not even blinking, as her gaze followed the young Twoleg.

That figures, Lionblaze thought. *WindClan cats are used to hunting without ground cover.*

Several moons seemed to pass before the Twoleg found the round thing and ran off with it. Gradually the noise from the Twolegs died away. The three cats slid down into the stream again; Toadfoot was waiting for his Clanmate with his neck fur bristling.

"Are you completely mouse-brained?" he demanded. "Do you *want* Twolegs to catch you?"

"Sorry," Tigerheart mumbled.

Whitetail glared at Sedgewhisker, who ducked her head apologetically.

"Let's get a move on," Toadfoot meowed. "We've wasted enough time here." He set off at a run, glancing back to add, "The brown animals won't be anywhere around here, right?"

"Er . . . right," Dovepaw stammered.

The stream skirted the green expanse where the Twolegs were playing, then ran between rows of Twoleg nests, with neat patches of grass that stretched down to the bank. Trees overhung the channel; Lionblaze was thankful for the shade and the cover, especially when he heard the yowls of young Twolegs coming from their nests.

Popping his head up above the bank from time to time, he spotted Twoleg kits chasing one another or kicking more of the smooth, round things. Once he saw a young Twoleg screeching happily as it swung from a tree on a piece of wood suspended between two long tendrils.

"What do you think that is?" he asked Whitetail, who had climbed up beside him.

"I have no idea." The WindClan she-cat shrugged. "Whatever it is, the kit is having fun."

Sunhigh came and went as the cats padded onward up the stream. Lionblaze's belly began to rumble; it seemed a long time since their fresh-kill in the early morning. Whitetail and Sedgewhisker seemed excited by something; their ears were pricked and their whiskers quivered, and they kept whispering to each other.

"Is something the matter?" he asked.

Sedgewhisker turned to him, her eyes glowing. "We can scent rabbits!"

"What?" Toadfoot halted with a scornful flick of his tail. "Have you got bees in your brain? Rabbits wouldn't live this close to Twolegs."

"Yeah, the Twolegs would probably hunt them," Tigerheart added.

"There *are* rabbits," Whitetail insisted, giving the Shadow-Clan cats a withering glare. "And not far away, either." She began stalking up the streambed, nostrils twitching; Sedge-whisker padded at her shoulder.

Lionblaze turned to Dovepaw. "Are they right?"

To his disappointment, his apprentice just gave a shrug. "I don't know. I've still got my senses blocked," she muttered. She looked up at him with a fierce glare. "I can't help it, okay? There's just too much noise to cope with!"

"Okay," Lionblaze soothed before the other cats wondered what they were talking about.

Suddenly Whitetail streaked away with Sedgewhisker hard on her paws. The WindClan warriors shot up the side of the bank and vanished through the thick grass that bordered the stream.

"Fox dung!" Toadfoot hissed, heading after them.

Lionblaze and the other cats followed, then stopped dead as they reached the top of the bank and peered through the clumps of grass.

"There *is* a rabbit!" Petalfur breathed. "Two rabbits!"

Water flooded Lionblaze's jaws as he eyed the creatures: They were young and plump, with thick black-and-white pelts. They sat nibbling on the patch of grass that stretched as far as the Twoleg nest, quite unaware that hunters were nearby. For some reason they were surrounded by a fence of shiny Twoleg stuff, but it was low enough for a cat to scramble over easily.

Whitetail and Sedgewhisker were already crouched on the grass, ready to spring; Lionblaze flattened himself to the ground and crept up to join them, aware of Toadfoot just behind him and the rest of the patrol fanning out to intercept any rabbit that might make a dash for safety. He saw Whitetail bunch her muscles to leap over the fence. A heartbeat later she froze as a loud yowl came from a tree a few tail-lengths away.

"Hey! You! Hold it right there!"

Lionblaze stared in astonishment as three kittypets leaped down from the tree and raced across the grass to stand between the WindClan cats and the rabbits. In the lead was an orange tom with glaring yellow eyes, followed by a small white she-cat and a fat black-and-brown tabby tom.

The orange tom planted himself right in front of Whitetail; his two companions stood just behind him. They both looked terrified, their fur fluffed out and their ears flattened.

"You can't hunt these rabbits," the orange tom declared, baring his teeth in the beginnings of a snarl.

"Oh, yeah?" Sedgewhisker rose from her hunter's crouch to stand nose to nose with the kittypet. "We'll fight you for them, if that's what you want. You should lay more scent markers if you want cats to stay out of your territory!"

"Territory?" The white she-cat sounded confused. "What are you meowing about?"

"Territory!" Toadfoot snarled, padding up to stand beside Sedgewhisker. "Don't pretend you're so dumb that you don't know what territory is."

"This is my housefolk's nest," the black-and-brown tom mewed.

"But the rabbits aren't in the nest, are they?" Whitetail sounded as if she was talking to particularly stupid kits. "Unless this territory is scent-marked, they're free for any cat to hunt."

"No, they're not," the orange tom insisted, his neck fur bristling up.

Tigerheart narrowed his eyes. "Look, kittypet—"

"This is ridiculous," Sedgewhisker interrupted impatiently. "There are two perfectly good rabbits waiting to be caught, and all we can do is argue. Are *you* hunting them?" she asked the kittypets. "Because—"

All three kittypets let out gasps of horror, their eyes stretched wide.

"No!" the tabby tom exclaimed. "Those rabbits belong to my housefolk."

"We would be in big trouble if we hunted them," the orange tom added.

"That's right," the white she-cat meowed. "Every cat around here knows about the tom who hunted his housefolk's rabbit." Her voice grew hushed. "They took him to the Cutter, and he was never the same afterward."

Lionblaze and the other Clan cats exchanged puzzled glances. "Now I've heard everything," Rippletail remarked. "Kittypets guarding Twoleg rabbits!"

"So what?" Toadfoot growled. "I'm going to get the rabbits anyway. They look fat and slow enough for any cat to catch, not just WindClan."

He hurled himself at the shiny fence and started to claw his way up it. Immediately the orange tom grabbed Toadfoot's tail in his teeth and yanked him down again.

Toadfoot scrambled to his paws and spun around, claws extended. "Back off, kittypet!" he spat. "Do you think I'll let you stop me?"

"No." Lionblaze shouldered his way between the two cats. "We'll look elsewhere for prey."

"Right." Whitetail sounded disappointed, but her voice was firm. "These rabbits are too well protected. We can't risk getting injured now."

Toadfoot went on glaring at the orange tom for a heartbeat longer, then shrugged angrily and turned away. The three kittypets stood in front of the fence and watched as the Clan cats padded across the grass and toward the streambed.

Even though Lionblaze had prevented the fight, he was still finding it hard to control his anger. *What a waste of rabbits. We could all have had a good meal.*

"Those kittypets think they've won!" Toadfoot exclaimed. He cast a last glance over his shoulder before he leaped back into the stream. "Look at them! I'd like to wipe those smug looks off their faces."

"But Whitetail's right: We can't," Petalfur reminded him.

"We have to stay safe until we find the water."

"Right," Toadfoot muttered darkly. "But just wait till we're on the way back. . . ."

The patrol continued in silence until they left the Twoleg nests behind. The gardens gave way to a prickly copse with young trees poking out of a tangle of undergrowth.

"I think we should stop here and find something to eat," Rippletail suggested.

Lionblaze could see that he and Petalfur were looking dull-eyed with exhaustion again. "Good idea," he agreed, seeing Toadfoot curl his lip in frustration. "We don't know when there'll be another chance."

The ShadowClan warrior let out an exaggerated sigh. "All right, let's get it over with. And let's hope we don't have any more dumb kittypets getting in our way."

Dovepaw's tail shot up. "I can hear a bird over there," she murmured to Lionblaze, angling her ears toward the other side of the copse. "It's banging a snail against a stone."

Lionblaze listened, but he couldn't hear a thing. "Go for it," he meowed, pleased that his apprentice was managing to use her extra-keen senses again.

Dovepaw scampered off happily, while Lionblaze stood for a moment tasting the air until he detected a squirrel near the top of a nearby tree. Swarming up the trunk, he had reached the branch underneath his quarry when a loud meow rang out from the ground below.

"Hello again!"

The squirrel sat straight up, startled, then bolted, hurling itself into the air and vanishing into the foliage of the next tree. Lionblaze let out an exasperated snort. Looking down, he spotted the white she-cat from the Twoleg nest with rabbits; she stood at the foot of his tree, gazing up at him with friendly green eyes.

"You just scared off my next meal," Lionblaze complained, scrambling down to join her.

"Sorry." The white kittypet blinked at him. "I just wanted to watch you hunting. I figured you'd stop here, since you tried to get those rabbits. Do you *really* have to feed yourselves? We sometimes catch mice, but it's not like we have to. I mean, who'd want to eat fur and bones?"

Plenty of cats, Lionblaze thought when the kittypet paused for breath. Could she truly be that clueless? Spotting another squirrel at the edge of a bramble thicket, he gave her a quick nod of farewell and stalked off after it.

But the white she-cat followed him. "Are you hunting that squirrel?" she asked. "Can I watch? I'll be quiet."

Too late! Lionblaze groaned as the squirrel's ears pricked; it leaped up the nearest tree to sit and chatter angrily at them from a low branch before disappearing.

"My name's Snowdrop," the white cat gabbled on, oblivious of what she had done. "The orange tom is called Seville, and the black-and-brown tabby is Jigsaw. Thanks for leaving the rabbits alone. It's true about what happened to that other cat, the one who ate his housefolk's rabbit."

Lionblaze took a deep breath and turned to face her. "It's nice to chat and all," he mewed through gritted teeth, "but I'm kind of busy."

He could have saved his breath; he could see Snowdrop

wouldn't have recognized a hint if it hit her over the head.

"What are you all doing here?" she meowed, peering through the trees at the other cats who were stalking their prey in peace. "Have you run away from your housefolk? Did you get lost? Are you looking for the way home?"

Lionblaze raised his tail in an effort to stem the flood of questions. "No, we're not kittypets," he meowed, trying not to feel offended. "We live in Clans, by a lake downstream from here."

"Clans?" Snowdrop sounded bewildered.

"A whole bunch of cats who live together," Lionblaze explained. "We have a leader—"

"What's all this racket about?" Fronds of bracken parted to reveal Toadfoot, his fur bristling in annoyance. He dropped the mouse he was carrying. "For StarClan's sake, you're making enough noise to scare away all the prey between here and the lake."

"Hello." Snowdrop seemed quite unworried by the Shadow-Clan cat's bad temper. "My name's Snowdrop. What's yours?"

Toadfoot exchanged a surprised glance with Lionblaze. "Never mind that," he mewed briskly to Snowdrop. "We're on a mission, and you can't help us, so please leave us alone."

Snowdrop's eyes stretched wide. "Oh, wow, a mission!"

"We're looking for the water," Lionblaze explained as the rest of his patrol padded up to find out what was going on. Dovepaw brought her thrush, and Rippletail proudly deposited a vole beside it. "We think there are some brown animals blocking the stream."

"Oh, really? I've often wondered what happened," Snowdrop chirped. "I used to like the stream. It was good to lie on the grass and watch the insects buzzing over the water."

Toadfoot rolled his eyes.

"Can I come with you?" Snowdrop mewed suddenly. "It would be fun! Maybe the brown animals are dogs—do you think so? Or giant rabbits!"

"No, sorry, you can't come," Rippletail meowed. "You wouldn't be able to look after yourself."

Snowdrop's gaze fell on the few pieces of fresh-kill the Clan cats had managed to catch. "You don't seem to be too good at that yourselves," she commented.

"We're fine," Rippletail replied. "Now run back to your housefolk."

Toadfoot waved his tail for the patrol to move off. "We'll eat later," he growled.

Whitetail grabbed Dovepaw's thrush while Petalfur picked up the mouse and Lionblaze took the vole. Before jumping into the stream again, he glanced back to see Snowdrop sitting where they had left her, watching them go. Her head was drooping unhappily.

Feeling guilty for abandoning her, Lionblaze darted back. "Here, would you like a bite of vole?" he offered, dropping it at her paws.

Snowdrop's gaze filled with horror. "With *fur* and everything? No way!"

Lionblaze heard snorts of amusement coming from his companions. "Okay, bye then," he mewed hurriedly and ran off to join them, remembering at the last moment to take the vole with him.

The sun had gone down by the time the patrol set out again. In the twilight they came to a steep-sided valley where the trees were much older, with spreading trunks and gnarled branches. Whitetail, scouting ahead, found a split in a huge hollow tree, the floor covered in a thick layer of dead leaves, where there was room for all of them to curl up and sleep.

"Well done!" Lionblaze yawned. "We'll be safe in here from anything."

He still thought it best to set up a lookout; exhausted from the night before, when he had taken Dovepaw's shift as well as his own, he didn't argue when Rippletail volunteered to take the first watch. He crawled inside the tree, noticing that no cat seemed to be particularly bothered now about whose pelt they brushed against as they lay down, and curled up gratefully beside Dovepaw. He was asleep within moments.

After what felt like just a heartbeat, Lionblaze was awakened by a prodding in his ribs. Moonlight trickling through the split in the trunk revealed Dovepaw looking down at him, her eyes shining.

"What's the matter?" he muttered.

"I can hear the brown animals!" Dovepaw told him, twitching her tail with excitement. "We're nearly there!"

CHAPTER 17

❦

Jayfeather lifted his head and tasted the air, which had cooled a little as evening approached. A faint breeze rustled the branches of the trees above the stone hollow and stirred the dust on the floor of his den. A few cats were gathered around the meager fresh-kill pile; their soft voices drifted through the bramble screen, reaching Jayfeather in a blur of sound.

Sighing, he wished that he had Dovepaw's far-reaching senses, so that he could track her and Lionblaze and the rest of the patrol. They had been gone two days now, and Jayfeather had no idea whether they were still searching, or whether they had found the brown animals and the trapped water. The night before, he had tried to walk in Lionblaze's dreams and had found himself padding up the dry bed of the stream, with unfamiliar trees arching their branches overhead. He had picked up his brother's scent, and once he thought he spotted the tip of a golden tail whisking away around a boulder just ahead of him. But however fast he ran he couldn't catch up, and Lionblaze didn't respond when he called out.

He's too far away, Jayfeather thought regretfully as he woke, his legs aching as if he really had tried to pursue his littermate.

There's no way you can catch him now.

His pelt itched with the longing to tell Lionblaze about his encounter with Breezepelt on the lake the day before. He was still shaken by the hatred that had emanated from the Wind-Clan cat, and he seemed to hear the voices of the Ancient Clan, whispering warnings that he couldn't quite make out.

I can't believe that mangy flea-pelt is my half brother!

The bramble screen rustled as a cat brushed past it; Jay-feather recognized Dustpelt's scent.

"I've come for more of those herbs," Dustpelt announced, then added reluctantly, "My back feels much better today, so they must have done some good."

"I'm glad to hear it," Jayfeather replied. "Hang on, and I'll get them."

As he headed for the storage cleft at the back of the den, Dustpelt called after him, "I don't want them if another cat needs them more."

"No, it's fine," Jayfeather replied. He collected a few leaves of tansy and some of daisy from the store and headed back to the tabby warrior. "Eat those," he ordered, pushing the tansy toward his Clanmate.

While Dustpelt was licking up the herbs, Jayfeather chewed up the daisy leaves and made a poultice to spread on the base of the ThunderClan warrior's spine, where the pain was worst.

"Thanks," Dustpelt meowed. As he was heading out of the den he paused, acute embarrassment flooding from his pelt. "Ferncloud said I had to thank you from her, too. She said I was being really annoying, complaining about backache without doing anything about it."

"Surely not," Jayfeather murmured, faintly amused, as the tabby warrior padded off toward the warriors' den.

The sound of Dustpelt's paw steps had hardly died away when another cat popped her head around the bramble screen.

"Hi, Cinderheart," Jayfeather mewed, breathing in her scent and picking up her anxiety along with it. "Is something wrong?"

"I'm fine, but I'm worried about Poppyfrost," the gray she-cat replied, slipping into the den.

"What's the matter with her?" Alarm leaped in Jayfeather like a jumping fish. "Is it her kits?"

"Oh, no, she's doing well physically," Cinderheart told him. "Her belly is about the right size, and there's no sign of fever or vomiting."

"Good," Jayfeather murmured. *And you would know—Cinderpelt*, he added privately to himself. Only he and Leafpool knew the strange truth about Cinderheart, that she had lived in ThunderClan before as the medicine cat Cinderpelt, who had died saving Sorreltail from a badger at the moment Cinderheart was born. Cinderheart had no idea why she knew so much about herbs, or why memories of ThunderClan's former home haunted her dreams. Leafpool and Jayfeather had agreed long ago not to tell her; she was a warrior in her own right, and if StarClan had chosen to give Cinderpelt a second chance, they would not interfere.

"It's just that she's so quiet and sad," Cinderheart went on.

"Is there anything you can do to help?"

Jayfeather was puzzled. *What sort of help does she expect?* "I don't want to give Poppyfrost herbs," he began, "not when she's expecting kits, unless it's really urgent."

"Yes, but—"

"You told me she's not ill," Jayfeather went on, ignoring the she-cat's protest. "If everything's okay—"

"It's *not* okay," Cinderheart interrupted in her turn. "Nothing's okay," she added wretchedly. "Oh, Jayfeather, I miss Hollyleaf so much!"

Jayfeather felt as though some cat had hurled a rock into his belly. He tried hard every day not to think about his sister, and every day he failed. "So do I," he replied quietly.

"Yes, you must." Cinderheart's tone was full of sympathy. "Losing a littermate is the worst thing ever. Maybe that's why Poppyfrost is so sad, because Honeyfern's gone." She let out a long sigh. "I'm sorry for disturbing you, Jayfeather."

She turned and padded out of the den; Jayfeather pictured her head drooping and her tail trailing in the dust. When she had gone, he slipped inside the storage cleft again and turned over his dwindling stock of herbs. Poppy seed . . . tansy . . . borage . . . *No, there's nothing here that will help a cat who's just sad.* And there was nothing any cat could say or do that would stop Poppyfrost from grieving for her dead sister.

Curling up in his nest of moss and fern, Jayfeather let himself drift into sleep and turned his paws in the direction of Poppyfrost's dreams. To his surprise, he found himself on the steep, rocky path leading to the Moonpool. The moon shed its pale light over the boulders and moorland grass on either side, and it gleamed on the tortoiseshell fur of the young cat slipping quietly ahead of him.

"Poppyfrost!" Jayfeather called.

The young cat started, then slowly turned to face him; starlight glittered in her eyes.

"What are you doing here?" Jayfeather asked her.

Poppyfrost seemed unsurprised to see that he was the cat who was following her. "I've dreamed of this mountain path so many times since Honeyfern died," she explained. "I want to see her so much, and I can hear her calling to me from somewhere up there." She nodded to the top of the ridge, silhouetted against the star-filled sky.

Jayfeather pricked his ears, straining in an effort to hear the young she-cat's voice. But there was nothing except the faint whisper of the wind over the grass. "I can't hear her," he meowed.

"I can." Poppyfrost was calm and clear-eyed as she spoke, though her voice betrayed her longing for her dead sister.

Jayfeather's paws tingled. Poppyfrost had set her paws on a path that was walked only by medicine cats. "You should come back to the hollow," he told her. He remembered how he had saved her life a long time ago, by guiding her back from StarClan when she was a tiny kit with greencough. She had come willingly enough then, not ready to leave behind the Clanmates she had only just begun to know. "This place isn't for you."

"No, I must go on!" Poppyfrost spun around and ran up

the narrow track, faster and faster until she vanished into a swirl of mist. Her voice drifted faintly back to him. "I have to see Honeyfern!"

Jayfeather woke with a jolt, his paws scrabbling among churned-up moss. Warm air stirred against his face, telling him that the sun was already up. His pads ached as though he had really spent the night trekking into the mountains. Yawning, he dragged himself out of his nest and padded into the clearing. Sunrays were spilling through the trees above the camp, scorching the bare ground. Jayfeather tried to picture the hollow as it had been, green and cool, knowing that everything now would be parched to a brittle brown.

A worm of worry was gnawing at his belly. Trying to ignore it, he padded across to the nursery and stuck his head inside the entrance. He could hear the soft breathing of sleeping cats, and he scented Ferncloud, Daisy, and Poppyfrost huddled together in a mound of fur. Slightly reassured, he crept away without disturbing them.

But I'll keep an eye on Poppyfrost, he decided.

"This is a dock leaf," Jayfeather announced, snagging it in his claws and holding it up so that all the apprentices could see it.

"Like we don't know," Ivypaw muttered.

Jayfeather bit back a stinging rebuke. He knew that the young apprentice was still grumpy because Dovepaw had gone on the mission without her, and he couldn't entirely blame her. But Firestar had asked him to give all the apprentices some basic training in the use of herbs, and Ivypaw had to learn the same things as the others, whether she liked it or not.

"Dock leaves are good for rubbing on sore pads," he went on, ignoring the young cat's bad temper for now. "And you can find them pretty well anywhere, so they're one of the most useful herbs."

"So, like, if we went on a long journey, we should look out for dock?" Bumblepaw asked.

Oops, you shouldn't have said that, Jayfeather thought, as Ivypaw let out an angry hiss at her denmate.

"That's right," he replied. "Or if you step on a sharp stone," he added, trying to take the focus off traveling.

"Wouldn't we need cobweb for that?" Briarpaw mewed.

"Only if the skin has broken," Jayfeather told her. "And that's true of all wounds, of course, especially serious ones where the cat is losing a lot of blood. For smaller scratches and scrapes, we use marigold or horsetail to stop the bleeding. These are leaves of marigold," he went on, holding one up. "I don't have any horsetail right now; you should ask your mentors to look for it when you go out for training, and it would be great if you could bring some back."

"And what if some cat eats bad food, or some nasty Twoleg stuff like our mother told us RiverClan cats did once?" Blossompaw chirped. "What do you give them then?"

"That's a bit complicated for now," Jayfeather mewed. "Today we're learning about soreness and minor wounds. You'll meet those almost every day, whereas cats are only poisoned once a season, if that."

"But we should know what to do, right?" Bumblepaw argued.

"You're not going to be medicine cats," Jayfeather began. "More serious illnesses—"

To his relief he heard paw steps approaching and picked up Thornclaw's scent as the tabby warrior poked his head around the bramble screen.

"Are you done?" he meowed. "The other mentors and I want to go out for some hunting practice."

"Yes! Hunting!" Blossompaw sprang to her paws. "I'll catch the biggest rabbit in the forest!"

"Don't make promises you might not be able to keep," Thornclaw mewed drily. "Can I take them, Jayfeather?"

"You're welcome to," Jayfeather replied with feeling. "Remember that horsetail!" he called after the apprentices as they bundled out of the den and dashed off across the clearing.

Once they had gone, Jayfeather padded out and headed for the elders' den. When he pushed his way under the hazel boughs, he found Mousefur and Purdy still sleeping, curled up companionably near the trunk of the bush. Longtail was awake, and he stretched as Jayfeather entered.

"Hi," he meowed. "I was hoping you'd stop by."

Anxiety pricked Jayfeather like a nettle when he heard how frail the elder sounded. He had always thought of Longtail as a young cat, living in the elders' den only because of his blindness, but now he realized that he was growing old as well.

"What can I do for you?" he asked Longtail.

"I wondered if there's any news about the cats who went upstream," the blind warrior replied. "Has any cat discovered what is stopping the water?"

"We haven't heard anything more," Jayfeather told him. *I'm certainly not going to give away Dovepaw's secret!* "You know as much as I do."

Longtail sighed. "It's not enough. No cat will be happy until they're home safe."

"I know, but there's nothing—"

"Jayfeather!" The loud whisper interrupted what he had been about to say; Jayfeather detected Ferncloud's scent and turned to face her.

"What's the matter? Is some cat ill?"

"No, but we can't find Poppyfrost. Have you seen her?"

Jayfeather didn't bother reminding her that he couldn't *see* anything. "She was asleep in the nursery earlier."

"Well, she's not there now." Ferncloud sounded puzzled rather than worried.

"She hasn't been here, either," Longtail told her.

"I can't find her anywhere!" Daisy pushed her way through the branches, nearly knocking Jayfeather onto Mousefur's sleeping body. "She's not in the apprentices' den, and she hasn't gone to make dirt, and—"

"It's getting too crowded in here." Jayfeather gave the she-cat a gentle push back toward the clearing. "If we're not careful, we'll wake Mousefur and Purdy, and then we'll never hear the end of it." As he herded Daisy and Ferncloud back into the clearing, he turned his head and meowed to Longtail,

"If I find out anything about the blocked stream, I'll let you know, I promise."

"Thanks, Jayfeather," the blind elder meowed.

Outside in the clearing, Jayfeather faced the two queens. "Right, tell me from the beginning."

"When I woke up, Poppyfrost wasn't in the nursery," Daisy mewed. "Ferncloud didn't know where she'd gone. We weren't worried at first, but when she didn't come back we started to look for her."

"She's not in the camp," Ferncloud added.

Jayfeather wasn't sure how worried he ought to be. Poppyfrost was at least a moon away from having her kits, so she wouldn't do herself any harm if she had just gone for a walk.

"We ought to tell some cat," Daisy suggested.

"But who?" Ferncloud asked reasonably. "Firestar has taken a patrol to fetch water; Brackenfur and Sorreltail are out hunting with Brambleclaw—"

"Cinderheart is training her apprentice," Jayfeather added. *And it won't do any good to tell Berrynose,* he thought, remembering how brusquely the cream-colored warrior had treated his mate when they met by the lake. "I don't think you ought to worry," he went on. "Poppyfrost has probably gone to stretch her legs, or maybe to get a drink of water."

"You're probably right," Ferncloud meowed, sounding relieved.

Waves of anxiety were still coming from Daisy's pelt, but she didn't protest when Ferncloud urged her gently back to the nursery.

Jayfeather padded back to his den and headed for the storage cleft to sort out some herbs for Dustpelt. He hadn't exactly been telling the truth when he told the tabby warrior he had plenty of what he needed to ease the stiffness in his back. He hadn't wanted to admit that the stocks of tansy were getting dangerously low, in case Dustpelt refused to take any more.

His head deep in the storage cleft, Jayfeather sensed rather than heard movement outside the den. As he backed out, he picked up Daisy's scent. "Come in, Daisy," he mewed, stifling a sigh. He wasn't surprised that she had come to see him; he knew she was making herself frantic over the absent queen.

The she-cat brushed past the bramble screen and halted in front of Jayfeather, her claws working in the dry ground. "I'm so worried about Poppyfrost! She's been really down lately."

"Why do you think that is?" Jayfeather asked, remembering what Cinderheart had told him. "There's nothing the matter with her kits. They're fine inside her; I've heard them squirming around. And the warriors are making sure she gets plenty of water and fresh-kill."

"It's not that," Daisy meowed with an impatient flick of her tail. "It's Berrynose. Poppyfrost thinks he doesn't love her."

Jayfeather stifled a groan. *I really don't have time for this!* "Well, Berrynose did love Honeyfern first."

Daisy let out a shocked gasp. "I can't believe you said that, Jayfeather! It shouldn't matter who Berrynose loved before, now that he's with Poppyfrost."

Jayfeather shrugged. "Maybe it does." *It seems logical to me. Every cat knows that Berrynose wanted Honeyfern for his mate, and then she was killed by the snake.*

"Poppyfrost is afraid that Berrynose doesn't want her or the kits," Daisy went on. "She thinks he wants Honeyfern back."

"Well, that's not going to happen," Jayfeather pointed out.

"I know that!" Daisy snapped. "But Poppyfrost isn't being logical."

You can say that again! Jayfeather sighed inwardly.

Daisy scraped the packed earth with her claws. "What if she's decided to leave the Clan forever?"

"She wouldn't do that," Jayfeather reassured her. *StarClan save me from fussing she-cats!* "But I'll have a word with Firestar when he gets back from his water patrol. Maybe some cats can go looking for her." *Though I'm not sure which cats we can spare, with so many needed for hunting and training and water patrols.*

Gently he guided Daisy out of his den and across the clearing to the nursery. He could sense that she still wasn't happy, but he didn't see what more he could do.

Once she was back inside, Jayfeather headed for the rock wall to check the holes for any sign that the snake might have paid another visit. Sunhigh was just past, and the ground was scorching hot, burning his pads; the basking rock was far too hot for the elders to be sunning themselves there.

At least I don't have to deal with Purdy this time!

As he pulled out the stones that were blocking the holes so that he could get a good sniff, Jayfeather pictured the day when Honeyfern died. Wincing, he let Berrynose's horror flood over him as he watched the young she-cat writhing in agony from the poison. The warrior's grief lingered at the foot of the cliff like a memory, soaking into the stones themselves.

It was enough to make Berrynose wish that he had been bitten by the snake instead of Honeyfern. If Poppyfrost knows that, she has good reason to run away.

Jayfeather paused halfway through rolling the last stone back into its hole. He suddenly had an awful suspicion about where Poppyfrost might be.

Leaving the hollow, he slipped under the forest trees, thankful for the cool shade and the air that felt so damp he could almost drink it. Poking out his parched tongue, he tried to lap it, but that only made him feel thirstier than ever.

Mouse-brain! What are you, a kit?

Giving himself a shake, Jayfeather headed through the trees up to the ridge that overlooked the lake. The air was hot and dry, sweeping across him in a scorching wind that carried the scents and sounds of cats up from the waterside. He knew what the lake looked like from his dreams; now he tried to picture it as much smaller, surrounded by dried mud and stones.

Even the underground tunnels will be dry by now.

Padding along the ridge, Jayfeather stopped every few paces to taste the air. Finally he picked up Poppyfrost's scent on a clump of long grass. *Yes! I was right.* He followed the traces along the spine of the hill until he reached the WindClan border. Poppyfrost's scent was just discernible beneath the WindClan scent markers.

Jayfeather's heart sank as he confirmed what he had suspected all along. Poppyfrost was trying to retrace the path she had followed in her dreams, all the way to the Moonpool.

Mouse-brained cat!

Following his Clanmate's scent, Jayfeather set off along the path to the Moonpool. But before he had taken many paw steps, he picked up another scent, slightly fresher than Poppyfrost's and overlying it, as if the cat it belonged to was following her.

Breezepelt! What's he doing here?

CHAPTER 18

Dovepaw felt her pelt stand on end with excitement as she looked at her mentor, his eyes glimmering in the moonlight that shone through the cleft in the hollow tree.

"What can you sense?" he asked in a murmur low enough not to wake the sleeping cats, or to reach Petalfur on watch outside.

Dovepaw closed her eyes. "Scraping sounds through the ground," she whispered. "The sound of teeth gnawing wood . . . and the crash of trees falling! The brown animals are dragging the trees to the stream and setting them in place, lodged tightly together like a wall." She took a deep breath. "Oh—I can sense the water! It's trapped behind the trees. . . . What are these creatures?"

She opened her eyes again to see Lionblaze looking alarmed, though his expression quickly changed to a look of determination when he saw she was watching him. "How many animals are there?" he meowed.

"I'm not sure. . . ." Dovepaw tried to concentrate on the brown animals as they moved among the fallen trees, but she couldn't get the picture clear enough to count them all.

"Fewer than our patrol, I think."

Lionblaze touched her shoulder with the tip of his tail. "It'll be okay," he reassured her.

Dovepaw couldn't share his confidence. What she hadn't told her mentor was that these animals wouldn't be easy to fight. They were much heavier than cats, dense and low to the ground, so it would be hard to flip them onto their bellies. They had long, sharp teeth and powerful clawed feet; she shivered at the thought of the wounds they could inflict. The fear that she could be leading the patrol into a battle they couldn't win weighed in her belly like a stone.

Lionblaze crept out of the hollow tree to relieve Petalfur on her watch. Dovepaw had already done her shift, so she settled down to sleep, but she couldn't block out the sounds from further upstream. She jerked back into wakefulness every time a tree crashed down, or a branch grated harshly as it was dragged across another. She was still trying to rest when pale dawn light filtered into the hollow tree and the other cats began to stir around her.

"Great StarClan!" Tigerheart exclaimed, sitting up and shaking dead leaves from his pelt. "Dovepaw, you're wrigglier than a pile of worms!"

"Sorry," Dovepaw muttered.

Tigerheart pushed his nose briefly into her fur to show that he hadn't meant to be unkind, before squeezing through the cleft and out into the open. Dovepaw and the other cats followed him out, and they finished off the rest of the fresh-kill pile. Dovepaw noticed that Rippletail and Petalfur didn't look so hollow and frail anymore.

They must be really starving in RiverClan if they're fattening up on what we've managed to catch out here!

Above the trees, the sky was milky-pale. A cold wind drove gray clouds across the sky, ruffling the cats' fur the wrong way.

"It's moons since it's been as cold as this," Petalfur meowed, shivering. "Maybe the weather is changing at last."

"We can deal with it," Toadfoot grunted.

When the cats had finished eating, Lionblaze took the lead, waving his tail for the others to follow him. "It's not far now," he encouraged them. "We're really close to the brown animals."

"How do you know?" Toadfoot demanded, his eyes narrowing in suspicion.

"The dream from StarClan said that they were just beyond the Twolegplace," Lionblaze explained, with a discreet nod to Dovepaw.

Even though she was worried about what other cats would say if they knew about her abilities, Dovepaw found she was annoyed by her mentor's secrecy. *He's willing enough to use my power, so why is he treating it like it's some sort of embarrassment for ThunderClan?*

"Don't forget to watch out for falling trees," she warned them. "And when we get to the place, the water will be really deep, so be careful not to fall in."

"All this was in your dream?" Toadfoot asked, sounding as if he didn't believe her.

"That's right." Lionblaze paused to give his chest fur a

couple of licks, as if he was thinking fast. "She saw the brown animals pushing trees over, and—and StarClan warned her about the water, isn't that right, Dovepaw?"

Reluctantly Dovepaw nodded.

"That was some dream!" Rippletail exclaimed. "Firestar never said anything about that at the Gathering."

"Yeah, well, he didn't need to," Lionblaze mewed uncomfortably, with a glare at Dovepaw.

Dovepaw met his glare innocently. *You got yourself into this mess, so get yourself out of it!*

As the patrol made its way along the streambed, up the gently sloping valley, the rush of the rising wind in the trees made it hard for Dovepaw to hear what was up ahead. She strained to make out the sounds of the brown animals, and she jumped when she heard Tigerheart's voice close beside her.

"Isn't this cool?" he mewed. "We're going to find these animals, and then—*pow!* Give us back our water! They won't refuse. If they do—well . . ." He crouched down, then sprang into the air, swiping his forepaws in a strong clawing move.

Dovepaw didn't think it would be as easy as that, and she wished that the chatty young warrior would just shut up. She stifled a sigh as Sedgewhisker came bounding up on her other side.

"Boasting—just like ShadowClan!" she meowed. "Watch this." Turning to face Tigerheart so the young warrior nearly tripped over her, she launched herself into the air with a terrifying shriek, twisting as she leaped and landing just behind him.

"Ha—missed!" Tigerheart exclaimed.

"I wasn't trying to grab you," Sedgewhisker retorted. "You'd know about it if I was."

"Oh, would I? Try it, then, and see!"

Dovepaw dodged aside as Tigerheart launched himself at the WindClan she-cat and cuffed her around the head, with his claws sheathed. Sedgewhisker let herself fall on one side, hooking Tigerheart's paws out from under him so that he lost his balance. The two young cats rolled over and over in the narrow streambed; Petalfur had to scramble up the bank so she wouldn't be squashed.

"Stop that right now!" Lionblaze growled, wading into the middle of the fight. "Mouse-brains! Do you want to get hurt before we even arrive?"

The two young cats broke apart and sat up; their fur was sticking out all over the place and coated with dust.

"I'd have won with the next move," Tigerheart muttered.

"In your dreams!" Sedgewhisker gave him a parting flick over the ear with her tail before drawing back.

Dovepaw spotted Lionblaze giving Sedgewhisker a worried look; she seemed to be moving awkwardly, as if she'd wrenched her shoulder again. Then his gaze swiveled back to Tigerheart; the look he gave the younger warrior was unreadable.

Now what's on his mind? Dovepaw wondered.

At the top of the valley, the land opened out into flatter, sparser woodland. The wind had dropped, and Dovepaw could hear the scraping and gnawing of the brown animals even more clearly than before. Her sense of urgency seemed to spread to the others, and Toadfoot, who was in the lead, picked up the pace until the cats were almost running along the stream bottom.

Lionblaze jumped onto the bank of the stream to look ahead and halted, his tail flicking up in surprise. "Look at that!"

"What?" Whitetail called up to him.

Lionblaze didn't reply; he just signaled with his tail for the rest of the patrol to join him on the bank.

As she scrambled up beside him and looked, Dovepaw felt her heart start to pound. She had known from the beginning of their journey what they would find, and yet it was all so much clearer and more frightening now that she was faced with it.

Ahead of them, the stream led through a stretch of patchy woodland. Several of the trees had been lopped off neatly about two tail-lengths from the ground, the top of the stump rising to a sharp, splintered point. It looked as if an enormous animal had crashed along the streambed, flattening the trees on either side.

But that wouldn't look so . . . so deliberate.

Stretching across the stream, clearly visible above the fallen trees, was an enormous barrier of logs. It rose in a curve like a hill, almost as big as a Twoleg nest.

Dovepaw shrank down, closing her eyes and pressing herself to the ground. The noise that surged through her was deafening: grunts and scratches, gnawing and scraping, the thump of heavy paws on wood. It took all the strength she had to control the sounds until she could cope with them and still stay aware of what was going on around her.

"So that's what's blocking the stream," Rippletail whispered.

A moment of shocked quiet followed his words; it was broken by Petalfur. "We'll have to push the logs away."

"No, better drag them out of the stream," Toadfoot argued. "Otherwise who knows where they'll end up?"

"Whatever, as long as we let the water out," meowed Lionblaze.

"And we'll need to keep well back when the logs give way," Whitetail pointed out.

"Wait." Dovepaw's voice was a hoarse croak as she struggled to her paws again. "The brown animals are still here. They *built* that barrier deliberately to trap the water."

Another shocked silence greeted her words. Then Toadfoot shrugged. "We'll just have to chase them away, then."

Dovepaw was sure it wouldn't be as easy as that, but she couldn't think of anything helpful to say.

"Don't be scared," Tigerheart whispered, padding up to stand beside her, with his pelt brushing hers. "I'll look after you."

Dovepaw felt too shaken to protest. She followed Lionblaze as he beckoned the rest of the patrol back into the cover of the streambed.

"I suggest that we wait until after dark before we attack," he meowed. "First we need to scout around on both sides of the logs, because right now the brown animals have the advantage of knowing the territory much better than we do."

"That's a good idea," Whitetail commented.

"And we have to remember that each Clan should fight to its strengths," Lionblaze added. "We—"

"I'm confident of my strength, Lionblaze," Toadfoot interrupted. "You just worry about yours."

Lionblaze held the ShadowClan warrior's gaze for a couple of heartbeats, but he didn't rise to the veiled challenge. Dovepaw was unnerved by the tension between the two cats, as well as the anxiety she could sense from the rest of the patrol. They couldn't argue now! More than ever, they needed to work together to free the water.

Whitetail took the lead as the cats crept out of the streambed and up a slope through the trees, circling around the fallen logs. She paused at the first of the lopped-off trees and gave it a curious sniff. "Big teeth," she murmured to Lionblaze, angling her ears toward the spiky top of the stump, where the jaw marks of the brown animals were clearly visible.

Lionblaze replied with a cautious nod, while Dovepaw's belly churned at the thought of those teeth meeting in her pelt. The scent of the brown animals was everywhere; Dovepaw had been aware of it before now, but the reek here was much stronger, a mixture of musk and fish.

"Hey, they smell a bit like RiverClan!" Tigerheart whispered with a playful gleam in his eyes.

"Don't let Rippletail or Petalfur hear you say that," Dovepaw warned him, in no mood for jokes.

Following Whitetail up the slope, she gradually became aware of something else up ahead. *Twolegs!* She nearly called out the word, but she realized that she would be in trouble again, trying to explain how she knew. *There are green pelt-dens, too, like the ones on the ShadowClan border.*

Putting on a spurt, she caught up to Whitetail and hissed, "I think I can scent Twolegs."

"Really?" The white she-cat halted and opened her jaws to taste the air. "Yes, I think you might be right." Turning to the rest of the patrol, she added, "Twolegs up ahead. Be careful."

The cats padded on more slowly, using the logs and stumps for cover. At the top, Whitetail signaled with her tail for the others to crouch down, and they crawled the last few tail-lengths on their bellies. Gazing out from the shelter of a clump of grass, Dovepaw made out several pelt-dens in the clearing ahead. A full-grown Twoleg was sitting outside the entrance to one of them, while two others were examining something on the ground a few fox-lengths away. There didn't seem to be any of the young Twolegs playing about, like the ones in the other clearing.

Just as well, Dovepaw thought with a sigh of relief.

"What do you think the Twolegs are doing here?" Ripple-tail asked, getting up to pad a little farther forward. "Do you think they have anything to do with the brown animals?"

"Maybe they've come to watch them," Petalfur guessed.

Around the edges of the open space were hard, black Twoleg things, with long black tendrils trailing along the ground. More of the Twolegs were gathered around them, muttering and occasionally touching the black things, which made sharp clicking sounds. Dovepaw bent down to lick one of the tendrils that was snaking past her, and jumped back at the bitter taste, which was similar to the stench on the Thunderpath.

"Hey, look!" Tigerheart padded up to her. "Some of those Twolegs have fur on their face! They look weird."

"Twolegs are weird," Toadfoot pointed out sourly from just behind him. "We don't have to go on about it."

"I wonder what they have in that den," Sedgewhisker murmured, peering around the trunk of a tree. "It smells so good!"

Dovepaw gave a long sniff, her nose twitching as she picked up the scent from the farthest pelt-den. It smelled like some sort of fresh-kill, though it was mixed up with Twoleg scents as well. Her belly rumbled. She was hungry enough to eat anything.

"I'm going to check it out," Sedgewhisker announced, bounding into the clearing toward the pelt-den.

"Hey, wait!" Whitetail called, but her Clanmate didn't reappear.

"I'll get her," Petalfur meowed, heading off in the Wind-Clan cat's paw steps.

"Now there are two of them in danger." Whitetail lashed her tail angrily.

Dovepaw watched, holding her breath. Sedgewhisker was heading straight for the pelt-den; Petalfur followed, but she was focused so closely on the WindClan warrior that she didn't spot the Twoleg moving toward her.

"Oh, no!" Dovepaw whispered. She didn't want to see what happened next, but she couldn't tear her gaze away.

The Twoleg yowled something, bent down, and scooped

up Petalfur in its huge paws. Petalfur let out a startled squeal and began wriggling, but the Twoleg held her firmly. The Twoleg was meowing something to her; Dovepaw didn't think it sounded hostile.

"I'll claw its ears off!" Toadfoot hissed, bunching his muscles to leap out into the clearing.

"No, wait." Lionblaze blocked the ShadowClan warrior with his tail. "Look."

Petalfur had stopped struggling. Instead, she pushed her face up to the Twoleg's, and batted gently at its ear with one paw. Dovepaw could hear her purring as the Twoleg stroked one paw down her back.

"I don't believe I'm seeing this," Tigerheart meowed gleefully. "Wait till I tell them back home."

The Twoleg put Petalfur down and made patting motions at her with its paws, as if it was telling her to stay where she was. Petalfur sat down, still purring. The Twoleg strode across to the pelt-den, passing Sedgewhisker, who was watching, frozen with horror, near the entrance.

The Twoleg ducked inside and reappeared a moment later with something in its paw; the Twoleg carried the object over to Petalfur and put it down in front of her. Petalfur picked it up and rubbed herself against the Twoleg's leg, then darted away, back to the edge of the clearing.

"What are you all staring at?" she demanded, dropping the thing the Twoleg had given her.

"Er . . . *you*, being so friendly with that Twoleg," Toadfoot replied.

"So?" Petalfur challenged him. "It got us out of trouble, didn't it? Oh, yuck!" she added, scraping herself against the nearest tree. "I'm going to stink of Twoleg for a moon!"

"I'm so sorry!" The undergrowth rustled as Sedgewhisker bounded up to them. "I didn't think they'd be bothered about us."

"No harm done," Lionblaze murmured, while Petalfur was still trying to get the Twoleg scent off. "But let's be a bit more careful from now on."

Dovepaw curiously sniffed the Twoleg thing. It smelled like fresh-kill, mixed with Twoleg scents and herb scents, and it was shaped like a fat twig. "I've never seen an animal like that before," she meowed.

"It must be Twoleg prey," Tigerheart suggested. "Hey, Petalfur, can I have some?"

"You all can," Petalfur replied. "I don't know what it is, but it smells tasty."

Dovepaw crouched down to eat her share. Petalfur was right; it was tasty and felt warm in her belly after the scant pickings that morning.

"Too bad there's no more," Tigerheart announced, swiping his tongue over his jaws and looking out into the clearing with a speculative gleam in his eyes.

"If you go out there, Tigerheart," Toadfoot growled, "I will personally shred your ears and feed them to the brown animals."

"I never said—"

"You didn't have to," Whitetail interrupted, sounding

concerned. "The Twolegs already know we're here, and that's bad enough without looking for trouble."

"I wouldn't worry." An unfamiliar voice spoke behind them. "The Twolegs are far more interested in the beavers."

Every cat spun around. Dovepaw found herself staring at a long-legged tom with shaggy brown fur. He looked them over with sharp yellow eyes, his gaze flicking from one cat to the next.

"So who are you?" he asked eventually.

"We could ask you the same thing," Toadfoot replied, his neck fur beginning to bristle. "And what do you know about these Twolegs?"

The cat seemed unimpressed with Toadfoot's show of hostility. "My name's Woody," he replied. "I've been getting food from the Twolegs for the last few moons."

With a warning glance at Toadfoot, Lionblaze stepped forward and dipped his head. "We haven't come to steal food from you or the Twolegs," he meowed. "We're here because of the blocked stream."

Woody's ears flicked up in surprise. "You mean the beavers?"

"Beavers?" Whitetail echoed. "Are those the brown animals? Is that what they're called?"

The loner nodded. "Big, mean animals with sharp teeth," he mewed, confirming the impression Dovepaw had received through her senses. "I came across some of them once before, when I was traveling."

"Have you ever fought one?" Toadfoot demanded.

The brown tom stared at him as if he had taken leave of his senses. "No way! Why would I need to? What do I want with a bunch of fallen trees?"

"We need the trapped water to fill the lake," Rippletail explained.

Woody looked completely baffled. "Lake? What lake?"

"The lake where we live," Lionblaze explained. "A couple of days' journey downstream."

"And you came all this way to find it?" Woody's ears twitched. "Why not just go to a different lake?"

Dovepaw examined the cat curiously. He didn't smell like a kittypet, and he didn't have the soft, groomed look that the cats in the Twolegplace had. Was he a loner? He seemed quite confident to be in these woods, even though he was badly outnumbered by the patrol. He seemed to know a lot about the brown animals, too. *Maybe he'll help us free the water.*

"You don't understand," Lionblaze replied to Woody, waving his tail to draw all the cats deeper into the undergrowth, well out of sight of the Twolegs. "There are a lot of us by the lake—far too many to give up our homes and find somewhere else to live."

"And StarClan told us to come here and find what's blocking the stream!" Tigerheart put in.

Mouse-brain! Dovepaw thought. *Woody won't understand about StarClan.* She was surprised to see that the brown tom just nodded briefly, as if he understood very well. *Maybe he's heard of Clan cats before?*

"We've got to chase these . . . these beavers away," Whitetail meowed determinedly. "Then we can get rid of the blockage and we'll have our water again."

Woody shook his head. "Bees in your brain," he muttered.

"Then you won't help us?" Lionblaze asked.

"I didn't say that. I'll take you down to the river and show you the dam—that's what they built to block the stream and make a pool deep enough for their den. You might change your mind when you've had a good look at it up close."

"Thanks," Rippletail purred; he was working his claws in the leaf-mold, as if he couldn't wait to get close to the sound and scent of water again.

"There'll be Twolegs around," Woody warned them, turning to lead the way down the hill. "But you don't need to worry about them. They're only interested in watching the beavers. In fact, the Twolegs brought them here."

"What?" Toadfoot halted, his jaws gaping in astonishment. "*Twolegs* brought them? In StarClan's name, why?"

Woody shrugged. "How do I know? Maybe they wanted some trees chopped down."

The brown tom led them around more of the black Twoleg things with the trailing tendrils, down into the valley, and across the dry streambed just below the wall of logs. This, then, was the beavers' dam; the reason the water had stopped flowing into the lake. Dovepaw looked up at the looming pile of tree trunks as she padded past. *It's so big! Can we really shift something that size?*

On the other side, Woody led them in a circle through the woodland until they approached the stream again. "There are no Twolegs on this side," he explained. "But watch out for the beavers. You won't be welcome here, you know."

He stopped halfway down the slope, in a patch of fallen trees, and the cats lined up beside him to stare across the trapped stream above the dam. It had overflowed the riverbank on this side and spread out into a wide, flat pool, reflecting the gray sky. Here and there circles appeared, spiraling outward as if a fish had risen to take a fly.

Toward the upstream edge of the pool was a mound of mud, twigs, and bark, jutting out from the bank but not blocking the stream like the dam. Dovepaw detected strong beaver scent coming from it.

"What's that?" Whitetail asked Woody, flicking her tail toward it.

"It's where the beavers live," the brown loner explained. "It's called their lodge, and they—"

"Oh, look!" Petalfur interrupted, her voice rising to the squeak of an excited kit. "So much water . . . it's wonderful!"

Before any cat could stop her she bounded down to the water's edge, with Rippletail hard on her paws, and she plunged in, splashing her paws rapturously and ducking her head under the water.

"They're like furry fish," Tigerheart grumbled, padding up to stand beside Dovepaw and Sedgewhisker. "Say what you like, it's not right for cats."

"They look as if they're having fun." Dovepaw felt a little wistful.

She was so busy watching the two RiverClan cats play in

the water that she stopped remaining alert to her surroundings. Suddenly she sensed movement on top of the dam. Spinning around, she saw that two heavy brown shapes had appeared on the logs. Their bodies were sleek and rounded like a bird's egg, with tiny black eyes and ears like furled leaves. Their tails spread out behind them, broad and flat like a solid wing. They were much bigger than a cat, and as broad and sturdy-looking as the logs that they stood on.

"Beavers!" she yowled. "Look—up there!"

"Oh, great StarClan!" Tigerheart muttered. His neck fur fluffed up and his tail bristled to twice its size. "They're *weird*!"

Still happily swimming in the pool, the RiverClan cats didn't notice the two animals, even when they clambered down the dam and slipped into the water, slapping the surface hard with their tails and sending up a shower of drops.

"Rippletail! Petalfur!" Dovepaw screeched, hurling herself down to the edge of the pool. "Beavers! Get out now!"

The beavers glided across the pool, their huge bodies making scarcely any ripples. Dovepaw could hear their paws churning through the water and felt their massive tails steering them toward the cats.

Rippletail and Petalfur spotted them and began splashing madly toward the edge of the pool. The beavers swerved effortlessly in pursuit, lifting their heads to avoid the waves behind the cats. Dovepaw dug her claws into the ground as she watched the gap between them grow smaller and smaller.

Oh, StarClan, help them!

The two RiverClan cats scrambled out of the water just ahead of the beavers' noses. Their fur was dripping and plastered to their sides, and their eyes were wild with fear.

"Run!" Lionblaze yowled.

Every cat bolted for the trees at the top of the slope. Glancing back, Dovepaw saw the beavers haul themselves out of the water, raising their muzzles and baring long yellow teeth. On land they were much clumsier than they were in the water; Dovepaw realized the cats could easily outstrip them if they gave chase.

But the beavers stayed where they were on the bank of the pool, gazing after the cats and not making any move to follow them. The patrol gathered close together under the trees, Petalfur and Rippletail shivering and shaking water from their pelts.

"That was close," Rippletail muttered. "Thanks for warning us."

"Oh, StarClan," Toadfoot breathed. "This isn't going to be as easy as we thought."

Dovepaw caught Lionblaze's gaze on her. He didn't speak, but she could guess what he was thinking.

Why didn't you tell us it was going to be this hard?

CHAPTER 19

❧

Lionblaze led the patrol away from the water and into the cover of denser trees. He could see his own shock reflected in the wide, scared eyes of his companions. The two RiverClan cats were still trembling, huddling close together, their gaze flickering down the side of the valley as if they expected beavers to burst out of the undergrowth at any moment.

Woody followed them and sat down with his tail wrapped around his paws. "Don't say I didn't warn you," he observed with a yawn.

Lionblaze drew a deep breath, knowing that if some cat didn't come up with a plan then they would all give up and go home. "Woody, do the beavers sleep at night?"

The loner shrugged. "I don't know. That's when I'm asleep, too. The Twolegs would know."

"Yes, but we can't ask them," Toadfoot snapped, curling his lips back from his teeth.

"At least the Twolegs won't be around when it's dark," Lionblaze meowed. "And the beavers *might* be asleep. I think that would be the best time to attack."

The air tingled with tension as the cats looked at one

another. Petalfur and Rippletail stared through the trees in the direction of the pool.

"That's *ours*," Rippletail murmured.

Lionblaze knew that they couldn't leave now. After they had come all this way, they had to do something to get the water back, for the sake of their Clans.

"Look," he began, scraping up a few twigs into a heap. "This is the dam. Here's the pool, and this"—he drew a long scrape in the earth—"is the streambed on the other side."

"We should divide ourselves up," Toadfoot mewed, touching the ground with one paw on each side of the heap of twigs. "Attack from two directions at once."

Lionblaze nodded. "Good idea. Once we're on top of the dam, we start to take it apart until the water can get through. Woody, do you know if the dam is hollow? Would the beavers be hiding inside it?"

Woody shook his head. "No idea. And don't think that *I'm* going to take part in this attack," he added. "This is your battle, not mine."

"We wouldn't ask you to," Lionblaze responded, though he felt a twinge of regret. Woody would be a valuable ally to have on their side.

"Okay, let's hunt now," Toadfoot suggested. "Then we'll get some rest until nightfall."

"But don't go off alone," Lionblaze warned. "And if you see a beaver, yowl to warn the rest of us."

He padded into the woods with Dovepaw at his side, and he halted after a few tail-lengths to taste the air. "I can't scent anything except beavers," he complained.

"Same here," Dovepaw meowed. "Look at this." She stopped in front of a large pile of mud mixed with twigs and grass. Large paw prints were set into the dried mud. "I wonder what it's for?"

Lionblaze padded up and gave it a cautious sniff, recoiling a pace or two at the strong reek of musky, fishy beaver scent. "Maybe it's a scent marker," he guessed. "If we get farther away from it, we might be able to pick up some prey."

To his relief, the beaver scent faded as they stalked farther into the woods and left the last of the felled trees behind. Lionblaze began to recognize the familiar scents of mouse and squirrel. Hearing a scuffling sound from underneath a bush, he pinpointed a mouse and glided up to it, careful to set his paws down lightly. The mouse tried to dart off at the last moment, but Lionblaze trapped it under his paw and killed it with a bite to the back of the neck.

"I've got one, too!" Dovepaw announced, trotting up with a mouse in her jaws.

Lionblaze scraped earth over the fresh-kill. "The hunting is much better here," he commented, pleased that they had found prey so quickly. "I suppose it's because the water is so near."

It didn't take much longer for him to catch a squirrel and Dovepaw to track down a couple more mice.

"I never knew hunting could be this easy," she mumbled around her mouthful of fresh-kill as they carried the prey back to the stream.

Lionblaze realized that Dovepaw had still been a kit when

the drought began. She'd never known what it was like to hunt when there was plenty of prey. "It'll be like this in the forest once we bring the water back," he promised.

Back in the undergrowth above the pool, they found that the other cats had all hunted well, and for once the patrol was full-fed when they settled down to sleep until nightfall.

"I'll keep watch," Dovepaw offered. Her eyes were wide and her whiskers quivered.

"No, you need to rest," Lionblaze told her. "*I'll* keep watch."

"But I don't think I'll be able to sleep," Dovepaw protested in a whisper, glancing at the rest of the patrol to make sure they couldn't overhear. "I can still hear the beavers, gnawing and scraping. . . ."

"Then block your senses like you did before," Lionblaze told her. "We know the beavers are here now, so we don't need you to be on the alert all the time." When she still looked unconvinced, he bent his head and gave her ear an approving lick. "You've done well, Dovepaw. You were right! The stream has been blocked by brown animals—and we can do something about that. When we defeat the beavers and release the water, the Clans will owe everything to you."

Dovepaw sighed. "I hope that's going to happen." Without arguing anymore she curled up; after a few moments Lionblaze realized she was asleep.

Wind ruffled the surface of the pool, sending clouds scudding across the waning moon. The woods were dappled with light and shadow as the patrol crept down to the water's edge.

Lionblaze halted at the edge of the pool; the dam looked even bigger and more threatening in the darkness, blotting out the stars behind the topmost logs. His belly churned. *Star-Clan, are you with us now? Do you even walk these skies?* He scanned the bank carefully in both directions and tasted the air, but he could see nothing moving, and the beaver scent clinging to everything was no help in telling him whether the beavers themselves were anywhere around. *With any luck, they're all asleep in that mudpile upstream.*

"Right," he whispered as the other cats gathered around him. "Dovepaw and I will cross the stream with Whitetail and Sedgewhisker. The rest of you stay on this side."

Toadfoot gave him a curt nod.

"We climb up onto the dam and pull the logs down," Lionblaze went on. "If the beavers try to stop us, we fight."

"Yes!" Tigerheart hissed, his eyes gleaming pale in the moonlight.

"Okay, let's go," Lionblaze mewed. He padded down to the bottom of the dry streambed and up the other side, with half of the patrol following closely. Now that the waiting was over, his worries had faded, replaced by a hard resolution. *This is the night when we get our water back!*

Once across the stream, Whitetail let out a yowl. It was answered by another yowl from Toadfoot on the far bank.

"Now!" Lionblaze growled.

He bounded down the slope and sprang onto the dam. A heartbeat later his paws skidded from under him and he slithered halfway down the pile of logs, barely saving himself from falling into the pool. Beside him, Dovepaw had slipped down to a lower branch; Lionblaze leaned over, grabbed her scruff, and hauled her up again.

"Be careful!" he gasped as he recovered his balance. "These logs are slippery."

He realized something that he hadn't noticed before: The beavers had gnawed all the bark off the tree trunks, leaving the shiny pale wood exposed. Whitetail was edging along one long trunk, setting her paws one in front of the other in a straight line and digging her claws in, while Sedgewhisker tried to jump, dislodged one log, and managed to scramble out of the way before it swept her into the pool.

Yowls and furious growling from the other side told Lionblaze that the rest of the cats were having the same trouble. *How can we destroy the dam if we can't even move around on it?*

He and Dovepaw were struggling to drag one log out of the pile when Lionblaze heard a splashing sound, followed by the heavy padding of paws. Every hair on his pelt lifted with horror as two beavers lurched up in front of him, their blackberry eyes and curved teeth gleaming in the moonlight.

"Oh, no . . ." Dovepaw muttered.

Lionblaze let out a yowl and hurled himself at the nearest beaver, slashing at its side as he sprang past it. To his dismay, his claws glanced harmlessly off its pelt, which felt thick and greasy, like mud. As he spun around, he saw both beavers heading for Dovepaw; the apprentice faced them bravely, leaping into the air as they rushed at her. She landed on the shoulders of the leader and cuffed him over the head and ears, but the beaver ignored her. Tossing its head, it shook her off as if she were a fly, sending her crashing into the logs.

The beavers slithered up to the top of the dam where Whitetail and Sedgewhisker were waiting, outlined against the sky. The she-cats' backs were arched and their fur was bristling as they let out caterwauls of defiance.

Lionblaze checked that Dovepaw was unhurt and left her scrambling to her paws while he flung himself back into the battle. When he reached the top of the dam, he saw one beaver swing on its forepaws and deal a massive blow to Sedgewhisker with its tail. The WindClan warrior let out a shocked yowl as she fell backward. In her fall she brushed against Whitetail, who sank her claws into the nearest log so she didn't follow her Clanmate.

Peering down into the darkness, Lionblaze spotted Sedgewhisker lying on the dry streambed below. She was moving, so he guessed she was just stunned; there was no time to go check. As he whirled to face the beavers again, Whitetail clambered up and stood at his side.

"Fox dung, I've torn a claw," she muttered.

One beaver had disappeared, but the other was coming at them; it reared up on its hind legs and let out a furious hiss. As it lunged forward, Lionblaze slipped to one side while Whitetail sprang at it from the other. The beaver's teeth slammed together a whisker's width from Lionblaze's ear; Whitetail managed to aim a slashing blow at its head before it could turn to face her.

"Well done!" Lionblaze gasped.

Briefly he spotted Dovepaw fleeing from the second beaver, leaping and scrambling across the slippery logs while the heavy animal lumbered after her. Lionblaze wanted to spring down to help her, but he was nearly knocked over by the slap of a flat tail as the beaver he was fighting turned on Whitetail.

"Lionblaze, help!" Whitetail screeched.

She lay sprawled on the logs; the beaver's vicious teeth were snapping at her throat. Lionblaze hurled himself at the creature's side; the impact felt as if he had tried to shift a tree, but he distracted the beaver for a heartbeat, enough for Whitetail to wriggle free, aiming a blow at their adversary's ear on the way.

This is hopeless! Lionblaze thought. *They're too strong for us! And where are the others?*

Scrambling out of range of the beaver, he reached the top of the dam and gazed across to the far side. His heart lurched when he saw the other four cats fighting for their lives against another pair of beavers at the bottom of the dam near the pool. As he watched, he saw Petalfur knocked off her paws and pitched backward into the water. She resurfaced, swimming strongly, but she was having trouble climbing out again onto the smooth logs.

Toadfoot and Tigerheart were fighting like a whole patrol, but these beavers were even bigger and stronger than the ones on the top of the dam. *We can't win,* Lionblaze realized, bitter failure sweeping over him. Glancing back, he spotted Whitetail with Dovepaw crouched just behind her, looking terrified but determined. Both the beavers were advancing on them, letting out their threatening hisses.

"Get back!" Lionblaze yowled. "Get back to the bank— climb a tree! I'm going to help the others!"

"No!" Dovepaw screeched back. "We're not leaving you!"

"I'll be okay!" Lionblaze fixed his eyes on his apprentice, hoping she would remember that he couldn't be killed in battle. "Now go!"

To his relief, Whitetail spun around and gave Dovepaw a push along the dam; both she-cats fled for the bank, scrambling over the logs, with Whitetail limping on three legs. There was still no sign of Sedgewhisker; Lionblaze assumed she was still lying stunned on the streambed.

Let's hope she stays there.

Lionblaze turned back to head for the opposite side of the dam and found himself face-to-face with the beavers; their eyes gleamed as they crept up on him.

"You think you're getting an easy victory?" Lionblaze taunted them, fluffing up his fur. "Think again!"

He hurled himself at the beavers, aiming for the narrow gap between them. As he slid through, helped on his way by their slimy pelts, he ducked his head to avoid their stabbing teeth and dodged from one side to another as they tried to claw him. He jumped over their tails as they swept around, trying to knock him off his feet, and then he was through. His sides felt battered, and as he landed he almost lost his balance and fell off the dam, but he managed to stay on his paws.

"See?" he yowled triumphantly. "Not a scratch on me!"

The words were scarcely out when he felt a heavy blow from behind, knocking his legs from under him. Another beaver had arrived, and it stood over him, its tiny front paws quivering as it lunged down to bite his neck.

Lionblaze rolled away, paws flailing as he slid down the side of the dam, ending up at the bottom, where Toadfoot and the others were still fighting.

"Retreat!" Lionblaze gasped. "It's over!"

"Not while I'm on my paws!" Toadfoot snarled, aiming a blow at a beaver that was trying to thrust him off the dam.

"Or me!" Tigerheart asserted through gritted teeth.

Lionblaze could see that both ShadowClan warriors were injured: Toadfoot had blood trickling from above his eye, while deep claw marks were scored across Tigerheart's pelt.

There was no time to argue. Lionblaze slid down to Petalfur, who was still trying to balance on the lowest logs, grabbed her by the scruff, and threw her onto the bank. He watched for a couple of heartbeats, until he saw her scrambling up the slope to safety. Then he glanced around for Rippletail. His heart slammed into his throat as he spotted the RiverClan warrior, who was cornered by the biggest beaver of all at the point where the dam met the bank. Rippletail was facing the creature defiantly, with teeth bared and claws extended, but Lionblaze could see that he didn't have a chance.

Just as he hurled himself at the beaver, the creature lunged forward. It fastened its long, cruel teeth in Rippletail's shoulder and tore a ragged wound; the RiverClan warrior let out a shriek of agony. Lionblaze flung himself at the beaver's head, digging his claws into its ears. The beaver let out a bellow of pain and backed off, its tail flailing at Lionblaze. Rippletail was able to slip past them, slither over the log where they were struggling, and plunge into the water.

"Help him get out!" Lionblaze screeched, clinging desperately to the beaver's head while it tried to slash his flank with its hind claws. He spotted Petalfur racing back down the slope.

"Rippletail! Rippletail!" she yowled.

Just then the beaver reared up and flicked Lionblaze off; he lay helplessly on the logs, struggling to catch his breath while the beaver bore down on him with glittering eyes and wicked teeth.

Then Toadfoot thrust himself between Lionblaze and the beaver; distracted, the creature turned to pursue the ShadowClan warrior. Toadfoot stood just out of range, snarling and batting at the beaver with his forepaws, until Lionblaze managed to scramble to his paws and flee.

Lionblaze and Toadfoot jumped off the dam and ran to the edge of the water, with Tigerheart hard on their paws.

Petalfur was crouched on the edge of the shore. "I'm going to help Rippletail," she yowled, launching herself into the water and swimming out to where her Clanmate was flailing. Lionblaze couldn't help remembering how happily the two RiverClan cats had played in the water the day before.

All five beavers were clustered together on top of the dam, watching the cats below. Lionblaze and Toadfoot turned to face them, ready to fight if they attacked again before Petalfur could rescue her Clanmate.

The RiverClan she-cat reached Rippletail, grabbed him by the scruff, and began towing him back to the bank. Meanwhile, Whitetail limped up to them from the streambed on the other side of the dam; her paw was bleeding heavily from where she had wrenched out her claw. Dovepaw and Sedgewhisker padded just behind her, with Sedgewhisker leaning on Dovepaw's shoulder; she still looked half-stunned from her fall off the top of the dam.

As Petalfur swam into the shallows with Rippletail, Lionblaze and Toadfoot waded out into the pool and helped her drag him onto the bank. The RiverClan tom was barely conscious; his paws wouldn't hold him up and his head drooped. Lionblaze and Toadfoot gripped his shoulders, while Dovepaw and Petalfur held up his hindquarters, and together they maneuvered him up the slope, back to the fern thicket where they had rested earlier. Whitetail and Sedgewhisker struggled up after them.

When they reached their makeshift shelter, Dovepaw tore up some bracken to make a nest, and the cats laid Rippletail down. The shoulder where the beaver had bitten him was bleeding heavily, the blood running down into his wet fur. Lionblaze felt his belly clench as he looked at the long, deep wound.

"We have to stop the bleeding," Dovepaw mewed. "Does any cat know the proper herbs?"

Lionblaze tried to think. *Surely Jayfeather must have said something, sometime, that would be useful now?* But between fear and exhaustion, he couldn't think.

"Rippletail was the cat who knew most about that." Petalfur's eyes were wide and frightened. "Mothwing gave him some training before we left."

Lionblaze's claws raked the ground in frustration. "Rippletail?" he hissed. "Rippletail, can you hear me?"

But the RiverClan warrior didn't respond. His eyes were closed now, and his breathing was shallow.

"Cobwebs stop bleeding," Whitetail meowed.

Dovepaw sprang to her paws. "I'll go find some." She plunged into the undergrowth.

Petalfur bent over her Clanmate, gently licking his wet fur as a mother would have cared for her kit. The rest of the cats watched in silence. *Oh, StarClan!* Lionblaze prayed. *Don't let him come to you yet.*

He looked up as a clump of bracken waved wildly, expecting to see Dovepaw returning, but instead it was Woody who stepped into the open, a vole dangling from his jaws. He gaped, dropping his prey, as his gaze fell on Rippletail, and his eyes stretched wide with horror.

"What happened?" he croaked.

"The beavers happened," Toadfoot replied tersely.

Woody padded up and gave Rippletail's wound a cautious sniff. "I can't believe you cats would put yourselves in such danger," he meowed.

"It's what we do." Lionblaze had to restrain himself from snarling at the loner. "The warrior code says that you must fight for your Clan to the death."

"In that case, you're fools," Woody snorted.

Tigerheart let out a snarl of fury and lunged at the loner. "Can't you see how brave this cat was?"

Woody whipped around to face him, sliding out his claws, but before Tigerheart could reach him Whitetail darted between them and thrust the young warrior back. "This won't help Rippletail," she pointed out.

As Tigerheart sat down, breathing hard and glaring at Woody, the bracken parted again and Dovepaw reappeared, hobbling along on three legs while she held up a pawful of cobweb.

"Thanks, Dovepaw." Petalfur took the cobweb and packed it into Rippletail's wound, but his blood quickly soaked it. His breathing had grown shallower still.

"His fur is burning," Petalfur whispered.

Lionblaze realized that the moon had set and the sky was growing pale with the approach of dawn. All the cats, even Woody, sat in silence around Rippletail, listening as his breathing grew fainter and more ragged. At last, as a golden line appeared on the horizon, it stopped.

Lionblaze bowed his head. Rippletail had been a young warrior, with so much to offer his Clan. And in the time that they had traveled together, Lionblaze had begun to think of him as a friend. The beaver had ripped all that away.

"He hunts with StarClan now," Toadfoot murmured; he reached out with his tail and touched Petalfur's shoulder.

Petalfur crumpled to the ground with a choking sound of grief. Whitetail and Sedgewhisker pressed close to her, one on each side, and the three she-cats huddled together beside Rippletail's body. Tigerheart looked on appalled, as if he couldn't believe that a warrior's life could end so quickly.

Dovepaw sprang to her paws and padded away, brushing blindly through the grass and ferns. Afraid that in her grief she wouldn't watch out for danger, Lionblaze followed and caught up to her at the top of the slope, above the huge mound of the dam. The beavers had vanished. Apart from a few scattered logs, there was no sign of the battle that had taken place there such a short time before.

Staring down at the dam, Dovepaw whispered, "We never should have come!"

CHAPTER 20

❧

What in the name of StarClan made her come all this way?

Jayfeather trudged up the rocky path toward the Moon-pool, following the scents of Poppyfrost and Breezepelt. His fur prickled as he thought how unlikely it was that the two of them would be together willingly.

What could he possibly want with her?

The sun had gone down, and the wind was rising, bringing with it the damp scent of rain. At last the drought seemed as if it could be coming to an end. *That's one good thing,* Jayfeather thought.

One last hard scramble brought him to the ring of thorn-bushes that surrounded the Moonpool. Pushing his way through, he padded down the spiral path, feeling once more the prints of the ancient Clan beneath his paws. Their whispers surrounded him, but Jayfeather was too intent on finding Poppyfrost to listen to them tonight.

With the endless gush of the waterfall in his ears, he reached the edge of the pool and picked up Poppyfrost's scent. The she-cat was sitting at the waterside a little farther around. She was alone; there was no sign of Breezepelt.

He's here somewhere. But where?

"Poppyfrost?" Jayfeather whispered.

He heard her gasp of surprise. "Jayfeather! Did you follow me?"

"Yes." *But I won't tell her another cat might have followed her as well.* "Your Clanmates are worried about you," he went on. "You shouldn't have come up here alone."

"My kits are fine," Poppyfrost responded, her voice dull and listless. "Is Berrynose worried about me?"

Jayfeather hesitated. He hadn't seen Berrynose before he left; for all he knew the cream-colored warrior was still unaware that his mate had disappeared.

"You don't need to answer," Poppyfrost went on bitterly. "Of course he isn't! He doesn't care about me. He's still in love with Honeyfern."

Jayfeather searched helplessly for the right words to say, but Poppyfrost went on at once, seeming to assume that he agreed with her.

"I wanted to see Honeyfern so much. I miss her more than I can say, and I don't blame *her* that Berrynose doesn't love me." Poppyfrost let out a shuddering sigh. "I always loved him, even when he was with Honeyfern. But I would never have tried to take him away from her! Then when she died, I thought he might love me after all . . . but he doesn't."

"You don't know—" Jayfeather began.

"Oh, yes, I do!" Poppyfrost flashed back at him. "You can tell from the way he behaves that he doesn't care about me at all. Why else would he want me to go into the nursery so early? He doesn't even want to see me in the warriors' den!"

Jayfeather was at a loss for how to reply. No cat could make Berrynose love Poppyfrost if he still wanted her dead sister, and trekking up here to the Moonpool wasn't going to help.

"I'm going to take you home," he meowed. "Remember I brought you home once before from a forest you visited in your dreams?"

Poppyfrost was silent for a moment; Jayfeather could feel the memories stirring in her mind, flickering like starlight on water.

"Yes, I remember," she murmured, her voice scarcely audible above the sound of the waterfall. "I was sick, wasn't I? But I didn't really leave the stone hollow. So where was that forest?" She caught her breath, and her voice strengthened as she went on. "It was StarClan, wasn't it? I was dying, and you saved my life!"

"Yes, that's what happened," Jayfeather mewed. "And I've come to help you again."

He heard Poppyfrost rise to her paws and pad around the Moonpool until she was standing in front of him, her scent strong in his nose.

"If I went to StarClan once and came back, I can go there again! Please!" Jayfeather could feel her body tremble with longing. "I want to see Honeyfern. I want to tell her that I didn't mean to take Berrynose from her. Oh, Jayfeather, what if she hates me, too?"

Jayfeather stifled a sigh. "That's not possible," he began. "Warriors can't just stroll in and out of StarClan. I would have to hurt you or make you sick, and medicine cats can't—"

He broke off at the sound of a soft pad of footsteps from the edge of the hollow. Breezepelt's voice echoed coldly off the stone. "What's this? Another dilemma for ThunderClan? You cats should really learn to control your emotions, you know. Now you'll just have more kits who should never have been born," he added.

"Breezepelt!" Poppyfrost sounded shocked. "What are you doing here?"

"That's not very friendly." The WindClan cat's voice was soft. "The Moonpool isn't ThunderClan territory, you know."

"Leave us alone," Jayfeather snapped, trying to conceal the fear that was trickling like icemelt down his spine. "We don't need you here."

"Oh, I think you do." The soft voice was drawing closer. "I'm willing to help Poppyfrost get to StarClan, even if you're not."

Jayfeather gulped, picking up a wave of fear and bewilderment from Poppyfrost, as if the young she-cat couldn't understand why the WindClan warrior was threatening her. "Don't be ridiculous," he meowed. "You won't kill her, not when I'm here."

"Oh, really?" Breezepelt snarled; he was only about a tail-length away now. "And you, a blind medicine cat, think you can stop me, do you? When her body is found drowned in your precious pool, it'll be your word against mine. I was never here tonight. My Clanmates can lie as well as yours, Jayfeather."

Poppyfrost let out a gasp. Jayfeather stepped in front of her, guarding her from Breezepelt. The waves of hatred coming from his half brother were almost enough to knock him off his paws—and he realized that Breezepelt would do anything to punish him for being born.

"Your quarrel is with me, Breezepelt," he growled. "Let Poppyfrost go."

Breezepelt gave a snort of contempt. "Sending you to Star-Clan isn't enough of a punishment. You need to know what it's like to have every cat in your Clan stare at you, whisper about you. You need to know that you're surrounded by lies and hatred and things that should never have happened."

"You think we *don't* know that?" Jayfeather challenged him. "The worst of the lies were told about us. We didn't even know who our real parents were."

For a heartbeat he felt the force of Breezepelt's hatred falter. But the moment did not last.

"Don't try to talk your way out of this," Breezepelt hissed. "You're nothing but a coward."

StarClan help me! Jayfeather thought, knowing there was only one way forward. Unsheathing his claws, he sprang at Breezepelt. He felt the WindClan cat's surprise as he was bowled over; Jayfeather landed on top of him and battered at his neck and ears, ripping his claws down his pelt.

Breezepelt let out a yowl of pain and fury. But Jayfeather knew that he couldn't hope to win a fight against a seasoned warrior. The WindClan cat threw him off and flipped him over onto his back. Holding him down with one paw, Breezepelt landed several hard blows on Jayfeather's belly. Wriggling in a vain attempt to escape, Jayfeather realized dully his adversary was keeping his claws sheathed.

He's playing with me. He'll finish me off when he's ready.

Poppyfrost's terrified wail came close to Jayfeather's ear. "Stop it! You can't kill a medicine cat!"

"Watch me," Breezepelt growled.

Poppyfrost aimed a blow at his shoulder, but she was heavy with her kits and clumsy; Jayfeather could tell the blow had no force behind it.

"Get out of here!" he gasped as another blow to his belly winded him. "Think of your kits!"

Poppyfrost backed away, whimpering, but she didn't try to leave.

In the next heartbeat Breezepelt sprang away from Jayfeather, who scrambled, half-dazed, to his paws. Standing still, he tried to locate the WindClan cat, but between pain and fear he was losing control of his senses.

Then Breezepelt leaped back in front of him, lashing out with his paws, claws still sheathed as he just brushed Jayfeather's ears and muzzle. "Go on, see if you can hit me!" he taunted.

Jayfeather sprang forward, but before he reached the WindClan cat a heavy weight landed on him from behind and claws raked across his shoulders.

Another cat? Oh, great StarClan, no!

Remembering his battle training, Jayfeather let himself go limp, flopping down on the edge of the pool with the strange tom crushing him down. He lashed out with all four paws, clawing frantically at the other cat's belly.

Who is it? How many cats want to kill me?

The newcomer's scent was all around him, but Jayfeather didn't recognize it. The tom didn't belong to WindClan, or to any of the other Clans. *But he's not a rogue or a loner. I ought to recognize that scent, but I don't.*

The unknown tom's weight suddenly vanished; Jayfeather struggled to his paws, only to stagger as a massive paw swiped him toward the pool. Breezepelt blocked him and shoved him back; for a few heartbeats the two cats batted Jayfeather between them like a pair of kits playing with a ball of moss.

Poppyfrost was still hovering close by. "Breezepelt, don't!" she pleaded. "StarClan will be angry if you kill a medicine cat."

"Like I care!" Breezepelt snarled.

Yowling in fury, Jayfeather tried to lash out, but his blows were too wild and uncontrolled to do any damage. He felt blood start to trickle from one shoulder as Breezepelt scratched him.

They're getting tired of this. They'll finish me off soon.

He was close to keeling over with exhaustion when he felt another cat leap down beside him. His last hope died at the thought of yet another enemy attacking him. Then he heard a startled screech from Breezepelt, and he realized that the latest arrival had sprung at the WindClan cat, driving him back.

"Hi, Jayfeather," the new cat hissed through clenched teeth. "Having trouble?"

"Honeyfern!" Jayfeather gasped.

The StarClan warrior's scent wreathed around him as she jumped back to his side. The massive tom bore down on them again; this time Jayfeather slashed with rapid blows at his ears, while Honeyfern dealt the WindClan warrior a hard blow to the belly.

Jayfeather heard a furious growl coming from the unknown cat as he backed off.

"Get away!" Honeyfern snarled. "You're not wanted here! And as for you, Breezepelt—" She swung around to face the WindClan cat again. "You get out of here, too. Or do you want a couple of shredded ears?"

"You might have won this time," Breezepelt spat. "But don't think this is over, Jayfeather, because it's not."

Jayfeather heard his paws retreating up the spiral path; his scent faded. Breathing hard, Jayfeather turned to Honeyfern and realized that he could see her. She was sitting at the edge of the pool, with starlight shimmering in her pale tabby fur. Rows and rows of starry cats had appeared behind her, clustering around the Moonpool and up the sides of the hollow. Jayfeather didn't dare look at them too closely, in case he saw Hollyleaf among them. Or didn't—which might mean she was somewhere much, much worse.

Instead, he padded up to Honeyfern. "Thank you," he panted. "I thought I was going to join you in StarClan for sure."

Honeyfern twitched her tail. "It isn't your time yet, Jayfeather," she replied. "You still have much to do." Stretching forward, she gave his ear a friendly lick. "Thank you for saving my sister."

"Can she see you?" Jayfeather asked, with a glance at Poppyfrost, who was crouched a little way up the spiral path.

Honeyfern shook her head sadly. "Please tell her that I miss her just as much as she misses me. And I will love her kits as if they were my own." Her eyes glowed with love and sympathy as she went on. "Berrynose does love her. He's just scared of losing her as he lost me. I am watching over both of them."

Dipping her head once more, she melted back into the crowd of starry warriors. Another cat came forward, her tousled fur like smoke in the starlight.

"Yellowfang," he sighed.

"I know who was helping Breezepelt," the former medicine cat told him, without wasting time on any greetings.

"You do? Who was it?"

Yellowfang blinked her amber eyes. "You don't need to know that yet. But his presence is a sign of great trouble to come."

Jayfeather's belly twisted. "What do you mean?"

"Honeyfern fought beside you today," Yellowfang meowed. "And so will every warrior of StarClan when their turn comes. But the empty hearts of our enemies have filled up with hatred and hunger for revenge, and that gives them strength that cannot be measured."

Jayfeather stared at her in horror.

"The forces of the Dark Forest are rising." Yellowfang's voice vibrated with foreboding. "I am afraid that it will take a power greater than StarClan to defeat them."

CHAPTER 21

❧

Lionblaze and Toadfoot lowered Rippletail's body into the hole they had scraped out under an oak tree. Beyond the undergrowth, Dovepaw could just make out the pool behind the dam, glittering in the morning sunlight. She hoped that Rippletail's spirit was down there now, swimming and fishing just as he had wanted to.

Rage burned like a slow fire in her belly. *Rippletail shouldn't have died on this journey!* She wanted revenge on the beavers now, wanted it like a starving cat longed for a bite of fresh-kill. *We have to destroy the dam! The water belongs to the Clans!*

As she stepped up to the edge of the grave and began to push soil and leaf mulch down onto Rippletail's body, she paused to listen to the beavers. They were moving around quietly inside the lodge, and she imagined them smug and gleeful because they'd chased off the cats in such an easy victory.

Lionblaze's voice distracted her from her thoughts. "We can't fight the beavers again."

"I told you so," Woody muttered from where he sat on one of the oak tree's gnarled roots.

Lionblaze flicked an ear to show the loner he had heard, but he didn't reply. "We need to find a different way to free the water," he went on.

Petalfur looked up from covering her Clanmate's body. Her eyes were still stunned with grief, but her voice was hard and determined. "We could try luring the beavers away."

"And then what?" Toadfoot asked.

"Then we destroy the dam," Petalfur replied.

"But it's huge!" Tigerheart objected. "It would take days. We can't keep the beavers away for that long."

"We don't have to destroy it all." Petalfur sounded confident. "If we can move enough of the top branches that the water spills over, the force of the stream will wash the rest of the logs away."

Dovepaw nodded. "I see," she mewed. She supposed that a RiverClan cat would know what she was talking about when it came to water. She cast her senses as far as the dam, feeling for the way the trunks and branches were woven together, and she realized that Petalfur's idea might work.

"We must do it quickly," Whitetail put in, with a glance up at the sky. "The weather is going to break soon, and besides"— her gaze flickered to Petalfur—"we need to get back to our Clans to tell them what's happened."

"That's true," Lionblaze agreed.

"I know what we can do!" Tigerheart was looking around the clearing. "Let's practice moving these fallen branches. If we figure how to do that without losing our balance, we'll be able to dismantle the dam much quicker."

Toadfoot gave his Clanmate a nod of approval. "Good idea."

Dovepaw was impressed, too. Tigerheart could be annoying

sometimes, but she had to admit he wasn't stupid.

When they had finished filling in Rippletail's grave, the Clan cats scattered through the clearing and began trying to lift the branches. To Dovepaw's surprise, Woody went to help Petalfur. "I shouldn't have let you attack the beavers," he muttered as he stood beside her and helped her roll a moss-covered log. "I should have known they were too strong for you. I'm sorry."

"It's not your fault, Woody," Whitetail called to him. Petalfur said nothing, just concentrated on rocking the heavy branch onto its side.

Dovepaw followed Lionblaze across the clearing to a lightning-split tree trunk lying on the ground. Shock slashed through her when she saw that he was limping. "Are you okay?" she asked.

Lionblaze nodded. "I don't get hurt in battles, remember?" he hissed. "But I can't let the others know that."

Dovepaw sighed. "I wish we didn't have to keep everything a secret."

"It's for their own good." Lionblaze turned to face her, pinning her with his compelling amber eyes. "They have to let us help them, and they might not do that if they think we're different."

Dovepaw glanced over her shoulder at the other cats, who were spread out over the clearing, struggling with logs. *Would they really be afraid of me if they knew what I can do? Probably,* she decided sadly. *After all, if I hadn't sensed the beavers, we would never have come, and Rippletail would still be alive.*

She and Lionblaze began to roll the log; it was heavy, and

the grass growing up around it made it hard to shift.

"Let's try flipping it over," Lionblaze suggested. "You go to that end, and I'll lift it up from here."

"Okay." Dovepaw gave the log a doubtful glance. *It's so big! And some of the logs on the dam are even bigger!*

She watched as Lionblaze thrust his paws under one end of the log and started to heave it upward. "I'm going to push it up from this end," he hissed through gritted teeth. "You keep it steady, then push from your end and it should go over."

Dovepaw tried to get a grip on the log, but as soon as it started to move, her paws slipped; the log banged her chin as it dropped to the ground again. "Sorry," she puffed. "Let's try again."

But the second attempt was no better. This time the log rolled over toward Dovepaw, and she barely saved her paws from being crushed as she sprang backward.

Lionblaze lashed his tail in frustration. "I can't move it on my own," he snarled, though Dovepaw knew that he was more angry with himself than he was with her. "It's too heavy."

"This isn't going to work, is it?" Dovepaw jumped, startled to see that Toadfoot had padded over to them. "We'll need at least three cats to lure the beavers away," he went on, flopping down beside the log with a tired sigh. "That leaves just five to dismantle the dam, even if Woody helps. We'll never do it."

Dovepaw glanced across the clearing to see that all the others had given up trying to shift the logs and branches. They looked exhausted, especially Petalfur, whose eyes were still dark with grief for her Clanmate.

This is hopeless! What are we going to do?

Lionblaze rose to his paws. "We can't give up now," he growled. "We need help."

"But that's mouse-brained," Whitetail protested. "We can't go all the way back to the lake to fetch more cats. It's too far. We need water now!"

"There are cats who can help us much closer than that," Lionblaze reminded them with a flick of his tail.

Toadfoot's eyes stretched wide with astonishment. "You mean the kittypets?"

Lionblaze nodded. "It's worth a try. We only need to go downstream as far as that Twoleg nest with the rabbits."

"Yeah, but . . . they're kittypets," Tigerheart pointed out.

Whitetail murmured in agreement. "If you go looking for them and they won't come, then we've wasted time."

"That's the risk we take," Lionblaze responded.

Dovepaw's belly churned. *If the rest of the patrol won't agree, what can Lionblaze do?*

After a few heartbeats, Sedgewhisker broke the silence. "I think we have to try," she mewed. "We owe it to Rippletail."

Petalfur nodded. "I don't want to think that he died for nothing."

The cats looked at one another, and Dovepaw knew that all of them were grieving for Rippletail, regardless of their Clan.

"Then go for it," Toadfoot meowed. "I can't think of anything better."

"Right." Lionblaze pricked his ears. "Dovepaw, you can come with me. The rest of you, keep practicing. We'll be back as soon as we can."

Dovepaw followed her mentor as he raced down the slope to the pool and leaped down into the streambed below the dam. As she followed him along the pebbly channel, she realized that her pads had grown tough and hard from their long journey. She didn't even feel any pain when she trod on a sharp-edged stone.

The day was approaching sunhigh by the time they reached the copse where they had stopped to hunt. Lionblaze slowed his pace. "Snowdrop followed us here," he mewed. "Maybe she comes here often. Dovepaw, can you sense her?"

Dovepaw was already feeling confused by the sounds of the Twolegplace: monsters, Twolegs yowling, and the strange, harsh clatter of their lives. She longed to block it out as she had done before, concentrating just on the ground in front of her paws and the leaves rustling closest to her, but this time she knew she couldn't. She had to listen to everything, take in all the information that was filtering through her ears and her nose and her paws, until they found the cats. She cast out her senses, searching in particular for Snowdrop, but she couldn't pick up any trace of the white kittypet.

"Never mind," Lionblaze told her. "She's probably by those rabbits, or inside the Twoleg nest."

As they trotted downstream, Dovepaw soon picked up the scent of rabbit, and the two cats climbed out of the stream at the end of the Twoleg territory. The rabbits were still nibbling the grass behind their shiny fence, but there was no sign of the kittypets. Dovepaw couldn't pick up anything except a fading scrap of Jigsaw's scent.

"Where have they gone?" she wailed. "I thought they lived here."

Lionblaze's eyes reflected her own anxiety. "I thought this part would be easy," he muttered. He hesitated, then added, "They probably see the whole of this Twolegplace as their territory. Do you think you can find where they are?"

Dovepaw's belly lurched. *Three kittypets? In a place as big and noisy as this?* But she had found the beavers—and now she realized that she could do this, too. She had to use her senses again to make their journey worth Rippletail's loss. "I'll try."

Crouching down, she closed her eyes and let her senses range out through the Twolegplace. This territory was so unlike anything she'd seen before that at first she had only a very fuzzy idea of what lay between the Twoleg nests. Gradually she began to build up a picture of rows and rows of nests, with Thunderpaths between them, the roar of monsters echoing off the hard red walls. Twolegs were running and shouting and carrying things around. . . .

"The kittypets!" Lionblaze hissed urgently into her ear. "You're looking for the kittypets."

Dovepaw flung herself back into the swirling chaos of the Twolegplace. This time she slowed down, listening at each corner, letting the images fill her mind until she could see the smallest details: the shadows of leaves on the dark green bushes, the wide pink faces of Twoleg kits, the gleam of sleeping monsters.

Cats. You're looking for cats. . . . There's one!

Dovepaw picked up the whisk of a tail, the sound of paw steps scrabbling up a wall and down onto some grass. Carefully focusing, she let her senses follow it and tasted the scent.

No, it's not one of the kittypets we met. Too young and skittish.

As her senses reached out again, a meow a little farther away caught her attention. *That sounds familiar. . . .* Tracing the sound, she spotted Seville, the big ginger tom, calling out to Jigsaw as he basked in the sun. *And Jigsaw is . . .* Dovepaw heard the scrape of claws on wood, and she knew the fat black-and-brown tom was balancing on a fence above Seville.

"I've found them!" she exclaimed joyfully. Opening her eyes wide, she gazed at Lionblaze. "Come on!"

Taking the lead, she padded along the edge of the stream, past the place with the rabbits, until they reached a narrow path leading between two of the Twoleg nests. Dovepaw's fur bristled as she emerged onto a Thunderpath; the reek of monsters and the noise of Twolegs in their dens flooded over her until all she wanted to do was turn tail and run back to the forest to stuff leaves into her ears and nose.

The growl of a monster sounded from farther down the Thunderpath. Dovepaw leaped back, crashing into Lionblaze. "Sorry!" she gasped as the sleek, brightly colored monster swept past. "I don't know if I can do this."

"Yes, you can." Lionblaze pushed his nose into her shoulder fur. "You can do it for the Clans. Now, do we have to cross this Thunderpath?"

Dovepaw nodded. Her heart was thumping so hard she thought it would burst out of her chest as her mentor nudged her gently to the edge of the hard black strip.

"When I say run, run," he instructed her. He looked carefully both ways, his ears pricked for the sound of monsters, then raised his tail. "Run!"

Biting back a yowl of terror, Dovepaw launched herself forward. Her pads skimmed the surface of the Thunderpath; then she was safely across, shivering as she pressed herself into the shelter of a hedge.

"Well done!" Lionblaze purred. "Now where do we go?"

Pull yourself together! Dovepaw told herself fiercely. "This way." She led Lionblaze along the edge of the Thunderpath, slipping behind a tree to hide as a slow-moving monster prowled past. "Do you think it's looking for us?" she whispered.

Lionblaze shrugged. "I doubt it. But no cat knows what monsters are thinking."

Turning away from the Thunderpath, following her sense of Seville's and Jigsaw's presence, Dovepaw found herself in a maze of narrow paths between walls of red stone and high wooden fences. As she rounded a corner, she almost stepped on a sleeping kittypet; the black tom sprang up, hissing, and leaped onto a fence before vanishing into the next garden.

Dovepaw let out a gusty breath of relief, then jumped, startled by the sound of a dog barking behind the fence on the other side.

"It's okay," Lionblaze mewed, though Dovepaw saw that his neck fur was bristling. "It can't get at us."

"I hope you're right," Dovepaw muttered.

The crisscrossing paths didn't seem to lead anywhere. *Have*

I gotten us lost? Dovepaw wondered. Then, where two paths crossed, she scented the sharp tang of chopped grass and spotted a bush with strong-smelling red flowers. *Yes! I've scented those before . . . and I remember that pattern of shadows the bush is casting on the path.*

"We need to go around this corner," she explained to Lionblaze over her shoulder as she quickened her pace. "Now over this wall . . ."

She leaped up, with her mentor beside her, and down onto a square of smooth green grass. Seville was basking at the foot of the fence on the other side.

"Hi, Seville!" Dovepaw called, racing across the grass to touch noses with the big orange tom.

Seville's green eyes widened with surprise. "It's the journeying cats!" he meowed. "What are you doing here? Did you find the animals you were looking for? Did you free the water?"

"We found the animals," Lionblaze told him. "But we can't free the water. We . . . we need help."

"Do you mean *our* help?" a voice called from above. "Wow!"

Dovepaw looked up to see Jigsaw perched on top of the fence, his black-and-brown tabby pelt almost hidden in the shade of a holly tree. He jumped down, his fur fluffing up as he touched noses with Dovepaw and then Lionblaze.

Seville blinked, his eyes wary as he looked from Lionblaze to Dovepaw and then back again. "What exactly do you mean?" he rumbled.

"Do you know where Snowdrop is?" Lionblaze asked, avoiding the question. "We looked for you at the place with the rabbits, but we couldn't find any of you."

"I'm the only one who lives there," Jigsaw explained. "Snowdrop's housefolk live on the other side of that birch tree." He pointed with his tail at a tall tree over a wooden fence. "How did you find us?" he added, narrowing his eyes.

"Oh, it was easy," Lionblaze replied. "We're Clan cats, remember." He shot an amused glance at Dovepaw.

"Wow!" Jigsaw's eyes gleamed. "I'll go get Snowdrop for you," he offered. "She'll kill us if she misses a chance to help real wild cats." Without waiting for a reply, he scrambled up to the top of the fence and disappeared.

Seville stretched, gesturing with his tail to the patch of sun-warmed grass beside him. "Lie down and rest," he invited the Clan cats. "It's lovely and sunny here."

"We've had enough sun lately, thanks," Lionblaze replied.

He turned to gaze out over the garden, clearly keeping watch for dogs and Twolegs, while Dovepaw tore at the grass with her front claws. Several moons seemed to pass before Jigsaw plopped down beside them, with Snowdrop following.

"Hi there!" the white she-cat greeted them, running up to Lionblaze to touch his ear with her nose. "It's great to see you again." Suddenly she backed off a pace, her lip curling as if she'd scented something foul. "You're not going to make me eat fur and bones, are you?"

"No," Lionblaze mewed. "We've come to ask for your help."

"Great!" Snowdrop purred. "What do you want us to do?"

"We can fight, watch!" Jigsaw added. He leaped at

Snowdrop, trying to wrap his forepaws around her neck. Snowdrop reared up on her hind paws and lost her balance as she aimed a blow at Jigsaw's ear. Both cats toppled over onto the grass in a heap of fur.

Seville rolled his eyes.

"Er . . . that's great," Lionblaze meowed. "But we don't need you to fight, actually. We need you to dismantle a dam."

Snowdrop sat up, shaking scraps of grass off her pelt. "What's a dam?"

Lionblaze described the huge mound of logs blocking the stream. "We fought the beavers, but they were too strong for us," he explained. "So some of us are going to lure them away while the rest take the dam apart and free the water."

Jigsaw blinked. "Will it be dangerous?"

Lionblaze nodded. "Yes," he mewed.

The black-and-brown tabby's eyes gleamed brighter still. "Good! We're awfully bored, lying around here all day."

Dovepaw's conscience pricked her like a thorn in her pad. "This isn't going to be fun," she warned the kittypets. "A—a cat died."

Snowdrop gasped and Jigsaw's neck fur stood on end.

"But we won't be fighting the beavers again," Lionblaze reassured them, with a glare at his apprentice.

Dovepaw met his gaze. "We can't ask them to come with us unless they know what might happen." *But what if they don't come?* she asked herself anxiously. *What will we do then?*

"We'll come, won't we, Jigsaw?" Snowdrop meowed.

Jigsaw nodded, though he looked less certain.

Seville let out a grunt and rose to his paws, arching his back in a long stretch. "I can't let you young 'uns go off on your own," he growled. "Who knows what you might get up to? I'll come, too."

"Thank you," Dovepaw mewed. "Our Clans thank you."

"Follow us." Jigsaw bounced on his paws. "We know a quick way back to the stream."

Dovepaw was amazed at how confident the kittypets were as they traveled through the Twolegplace. When they came to a Thunderpath, Jigsaw jumped right over a sleeping monster, leaving dusty pad marks on its gleaming snout. Seville and Snowdrop followed, then turned to wait for the Clan cats on the other side of the Thunderpath.

"Come on!" Seville called. "I thought you were in a hurry!"

Lionblaze gave Dovepaw a sidelong look. "Are we going to let those kittypets think we're scared of monsters?"

"No way," Dovepaw replied. *Even if we are!*

Lionblaze bunched his muscles and leaped up onto the monster's hindquarters. Dovepaw followed, trying not to flinch as her pads struck the smooth, hot surface. She jumped onto its back, then down onto its snout. In a heartbeat, she was on the ground, panting with relief. Glancing back once she reached the other side of the Thunderpath, she realized that the monster hadn't woken up, even after five cats had leaped over it.

Maybe monsters are stupid.

By now Dovepaw was completely lost, but she didn't have time to stop and sense the direction they should be going. Then she spotted a line of trees, and through them the streambed.

They emerged from the maze of the Twolegplace a few fox-lengths upstream from the place with the rabbits.

"Which way now?" Seville asked.

"Just keep following the stream," Lionblaze replied. He took the lead, picking up the pace until he was racing up the channel.

"Hey, take it easy," Jigsaw protested, wincing as he held up a paw. "These stones are sharp."

"Okay, sorry." Lionblaze slowed to a steady trot.

Dovepaw brought up the rear to make sure that none of the kittypets was falling behind. She could feel the tension rising as they drew closer to the dam—not just from the kittypets, from the air itself, as if something huge was about to happen. Above them, clouds were piling up in the sky, covering the sun, and a claw scratch of lightning flickered on the horizon. As they padded through the copse, Dovepaw could see how spooked the kittypets were, jumping whenever the branches rattled in the rising wind.

Putting on a spurt, she caught up to Jigsaw and fell into step beside him. "Are you okay?"

The tom's only reply was a tense nod.

I hope that's true, Dovepaw thought. Guilt and fear squirmed beneath her fur.

Oh, StarClan, am I taking more cats into a battle from which they'll never return?

CHAPTER 22

Lionblaze jumped up onto the bank of the stream and turned to look back down at his ragged patrol. Seville, Snowdrop, and Jigsaw were standing with their mouths wide open as they stared up at the dam.

"That's seriously *huge!*" Jigsaw breathed.

Snowdrop blinked at Lionblaze. "You really think we can move that?"

Lionblaze nodded, trying to hide his own doubts and give the kittypets confidence. "With all of us working together, yes, I do."

"Come on," Dovepaw urged them, leaping up to stand beside Lionblaze. "Let's go find the others."

Lionblaze led the way up the slope and into the clearing where he had left the other Clan cats. Pushing through the undergrowth into the open, he halted, eyes wide with surprise at the sight of a pile of logs in the middle of the clearing. Sedgewhisker was just heaving a branch onto the top of the stack, before leaping lightly down.

"Hi, you're back," she panted.

"I figured if we could stack branches, we could work out how to pull them apart," Toadfoot explained, padding over to meet Lionblaze. His pelt was covered with scraps of twig and bark and he was breathing hard.

"Good idea," Lionblaze meowed admiringly. "You're doing a great job."

At the opposite side of the clearing Petalfur was dragging a branch that was far, far bigger than she was. She didn't stop until she reached the stack of logs and pushed her branch up to the foot of it. Then she limped wearily across the clearing to join Lionblaze and the others; her eyes as she gazed at the new arrivals were old and full of determination.

As Tigerheart and Whitetail trotted up with Woody, Lionblaze began to introduce the kittypets.

"I'm not a Clan cat," Woody explained. "I'm just passing through."

"I think I've seen you before, in the woods," Seville meowed; he looked relieved to meet a cat who was even slightly familiar.

"We've got to discuss the plan," Toadfoot announced as soon as the introductions were over. "We need to decide—"

"Hunt first," Whitetail interrupted with a flick of her tail. "We can't do this if we don't eat and rest for a bit."

Toadfoot looked briefly offended at being contradicted, then gave the WindClan she-cat a nod. "Okay," he agreed. "But we'd better be quick about it."

To Lionblaze's relief, there was still plenty of prey in the woods, and it wasn't long before the cats had gathered in the clearing again, crouching to eat their catch.

"We've already eaten, thanks," Seville mewed when Whitetail offered him a mouse.

Snowdrop drew back, her green eyes wide with horror, but

Jigsaw looked cautiously interested, and he leaned over to sniff the squirrel Dovepaw had caught.

"Go on, take a bite," she encouraged him.

Jigsaw hesitated, then buried his teeth in the squirrel and tore off a mouthful.

"What do you think?" Dovepaw asked as he gulped it down.

"Er . . . not bad," the tabby tom replied. "Just a bit . . . fluffy."

Night was falling by the time the cats had finished eating. The moon shone fitfully from behind drifting banks of cloud, and the air felt damp and heavy.

"I think Whitetail and Sedgewhisker should be the ones to lure the beavers away," Lionblaze began as the rest of the cats clustered around him beneath the trees.

"Why?" The tip of Whitetail's tail twitched. "We're not scared to work on the dam." Sedgewhisker nodded.

"Because WindClan cats are the fastest runners," Toadfoot replied. "We all have to do what we're best at."

"Oh . . . okay." Whitetail looked satisfied.

"I'll come with you," Woody meowed. "I know these woods. We'll start off from the beavers' lodge, and then go this way. . . ." Picking up a twig in his jaws, he traced a line in the leaf-mold to represent the stream, and then a winding route through the trees. "There's plenty of cover; they'll have no idea what's happening back at the dam," he added, dropping the twig.

"That's great, Woody," Lionblaze told him.

"We'll distract the beavers for as long as we possibly can," Whitetail mewed.

"And if they do decide to come back, I'll run ahead and warn you," Sedgewhisker added.

Lionblaze nodded, with a sideways glance at Dovepaw. *She can use her senses to track the beavers, too.*

"So what about the dam?" Tigerheart prompted. "Once the beavers are out of the way—what then?"

"We'd be better off tackling it from the other side," Lionblaze meowed. "That way we'll be even farther from the beavers."

"That's a good idea," Petalfur agreed. "And I've been thinking. Look at this." She pointed with her paw to a small pile of twigs. "It's easiest to knock the top logs off the dam"—she demonstrated by swiping at the topmost twig with a claw—"but if we can somehow get inside and shift the logs farther down, then the whole thing might collapse." Delicately she removed a twig from the middle of her pile, and the heap crumbled, sending twigs rolling down the slope. "The weight of water would crush it."

"Brilliant!" Tigerheart exclaimed.

"Hang on a moment." Seville, the orange kittypet, spoke up. "You want us to go inside the dam and collapse it . . . and we would still be inside it, yes?"

Lionblaze nodded. "It's risky, but it looks like it's the only way." He hesitated, gazing around at the worried faces of his friends. "We'll just have to see what it's like when we get there," he ended with a shrug.

With a last glance at their companions, Whitetail, Sedge-whisker, and Woody headed upstream toward the lodge, while Lionblaze led the rest of the cats across the stream below the dam to the bank on the opposite side. Farther up the slope, they could see the Twoleg pelt-dens glowing with light and echoing with murmuring voices.

"What about them?" Toadfoot asked, flicking his tail in the direction of the pelt-dens.

Lionblaze paused at the bottom of the dam. "There's nothing we can do about them," he replied at last. "We don't have enough cats to distract them. We'll just have to hope that they don't cause any trouble."

"Hope's the easy part," Toadfoot responded caustically.

Lionblaze's pelt prickled with tension as he waited for the signal from Whitetail. He could tell that the other cats felt the same. Dovepaw was scraping at the ground with the tips of her claws, while Tigerheart's tail twitched back and forth. All three kittypets looked terrified, their eyes wide and their ears laid back.

Come on, Whitetail, Lionblaze urged. *Get a move on, before one of us starts to panic.*

"Remember," he mewed aloud. "No cat is to fight. If the beavers come back and challenge you, don't try to be a hero. We've learned that lesson the hard way."

"Right," Toadfoot agreed. "If the beavers attack, run. Climb a tree. I don't think they can—"

A piercing yowl from across the stream interrupted him.

"Something's happening," Lionblaze murmured, with a glance at Dovepaw.

She nodded. "The beavers are moving inside their den," she whispered, so faintly that no other cat could hear.

Lionblaze peered upstream toward the lodge. At first the night was so black that he could see nothing. Then the moon drifted out from behind a cloud, and he spotted movement beside the mound of sticks. The beavers' heads broke the surface of the pool and they scrambled up onto the outside of the lodge, their bodies swarming over the logs like bulky shadows.

On the bank, Lionblaze made out Whitetail's pale pelt, with Woody and Sedgewhisker dark shadows beside her. He could just hear their mocking hisses, taunting the beavers to draw them off their den and away from the pool. One of the beavers grunted, then waddled down the hill of sticks and onto the bank. It started bustling toward the cats, its tail whispering over the leaves. The other beavers followed, clumsy but surprisingly fast. Sedgewhisker darted forward and dealt the leader a swift blow on the nose before dancing away again.

"Great StarClan!" Toadfoot spat. "Has she *no* sense?"

The beavers lumbered in pursuit as Whitetail and the others slipped back into the trees, drawing them deeper into the forest. Within a few heartbeats, Lionblaze lost sight of them.

"Go!" Toadfoot hissed.

As the cats jumped up onto the dam, a claw of lightning split the sky from top to bottom, and thunder cracked above their heads. Snowdrop flinched, pressing herself to the log where she was balancing, then forced herself to her paws again and kept climbing.

"We should split up," Petalfur panted. "Some cat should come with me and start looking for a gap where we can get inside. The rest of you can start pushing logs off the top."

"I'll come with you," Toadfoot offered.

Petalfur led the way across the dam, just above the level of the pool, with Toadfoot following her. Lionblaze watched as she halted and started prodding one of the logs; then he headed for the top of the barrier. Lightning crackled out again; Lionblaze was almost deafened by the roll of thunder that followed it, and his ears kept ringing afterward. He shook his head impatiently. Then fat drops of rain began to fall, splashing on the logs and on the cats' pelts.

"This is all we need," Tigerheart grumbled.

"We'd have been happy about it back at the lake," Dovepaw pointed out. "I hope it rains there, too."

As Lionblaze scrambled over the topmost log and stood looking down at the pool, the clouds burst. Rain poured down in a hissing screen that blotted out everything except the logs beneath his paws. His pelt was drenched within heartbeats; he shivered as the cold rain reached his skin.

"Okay," he yowled, raising his voice to be heard above the drumming of the raindrops. "See if you can loosen some of these logs and branches. Push them down into the streambed."

He grabbed a long, thin branch in his jaws and hurled it down, then bent his head to grapple with a bigger log. Jigsaw pushed at it from the other end; it rolled slowly to the edge and landed in the stream with a satisfying crash.

"Yes!" Jigsaw yowled.

Farther along the dam Tigerheart and Snowdrop were struggling with a tree trunk, while Seville was showering down twigs and smaller branches into the streambed. Dovepaw was crouched close to Lionblaze, her eyes closed; he guessed she was sending out her senses to find out what the beavers were doing.

"Everything okay?" he asked.

Dovepaw blinked up at him through the driving rain. "Fine," she replied. "Whitetail and the others are keeping the beavers busy."

Lionblaze twitched his ears. "Good. Now come help me with this log. Otherwise every cat will start wondering what you're doing."

Dovepaw glared at him; Lionblaze knew how she felt about keeping her powers a secret, but he didn't see what else they could do. Slipping on the wet logs, she struggled to his side and put her shoulder to the log he was trying to shift. Lionblaze thrust hard at it and felt it start to move, rolling faster and faster until it tipped over the edge and fell into the stream.

"Well done!" Lionblaze panted. "We—"

He broke off as the terrified screech of a cat cut through the hiss of the rain. A couple of tail-lengths farther along the dam, Lionblaze spotted Tigerheart's paws skid from under him; the young warrior went plummeting down toward the stream, landing with a splash where rain was pooling on the stony bed.

Before Lionblaze could find a way to help him, he made out movement down below and Tigerheart appeared, clawing his way determinedly up the stack of logs. His mud-soaked fur stuck out in spikes, but his eyes gleamed with determination.

"Are you okay?" Lionblaze called out.

"No, I'm furious!" Tigerheart hauled himself onto the top of the dam. "I'd like to turn every one of those beavers into fresh-kill."

"He's okay," Dovepaw murmured.

Lionblaze waved his tail at the ShadowClan cat, then began testing which of the logs around him could be dislodged next. They all seemed to be stuck fast, bound together with mud and twigs.

Then he heard Petalfur calling from farther down the mound. "Hey, we need some help down here!"

Heading toward the sound of the she-cat's voice, Lionblaze was joined by the three kittypets. Their fur was plastered to their bodies and their eyes were wild with fear. But they didn't hesitate, scrambling across the logs to answer Petalfur's call.

I'll never feel the same about kittypets after tonight, Lionblaze thought.

Petalfur and Toadfoot were clinging to the dam two or three tail-lengths above the pool. Rain stippled the surface while black water sucked at the lowest logs. A dark hole gaped in the mound beside Toadfoot and Petalfur, with a huge tree trunk poking out of it. "We pulled out some of the mud and twigs," Petalfur explained. "If we can shift that trunk, I think a lot of the dam will go with it."

"Okay, let's try," Lionblaze meowed.

Glancing around, he saw that Dovepaw and Tigerheart had also clambered down to join them. "Dovepaw, you're the smallest," he called. "Can you go right inside and push from there?"

Dovepaw gave him a tense nod and vanished into the hole. The rest of the cats lined up against the tree trunk and started to push. At first Lionblaze couldn't feel it move at all.

"Harder!" he yowled. "Jigsaw, push more from your end! Toadfoot, can you wriggle underneath and pull out more of the mud?"

Gradually, as all the cats struggled and panted, the tree trunk began to shift. The outer end swung around; Lionblaze heard a crunching sound from inside the dam.

"Dovepaw, get out!" he screeched.

The apprentice popped out into the open again as more mud poured down into the hole, which quickly closed up. The tree swung further, tearing several more logs along with it, then ripped free and tumbled down the slope. Jigsaw was knocked off his paws as it slid past him; Snowdrop fastened her teeth in his shoulder and hauled him upright again. Tigerheart flung himself flat and the tree trunk bounced right over him, skimming his bristling fur. Lionblaze suddenly realized that the log under his paws was moving. He looked around for a solid place to jump to, but there was no time. As the log where he had been standing fell into the pool, he dug the claws of one paw into another branch and hung there, dangling in the air, with water lapping against his tail.

The pool was pushing hungrily at the dam. Lionblaze clawed his way onto a bigger log, feeling it shift under his weight. The whole structure was starting to shiver.

"Pull out those twigs!" Petalfur ordered Seville, gesturing with her tail. "Tigerheart, scoop the mud out of that hole.

Toadfoot, you and Jigsaw help me roll this log down."

Lionblaze took a gulping breath. *How does Petalfur know what the water is going to do?* He started to claw out pawfuls of twigs, realizing as he did that the level of water in the pool was rising—or was the dam sinking into it? A wave lapped over his head, leaving him spluttering; he caught a glimpse of Dovepaw and Snowdrop, working side by side, under the level of the trapped water.

We've got to work faster! he thought as Dovepaw popped her head up to take a breath. His legs ached as he forced them to tear at the branches and kick the debris away behind him as he worked. Suddenly he realized that Dovepaw was beside him again, water streaming from her pelt.

"The beavers!" she gasped. "They're coming back!"

A heartbeat later, Lionblaze heard terrified yowling; Whitetail, Sedgewhisker, and Woody dashed onto the top of the broken dam. Peering through the rain, Lionblaze made out the bulky, menacing shapes of the beavers just behind them.

"Quick!" he screeched. "Pull the logs out!"

Every cat was tearing and scrabbling at the branches, but they were too tightly woven. Fury surged up in Lionblaze as he realized that they were going to fail, only because their time was running out.

Then he heard a rumbling sound coming from farther upstream. The dam began to shake.

"Flood!" Toadfoot shrieked. "Coming straight at us!"

Lionblaze whipped around, almost losing his footing on

the unsteady logs, and saw a surge of water traveling downstream, a huge swelling wave that rose higher and higher as it drew closer. "Get off the dam!" he yowled.

Snowdrop was nearest to him; he grabbed her by the scruff, ignoring her outraged screech, and swung her down to the safety of the bank. Seville and Jigsaw leaped after her, followed by Woody.

Farther up the slope, yellow beams of Twoleg lights were slicing through the trees. Lionblaze spotted Twolegs charging down toward the stream, their voices raised. One beam of light picked out Dovepaw, clinging to a branch in the middle of the dam with all four sets of claws.

"Get back to the bank!" Lionblaze ordered.

But it was too late. The rumbling grew louder until it filled the whole world, cutting off the yowling of the Twolegs and the screeches of the cats. The dam was shaking too much to jump off now. Rushing water roared in Lionblaze's ears as the storm surge struck.

"Hang on!" he shrieked.

He drove his claws hard into a log as the dam exploded, logs and branches flying up like twigs. The trapped water gushed through, pouring into the streambed and overflowing the banks. Lionblaze caught a glimpse of Woody and the three kittypets huddled together halfway up the slope, their jaws gaping, as the wall of water swept him away.

CHAPTER 23

❧

Jayfeather groaned as he forced his eyes open on darkness. Poppyfrost's scent was all around him and he felt her tongue rasping busily at his scratches.

"Jayfeather, please wake up!" she begged. "Please! I can't carry you back to the hollow on my own."

"Wha . . . ?" For a heartbeat Jayfeather couldn't remember where he was, or why his Clanmate was panicking.

"Oh, thank StarClan!" Poppyfrost exclaimed. "You're not dying! I'm so sorry I caused all this trouble," she went on, giving him rapid licks between words. "I had no idea Breezepelt had followed me all this way."

Breezepelt . . . all this way . . . Jayfeather realized that he could hear the gentle sound of the waterfall cascading into the Moonpool. The memory flooded back, of his battle against Breezepelt and the mysterious cat who had joined in the fight against him. And the cat who had come to his rescue. *If it wasn't for Honeyfern, I'd be crow-food.*

Jayfeather struggled groggily to his paws. "I'm okay, Poppyfrost. Stop fussing." *How much does she know?* he wondered. *Did she see the other cats in the battle?*

270

"But you're not okay!" Poppyfrost still sounded distraught. "You have a really deep scratch down this side."

"Yeah, I've got Breezepelt to thank for that," Jayfeather mewed. "It's a good thing he didn't bring any other cats with him," he added, wondering if Poppyfrost would mention Breezepelt's ally.

Poppyfrost shuddered. "I know. I couldn't believe that he would attack a medicine cat. You were so brave, Jayfeather, fighting him off all by yourself."

Relief tingled in Jayfeather's paws. *She didn't see the others. But there was still something she needed to know.*

"Honeyfern came to me just now," he told her.

Instantly he felt the sharp stab of the she-cat's emotions: a mixture of hope and fear.

"Did she . . . did she speak to you?" Poppyfrost asked nervously.

Jayfeather nodded. "She told me that she's delighted that you're with Berrynose. And she said that she'll watch over your kits."

"Really?" Poppyfrost's voice softened to a purr. "Oh, I'm so glad!"

"Oh, and she told me that Berrynose really loves you," Jayfeather added.

Poppyfrost's purr faded. "I wish I could believe that. . . ." She sighed. "But I don't see how Honeyfern could possibly know."

Jayfeather stifled an exasperated hiss. "She's a StarClan cat. She knows lots of things that you don't." He stopped himself from adding, *mouse-brain*.

"I suppose we'd better get back to camp," Poppyfrost mewed. "I'll help you, Jayfeather."

"I'll be fine, thanks."

But as he struggled up the spiral path he became more aware of the throbbing pain in his side. His legs felt as weak as a newborn kit's, and by the time they reached the line of thornbushes he had to lean on Poppyfrost's shoulder.

They limped slowly down the path that led back to the forest, taking frequent rests along the way. Even though he was exhausted and in pain, Jayfeather's mind was still working, and he began to realize just how strange it was that Breezepelt had followed Poppyfrost to the Moonpool.

Why? She never crossed into WindClan territory, and even if she had, the right thing to do would have been to chase her off. And why did Breezepelt threaten to kill her? He doesn't hold any grudge against Poppyfrost. She's not half-Clan, and she didn't have anything to do with the lies Leafpool and Squirrelflight told.

Jayfeather let out a sigh. There was a lot that he didn't know, but he needed to find it out, and quickly. The appearance of the cat he hadn't recognized troubled him deeply.

"Are you okay? Do you want to rest again?" Poppyfrost asked.

"No, I can keep going."

Warmth on his pelt told Jayfeather that the sun had risen, though a damp wind was sweeping over the moorland, flinging the occasional spatter of rain. The air felt heavy. His pelt prickled. *There's a storm coming.* As they reached the WindClan border, Jayfeather kept tasting the air for Breezepelt's scent, in case he was waiting to ambush them on their way home. But all he could pick up was the scent from the WindClan markers: strong and fresh, as if a patrol had been by not long before.

Poppyfrost jumped, interrupting his train of thought.

"What's the matter?" he growled, his neck fur rising.

"Sorry, it's nothing," the she-cat replied. "I saw a flash of lightning over the trees, and it startled me, that's all."

Jayfeather forced his fur to lie flat again. *Are you a scaredy-mouse kit?* he scolded himself. *You'll be frightened of falling leaves next!*

But the danger was real, even if it wasn't hard on his paws right now. Jayfeather's pelt prickled as he wondered whether the cats of the Dark Forest were watching him now. The Dark Forest, the Place of No Stars, where the spirits of cats who had not been welcomed by StarClan walked alone. . . .

Is that where the strange cat came from? It wasn't Tigerstar or Hawkfrost. And what did Yellowfang mean? Was she warning me there will be a war between the cats of the Dark Forest and StarClan? And if there is, will the Clans have to fight?

Jayfeather let out a sigh. "I need a rest," he muttered, sinking into the grass beside the stream. Battered and weary, he wondered how he ever could have imagined that he had the power of the stars in his paws.

Where are Lionblaze and Dovepaw? he wondered. *I hope they're safe, and on their way home.*

* * *

Sunhigh was long past by the time Jayfeather and Poppyfrost staggered back into camp. As soon as they emerged from the thorn tunnel, Jayfeather heard paw steps racing from the nursery; Berrynose's scent, sharp with anxiety, swirled around him.

"Where have you *been*?" the warrior demanded. Jayfeather heard the rasp of his tongue as he licked Poppyfrost's ears. "I've been worried out of my fur!"

Poppyfrost broke into a puzzled purr. "It doesn't matter. I'm back now."

Berrynose pressed himself close to her side. "I couldn't bear to lose you, too," he murmured.

"Don't worry." Poppyfrost's voice shook a little. "I'm not going anywhere."

"Yes, you are. You're going back to the nursery *right now*." Berrynose nudged her. "I'll bring you some fresh-kill, and then you're going to rest."

Jayfeather stayed where he was as their paw steps retreated. Daisy and Ferncloud came out of the nursery to greet Poppyfrost, and Berrynose guided her inside, still scolding her gently.

Berrynose is a real pain in the tail, and yet he gets two *apparently sensible she-cats padding after him,* Jayfeather thought with a shake of his head. *Weird.*

Turning away, he limped across the clearing to his den, but as he settled down in his nest he knew he wouldn't sleep. He felt as restless as the trees clattering their branches above his head. *There's a storm coming, and more than rain and thunder. The forces of the Dark Forest are rising. . . .*

Finally, after squirming around in his nest, failing to get comfortable or to put his worries out of his mind, Jayfeather decided to go down to the lake and find his stick. *Maybe Rock knows something about the battle.*

On the way out of his den he encountered Cinderheart, who was padding across the clearing toward the thorn tunnel.

"Thanks for bringing Poppyfrost back," she mewed, touching his ear with her nose. "We were all so worried."

"You're welcome," Jayfeather mumbled, just wanting to get away.

But Cinderheart stopped him as he tried to move off. "Are you okay?" she queried, her voice growing sharper with anxiety. "You seem . . . sort of upset. And—oh!" She gasped. "You've got an awful scratch down your side."

"It's nothing," Jayfeather muttered.

"Nonsense!" Cinderheart meowed. "You're a medicine cat; you know very well it's not nothing. Come on. You'd never let any of us leave camp without having that treated."

Taking no notice of Jayfeather's protests, she herded him back into his den and headed for the storage cleft. A moment later she came back with a bunch of chervil leaves in her jaws. "This should stop any infection," she announced, beginning to chew them up.

When the poultice was ready, Cinderheart's paws moved deftly and confidently as she plastered it on Jayfeather's side. He let out a sigh of relief as the throbbing pain ebbed.

Does Cinderheart ever wonder why she feels so comfortable in the medicine cat's den? She knew exactly which herb to use and what to do with it.

Will it ever be the right time to tell her that she used to be Cinderpelt?

Another pang of foreboding shook him. *If there is a battle coming that involves every warrior since the dawn of the Clans, we'll need all the medicine cats we can get.*

Once Cinderheart was satisfied, Jayfeather headed out again, his pelt sticky with her poultice. Branches rustled above his head, and huge plops of cold water began to fall, splashing on his fur and flung against the trees by the rising wind.

"It's starting to rain!" Foxleap's voice came from among the trees, and a moment later a patrol caught up to Jayfeather, with Squirrelflight, Rosepetal, and Icecloud.

"Hey, Jayfeather!" Foxleap chattered on. "Isn't this great? If it keeps raining, we won't have to go get water anymore."

An irritated hiss came from Squirrelflight. "Foxleap, now look what you've done! You've dropped your moss, and it's all dirty. Stop getting so excited, and concentrate."

"Sorry," Foxleap meowed, though he didn't sound at all subdued. "I'll wash it off when we get to the water."

Jayfeather padded beside the patrol until they drew closer to the lake. Then he veered off, heading for the place where he had hidden his stick, and dragged it out from under the roots of the elder bush. Dropping it into the shelter of the bank, he sat down beside it and ran his paws over the scratches.

The voices of the ancient cats were faint and far away.

"Rock . . ." Jayfeather murmured. "Were you at the Moonpool last night? Do you know what is happening in the Dark Forest?"

"Yes, I know." A voice breathed in Jayfeather's ear, sending a shiver through him from ears to tail-tip. "But I cannot stop it—and even if I could, I would not. This is a storm that needs to break, Jayfeather."

Jayfeather's ears twitched up in shock. "Why?"

"There have been too many lies," Rock replied. "Too much pain has been caused among the Clans. Cats will have their revenge, and the oldest grievances will be settled."

Jayfeather turned his head toward the voice, and he saw the hazy shape of the ancient cat, with his hairless body and sightless, bulging eyes.

"Did you know?" he demanded. "About Leafpool and Crowfeather?"

Rock let out a sigh that stirred Jayfeather's whiskers. "Yes, I knew."

Jayfeather sprang to his paws. "Then why didn't you tell me? Don't you know how much pain we went through?"

"It was not your time to know, Jayfeather." The ancient cat's voice was calm and matter-of-fact. "You had to be raised as a ThunderClan cat, trained in medicine by your mother, Leafpool. That was your destiny, Jayfeather."

"It's not the destiny I wanted!" Jayfeather snapped.

"There was no room for you to be half-Clan from birth," Rock went on, as though Jayfeather hadn't spoken. "No room for you to be rejected because your mother had broken the code of the medicine cats and the warrior code."

Jayfeather stared at him, hardly able to believe what he was hearing. "So you lied, and every cat lied, for the sake of the prophecy?" Rage was building inside him until he was angrier than he'd ever been before in his life; he dug his claws hard into the ground to stop himself from raking Rock's eyes out. "Do you think it was worth it? Do you? I thought you were my friend!"

Slowly Rock shook his head. "I am no cat's friend. I know too much for friendship. Be glad that you will never be burdened with the knowledge that I have. My curse is to live forever, knowing what has been and what has yet to be, powerless to change anything."

His outline began to fade. As it vanished, Jayfeather's fury erupted. He felt around on the ground until he located a sharp stone. Then he snatched up the stick, balanced it across the stone, and brought his forepaws smashing down on one end. He heard the stick break, and splinters pierced his paws. Rock and the ancient Clans had betrayed him, too. Did no cat tell the truth, ever?

In the same heartbeat, thunder crashed out overhead, rolling around the sky. Rain cascaded down onto the lakebed. Jayfeather crouched under the bank, his jaws wide in a soundless wail, and wrapped his paws over his ears.

CHAPTER 24

♣

Dovepaw sank her claws into a branch as the wave of floodwater swept her downstream. The yowling of terrified cats was all around her, but she could see nothing except the heaving dark water and the tops of the trees as they spun past. Her pelt was drenched, she was shivering with cold, and she was more afraid than she had ever been in her life.

"Hold on!" Lionblaze's voice rose above the chaos of the storm.

"Where are you?" Dovepaw wailed, but there was no reply.

A wave crashed over her, filling her mouth and nose with water. Still managing to cling to the branch, she forced her head to the surface, spluttering and coughing as she fought to breathe. Harsh yellow light flashed across her vision, and Dovepaw realized that she was being carried past the dens of the Twolegplace. *I hope the kittypets get home safe,* she thought fuzzily.

Something dark loomed up ahead of her: the branches of an overhanging tree, dipping down and trailing in the surge of water. Dovepaw kicked out frantically, trying to avoid it, but the floodwater drove her right into the middle of the branches.

They scraped at her fur as she was carried past, almost sweeping her off her branch.

Gripping as hard as she could, until she thought her claws would be ripped out, Dovepaw was suddenly jerked into open water again. A bundle of tabby fur, dark from the water, whisked past her with a wail.

Tigerheart!

Blinking water out of her eyes, Dovepaw watched with horror as the young ShadowClan warrior vanished under the surface.

StarClan, no!

Taking a deep breath, she let go of her branch and plunged after him. Catching at memories of Rippletail and Petalfur swimming in the pool behind the dam, she tried to copy their movements. But it was hard. Her soaked fur was heavy and her legs ached with exhaustion. She kept banging into more floating branches that pushed her under the water, and when she resurfaced, waves spat in her eyes.

Dovepaw had almost given up hope of ever finding her friend when she caught a glimpse of Tigerheart bobbing up again less than a tail-length from her, before vanishing almost at once. She swam toward him, then dived under the surface.

Above, the water had been dark, with only fitful gleams of moonlight flickering on the surface. Down here, Dovepaw felt as blind as Jayfeather, sending out her senses to locate Tigerheart and pushing through the murky water until her paws touched his pelt.

He's not moving! Am I too late?

Grabbing a mouthful of his fur, Dovepaw paddled frantically upward. As her head broke the surface, a branch bobbed past her and she wrapped her front legs around it. Tigerheart's weight threatened to drag her under the water again, but Dovepaw wouldn't let go. Relief flashed through her when she spotted Petalfur swimming strongly toward her.

"Rippletail will not die in vain," the RiverClan cat hissed through gritted teeth. "StarClan will not take any more warriors from us."

She gripped Tigerheart by the scruff, relieving Dovepaw of his weight. Dovepaw was able to haul herself a little higher out of the water, where she caught sight of a flat piece of wood being whirled toward them on the current. Floundering through the flood, she managed to grab it and pushed it toward Petalfur.

Together the two she-cats hauled Tigerheart onto the flat wood and crouched beside him, clinging on as the water carried them across the stretch of green grass at the edge of the Twolegplace, and into the woods beyond.

Dovepaw realized that she could see more clearly; the rain-filled sky was growing gray with the first pale light of dawn. The water was calmer now; it still overflowed the stream banks, but the first terrifying wave had died down. Looking around, Dovepaw spotted branches scattered over the surface, and here and there, bobbing up and down, the heads of cats.

"Yes!" she gasped, reaching out her tail to touch Petalfur on the shoulder. "There's Toadfoot! And Lionblaze! And there's Whitetail and Sedgewhisker, hanging on to the same branch."

"Thank StarClan," Petalfur mewed. "They're all safe!"

As she spoke, Tigerheart began to thrash and splutter, tilting the piece of wood dangerously so that water surged over them.

"Lie still," Dovepaw told him. "You're safe. And we'll be home soon."

At last the current slowed enough for the cats to leave the branches they were clinging to and wade through the shallows to solid ground. All seven cats huddled together, panting and watching as the floodwater gradually washed back between the banks of the stream.

Rain was still pouring steadily down, but Dovepaw scarcely noticed it. She was wetter than she had ever been, and she had swallowed so much water she couldn't imagine ever being thirsty again. Drawing a deep breath, she listened to the water glugging and pooling and splashing through the woods, through ShadowClan territory, and finally down to the lake, where it swelled over the dried mud and stones, rippling into every crack and hollow, spreading silvery twigs across the parched surface.

We did it, she thought. *We brought back the lake.*

Tigerheart was sprawled on the ground, coughing up mouthfuls of water while Petalfur rubbed his back.

"Will he be okay?" Dovepaw asked anxiously.

"He'll be fine," Petalfur assured her. "This is what we do in RiverClan if kits fall into the lake before they can swim.

It always seems to work."

Tigerheart coughed up more water, then turned his head to look blearily up at Dovepaw. "Thanks," he rasped.

When he had recovered enough to stagger to his paws, all the cats gathered and stood in a circle with their heads bowed.

"StarClan, we thank you," Whitetail meowed. "You helped us to destroy the dam and protected us in the flood. We ask you to honor Rippletail, the warrior who will never come home."

Dovepaw lifted her head and caught Lionblaze's eye. She wondered if he was thinking the same thing.

StarClan didn't save us. We did.

CHAPTER 25

❧

The daylight grew stronger as the cats headed back through the woods, following the edge of the stream. Branches were strewn everywhere, left behind by the retreating wave; they had to scramble over them or wriggle underneath, until Dovepaw felt as if her paws wouldn't carry her a step farther.

I wish I was back in my nest. I'd sleep for a moon!

Gradually the rain eased off, and though it didn't stop, patches of blue sky appeared as the wind tore the gray cloud into strips. In the shelter of the trees, the cats' fur began to dry in untidy clumps.

"When I get back, I'm going to groom myself like I've never groomed before," Whitetail muttered. "My pelt has never been as filthy as this."

Suddenly Toadfoot halted with his head raised and his jaws parted to taste the air. "I can smell ShadowClan scent markers!" he announced.

Strength seemed to flow back into Dovepaw's paws, and all the cats picked up speed. Soon they crossed the border.

"I never thought I'd see the day when I was glad to be in ShadowClan territory," Lionblaze murmured to Dovepaw.

She nodded. *This journey has changed the way we think about the other Clans, forever.*

A few heartbeats later, she picked up the scent of approaching ShadowClan cats, and soon they appeared through the trees: a patrol led by Tawnypelt, with her apprentice, Starlingpaw, and the warriors Owlclaw and Redwillow.

"Toadfoot! Tigerheart!" Tawnypelt exclaimed, bounding forward through the rain. She touched noses with Toadfoot, and she pushed her muzzle into Tigerheart's fur, murmuring, "You're safe!"

A shiver went through Dovepaw as she imagined what this meeting would have been like if Tawnypelt's son Tigerheart had not returned.

"This is wonderful!" Tawnypelt went on, drawing back to gaze at the rest of the cats. "You brought the water back! Starlingpaw, run back and let Blackstar know right away."

Her apprentice took off through the forest, his paws skimming over the pine needles and his tail waving excitedly.

"Come on," Tawnypelt urged. "You've got to come back to our camp and tell us everything."

Dovepaw exchanged a glance with Lionblaze; she wanted to be home in the stone hollow, but at the same time she was reluctant to say good-bye to the rest of the patrol.

Whitetail and Sedgewhisker whispered together for a heartbeat; then Whitetail nodded. "We'll be glad to visit with you," she mewed.

Lionblaze agreed too, and though Petalfur seemed reluctant, she followed the others as they were escorted through the forest by Tawnypelt and the rest of her patrol.

Dovepaw could hear the yowling of excited cats long before they reached the camp. Through the trees she saw the ground slope upward to a line of bushes where Blackstar stood, flanked by his warriors. More cats were emerging from the bushes around them.

"Welcome to our camp!" Blackstar called, beckoning them with his tail. "Rest here and take your pick of the fresh-kill pile."

"Who are you, and what have you done with Blackstar?" Lionblaze muttered into Dovepaw's ear as they padded up the slope.

Flametail and Dawnpelt, Tigerheart's littermates, dashed up to touch noses with him.

"I just went down to the lake!" Dawnpelt announced excitedly. "The water is flowing back."

"It'll take a while to fill up," Flametail added, rubbing his muzzle against his brother's shoulder. "But the Clans have been saved, and you did it!"

"We all did it together," Tigerheart meowed.

Dovepaw felt strange to be welcomed like this, especially when the cats of ShadowClan had been so secretive and suspicious in the past. Besides, she didn't feel as if she deserved this much praise. *We lost Rippletail, and we nearly didn't destroy the dam at all. And we couldn't do it on our own—we needed kittypets and a loner to help us.*

"Come into the camp." Blackstar repeated his invitation as he padded forward to meet the patrol.

Petalfur dipped her head. "Thank you, Blackstar, but no. I have lost my Clanmate, and I must go back to RiverClan and tell them how he died."

"We'll go with you," Lionblaze offered immediately; Whitetail and Sedgewhisker murmured agreement.

Petalfur held her head high. "Thank you, but I will go alone." Without waiting for a reply, she dipped her head once more to Blackstar, then to the rest of the patrol, and walked away. Dovepaw watched her until she disappeared among the trees.

"It's time for us to go, too," Lionblaze told Blackstar. "Whitetail, will you and Sedgewhisker travel back with us?"

"Yes, we will," Whitetail replied. "Blackstar, thank you for asking us into your camp, but it's time we went back to our own Clans."

A pang of regret clawed through Dovepaw as she turned to say good-bye to Toadfoot and Tigerheart. They seemed different, somehow, now that they were back with their Clanmates. Already their scent was sharpening, had become less familiar, and their expressions were harder to read. *They're more . . . more ShadowClan now. When we were traveling together we were all one Clan.*

Toadfoot was standing beside Tawnypelt; he gave Lionblaze and the others a dignified nod. "I'm proud to have traveled with you," he meowed. "And prouder still that we achieved what we set out to do."

To Dovepaw, it sounded like the kind of formal report a leader would make at a Gathering; not for the first time, she wondered how Toadfoot really felt, and if his loyalty had ever really extended beyond his own Clan to the cats who had traveled with him.

With a sidelong glance at his Clanmates, Tigerheart bounded up to Dovepaw and rubbed his muzzle against hers. "I'll miss you," he whispered. "I'll see you at the Gatherings, right?"

Dovepaw just had time to reply, "Yes, I'll miss you, too," before Toadfoot beckoned the younger warrior away with a jerk of his head. Tigerheart bounded back to his Clanmates.

"Keep practicing that battle move I showed you," Sedgewhisker reminded him. "I'll beat you at the next Gathering!"

Tigerheart gave a last wave of his tail as the ThunderClan and WindClan cats turned away, heading back through the drenched pine trees toward the stream. With Lionblaze in the lead, they walked silently along the bank, still keeping to the ShadowClan side, until they reached the lake.

Dovepaw had half expected to see it brimming full, as it had been in her dream, but the water's edge was still far away across the stretch of mud. The stream was spilling out onto the dry stones of the lakebed; *I don't suppose any of us will mind getting our paws wet in future,* Dovepaw reflected as they splashed through the water and padded along beside ThunderClan territory.

When they reached the point where she and Lionblaze would need to turn in to the forest to head for the stone hollow, they said good-bye to the WindClan cats.

This is really the end, Dovepaw thought sadly. *We're not a patrol any longer. Just cats from different Clans.*

"Good-bye," Whitetail mewed; her eyes were full of regret, as if she too was sad that their journey had come to an end. "May StarClan light your path."

"And yours," Lionblaze replied.

He and Dovepaw stood close together for a few heartbeats, watching the two WindClan cats trek wearily along the edge of the lake. Then the ThunderClan cats scrambled up the shore and headed into the dripping trees. Before they had taken more than a couple of paw steps, Dovepaw heard a yowl behind them and spotted Sandstorm racing across the lake-bed, with Foxleap, Icecloud, and Toadstep following her. All four cats carried bundles of soaked moss in their jaws.

"Hey, it's Lionblaze and Dovepaw!" Foxleap exclaimed, dropping his moss and putting on a spurt to pass Sandstorm and reach his Clanmates first. "You're back! You brought the water!"

Icecloud raced alongside her brother. "What happened?" she mumbled around her mouthful of moss. "Did you find the animals?"

"Was it scary?" asked Toadstep, his eyes shining as he crowded around with the others.

"Give them some space," Sandstorm meowed. "There'll be plenty of time to hear their story back in the hollow. Foxleap, run ahead and tell Firestar that they're back."

Foxleap took off through the trees with a joyful flick of his tail, while Lionblaze and Dovepaw followed more slowly, escorted by the water patrol. By the time the thorn barrier across the entrance to the hollow came in sight, cats were spilling out through the thorn tunnel. *Just like the floodwater breaking through the dam,* Dovepaw thought. Briarpaw, Bumblepaw, and Blossompaw were scampering around, play fighting with one another in their excitement. The older warriors followed more slowly, their tails erect and their eyes shining. Poppy-frost emerged, heavy with her kits, escorted by Ferncloud and Daisy. Even the elders appeared, Mousefur guiding Longtail with her tail across his shoulders, and Purdy lumbering along behind.

As Firestar pushed his way through the thorns, the other cats drew back to each side to let him pass. The ThunderClan leader padded forward until he stood in front of Lionblaze and Dovepaw, and he reached out to touch each of them on the shoulder with the tip of his tail.

"Congratulations," he mewed, his green eyes shining with pride. "You have saved the lives of all the Clans."

Gesturing with his tail, he invited Lionblaze and Dovepaw to enter the camp ahead of him. The rest of the Clan poured in behind. Cloudtail dragged an enormous rabbit from the fresh-kill pile and dropped it at Lionblaze's feet.

"Here, eat," he meowed. "You both must be starving."

"Later, thanks." Lionblaze dipped his head to the white warrior. "We've got to report to Firestar first."

But it was impossible to move because more and more cats pressed around them.

"What was blocking the stream?"

"Were there really brown animals?"

"Did you have any trouble with the Twolegs?"

Trying to ignore the excited questions, Dovepaw strained upward on the tips of her paws, peering over the heads of the cats who surrounded her.

Where is she?

At last she spotted Ivypaw hanging back from the crowd, casting a shy glance at her sister and then gazing down at her paws. Dovepaw shouldered her way through the cats until she reached her sister.

"Ivypaw!" she mewed. "I've missed you so much!"

Ivypaw looked up at her with sad eyes. "I was afraid you wouldn't!" she confessed.

"Don't be such a mouse-brain," Dovepaw murmured affectionately. "We're best friends, aren't we? I thought of you all the time!" *Well, lots of the time at least.*

"Hey, Dovepaw!"

At the sound of her mentor's voice, Dovepaw turned. Lionblaze was standing with Firestar and Brambleclaw near the bottom of the tumbled rocks.

"We need to make our report," he called. "Firestar wants us to tell the whole Clan what happened."

"Coming," Dovepaw replied.

As she padded toward him, she saw Lionblaze's gaze shift to focus on something behind her. "Jayfeather," he mewed with a nod.

Glancing back, Dovepaw saw Jayfeather approaching from the direction of his den. She swallowed a gasp of shock: The medicine cat looked seasons older than when she and Lionblaze had left the camp. His eyes were haunted, his body had the gaunt look of an elder, and he had a fresh scar down one side. He put one paw slowly in front of another, as if he wasn't sure his legs would hold him upright.

"Welcome back," he rasped.

"Thanks, Jayfeather." Dovepaw couldn't take her eyes off him. What had happened while they were away to make him look like that?

Looking back at Lionblaze, Dovepaw saw her own shock reflected in his eyes. She followed Jayfeather as he headed over toward the Clan leader and the other cats, with a quick glance over her shoulder at Ivypaw.

"I'll be back soon," she promised.

"That's very bad news about Rippletail," Firestar meowed when Lionblaze and Dovepaw had finished their report. "We are all Clanmates in this. We have lost a brave warrior."

All the Clan bowed their heads in silence.

Spiderleg was the first to break it. "You mean you actually asked *kittypets* for help?"

"And you fought these . . . what did you call them, beavers?" Dustpelt meowed. "You'll have to teach us the right battle moves in case they come here."

"They'd better not, or I'll give them somethin' to think about," Purdy grunted.

Firestar raised his tail for silence. "That's enough for now," he meowed. "There'll be plenty of time to talk to Lionblaze and Dovepaw later. Let them eat and rest first."

Lionblaze retreated to the fresh-kill pile, where he tucked

into Cloudtail's rabbit with Jayfeather and a few of the other warriors. Even though she couldn't remember when she had last eaten, Dovepaw felt too exhausted to join them. She tottered across the clearing and pushed through the ferns into the apprentices' den.

Briarpaw followed her in. "Look!" she mewed proudly, pointing with her tail toward Dovepaw's nest. "We made it especially comfortable for you."

Dovepaw saw that her nest was lined with soft gray feathers. "Thank you," she purred, warmed by the friendship of the older apprentices. "That looks great. It must have taken you ages."

"You deserve it!" Bumblepaw added, poking his head through the entrance.

"Yes, you're a hero!" Blossompaw chirped, popping up beside him. "The Clans won't ever forget what you did."

The three apprentices left Dovepaw alone to settle down and rest. It felt strange to curl up in her own nest again. *Now that I'm back, I'm just an ordinary apprentice, aren't I? Shouldn't I be out on a patrol or something?*

Her nest had never felt so warm and comfortable, but Dovepaw kept shifting around in the feathers, unable to sleep.

What's wrong with me? I'm so tired my fur's dropping off!

She opened her eyes at a rustling sound to see that Ivypaw had pushed her head through the ferns.

"I thought you'd be asleep," she mewed.

"I can't," Dovepaw confessed. "I feel as if I've got ants in my pelt."

"Want to go for a walk?"

Maybe she needed to do something to make her even more tired. Dovepaw scrambled out of her nest and followed her sister through the thorns and into the forest. This was better than trying to sleep, alone with her thoughts. Her paws tugged her toward the lake and the water that she had freed. The sun had set, leaving the forest shrouded in twilight. The rain had stopped and the wind had died down; the air was damp and fresh, moving softly against her pelt. The grass already felt lush and juicy under her paws.

The drought is over. The Clans will survive! Dovepaw paused briefly, blinking in surprise. *I did that,* she realized. *If it wasn't for my senses, the Clans would still be dying of thirst.* Pride flooded over her with the force of the freed water surging down into the lake. *Maybe it won't be so bad, having these powers, if I can use them to help my Clan.*

Reaching the lake, the two she-cats leaped down from the bank to stand on the very edge of the mud, looking out toward the distant ripple of water.

"Am I imagining it, or does it look closer?" Dovepaw whispered.

"I think it does," Ivypaw replied. She gave an excited little skip. "I can't wait to see what it looks like when it's really full, with the water all the way up here."

Dovepaw took a pace forward and halted as something sharp dug into her pad. "Ow! I've trodden on something." Looking down, she saw two parts of a stick marked with scratches, the broken ends splintered. With an annoyed flick of her tail, she pushed the scraps away and examined her pad.

"Are you okay?" Ivypaw mewed.

"Yes, fine." Dovepaw swiped her tongue over her pad. "The skin's not even broken."

She stood close to her sister again, their pelts brushing. Ivypaw twined her tail with Dovepaw's, letting out a soft purr. "I'm so glad you're back, Dovepaw."

"So am I." Dovepaw buried her muzzle in her sister's soft pelt. "I'll never leave you behind again," she promised.

CHAPTER 26

❧

"*What's happening?*" *Berrynose poked his head* into the entrance of the nursery. "Why aren't the kits born yet?"

Jayfeather paused with his paw resting gently on Poppy-frost's belly and let out an exasperated sigh. "Because it's not quite time, Berrynose," he meowed, forcing his voice to remain calm. "You don't need to worry."

He could feel powerful ripples passing through Poppy-frost's body as her kits prepared themselves to be born. The young she-cat lay on her side on the soft moss of the nursery; Daisy was crouched beside her head, licking her ears, while Ferncloud stroked her pelt with a calming paw.

"Yes, Berrynose, why don't you go catch a shrew or some-thing?" Daisy suggested. "We're getting on just fine."

"Then why is it taking so long?" Berrynose demanded.

Jayfeather rolled his eyes. When Daisy had first roused him to come to the nursery, Berrynose had insisted on stay-ing with his mate. But he had been such a nuisance, getting in the way and questioning everything the medicine cat did, that Jayfeather had sent him outside. But it annoyed Jayfeather almost as much to hear him pacing up and down, and sticking his head in every few heartbeats to ask stupid questions.

Any cat would think no queen had ever kitted before!

Berrynose withdrew, and Jayfeather could hear his nervous pacing start up again. Outside the nursery, night lay over the stone hollow, with a gentle breeze stirring the trees and the scent of leaf-fall in the air. Two nights before, Jayfeather had traveled to the Moonpool to meet with the other medicine cats. He had hoped to learn more about Yellowfang's warning, but none of the other medicine cats spoke about messages from StarClan, or dreams of the Dark Forest. When Jayfeather settled down to sleep by the lake, he had found himself padding through the sunlit territory of the Clans' ancestors, but no starry warriors had answered his calls.

A grunt of pain from Poppyfrost distracted Jayfeather, and another powerful ripple passed through her belly.

"It won't be long now," he promised.

Daisy stopped licking to give Poppyfrost a drink from a clump of soaked moss, and the she-cat relaxed with a long sigh. "No cat told me it would be such hard work," she murmured.

"What happened? I heard something! Are they here yet?" It was Berrynose again, thrusting his head and shoulders into the nursery.

"Berrynose, you're blocking all the light," Ferncloud pointed out gently. "It really isn't helping."

"These are *my* kits, you know," Berrynose protested.

"Yes, and I'm the one having them!" Poppyfrost meowed sharply. "Honestly, Berrynose, I'm fine."

At that moment, Jayfeather heard his brother's voice calling from outside the nursery. "Is there anything I can do to help?"

"Yes," Jayfeather called back. "Keep Berrynose out of my fur!"

Berrynose drew back with an offended snort, and Jayfeather heard Lionblaze talking quietly to him. The paw steps started up again, but this time there were two sets, drawing a little farther away from the nursery.

"Right," Jayfeather mewed. "Now we can get on with it."

Poppyfrost grunted as she strained to bring her kits into the world. "I don't think they're ever coming," she panted as the spasm passed.

"They will," Jayfeather told her calmly. "This first kit is a big one; that's why it's taking longer. But it'll be here soon."

The she-cat gasped for breath; Jayfeather felt her belly convulse, and a kit slithered out onto the moss.

"Oh, look!" Ferncloud exclaimed in a delighted purr. "A tom—and he's beautiful, Poppyfrost."

Poppyfrost gave a grunt of acknowledgment as another spasm passed through her. Jayfeather carefully felt her belly. "Just one more to come," he told her.

She's getting tired, he thought. *Come on, kit, get a move on. Your mother needs to rest.*

Daisy gave Poppyfrost another drink, while Ferncloud bent over her, murmuring encouragingly. But Poppyfrost was barely conscious by the time the second kit, a little she-cat, slipped out to join her brother.

"Oh, they're just beautiful!" Daisy whispered; she and

Ferncloud bent their heads to lick the kits into wakefulness. "Look, Poppyfrost. Aren't they lovely?"

Poppyfrost let out an exhausted murmur and gathered the two kits toward her belly. Jayfeather could hear their tiny squeaks that faded into silence as they began to suckle.

"All done," he stated with satisfaction. "Here, Poppyfrost, eat these borage leaves. They'll help your milk to come."

Listening to the new mother licking up the herbs, Jayfeather suddenly had the sensation that the nursery had grown more crowded. "Okay, Berrynose, you can come and meet your kits," he meowed.

He turned, expecting to pick up Berrynose's scent. Instead he realized that he could see the branches of the nursery, intertwined with bramble tendrils to keep out the drafts.

Am I dreaming?

There was no sign of Berrynose, but three other cats were sitting beside the nursery wall. Horror stiffened every hair on Jayfeather's pelt when he saw the muscular tabby shapes of Tigerstar and Hawkfrost, one with gleaming amber eyes, the other with ice blue. The third cat was a big brown tom with a crooked tail. Jayfeather had never seen him before, but he recognized the scent of the cat who had attacked him at the Moonpool during his fight with Breezepelt.

There was hunger in the eyes of the three spirit cats as they stared at the newborn kits.

Jayfeather was still frozen with shock when Lionblaze pushed his head into the den. "Can Berrynose come in yet?" he asked.

Then his eyes narrowed and he turned his head toward

the three cats from the Dark Forest. "You will not have these kits!" he hissed.

Jayfeather's heart began to pound. "You can see them?"

Lionblaze nodded. "Yes. I can see them." He let out a snarl, baring his teeth.

"Lionblaze, what in the name of StarClan are you doing?" Daisy asked. "Go get Berrynose."

At the sound of the she-cat's voice the three cats vanished, and Jayfeather's sight went dark once more. He crouched down, trembling, as Lionblaze withdrew, and forced himself to turn back to the kits. The sound of healthy suckling calmed him, and he managed to pull himself together as Berrynose came into the nursery.

The young warrior was quivering with excitement. "Oh, wow! A son and a daughter!" he exclaimed. He pressed himself close to Poppyfrost, covering her face with licks. "You're so clever, so beautiful," he kept repeating. "Our kits are going to be the best in the Clan!"

As Jayfeather listened, he became aware of Honeyfern's scent wreathing around him, and a faint murmur reached his ears.

Thank you.

His head still spinning, Jayfeather slipped into the clearing. Lionblaze was waiting for him. "Do you know who that third cat is?" he demanded.

Jayfeather shook his head. "I don't know his name, but I've met him before. He attacked me at the Moonpool when I was fighting against Breezepelt."

"*What?*" Lionblaze sounded horrified, and his claws scraped against the earth of the clearing.

Quickly Jayfeather told him what had happened when he had followed Poppyfrost to the Moonpool. "Breezepelt seems to want vengeance on every cat in ThunderClan," he finished, "because of what Leafpool and Crowfeather did."

"I can understand that . . . in a way," Lionblaze meowed. "But where did the other cat come from?"

"Yellowfang spoke to me in a dream," Jayfeather told his brother. "She seems to know this cat—he comes from the Dark Forest, like Tigerstar and Hawkfrost—but she didn't tell me his name." He let out a frustrated sigh. "I don't understand why cats from the Dark Forest are suddenly appearing among the Clans. Do they really want to get involved in new quarrels?"

But that's what Rock told me, he suddenly remembered. *He spoke about ancient grievances that will be answered. Is this what he meant?*

"Jayfeather, there's something I need to tell you." Lionblaze led his brother out through the thorn barrier and into the forest, halting to face him on the mossy ground beneath an oak tree. The branches creaked peacefully above them in the breeze.

"I have a confession to make," Lionblaze began.

Jayfeather listened, his mouth dropping open with horror, as Lionblaze told him how Tigerstar used to visit him at night, and how the vengeful cat had trained him to fight better and more strongly than his Clanmates. Not for the sake of his Clan—but to satisfy Tigerstar's own hunger for power.

"Why didn't you tell me?" Jayfeather croaked when Lionblaze had finished.

"Because I thought it was my destiny," Lionblaze replied. "Tigerstar told me he was my kin, but he knew all along that he wasn't. So he lied, he lied to get me on his side, as one of his warriors for a battle among the Clans."

"It's coming," Jayfeather whispered. "A battle between StarClan and the Dark Forest, and every warrior will be called upon to fight." Ice-cold fear raised every hair on his pelt. "Did the three cats come tonight in case one of Poppyfrost's kits died, so they could take it to the Dark Forest?"

"They don't need dead kits," Lionblaze meowed. "They can visit the living, just like they visited me." He hesitated. "I—I think they're training Tigerheart already. In the battle against the beavers, I saw him use a battle move that Tigerstar taught me."

Jayfeather's thoughts flew back to the Moonpool, and how Breezepelt hadn't seemed at all surprised to be fighting alongside the shadowy warrior. "They've recruited Breezepelt, too," he realized. "Feeding off his hatred of us, and his hunger for revenge. But how? Warrior ancestors have never been able to touch the living world before now."

"They have." Lionblaze's tone was grave. "When I trained in my dreams with Tigerstar, toward the end, I woke up with real injuries." Jayfeather felt his brother's tail-tip rest on his shoulder.

"They're breaking through," Lionblaze growled. "And when the battle comes, it will be for real."

Turn the page to play the first adventure
in the

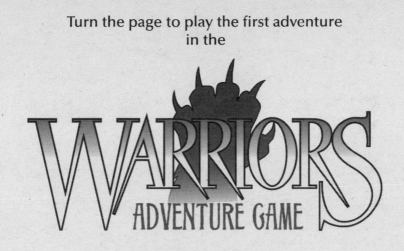

WARRIORS
ADVENTURE GAME

*Visit www.warriorcats.com to
download game rules, character sheets,
a practice mission, and more!*

Written by **Stan!**   •   Art by **James L. Barry**

FEVER DREAMS

Several moons have passed since the end of the "Saving the Kits" mini-adventure, found at the end of the Warriors Adventure Game rules on warriorcats.com. If the players' cats went through that adventure, they are all now 4 moons older. Before starting play, everyone (including the person who will take the first turn as Narrator) should use the information found in the "Improving Your Cat" section of Chapter Four in the game rules to give their characters the benefits of that passage of time.

Unless you are going to be the first Narrator in this adventure, stop reading here. The information beginning in the next paragraph is for the Narrator only.

The Adventure Begins

Hello, Narrator! It's time to begin playing "Fever Dreams." Make sure all the players have their character sheets, the correct number of chips, a piece of paper, and a pencil. Remember that the point of the game is to have fun, so don't be afraid to go slow, keep all of the players involved, and refer to the rules if you aren't sure exactly what should happen next.

When you're ready, begin with **1** below.

1. A Dream of Death

Special Note: This section presumes that the players' cats come from different Clans. You should modify this section if all the players' cats are from the same Clan. In that case, only one medicine cat needs to be present, and the fever only needs to affect that Clan.

Read Aloud: "It's a troubling time for the cats in every Clan.

Despite the fact that it is the height of greenleaf, usually a time of good health and full bellies, a mysterious disease has swept through the territories. Cats in every Clan, from the smallest kit to the strongest warrior, have been coming down with a fever that, if not treated quickly, can be deadly. You've been called into a meeting with several Clan leaders and medicine cats."

Narrator Tips: Your job in this scene is to have these Clan leaders and medicine cats tell the characters about how big the fever problem is and to answer the players' questions. Give the players an idea of what's going to happen in this adventure—what the goal is, what the stakes are, and what is expected of their cats.

In this meeting are the leaders of two Clans and the medicine cats from the other two. (You can find a list of the current Clan leaders and medicine cats on warriorcats.com.) If the characters ask where the other leaders are, tell them that they are absent because they have come down with the fever and are unable to leave their nests. (If all the cats are from one Clan then this detail is unimportant—everything will focus around that Clan. However, you can still make it so that the Clan leader is one of the cats who is sick.)

The medicine cats are all baffled by the current fever. It is different than greencough—easier to cure, but more deadly if medicine is not given in time. Luckily feverfew, the herb usually used for fevers, works, but so many cats are sick that the Clans are running through their supplies quicker than they can be replenished from local sources.

All of the medicine cats have had the same dream from StarClan—a dream that says if the medicine runs out, many cats will die. The dream also hints at the location of a new supply of feverfew, an untouched patch of the herb that could save

the Clans. But the patch is far away, and the medicine cats have to stay with their Clans to treat the sick.

The players' cats have been chosen because they are young, strong, and haven't contracted the fever—yet. Their vital mission is to find this new patch, gather as much feverfew as possible, and bring it back quickly. Unfortunately, as dreams from Star-Clan often are, this one was short on specifics. The medicine cats can only repeat StarClan's words to the characters:

To the north, the Hill That Cries holds what you need. . . . Along a winding face, topped with dozens of eyes, you will find one special pool with a garden of the herb you seek.

The medicine cats have no more information, but will teach the characters how to wrap feverfew in leaves to make it easier to carry back. They stress that this is one of the most important missions in the history of the Clans. If the characters cannot bring back a new supply of medicine within a week, many cats will die. Because of that timeline, the medicine cats are sure that the Hill That Cries must be within three days' travel from the lake; otherwise, it would be impossible for the cats to go there and return in time.

What Happens Next: When the players understand the situation and their assignment, continue with **2**.

2. A Long Journey

Special Note: There is no Read Aloud section in this scene as it involves mostly the Narrator improvising the first part of the journey.

Narrator Tips: At this point, you can either lead the characters through a journey to the Hill That Cries, or you can decide to skip that time and get right into the adventure. Some players will want to spend time on the journey, hunting and figuring out where to go, and other players will not. It's up to you, as

Narrator, to figure out what your players would enjoy most. If they want to take time to go through the journey, use the snippets of information below to build the scene.

- The trip takes them along the edge of some Twoleg nests, and the cats may meet up with rogue cats or kittypets on the way. Those cats don't know of any Hill That Cries, but they can say that the nearby hills do have a lot of small lakes and ponds.
- If extra excitement is needed, the cats may be chased by a dog or have to cross a Thunderpath.
- The cats may want to do some hunting for fresh-kill along the way. Use the information in Chapter Five of the rules to lead the players through that activity.

When the scene feels complete, the cats have arrived at the Hill That Cries—a thickly wooded hill that has a pair of thin, quickly rushing streams coming down it side by side, making it appear as though the hill is indeed crying.

What Happens Next: There are three ways to head up the hill—follow the rocky shore of the streams, go directly into the woods, or go along a dirt path that was clearly made by Twolegs.

If the cats walk beside the streams, continue with **6**.
If the cats go directly into the woods, continue with **7**.
If the cats follow the Twoleg path, continue with **8**.

This marks the end of the chapter. After the characters have made their decision about which way to go, hand the adventure to the next person who will take the role of Narrator, tell him or her what number to continue with, pick up your cat's character sheet, and resume playing the game.

3. The Grumbling Cliff
Read Aloud: "The cliff is made of very soft rock. Although that

means that your claws can grab tight, it also means that the rocks sometimes crumble when you grab them."

Narrator Tips: Climbing the cliff is practically impossible, but the cats may not figure that out right away, and finding out the hard way can be bad for their health. Make sure the players understand that falling from the cliff may cause their cats to be seriously injured.

Climbing the cliff requires a total of five successful Climb Checks. Each Check will be harder than the previous one. The first Check only requires a total of 4 or higher to succeed, but each Check after that increases in difficulty by +2. So the second Check requires a total of 6, the third Check requires a total of 8, the fourth a total of 10, and the final Check requires a total of 12 or higher to succeed.

You, the Narrator, should stress to the players how difficult the Check will be *before* their cats decide whether or not to attempt it. They should know how difficult the task will be because failure has a severe penalty.

If a cat fails a Climb Check, he or she has slipped or the rock has crumbled—the cat is falling off the cliff. That cat must immediately make a Jump Check. If the total is equal to or higher than the difficulty of the current Climb Check, the cat is okay. For example, if it was the third Climb Check (which would need a total of 8 to succeed), then the Jump Check must also be 8 or higher in order to succeed. If the Jump Check is too low, the cat will sustain injuries. He or she loses a number of chips equal to the difference between the Jump Check total and the target number. For example, if the cat needed an 8 to succeed but the Check total was only 5, he or she loses 3 chips! (The player may choose which type of chip to lose.)

If a cat realizes that a Climb Check is too difficult and wants to go back down the cliff voluntarily, he or she may do so by making a Jump Check. If the total is 5 or higher, the cat gets down safely. If the total is 4 or lower, the cat is injured and loses 1 chip (player's choice).

What Happens Next: If any of the cats are Knocked Out, continue with **12**.

If the cats decide to take the route by the river instead, continue with **6**.

If the cats decide to take the Twoleg path instead, continue with **8**.

If all the cats manage to climb the cliff safely to the top, continue with **5**.

4. A Strange Thunderpath

Read Aloud: "The thick forest of trees gives way to a large, open meadow. But this meadow is being patrolled by an angry group of Twoleg monsters!"

Narrator Tips: This is the meadow where the humans are riding their ATVs. They are driving as fast as possible then skidding to a stop, using small hills to cause their vehicles to jump into the air, going into the woods along narrow paths, and then returning to the meadow at full speed.

To the cats, this will be an almost inexplicably strange sight. Try to describe it in the weird and alien way it would seem to a cat—let the players make their own conclusions about what's really going on.

There is no more path to follow, but it is easy to tell which way the cats have to head in order to reach the top of the hill. If any cats try to use their senses to find clues as to where

to go next, they may uncover the following. Any of the following Checks must have a total of 5 or higher in order for the cat to perceive anything over the ruckus the monsters are making. A Listen Check can reveal the faint sound of splashing water just a little farther up the hill—a sign that the pools of water they're seeking may be nearby. A See Check can reveal a small stream running through the meadow—another sign that pools of water may be nearby. A Smell Check can reveal the scent of fresh herbs wafting down from the woods beyond the meadow—perhaps even the distinct scent of feverfew.

Unfortunately, the only way to get to the woods is to cross this grassy meadow and, hopefully, avoid the monsters along the way. If the cats try to sneak around the outside of the meadow, they keep finding that monsters suddenly appear out of the woods and force them back the way they came. Their only real hope is to cut across the meadow or go back toward the dirt path. Of course, they can also head back down the hill and try a different route entirely.

If the cats decide to try to cross the meadow, it's just a matter of timing and luck. Each cat in turn must do the following.

1. **Make a Focus Check**—This is to help them concentrate on this important task. If the total is 4 or higher, the cat gets a +1 bonus to the Checks in steps 2 and 3 below. If the total is 7 or higher, the bonus increases to +2.

2. **Make a See or Listen Check**—This is to recognize the pattern the monsters are following and time a safe sprint across the open field. If the total is 3 or less, the cat gets a –1 penalty on the Pounce Check below. If the total is 6 or higher, the cat gets a +1 bonus to the Pounce Check below.

3. **Make a Pounce Check**—This is to make the dash across the field. If the total is 7 or higher, the cat gets across safely. If the total is between 4 and 6, one of the monsters steps on the cat's tail and the cat loses 2 chips (player's choice) from the injury. If the total is 3 or less, one of the monsters swats the cat, doing damage that causes the cat to lose 4 chips (player's choice) from the injury. As

long as the cats aren't Knocked Out by this damage, they make it safely to the far side of the meadow.

What Happens Next: If the cats all make it across the meadow, continue with **5**.

If any of the cats are Knocked Out, continue with **12**.

If the cats decide to go back to the Twoleg path, continue with **10**.

If the cats decide to take the route by the river instead, continue with **6**.

If the cats decide to go directly into the deep part of the woods, continue with **7**.

5. You Give Me Fever

Read Aloud: "Despite the fact that it's a warm day in the middle of greenleaf, you feel cold. In fact, you find yourself beginning to shiver slightly."

Narrator Tips: Although the cats seemed completely fine at the start of the adventure, the truth is that they were already infected with the fever that is ravaging the Clans. But out here in the middle of a strange land, there is no medicine cat to take care of them, nor a comfortable nest to lie down in. The cats must press on. If they are successful in their mission, they will have feverfew to cool their brows. But until then, they must muddle through as best they can.

This isn't a dramatic scene so much as it is a time when the cats have to muster their willpower and press on despite the fact that their own bodies are working against them. Whenever the cats reach this point, each must make a Spirit Check.

The first time a cat plays through this scene, if the total of the Spirit Check is 5 or higher, nothing happens. If the total is 4 or lower, though, he or she is feeling ill and must lose 1 chip of the player's choice—as though the cat had taken damage in a fight (see Chapter Five of the game rules for details).

Each time the cat plays through this scene, the difficulty of the Spirit Check increases by 1. So the second time it must total 6 or higher in order to succeed, and it must total 7 or higher to succeed on the third time. This continues until the cat is cured of the fever.

What Happens Next: If the cats have just finished following the river or climbing the Twoleg path, this is the end of the chapter. Pass the adventure to the next Narrator and tell him or her to continue with **15**.

If the cats have just left one of the wrong ponds or successfully climbed the cliff, this is the end of the chapter. Pass the adventure to the next Narrator and tell him or her to continue with **16**.

If the cats have found the right pond, go back to **20** and follow the additional instructions.

6. Down by the River Side

Read Aloud: "As you go up the hill, the rocks grow bigger and the streams get wilder. So just as the climbing gets tougher, the rocks also become harder to navigate."

Narrator Tips: Your job in this scene is to give the characters some information, and then let them choose their path. There are three main paths the cats may take. They can walk along the slippery rocks, dangerous as it may be. They can move away from the stream to the forest's edge, but since the rocks along the stream are growing bigger, it will be impossible to see the water and the cats won't know if the streams point to anything important. Finally, the cats can decide that walking along the stream is not the way they want to go after all, and they can try one of the other ways up.

You should give the players a chance to discuss the matter. Each course of action has its own ramifications and possible dangers. Your job is to make sure they understand that all the choices have their own element of risk.

What Happens Next: If the cats decide to walk along the slippery rocks, continue with **13**.

If the cats decide to move to the edge of the woods, continue with **11**.

If the cats decide to leave the stream and go into the deep woods, continue with **7**.

If the cats decide to leave the stream and go up the Twoleg path, continue with **8**.

7. Into the Woods

Read Aloud: "The woods are unusually dense, with trees growing close together and the ground covered in a thick underbrush. Still, you're able to make steady progress."

Narrator Tips: This scene is about the cats moving through the woods on the lower part of the hill. The going is tougher than they might hope because they have to push their way through underbrush and wind their way between trees. However, the cats still seem to be making good time, which seems odd. Have the characters each make a Ponder Check, and anyone whose total is 3 or higher realizes that the reason things are going quickly is that they don't really seem to be going uphill very much—which is strange considering that they're supposed to be climbing a very tall hill.

Once the cats realize this and the players have had a chance to talk about what it might mean, continue below.

Read Aloud: "As you push through the underbrush, suddenly you find yourself stepping into a clearing. A short field of grass leads up to a sheer wall of rock that is nearly as tall as the trees themselves."

Narrator Tips: The reason this section of the woods has been so flat is that it runs directly up to this cliff. In order to continue to the top, the cats will have to either climb this cliff or go back and try one of the other routes up the hill. If the players ask, tell them that the cliff goes almost straight up and down and that there is not an obvious route or a series of ledges for the cats to use—climbing this cliff will be very difficult and very dangerous.

What Happens Next: If the cats decide to climb the cliff, continue with **3**.

If the cats decide to take the route by the river instead, continue with **6**.

If the cats decide to take the Twoleg path instead, continue with **8**.

8. Sounds and Smells

Read Aloud: "As you're walking along the dirt path, you notice the odor of the Twoleg monsters. That, in addition to how unnaturally flat, smooth, and uniformly wide the path is, makes you certain that this was made by Twolegs, rather than deer or other large animals. In the distance you can hear strange sounds, similar to but definitely different from those you've heard the monsters make along the Thunderpath."

Narrator Tips: Although you, as the Narrator, should probably not explain the situation in human terms to the players (because their cats would not perceive things in that way), the easiest way for you to understand this scene is to know what the humans are up to.

The path that the cats are climbing is a private dirt road up to a small cabin. The path is bumpy by human standards, but seems unusually smooth to the cats. Right now a group of Twolegs are visiting the cabin, and they brought some small 4-wheel all-terrain vehicles (ATVs). They parked their trucks by the cabin and are spending the day riding the ATVs through the meadows and paths farther up the hill. They've also left a dog by the cabin to guard the site and their equipment.

Of course, the cats don't know (and wouldn't understand) any of this. But use the knowledge to describe what the cats can see, smell, and hear as they climb the path. The clues will get stronger as the cats progress, and eventually they will have to decide whether they want to continue to follow the Twoleg path or go through the woods (which would lead them toward where the strange sounds are coming from). Of course, alternatively, they could decide to go back down the hill and take one of the other routes, but of all the ways up the hill, this one is the most certain and easy to follow.

What Happens Next: If the cats stay on the Twoleg path, continue with **10**.

If the cats cut through the woods toward the strange sounds, continue with **4**.

If the cats decide to take the route by the river instead, continue with **6**.

If the cats decide to go directly into the deep part of the woods, continue with **7**.

9. Cats *Can* Swim

Read Aloud: "With a splash, you're tumbling through ice-cold water and being carried down the hill and away from your friends. You've got to get out of the water fast!"

Narrator Tips: Any cat that's in the water must make a Swim Check that totals 5 or higher in order to get control of himself or herself. Then the cat must make a second Swim Check with a total of 4 or higher in order to successfully swim over to the edge of the stream. Finally, the cat must make a Climb Check that totals 3 or higher to get out of the water and back onto the

rocks. Any cat that gets safely out of the water in this manner automatically gains +1 in the Swim Skill, but this can only happen the first time. If the same cat falls in again, he or she gains no additional bonus from getting out.

Every time a cat in the water fails a Skill Check, that cat takes damage from being in the chilly river, and must lose one chip (player's choice). So being in the water too long makes it even more difficult to get out.

The other cats will probably want to follow along the shore and try to help their friends in the water. This is difficult and dangerous. If they try to follow along the rocks, the cats must make a Focus Check each round. If the total is 3 or lower, that cat slips and falls into the water, too. Alternatively, the cats can jump down from the rocks and follow by the forest's edge. This is safer, but they can no longer see their friends directly. In that case, they must make a Listen Check with a total of 3 or higher to hear where along the riverbank the swimming cats are.

What Happens Next: If the cats all successfully climb out of the water, continue with **11**.

If one or more of the cats are Knocked Out because of damage taken in the river, continue with **12**.

10. The Twoleg Nest

Read Aloud: "The path winds back and forth as it goes up the hill. Eventually it leads toward a Twoleg nest, and standing in front are a pair of monsters!"

Narrator Tips: The monsters the cats see are two parked trucks that the Twolegs have used to haul their ATVs up to the cabin. The Twolegs are now out riding the ATVs in the meadow, so the cabin is mostly quiet. However, sleeping in one of the truck beds is a dog who was left here to guard the trucks and other gear.

At first, you should describe the scene as being very quiet.

Tell the players that if their cats cross the yard and go behind the Twoleg nest, they should be able to continue up to the top of the hill. Also tell them that the monsters here are completely silent and still. Have the cats cross the yard, and ask them to each make a Smell Check to see if they notice anything odd. (Players may also ask if their cats can try other Checks like See or Listen, and you should certainly let them. However, those Skills will not reveal any further information—the dog is completely hidden from sight and although it's asleep, it isn't snoring.)

If the total is 5 or lower, the cats notice that the monsters don't smell as bad as they do when they're traveling on the Thunderpath, but they do still smell pretty awful. If the total is 6 or higher, they also notice the scent of a dog coming from on the back of one of the monsters.

If the cats cross the yard without taking any special precautions, there's a very good chance that the dog will wake up. Flip a coin twice. If it comes up heads on either flip the dog is awake. If the cats are at all noisy while crossing the yard—goofing around or, worse, talking loudly to one another—the dog should automatically wake up.

If the cats try to move stealthily across the yard, have them each make a Sneak Check. Add the totals from all the Checks together to get a group total. If that group total is equal to or higher than the number of cats x4, then they get across safely; otherwise, the dog has woken up. (Do not count the Narrator's cat in this total, only the cats of the players who are actively participating in the scene.) For example, if there are four cats actively trying to go across the yard, the group total of all their Sneak Checks must be 16 or higher (4 x 4 = 16) or the dog will wake up.

What Happens Next: If the cats get across safely, continue with **5**.

If the dog wakes up, continue with **22**.

If the cats decide to go into the woods toward where the

monster noises are coming from, continue with **4**.

If the cats decide to take the route by the river instead, continue with **6**.

If the cats decide to go directly into the deep part of the woods, continue with **7**.

11. At a Safer Distance

Special Note: If the players arrive here because some of the cats fell into the water, explain that their cats have realized this is the *only* safe way to follow the river. If they would rather follow one of the other paths, continue with the choices at the end of scene **2**, but tell them that they've lost almost half a day because of this delay.

Read Aloud: "The hill is steep, but traveling by the edge of the woods is much easier than crawling over the river rocks. However, from this vantage point you can no longer see the water."

Narrator Tips: As the cats go farther up the hill, the terrain gets rockier and they have to go around some boulders. It is easy, while doing this, to get turned around and lose track of where the river is. You should describe how the large stones and thick woods mix and overlap to create cliffs and roadblocks and detours that make it difficult to keep a good sense of direction. It's not even always clear which way is up the hill because of little groves and valleys that form in these remote places.

The group should have one cat take the lead. That cat must make a Ponder Check to see if he or she can correctly follow the path.

What Happens Next: If the Ponder Check total is 6 or lower, the cats are lost. Continue with **14**.

If the Ponder Check total is 7 or higher, the cats have successfully followed the river to its source. Continue with **5**.

12. Knocked Out!

Special Note: There is no Read Aloud section for this scene. If the cats have ended up here, it is because one or more of them have been Knocked Out or otherwise been so damaged that the group cannot continue.

Narrator Tips: It is up to you, as Narrator, to describe the results that led the cats to this end. If one or more of them get Knocked Out in the river, were their friends able to pull them from the water at the bottom of the hill or were they washed downstream to some unknown fate? If they were beaten in combat, do they manage to stagger back to their Clan camps or are they now wounded rogues in a strange territory? Were they captured by Twolegs and imprisoned in one of their nests?

The details are left up to you. The one thing that will remain true in every case is that the cats did not get the needed herbs, and the fever continues to ravage the warrior Clans. Many cats will die, and while it's certainly not the characters' fault, they had the chance to prevent it and they failed.

What Happens Next: The adventure is over for the cats. They acted bravely but, in the end, did not have what it took to overcome the dangers they faced.

Although they can be proud of the bravery they showed, the cats do *not* get any Experience rewards for this adventure. They *can*, however, play the adventure again, hopefully using the things they learned to bring about a better conclusion the next time.

13. Slippery When Wet

Read Aloud: "The higher up the hill you go, the bigger the rocks get. And wherever the water splashes on them, they're covered with some kind of slippery green plant."

Narrator Tips: Climbing over the rocks is not going to work out

for the characters. It just keeps getting tougher and tougher and eventually they are going to fall into the water. But, as the Narrator, you have to give them a chance to discover that for themselves.

Describe to the players that as they look up the hill, they see the stream turning into a river and the rocks getting bigger and bigger. Also, these bigger rocks are wet almost all the time, so they are completely covered by a thin layer of algae that makes them even harder to climb. Tell the players that the cats can change their minds and walk by the edge of the woods if they prefer.

If the characters want to continue on this route, have all the cats make Climb Checks. If any cat's total is lower than 2 that cat slips and falls into the water (see below for what to do if that happens). If everyone's total is 2 or higher, they can continue. Soon, though, they have to make another Check. Tell the players that this looks like it will be more difficult than the last one. Give them a chance to get off the rocks rather than attempt the Climb Check. If they do try to Climb, this time any cat whose total is lower than 3 slips and falls in.

Continue this process, always giving them a chance to opt out voluntarily and with each successive Check being 1 point more difficult than the last. Eventually, the cats will have to give up voluntarily, or some of them will fall into the water.

What Happens Next: If the cats decide to leave the rocks and go over by the edge of the woods, continue with **11**.

If any of the cats slip and fall into the water, continue with **9**.

14. Where'd the River Go?

Read Aloud: "That doesn't seem right at all. Shouldn't the river be where that giant oak tree is?"

Narrator Tips: The cats have gotten lost. This may not panic them terribly since they didn't really know where they were to begin with, but somehow they've got to get their bearings and head up the hill so they can find the pool that has the feverfew.

Let the players suggest ways their cats could find their way out of this predicament. Perhaps they want to listen for the river, or use their innate senses to tell which way is north, or which way is the bottom of the hill they started at. You, as Narrator, have a lot of flexibility to let this scene play out whatever way is most fun for the group. In the end, though, it should require a Skill or Ability Check (whichever one you think is most appropriate), and the total must be equal to or higher than 7 (just as in scene 11). However, in this instance it is possible for the cats to gather their efforts and work as a team.

Whatever Check is being attempted, one cat should perform it. The others can all perform Focus Checks to try to assist in the effort. For every assisting cat that gets a total of 4 or higher on the Focus Check, the cat performing the main Check receives a +1 bonus.

For example: In a group of five cats, one of them has to make a Ponder Check to figure out how to get to the river. The other four may make Focus Checks to assist. If three of these cats get 4 or higher on their Focus Checks, then the first cat will get a +3 bonus to the Ponder Check. If that total is 7 or higher, then the cats have found the river again.

The cats may try these Checks multiple times, but it doesn't get any easier. If they spend too many of their chips in failed attempts, the cats will end up in a situation where they no longer have any chance of success.

What Happens Next: If the cats succeed at the necessary Skill Check, continue with **5**.

If the cats are in a position where there is no chance for them to succeed at the necessary Skill Check, they remain lost and actually move deeper into the woods. They must rest for the night and try again in the morning. As the Narrator, you can play out this scene in as much detail as you like, but be sure to emphasize that this delay could be tragic if they don't get the feverfew back to their Clans in time. In the morning, the cats get the healing benefits of a night's sleep (as described in Chapter Five in the game rules). They also get to refresh their chips. They may now continue with **5**.

15. A Beautiful Pool

Read Aloud: "You're getting near the top of the hill and still you haven't seen any of the 'eyes' that the medicine cats told you about. Then, as you push through the brush, you see not one but literally dozens of pools of water. Some are no more than large puddles, while others are whole ponds."

Narrator Tips: Before they go any farther, tell the players that it is time to refresh their chips. Any chips they have spent can now be returned to their chip pool, though chips lost due to injury remain lost. (See Chapter Five of the rules for details on refreshing your chips.)

Now the cats must decide where to search for the feverfew. Let the players talk about it as much as they like. When they're ready to make a decision, each cat must make a Ponder Check. Add up all their totals to get a group total. If that number is equal to or greater than the number of cats x5, they have gotten an insight into the problem. (Do not count the Narrator's cat in this

total, only the cats of the players who are actively participating in the scene.) For example: If there are three cats actively Pondering, the group total of all their Ponder Checks must be 15 or higher (3 x 5 = 15) in order for them to get an insight.

What Happens Next: If the cats have gotten an insight into the problem, continue with **16**.

If the cats failed to get an insight, continue with **18**.

16. Guardian

Read Aloud: "Beneath the boughs of an elm tree, you see the most serene and beautiful pond yet. Perhaps this will turn out to be the right one."

Narrator Tips: Something just feels right about this pool, but before the cats can check it out they will have to deal with one last challenge. A badger has dug its den in the ground near the pool and it doesn't like to share the clean, clear water with outsiders. Before the cats approach the water, have them each make a Smell Check. Any cat whose total is 4 or higher catches the scent of an animal in the area. Those same cats (and *only* the ones who succeeded at the Smell Check) may then attempt a Ponder Check to determine what animal it is. If one of these cats has the Animal Lore Knack, this would be a perfect time to use it. If the Ponder Check total is 6 or higher, the cat recognizes the scent as that of a badger. If the total is 7 or higher, the cat remembers the following information about badgers.

<u>Badgers</u>—*Badgers are smart, tough animals. They are very protective of their territory, especially their dens. They don't like fighting, but once a fight is started a badger will not quit until it or its enemy is dead. If you happen upon a badger, do not act in an aggressive way. Stand your ground and try to show the badger that you are not an enemy, but you're also not afraid of it. If it senses fear or danger from you, the badger will attack.*

A cat with this insight knows that the best thing to do if a badger comes out is for a single cat to take the lead. That cat should stand facing the badger and perform an Arch Check, but, and this is very important, none of the cats should appear angry or Hiss at the badger. If the Arch Check conveys enough confidence and calmness, the badger will let the cats pass.

Read Aloud: "With a wuffling snort, a badger waddles out of the burrow. A squat beast with bristly fur, small eyes, and a large, sensitive nose, the most prominent feature on the badger are its long, deadly, sharp claws."

Narrator Tips: Let the players discuss what to do—don't rush them. Let any cat who does not have the Animal Lore Knack now attempt a Ponder Check. If the total is 7 or higher, the cat remembers the badger information listed above. The cat also knows that it's possible for the rest of the cats to help the one taking the lead. All the remaining cats can make Focus Checks. For each cat whose total is 5 or higher, the lead cat will get a +1 bonus to his or her Arch Check.

If the Arch Check has a total of 8 or higher, the badger snorts again and waddles back into its burrow. Otherwise, it will charge in for a fight.

What Happens Next: If the cats succeed in the Arch Check, continue with **20**.

If the Arch Check fails or if the cats try any other strategy, continue with **21**.

17. Delirious

Read Aloud: "Maybe it's the fever, or just exhaustion setting in, but you're finding it harder and harder to concentrate."

Narrator Tips: Even though they know with absolute certainty that the feverfew is somewhere around this pool, the cats haven't found it yet. By this point, several of them may be suffering the effects of the fever, and a few may even be Knocked

Out. Time is running out and you, as the Narrator, should make them fully aware of that.

There really is no action that takes place in this scene. The cats must continue their search. You should use this scene as a reminder that the cats are starting to feel more and more worn down. As you describe the upcoming scenes, stress how tired they are and how ill they are feeling. Try to get the players to think about what it feels like to be running a high fever—the disorientation and confusion and exhaustion—and convey that their cats are feeling just that way.

What Happens Next: If more than half of the cats are still awake and active, continue with **20**.

If more than half of the cats are Knocked Out, continue with **12**.

18. Not the Right Pool

Read Aloud: "You've found a beautiful pool—calm, clear water, tall grass growing around its banks. Surely this is where the feverfew will be found."

Narrator Tips: Let the cats search around the pond briefly, allowing them to make See or Smell or Ponder Checks, if they like. Cats with the Herb Lore Knack may use that in these efforts. Pretty quickly, though, they should realize that there is no feverfew around this pool, so they must be in the wrong place.

Let the cats make another group Ponder Check to gain an insight. This is just as described in scene **15** except that it is a little easier (since they have gained some experience from this wrong turn). This time they gain insight if the group total is equal to or higher than the number of cats x4. And, if they wind up trying this again later in the adventure, the target for the Ponder Check multiplier drops by 1 each time (so it's cats x3 on the third Check and cats x2 on the fourth).

What Happens Next: If the cats failed to get an insight, they must retry scene **18** again. Don't tell them that they are doing the same scene a second time. Improvise a slightly different Read Aloud section and make them feel like they have certainly found the right pool this time.

If the cats have successfully gotten an insight into the problem, continue with **5**.

19. Feverfew

Read Aloud: "Along the water's edge, hidden among the roots of tall grass and reeds, you finally find it—a thick, green, overflowing patch of feverfew!"

Narrator Tips: Success! The cats have found the feverfew!

Using the instructions given to them by the medicine cats, they can gather as much of the herb as they need. And the cats who are currently suffering from the ill effects of the fever can begin taking the medicine right away. They won't be completely healed, but they will feel a little bit better right away. (They get 1 chip of immediate bonus healing.)

The adventure is over, but let the players describe what their cats are doing and how they will get the feverfew back to the Clan territory. Then skip ahead over the two days of travel, and describe the scene when the cats return.

At first, the medicine cats will simply grab the herbs and get to work, perhaps leaving the characters to feel unappreciated. But later, the medicine cats and the Clan leaders and all the other healthy members of the Clans will come and thank them, telling them that they are real heroes. And it's true.

What Happens Next: The adventure is over. Well done!

20. One Special Pool

Special Note: The cats may come to this scene more than once. After the first time, there is no need to reread the Read Aloud section; just get to the meat of the scene.

Read Aloud: "The other pools are certainly beautiful, there's no doubt about it. But there is something special about this pool. And there is a fresh, hopeful scent in the air."

Narrator Tips: The cats are absolutely certain that this is the right pool. The scent of feverfew fills the area. Unfortunately, that makes it more difficult to determine where exactly the patch is. It will take a group effort to find it.

Each cat must make either a See or a Smell Check. Add their totals together to get a group total. Write that number down; you may need to remember it later. If the group total is equal to or greater than the number of cats x6, they have succeeded in finding the feverfew. If the group total is less than that number they have failed to find the herb.

It is possible that the cats will fail to find the feverfew on their first attempt. If so, they will have to visit this scene a second and possibly a third time. Each time they do, they build on the same group total. So, for example, if there are six cats, the group total must be 36 in order for them to succeed (6 x 6 = 36). If the first group total is only 15 points, then the next time the cats try they add their new group total to the old one. So if the second group total is 12, the overall group total is now 27 (15 + 12 = 27). That's still not enough to succeed, but it's getting close. They'll almost certainly succeed on the third try.

What Happens Next: No matter what the results of the search are, the cats must first face the ravages of the fever. Continue with **5**, but then come back here to see the final resolution.

If the cats succeed in finding the feverfew, continue with **19**.

If the cats fail to find the feverfew, continue with **17**.

21. Fight!

Read Aloud: "The badger launches itself straight at you, snorting and growling and baring its teeth. But as sharp and dangerous as those teeth look, you know that the real danger is the badger's claws!"

Narrator Tips: This is the big fight. Either the cats will win, or the adventure will end in tragedy for them and all the cats suffering through the fever back in the Clan territory.

The thing that makes the badger especially dangerous is that it's a vicious fighter with incredible speed. In each Round of this fight, the badger may be able to attack twice. It always attacks first; then all of the cats attack. If any of the cats try to Swat or Wrestle with the badger and fail on their attack Checks, the badger gets to make a second attack at the end of the Round.

When the badger makes a Swat Check, the total is 7. If the badger hits, its Strength Check has a total of 8 when determining damage. When the cats attack, the badger's Jump Check total is 7. Its Strength score, for determining how much damage the cats do, is 5. Once a fight starts, the badger will not quit until it is Knocked Out—it has a total of 15 chips that must be lost before this happens.

In most scenes, if one cat is Knocked Out, the whole team loses—even if they beat the enemy. Since this is the climax of the adventure, though, the group can still win even if one or two of their members are beaten. If half or more of the cats in the group are Knocked Out, though, then the whole team loses—there aren't enough cats left to bring back sufficient amounts of feverfew. If, however, the badger is beaten and more than half the cats are still standing, the team wins.

What Happens Next: If the cats Knock Out the badger and less than half the cats are Knocked Out, continue with **20**.

If half or more of the cats are Knocked Out, continue with **12**.

22. Dog Fight

Read Aloud: "With a roaring bark, a large brown dog leaps from the back of one of the monsters."

Narrator Tips: The cats have very few choices at this point. They can try to run up the hill and hope the dog doesn't follow them, they can fight the dog, they can climb a tree, or they can retreat down the hill and hope the dog doesn't follow them.

<u>Up the Hill:</u> This is the worst choice the cats can make. The dog will catch them and start a fight, but in the first Round, the target cat cannot make a Jump Check to avoid the dog's bite—he or she is automatically hit—and none of the cats may make attacks. It is basically just a free bite for the dog.

<u>Fight:</u> Fighting the dog works the same as any fight (see Chapter Five of the game rules). In each Round, the dog goes first and will attack one cat. It is probably best to use a random method (like Evens & Odds or Rock, Paper, Scissors) to pick exactly which cat gets attacked, though a particularly brave cat can volunteer to get the dog's attention. After that, all the cats get to go.

The dog does not Swat; it only Bites (and remember that Bites do extra damage). Its Bite Check has a total of 8. When the cats are attacking, the dog has a Jump Check total of 5. When it comes to inflicting or taking damage, the dog has a Strength score of 6.

The dog is really just a big bully. It's happy to pick on the cats

as a mean kind of game, but if the cats actually hurt it too much, the dog will run away. If the cats manage to do 6 chips worth of damage to the dog, it will give a loud yelp and run away to hide in the back of the truck. The cats can then safely get away.

<u>Climb:</u> There are plenty of trees around to climb. If the cats just want to get away from the dog's teeth, they only have to succeed at a Climb Check with a total of 4. Of course, once they're up in the trees, there's nowhere to go, and they have to make another Climb Check to stay balanced—if the Check fails, they have to come down out of the tree. If they have to or choose to come down, the cats will have to fight the dog.

Describe the situation like a scene in a scary movie. The dog is at the bottom of the tree, barking and howling. The cats are stuck in trees that are swaying dangerously in the breeze. Make the cats all attempt a total of 3 extra Climb Checks to see if they can keep from falling off their perches. If they do, the dog gets bored and goes back to the truck. Then the cats can come safely out of the trees and hopefully get away from the dog. They still have to make Sneak Checks (as described in scene **10**) to get safely across the yard.

<u>Down the Hill:</u> The dog will not chase the cats down the hill. They can choose which alternate route they want to take.

What Happens Next: If the cats get away from the dog, continue with **5**.

If any of the cats are Knocked Out, continue with **12**.

If the cats retreat and prefer to go directly into the deep part of the woods, continue with **7**.

If the cats retreat and prefer to take the route by the river instead, continue with **6**.

If the cats retreat and prefer to go into the woods where the monster noises are coming from, continue with **4**.

AFTER THE ADVENTURE

After the last scene of the adventure has been played, the game itself is not necessarily over. There still are a few things you can do if the players want to keep at it.

Play It Again

One of the great things about storytelling games is that you can always tell the story again. And, since so many of the events depend on Skill Checks, it won't always go exactly the same way.

There may be parts of the adventure that the cats never got around to exploring (especially if they only tried one path up the hill). Playing again will let everyone see all the parts of the story and give other players the chance to try their hands at being the Narrator.

In particular, if the adventure ended badly, you and the players may want to try a second time. Maybe starting back at the beginning, or perhaps picking up somewhere in the middle where it feels like things went wrong.

Experience

If the cats completed the adventure successfully, then they all get Experience rewards. It is important to note, though, that each cat can only get experience from this adventure *once*! If you play through and successfully finish the adventure several times, your cat only gains the rewards listed below after the first time he or she completes the adventure.

If you use different cats each time, though, each one can get the experience rewards. The rule is *not* that a player can only get experience once, it's that a *cat* can.

Age: Although the action in this adventure clearly all happens over the course of just a few days, the presumption is that this is the most interesting and exciting thing that happens to your cat during the whole of that moon. Increase your cat's age by 1 moon and make any appropriate improvements described in Chapter Four of the game rules.

Skill: On top of the improvements your cat gets from aging, he or she also gains 1 level in one of the following Skills (your choice!): Focus, Ponder, See, Smell, Swim.

More adventures can be found at the back of each novel in the Omen of the Stars series, and you can find extra information at www.warriorcats.com.

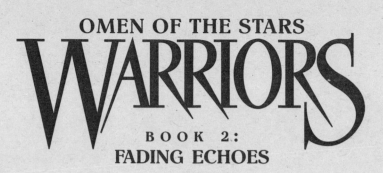

OMEN OF THE STARS
WARRIORS

BOOK 2:
FADING ECHOES

Dovepaw trembled in her sleep.

"Dovepaw! Dovepaw!" Voices wailed around her as she struggled in the current, dragging at her fur, swirling her through darkness. "Dovepaw!" The cries were jagged with fear. Trees and branches tumbled past her, sweeping away downstream. Darkness yawned below, stretching so far beneath her that horror caught in her throat.

"Dovepaw!" Rippletail's desperate, lonely whimper rang in her ears.

With a start, she blinked open her eyes.

Her sister, Ivypaw, stirred beside her. "Were you dreaming?" The silver-and-white tabby raised her head and gazed anxiously at Dovepaw. "You were twitching like a mouse."

"Bad dream." Dovepaw fought to keep her mew steady. Her heart was pounding and Rippletail's cry echoed in her mind.

She stretched forward and licked Ivypaw's head. "It's gone now," she lied.

As Ivypaw's sleepy eyes began to close, Dovepaw breathed in the soft scent of her sister. *I'm home,* she reminded herself. *Everything's okay.* Yet her heart still pounded. She stretched in her nest, a shiver running to the tip of her tail, and clambered to her paws. Padding carefully between the nests, she headed out of the den.

Moonlight bathed the deserted clearing, and above the rock walls that encircled the camp, the horizon was milky with dawn light. The mewls of Poppyfrost's newborn kits drifted from the nursery, and snores rumbled from the dens. The air felt strange, cool and wet on her muzzle. For many moons, Dovepaw had known nothing but the parched wind of drought, dry on her tongue. But now she could taste the green freshness of the forest, heady and mouthwatering.

Thin clouds drifted across the star-speckled sky, draping Silverpelt like cobwebs. She wondered if Rippletail was watching from among her starry ancestors.

I'm sorry. The words echoed in her mind like the lonely call of an owl.

Even though the long journey upstream was a quarter moon ago, the memory still ached in her muscles. Dovepaw had traveled with Lionblaze and two cats from each of the other Clans to track down the beavers that had blocked the stream and starved the lake of water. Together they had destroyed the dam and unleashed the torrent that had filled the lake once more. And now life was returning to the territories. She felt it in the rustling of the forest, heard it in the stirrings of prey beyond the edges of the camp.

Pride coursed through her. She had been the one to sense the beavers as they worked to block the stream. She had helped break their dam to pieces and now all the Clans would survive. But the memory was bittersweet, like yarrow on her tongue. The RiverClan warrior Rippletail had died fighting the large brown creatures, their heavy bodies stronger than foxes, their snapping yellow teeth deadlier than claws.

Memories of the journey had thronged in Dovepaw's mind since she'd returned, and Rippletail's death haunted her dreams. Did Lionblaze feel the same? She didn't dare ask. Nor could she confide in Jayfeather about how much the journey still clung to her thoughts. They might think she was weak. She had a great destiny ahead of her.

How could she ever live up to the prophecy that had been given to Firestar many moons ago? *There will be three, kin of your kin, who hold the power of the stars in their paws.*

Dovepaw was one of the Three, along with Lionblaze and Jayfeather. The realization still shocked her. She'd been an apprentice less than a moon and now she carried more responsibility than a senior warrior on her shoulders. What could she do but hone the power she'd been given, the power that made her one of the Three? She practiced each day, reaching out with her senses as deep into the forest as she could, listening, tasting, feeling for sounds and movements even Jayfeather could not detect.

Dovepaw crouched outside the den, her pelt ruffling in the

damp air, and closed her eyes. She let the sensation of earth beneath her paws slide away, reached beyond the sound of Poppyfrost's kits fidgeting in the nursery, and let her senses roam. The forest trembled with life, filling her senses with smells and sounds: birds shaking out their feathers before they began their morning song, an early ShadowClan patrol padding sleepily out of camp, their paws clumsy on the slippery, needle-strewn ground. The sharp scent of catmint growing beside the abandoned Twoleg nest bathed her tongue. The sound of water chattering over the rock-cluttered stream on the WindClan border stirred her ear fur.

Wait!

Why were two cats slinking beside the lake at this time of day?

DON'T MISS:

SEEKERS

THE QUEST BEGINS

Lusa

"*And over there you can see* Lusa, our youngest black bear, who is five months old. She was born right here in the zoo. Black bears actually come in a lot of different colors like cinnamon or gray, but Lusa's name means 'black' in the Choctaw language, and if you look closely you won't find one speck of another color on her coat. That's her mother, Ashia, and her father, King.

"All North American bears are suffering from the changes in their environment. For the most part, black bears are doing better than white bears and grizzlies, but we have had to rescue some of them when they run into trouble. We found King, for instance, wandering at the edge of the forest. He would have starved to death if we hadn't brought him here. Lusa's never known any other place, and she feels safe around humans, so she is certainly better off living in the zoo with us."

Patches of snow covered the bare rocks and grassy ground inside the Bear Bowl, but the smell of leaftime was in the air, and a few purple crocuses were already nudging their way through the dirt. Lusa stood on her hind legs and twitched her ears at the group of flat-faces on the upper ridge of the Bowl. Several flat-face cubs were leaning against the railing, pointing at her and chattering. They sounded like birds. She didn't understand most of what the zoo guide was saying, but she knew her name in the flat-face language. Her feeders called her Lusa when they brought her food, so she could tell when the guides were talking about her to the visiting flat-faces. The wind brought a whiff of their strange scent to her—a warm, milky smell covered over by sharp, almost flowery scents. Their high-pitched voices made her ears hurt, but she liked the sound of their laughter.

Dropping back down to her paws, she scrambled into the part of the Bowl where three tall trees grew next to a log that never rotted. Lusa called this the Forest. Raising herself onto her hind legs again, she batted her paws in the air, as if she were fighting a butterfly, to catch the attention of the flat-faces. When she was sure they were watching her, she jumped onto the log and ran along it, jumping down on all fours at the other end.

As she'd hoped, the flat-faces made the quick huffing sound that meant they were pleased, and the guide leaned over the rail to give her some fruit. Lusa had to stand on her back legs and stretch as high as she could to reach the pear.

"What you see Lusa doing here is similar to what bears like her would do in the wild—stretching up into the trees to reach food like fruit, nuts, berries, and honey," the guide chattered.

Lusa wrapped her paws around the piece of fruit and

nibbled at it. Suddenly she felt a paw cuff her shoulder. She knew from its size that it wasn't one of the bigger bears, so she had a good chance of defending her pear. With a snort, she tucked her paw around the fruit and turned to face Yogi, the other cub in the Bowl.

Yogi was one season-circle old, but he hadn't been born here. He talked sometimes about another zoo, where his mother lived, but he didn't remember it very well. He was almost as black as Lusa, but he had a pale splash of white fur on his chest.

With a huffing sound, he lifted himself onto his hind legs so he towered over her. "Lusa, share!" he demanded. "Give me some!"

"No!" she said. "It's mine!" She stuffed the fruit in her mouth and ran away across the enclosure. The flat-faces up above chattered and giggled as Yogi chased her.

Lusa scrambled up onto the Mountains near the back of the Bowl. She was better than Yogi was at balancing on the four large boulders. He huffed and grunted as he climbed after her. With a playful snort, Lusa leaped off the last boulder and tumbled straight into her father, King, who was dozing in the sun.

"*Hrr*—what?" her father mumbled. Then Yogi came bounding off the rocks after Lusa and crashed into King as well. This brought the giant black bear to his paws with a roar.

"Get off!" he bellowed, swatting at them. "Go away!"

Yogi fled to the Fence at the far end of the Bowl. On the other side of the Fence, Lusa could see the old grizzly rolling on his back, muttering to himself. Chuffing with laughter, Lusa followed Yogi.

"How can you find that funny?" Yogi asked, his fur standing on end. "Your father is so scary!"

"Oh, he's a big furball," Lusa said. "His bluster is worse than his bite."

"You don't know that," Yogi pointed out. "He's never bitten you—yet!"

"He wouldn't!" Lusa protested. "He was just startled, that's all. You know he's a bit deaf. He probably didn't hear us coming." She was pleased to see that Yogi had forgotten about the fruit. She sat down and finished eating it, licking the juice off her paws with her long tongue.

"Well, I'm not going to bother him again," Yogi said. "I'm going to stay over here and watch the white bears through the Fence." Lusa was glad that the bears in the Bowl were kept apart from one another by the cold gray webs of the Fences. She liked being with other black bears, but she was a little bit afraid of the big brown grizzly and the massive white bears. They were much, much bigger than she was, and their deafening roars sometimes kept her awake at night.

"That sounds like a good idea to me." Lusa turned and saw her mother, Ashia, lumbering toward them. "You two should learn not to disturb King, especially when he's resting."

"We weren't *disturbing* him," Lusa objected.

"Just stay out of his way and don't cause trouble," Ashia scolded.

"I don't want to watch the white bears," Lusa said to Yogi.

"They're boring. Let's go hide in the Caves."

They scampered off to the back corner of the Bowl, where a ledge of white stone hung over a rocky patch of ground hidden in shadow. Lusa and Yogi crowded into the shadows, each trying to keep their paws out of the sun. They crouched as low as they could get and held very still.

"*Shhh,*" Lusa whispered. "There's a grizzly crashing through the forest."

"It's coming after us," Yogi whispered. "It's going to chase us with its giant hooked claws."

"But if we stay very still, it won't know we're here," Lusa breathed.

"Whoever moves first loses," Yogi challenged.

"All right," Lusa said, pressing her muzzle to her paws. "I'm going to win."

They fell silent. Lusa willed every muscle in her body to stay perfectly still. She felt the wind tickling around her ears and nose. She could smell every other bear in her section of the Bowl: King dozing in the sun, Ashia snuffling around the bottom of the wall for anything the flat-faces had dropped, Stella scratching her side against one of the trees.

In the next enclosure, one of the giant white bears was swimming around and around in a circle, from one lump of stone to the next. Lusa had seen it do this for hours. The white bears were even less friendly than the grizzly, who lived on his own and didn't say much. Lusa didn't know their names. The white bears stayed on their island of gray stone or in the chilly water and ignored the bears on either side of them. Lusa was fine with that; they were nearly three times her mother's size, and she sometimes got the feeling that they'd be perfectly happy to have her for dinner instead of the slabs of meat the flat-faces threw over the wall.

Her nose was beginning to itch. Lost in thought about the white bears, she forgot about the competition and reached up to scratch it.

"Ha!" Yogi yelped, jumping to his paws. "You moved! I win!"

"Oh," Lusa said, feeling foolish. "Well, it doesn't matter anyway. If a grizzly spotted me, I would just run up a tree. I can climb much better than any old brown bear!"

ERIN HUNTER

is inspired by a love of cats and a fascination with the ferocity of the natural world. As well as having great respect for nature in all its forms, Erin enjoys creating rich, mythical explanations for animal behavior. She is also the author of the bestselling Seekers series.

Visit Warriors at
www.warriorcats.com.

For exclusive information on your favorite authors and artists, visit
www.authortracker.com.

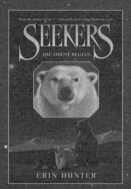